EXFIL

Alan Reynolds

Fisher King Publishing

EXFIL
Copyright © Alan Reynolds 2019
ISBN 978-1-913170-13-4

All rights reserved. No part of this publication may be
reproduced or distributed in any form or by any means, or
stored in a database or electronic retrieval system without
the prior written permission of Fisher King Publishing Ltd.
Thank you for respecting the author of this work.

This is a work of fiction. Names, characters, businesses,
places, events and incidents are either the products of the
author's imagination or used in a fictitious manner. Any
resemblance to actual persons, living or dead, or actual
events is purely coincidental.

Published by
Fisher King Publishing
The Studio
Arthington Lane
Pool in Wharfedale
LS21 1JZ
England

Also by Alan Reynolds

Enormous thanks to Rick Armstrong for his
unstinting support, guidance and friendship;
also to Samantha Richardson and
Rachel Topping at Fisher King Publishing,
thank you for your patience and great artwork
and to Lisa Slater at Make Your Copy Count
for editorial and proof-reading support.

Dedicated to my family and friends, and to all
those who have supported me in my writing –
your encouragement has been inspirational.

Much love

Chapter One

Gholhak Garden in Iran is the British diplomatic compound in the northern Tehran neighbourhood of Gholhak, about three miles from the main embassy in the city centre. The sprawling wooded area, bordered by high walls, houses British diplomats and their families. Parrots flutter between towering plane trees and foxes can frequently be seen frolicking on the landscaped lawns. The compound is also home to the Tehran Commonwealth War Cemetery, the British Council, and a French school. The entrance is dominated by an impressive tower and pointed archway, typical of Islamic architecture. It is closely guarded.

Gholhak Garden Compound, Tehran - Thursday April 6th 2006

At seven o'clock, Afareen Mahabadi approached the entrance to the compound. She wore a pink embroidered shawl over a black long-sleeve top and black leggings, completed by a white Hijab; fashionable in Tehran and complying with the strict local dress-code for women. She was anxious as she waited her turn. Sometimes she was searched; sometimes not. Today, two people in front of her were checked, but she was waved through unhindered. She exhaled, but not loudly enough to be heard. She had made this journey for the last four months as one of six women employed as cleaners allocated to specific residencies. Four weeks ago, she was finally assigned to the Dexter home.

Sophie Dexter was in her kitchen when Afareen arrived; her husband, David Dexter was already on his way to the embassy in town. At thirty-three, Sophie was four years younger than David, who was considered a high-flyer in diplomatic circles. As the wife of the Commercial Attaché, she was an active member of the community and one of the three teachers at the compound school, the École Française de Téhéran, where she taught English.

"Good morning, Afareen," said Sophie, as her cleaner entered through the front door of the three-bedroomed bungalow. "How are you today?"

"I'm ok, thank you," replied Afareen, with an accent that reflected her American tutelage. "I want to start with the bedrooms today, can you show me where you would like me to start?"

Sophie looked confused.

"Show me," whispered Afareen.

Still unsure about the request, Sophie led Afareen to the master bedroom. The duvet cover was pulled back, the sheets were untidy and the pillows askew. Discarded clothes were scattered on the two chairs next to the window; the dressing-table showed evidence of spilt powder and makeup.

Sophie detected a change in Afareen's demeanour today; she seemed nervous for some reason. Her dark eyes flitted from side to side, anxiously scanning the room as if she were looking for something.

"Are you ok?" said Sophie.

Afareen put her fingers to her lips to indicate silence. She removed one of her slip-on shoes and twisted the heel, revealing a hollow space. She extracted a piece of paper, which she pushed into Sophie's hand, repeating the motion to stay silent. Sophie nodded, unsure of what she had been handed but seeing the urgency in her cleaner's eyes.

The role of a Commercial Attaché is primarily to promote UK business and commerce in the country where they are based. In Iran, this was especially problematic given the fractious relationship between the two countries. Tensions had lessened over the last two years, so there were new opportunities to boost UK trade, which David Dexter was charged to do. Most of his days were spent meeting businessmen and government officials. He was constantly under surveillance.

David also had an ulterior motive for being there. Although paid by the government, his payslip originated in a different building from the Trade and Industry department. It came from Vauxhall Cross, home to the British Secret Service, MI6.

After another day of meetings, David Dexter was being driven through the Gholhak Garden arch in the Jaguar provided for him by the Foreign Office. Each of the two senior diplomats had one, the Ambassador had a Bentley; they came with the role. Dexter's diary was clear for the evening, which would give him some much-needed downtime. He was about to be disappointed.

"Hi, darling," he said, as he entered the house.

"I'm in the kitchen," was the reply.

David walked through from the living room. He and Sophie kissed fondly.

"How was your day?" said Sophie.

"The usual. Back-to-back meetings."

As they spoke, Sophie opened the cutlery drawer and

lifted out the tray of utensils.

She was aware of the possibility that the bungalow might be bugged. There were two areas which had been screened by the embassy tech people and declared 'safe' – the bathroom and master bedroom. It was something she complained about to her husband but recognised it went with the territory.

"Something smells good," David said.

"Oh, it's something Afareen cooked this afternoon. I only had to heat it up. I don't know what I would do without her," said Sophie. She took out the piece of paper from beneath the cutlery and handed it to her husband as discreetly as possible, putting her finger to her lips as she did so.

"Go and freshen up, dinner will be ready in ten minutes."

"Yes, ok. I won't be long," said David.

Once in the bathroom, he studied the small piece of paper. The writing was tiny – not decipherable using normal vision. Someone had gone to a lot of trouble to compose it.

He went to the second bedroom, which had been converted to a home office, and retrieved a magnifying glass from one of the desk drawers. He put the note on the top of the desk and scanned it.

"Shit!"

He called his driver, then returned to the kitchen.

"Sorry, darling, I need to go back to the embassy."

"Oh dear. How long will you be?"

"I don't know; I'll call you."

"What about your dinner?"

"I'll get a sandwich at the embassy."

Twenty minutes later, David was back in the Jaguar heading down the Modares Highway towards the British

Embassy. He knew there was a likelihood that he was being followed; a surveillance team might well have called in the unscheduled departure. It was unlikely, however, that he would be stopped. In the event of that possibility, David had hidden the note in the lining of his jacket, and it was as secure as it could be. His suit was bespoke; it had been specially made for precisely this purpose. The vent at the back of the jacket was not stitched at the bottom but fastened by a strip of Velcro, undetectable to the human eye. Today was the first time David had needed to use this customisation.

They drove down the tree lined Ferdowski Avenue; traffic was lighter now rush-hour had passed, but it was still busy. The high gates of the embassy opened as the Jaguar approached the entrance and stopped at the barrier to allow the usual checks; an official waved them through.

David's office was on the second floor of the building. He unlocked the door and closed it behind him. He needed to get the information back to London as soon as possible; it was a matter of life or death.

At this time of day, there was only a skeleton staff present, but one of the tech guys was always on duty in case of a hacking incident or any other disruption to web-based traffic. David picked up the internal phone.

"Ryan, can you spare a minute?"

Ryan Hudson was one of the most valuable team members at the embassy. As a senior communications officer, he was an expert in covert messaging systems. He defied the stereotypical computer geek image. He wore a suit and resembled a male model; strong, rugged features, sharp haircut, and toned from his five years working with special forces as a comms officer. His move into diplomatic service was a natural progression.

After receiving the call, Ryan headed straight to David's office. David was holding a small container.

"Ryan, I need to get this to Vauxhall as soon as possible."

"What have we got?"

David opened the container and showed Ryan the content.

"Hmm, someone's gone to a lot of trouble," said Ryan.

"Yes, it's extremely delicate. Can you encrypt it and get it off?"

"Of course, I'll get right on it. Anything else you need?"

"Not at the moment; let's see what Mother says."

Vauxhall Cross, MI6 Headquarters, London – Friday April 7th – 9:00 a.m.

Nick Houghton was at his desk, still wearing his jacket. It was one of those days when the office central-heating system wasn't sure whether to kick in or not, and the room felt chilly. His internal phone rang.

"Houghton," he responded. "Yes, ma'am, right away."

He took the lift to the twenty-second floor.

Commander Philippa Jenkins, Head of MI6, was in her office; her assistant, Andy Fellows, was seated on a chair in front of her desk. There was a vacant seat next to him.

"Ah, Nick, come in. You know Andy, don't you?"

"Morning, ma'am, yes," said Houghton and shook hands with Fellows.

"Sit down, would you like a coffee?"

"Thank you," said Nick and took the vacant chair.

Andy got up and poured Nick a drink from a coffee machine in the corner of the large office. The Commander stood at the green-tinted window, surveying the magnificent view of the Thames. She was a formidable woman who commanded respect throughout the community. She was dressed in her usual twin-set and pearls, but this morning she appeared on edge. She turned and addressed the two men like an old school ma'am, arms folded.

"Something's come up. It's big, very big." She sat down and picked up her half-drunk cup of coffee and took a sip. "Have you heard of Hassan Mahabadi?"

They looked blank.

"He's one of Iran's top nuclear scientists," the Commander informed them.

Nick raised his eyebrows.

The Commander continued; "Ok, let me fill in some background. As you are aware, Iran stopped Uranium enrichment in 2003, after the Paris agreement, but what you might not know is there are rumours that they have started production again."

"Is this still at Natanz?"

"Probably, but they also have a place at Esfahan. It's a Uranium enrichment facility, south of Tehran. We don't know for certain, but this is highly sensitive, and we haven't had confirmation yet. The Americans are monitoring it."

"I bet they are," said Houghton.

"As you can imagine, the loss of one of their top scientists would be incredibly damaging both scientifically and politically for the Iranians."

"Loss? What do you mean, loss?"

"That's why you're here," she paused, taking another sip of coffee. "We received some information yesterday; it appears that Mr Mahabadi is becoming disaffected with the regime. He wants to defect."

"Defect?" said Houghton. "Why?"

"We don't know exactly, could be any number of reasons, but he's virtually a prisoner there. It certainly can't be much of a life. Unfortunately, we don't have a great deal of information. Would you believe, his wife is working as a cleaner in the British compound in Tehran? She managed to smuggle a message to one of our people."

Houghton looked at Fellows. "Wow, she's one brave lady."

"Yes, she is. Having got this information, I spoke to the Home Secretary, and he's given the go-ahead to pursue this eventuality."

"You want us to spring this man?" said Houghton.

"If it's possible, yes, but first, we need to work on a strategy for me to put to the Home Secretary. We need it to look like an escape. In the present climate, we can't be seen to be aiding the defection of one of their key people."

"That's going to be difficult," said Houghton. "Where's he based; do we know?"

"Hmm, that's the other problem, we don't, not for certain. The Iranians also have a heavy-water production plant on a new site at Arak; just outside the town, started two years ago. He could be there, or either of the other two sites."

"I bet the Americans are all over this," said Houghton.

"Yes, they are, and that's another problem. We don't want to involve them."

"So basically you want us to extract this man…."

"And his family," interrupted the Commander.

"And his family," echoed Houghton, "without either the Americans or Iranians finding out?"

"Yes," said the Commander.

Houghton looked at Fellows.

"Do we have any more information?"

"Not much, I'm afraid. Mahabadi has an older brother, Mehran, in Cambridge. He's a professor in natural sciences; been here since the revolution in seventy-nine. Mehran fled the regime and was granted asylum; highly regarded, by all accounts. This is probably why Hassan has approached us and not the Americans. It might be worth speaking to the brother, we don't know what contact they have, if any. Whatever you do, don't mention a possible defection to him at this stage. We have no idea about Mahabadi's situation."

"He's going to wonder why we've contacted him."

"Yes, that's true, but he's been helpful to us in the past, so it should be a relatively open door." She looked at him; deadly serious. "I cannot stress enough, this must be handled extremely sensitively; there are people's lives at stake here, not to mention the possible political fallout. Can you work with Andy and come up with some ideas? Oh, and you might want to chat to Ahmad Qomi on the tech team, he's from Tehran; he could be quite useful. As I see it, the biggest problem is going to be communication. We don't know how long it's taken to get this message to us, and I have no idea how we can get a message back. I need something quickly; I want you to drop everything and work on this."

"Right, ma'am, I'll get on with it."

"I'm going to allocate you a secure office and comms; let me know what other resources you're going to need and give me a progress report by five o'clock. Good luck."

Houghton and Fellows left the Commander's office and took the lift down to the twelfth-floor where their secure office was located.

"Where do you want to start?" said Fellows.

"Well, I think I need to get up to Cambridge and see the brother. Can you do some digging and find out as much as you can about Natanz, Esfahan and this new place, Arak? You can speak to Ahmad; he might have some information. Then, see if we can outline a feasible exfil plan – how and where? Just possibilities at this stage," said Houghton. "Oh, and see if you can beg, borrow or steal a coffee machine from somewhere. I think we're going to need it."

"I'm on it."

While Fellows was hunting for a coffee machine, Houghton was tracking down the Cambridge professor. Unfortunately, the number on file was the switchboard of the University's Natural Sciences Department and not the professor himself. He called the number, but the receptionist politely explained that Professor Mahabadi was lecturing.

It was after eleven o'clock before Houghton was able to speak to the professor.

"Professor Mahabadi? Nick Houghton, Vauxhall Cross, is it possible for me to come up and speak to you... Yes, it's about your brother... No, he's ok, as far as I know... No, I would prefer to discuss it in person. As soon as possible – this afternoon, preferably? I can be there around four... Cambridge Arts Theatre, Italian coffee shop... Yes, ok, I'll find it... See you then, thank you."

"Any joy?" asked Fellows as Houghton ended the call. He was at his computer doing research; his desk piled high with files.

"Yeah, I'm going up to Cambridge this afternoon and meeting him outside the university at four."

"Well, I've spoken to GCHQ and managed to get some more background on him. Pretty much what Mother told us; they've been keeping an eye on him for a few years; nothing remarkable, just basic stuff, email traffic and phone calls. He hasn't made any contact with Iran in the last two years, that we know of."

Houghton emailed the Commander explaining the pending visit and suggesting an update meeting take place the following morning.

With the volume of traffic, it took the agent over three hours to get to Cambridge. He hadn't been before, but it was clear to see why it was such a desirable place to live; so different from London.

He found the University complex and, after some searching, pulled up outside the Italian Coffee shop next to the Cambridge Arts Theatre where the meeting would take place. He checked the photograph from the file again so he would recognise the professor.

There was a multi-storey car park a hundred yards on the right, and he drove away and parked up. He checked his watch, three forty-eight. The area was awash with students, easily identifiable with their college scarves, seemingly worn as trophies.

The café was elegant-looking from the outside; the window displaying various pictures of coffee and an array of cakes and pastries, all home-made, it said.

Inside reflected the style of the exterior. There were around twenty tables with four chairs at each; pictures of Tuscan landscapes decorated the walls. Staff were dodging from tables to the counter where two people wearing tee-shirts with the word 'Barista' printed on the back, were dispensing drink orders. It was about half-full, mainly with students, but there were some elderly people taking their afternoon tea. Houghton chose a seat in the corner, which would afford a degree of privacy.

A waitress descended on him within seconds of him being seated. "I'm waiting for someone," said Houghton and the girl moved on to another customer.

Professor Mahabadi walked in; Houghton recognised him straight away and watched him looking around the room. Eye contact was made; Houghton acknowledged him with a nod. He got up from his seat as the professor approached and held out his hand in greeting.

"Nick Houghton, we spoke on the phone."

The professor sat down, ignoring Houghton's offer of a handshake.

"Why are we here? I told you people I did not want to be contacted," said the professor gruffly.

The waitress re-appeared before Houghton had a chance to reply.

"What would you like?"

"A tea," said Mahabadi sharply.

"Two teas," said Houghton to the waitress. She took the order and went to the counter.

"Yes, I'm sorry, but we are hoping you can help. It concerns your brother."

"Yes, you told me, but I haven't spoken to him in over two years."

Houghton looked at him; he looked older than his fifty-seven years. His wavy hair was greasy, thinning and grey. There was a stern look about him; his face lined with past angst.

"Look, you know how these things work; I can't go into details, but I need as much information on your brother as you can give me."

"Is he in trouble?"

"I hope not, no," said Houghton, "but I could really do with your help here."

The waitress brought the teas, and Nick noticed the man visibly relax. His rather old-looking sports jacket gaped, and the pressure on his shirt-buttons was straining the cotton threads that attached them to his shirt. His accent was distinctly Farsi, but his English was good; his students would be able to understand him.

He poured some tea from the china teapot into the matching cup and took a sip. He was taking his time, considering Houghton's request.

"So, what is it you need to know?" he said in a measured way.

"As much as you can give me. What's his date of birth?"

"You do not have this on file? I am surprised."

"No," replied Houghton.

"Fourteenth October 1957." Houghton made a note.

"What about his wife, Afareen?"

"I do not know her birthday – why would I?"

"No, ok, forget that. It's fine. Do they have children?"

"Yes, two. What's this all about?"

"Like I said, I can't go into detail, but you will be helping your brother if you can answer my questions."

Mahabadi eyed up his interrogator. "Ok, what else do you want to know?"

"When did you last speak to him?"

Mahabadi took another drink. "It is over two years now."

"Do you know where he is? Which facility, I mean?" Houghton was fishing.

"I do not know. He could be anywhere."

Houghton raised his eyebrows in disbelief; the professor became defensive. "I told you I have not spoken to him, so how would I know where he is?"

"Have you tried to contact him?"

"Of course, but he no longer has a phone, as far as I know."

"What about his wife? Have you spoken to her?"

"No, it is not possible. I do not know where she lives or what she is doing. I don't have her number."

The questions continued for another thirty minutes before the professor declared a halt. "I have told you all I can, now if you will excuse me, I have another lecture. I need to go," he said and stood up.

Houghton also stood up. "Before you go, have you got a photograph you could let me have? I will return it to you."

There was a look of frustration from the professor. He rummaged around in his jacket, pulled out his wallet and dug out a picture from one of the leather pockets. It was a family shot; the edges of the photograph were dog-eared and frayed.

"That is Hassan and his wife and the children. It is over two years old, but it is the only one I have."

Houghton took the picture and looked at it.

"Thank you; I will return it in a few days. Can I have your address?"

"You know where to find me."

"Yes, of course. Thank you professor, you have been very

helpful. I really appreciate you seeing me today."

Houghton offered his hand again, but the professor just turned and walked out of the café.

Houghton went to the cashier's desk and paid for the drinks. It would take him another four hours before he was back on home territory. He was mulling over his conversation with the professor; it hadn't been as fruitful as he had hoped. The task ahead had not got any easier.

The following day, Houghton and Fellows were seated in the Commander's briefing room at eight o'clock, waiting for their boss. Houghton twisted the blind mechanism, so the outside was blocked from view.

"Good morning, ma'am," said Houghton and Fellows in unison as the Commander entered the small room.

"Good morning gentlemen. So, what have we got?" Straight and to the point, the Commander put a file down on the table. "Nick, your meeting with Professor Mahabadi, how did it go?"

"Not as easy or as productive as I'd have liked. He doesn't like British Secret Service, that's for sure."

"No, well, I can't blame him; we've not treated him that well," said the Commander.

"I did get some personal details on Hassan which will come in useful and something interesting about his wife. She's the daughter of Sadeq Pahlavi."

There were blank looks from his colleagues.

Just then, the door opened, and a bright-looking intern walked in with a tray, three cups and a large thermos; there was a small jug of milk and a sugar bowl to the side. Fellows took the tray, and the intern left.

"Carry on Nick," said the Commander while Fellows dispensed the drinks.

"As I was saying, Hassan's wife is the daughter of Sadeq Pahlavi. I did some research, and he was a cousin of the former prime minister and a prominent member of the pre-revolution government. Unfortunately, he was executed by the Ayatollah regime in 1979."

The Commander looked at the two officers and took a drink of coffee. "Hmm, that could prove a problem. Do you think she's being watched?"

"That's difficult to say, but we can't rule it out. Wife of a prominent nuclear scientist and daughter of a pre-revolution politician; my guess, they'll be all over her like a rash."

"Hmm," said the Commander, topping up her cup from the flask. "Although, if they had suspected her of anything, wouldn't they have picked her up by now?"

"That depends, you would have thought so, but if she is being watched, they'll probably keep her under surveillance to see what she's up to. I mean, applying for a job at the British compound; it would have set all manner of hares racing," said Houghton.

"You could be right," said the Commander. "So, where does that leave us? Any thoughts?"

Fellows picked up the narrative. "The real difficulty is going to be getting in touch with Mahabadi. I've had a chat with Ahmad Qomi, as you suggested, and we're going to see if we can set up some way of exchanging messages without alerting the Iranians. Unfortunately, we don't know what communication he has with his wife. There must be some; otherwise, we wouldn't have received the message in the first place. We really need to speak to her; she's the key."

"Yes, I agree with that, although given her situation, we will need to tread very carefully."

The room went quiet as the Commander finished the remainder of her coffee and looked up. "There is someone else who might be able to help us."

Houghton and Fellows looked at each other.

"Mayflower," said the Commander cryptically.

"Mayflower?" said Houghton.

"Yes, she's an asset we have in Tehran. She's been in deep cover for over three years."

"I wasn't aware we had anyone in Tehran," said Houghton.

"Few people know about it, just me, the DC and her handler; it's too risky."

"So, what's her story?" said Houghton.

"She's a nurse at Mardom Hospital. One of the embassy staff, Saunders, was admitted there just over three years ago with appendicitis and she was looking after him. As I understand it, she passed him a note as he was leaving, just her phone number. Saunders contacted her and, to cut a very long story short, we recruited her. We have kept her very low key through necessity, but occasionally she sends us useful information. The hospital in question is a private facility where government officials are sent if they need treatment. It's always useful to know who is feeling unwell in the regime."

"But why did she want to get involved? If she were caught, I can't imagine the consequences," said Fellows.

"I don't have a lot of information, but apparently her father was killed by Khomeini. Saunders arranged to meet her and eventually passed her on to us, but, given the situation out there, we have been very light-touch. Even the embassy staff are not aware of her, but she's already proved to be a reliable asset, and I think she could be very useful here. Have a word with Jordan Proctor; he's her handler. I'll let him know to expect you."

The Commander refilled her cup.

"Have you any ideas on how you might get them away?" said the Commander.

"Nothing definite; I'm working on a couple of scenarios, but it's going to take a lot of arranging," said Fellows.

"Well, bring Nick up to speed and give me an update later today."

"Yes, will do," said Fellows.

"I did get a photograph from the Professor," said Houghton. "I've passed it on to the tech guys. I'm hoping we can use it for passports. It has all four of the family on and isn't in bad condition."

"Yes, good, we'll certainly need passports, I doubt the Iranians have let them keep theirs," said the Commander.

She knocked back the remnants of her coffee and stood up. "Ok, Nick, speak to Proctor about Mayflower, then I think you need to get out there and see Hassan's wife. Meanwhile, I'll speak to the Foreign Office to see if we can arrange for one of the admin staff to take some leave; there should be no shortage of takers."

"Yes, ma'am."

Chapter Two

A few minutes later, Houghton was at the Iranian 'desk'. Actually, it was several desks; a small department with around fifteen specialists who would monitor anything of interest involving Iran; it was a twenty-four-hour operation. Most people were seated in front of screens wearing headphones, listening for keywords that would warrant a more detailed investigation. Much of it was boring and mundane work.

Jordan Proctor was head of this department. He was a highly-valued member of the central staff. Formerly a field agent based in Tehran, his knowledge of the Iranian political system and culture was vital to the running of the desk.

Houghton saw Proctor at one of the workstations listening to some telephone chatter with a pair of headphones held up to one ear. A female team member was seated next to him, watching him at work. Houghton attracted his attention and Proctor acknowledged him with a wave. He passed the headset back to his colleague, gave some instructions, and then spoke to Houghton.

"Hi Nick, take a pew."

Proctor was in his early forties with a taste for flamboyant clothes. Today he was his usual self, wearing a yellow shirt and lime green jeans. Houghton momentarily had visions of an unripe banana and had to bite his lip at the thought, but he composed himself. They exchanged pleasantries.

"I take it you know why I'm here?" said Houghton.

"Yeah, just had a call from Mother. Mayflower?"

"That's right. From what Mother was saying, she could be a big help with a project I'm running. Did she explain the situation?"

"Not in detail; just that you need to be in Tehran and wanted access to Mayflower."

"Yeah, I'll be heading out shortly. I think Mayflower could be a useful contact while I'm there."

"Ok, I'll arrange it from here. Let me know a date and a rough time, and I'll set it up."

"How will I know her?" said Houghton.

"You won't – she'll know you."

"Can you give me some background on her? Mother said that she made contact with one of the diplomats."

"Yes, one of them went down with appendicitis and Mayflower was the theatre nurse that looked after him. As he was leaving, she slipped her phone number into his hand. He called her, then passed her on to us. I was a field agent working out of Istanbul at the time. It took a while to arrange, but eventually, I met her in a coffee shop in Tehran and became her handler."

"Great, thanks," said Nick, even though he hadn't really learnt anything new.

"Will you be meeting David?" said Proctor.

"Dexter? Yes, they're arranging accommodation at the compound; he's my liaison there. I assume he doesn't know about Mayflower?"

"No, and for the moment we want to keep it that way. Although that might change if the circumstances dictate. We're working on the basis that the less anyone knows about Mayflower, the safer she'll be."

"Yeah, I get that," said Houghton. "Ok, thanks. I'll be in

touch when I get out there."

"Good luck," said Proctor. "David's a good guy; you two will get on well."

They shook hands. Houghton got up and walked back to his office.

London Heathrow Airport – Monday April 10th – 5:00 a.m.

Three days later, an admin member of the British Embassy staff was at Tehran Imam Khomeini International Airport, boarding a plane to London Heathrow. Nick Houghton was travelling in the reverse direction, posing as his relief. He sat in the executive lounge at Heathrow Airport, waiting for his flight. It had been a very early start and he felt weary, but the adrenaline prevented any chance of a nap.

The rain spattered down the windows of the terminal building; it was still dark, an hour and a half before sunrise. His trip to Iran was part of his job, but the mission filled him with a great deal of anxiety. He was not afraid; he had been on similar missions before, but each had its own degree of uncertainty, and this one had more than any he had previously undertaken.

Email traffic between the British Embassy and the Foreign Office was almost certainly being monitored by Iranian Intelligence. For sensitive information, the embassy used secure encryption. Normal channels were only used for non-sensitive information such as administrative issues, or when the embassy or Foreign Office wanted to distribute misinformation.

Houghton's arrival in Tehran fell into the latter category. A straightforward memo had been sent from the embassy stating that the mother of Leo Sinclair, one of the junior support staff, had been taken ill and he had requested an immediate return to the UK. A relief officer would be required, and after some emails back and forth, Nick Houghton was established as Sinclair's temporary replacement.

The five-hour flight was uneventful; Houghton viewed a couple of in-flight movies and dozed occasionally. It was his first visit to the Iranian capital. As the plane descended towards Tehran, he could see the city stretching below him from his window seat. The snow-topped Alborz Mountains loomed large in the background like giants guarding the city. Then the plane touched down, and Houghton felt a strange déja-vu; a nervous shiver ran through his body.

He exited the plane behind another hundred and fifty passengers, anonymous faces going about their business. He rode the escalator into terminal three and was surprised at the space and airiness of the arrivals hall. He'd never really thought about the airport's appearance, but it wasn't what he was expecting.

There were the usual queues at the passport control booths, and he waited in line for his turn. Other aircraft had landed, and there were now over two hundred people waiting to be cleared.

People around him were getting impatient at the delay. Children were screaming or running around; parents trying desperately to keep them under control. Tempers were rising; couples were arguing. It all seemed to add to the stress Houghton was feeling.

It was his turn; it had taken over half an hour. The officer was dressed in military uniform, complete with a sidearm. Houghton handed over his documents and waited as the officer examined them. Heavily-armed guards in green uniform watched the queues vigilantly; Houghton felt conspicuous.

He was blessed with twenty-twenty vision, but for this operation, he was wearing special photochromic spectacles which would darken in bright light. He hoped they would help to confuse security cameras.

The customs man looked at Houghton. "Glasses, move," he ordered. Houghton complied and blinked as his eyes became accustomed to the light. The officer looked closely at the picture on the passport.

"Reason for visit?"

"I have business here," said Houghton.

"What business?"

"British Embassy staff. I have a visa."

Houghton held his breath. The man flicked slowly through the passport and visa, continuing his scrutiny, looking up and back to the documents. After what seemed an inordinate amount of time, he reached the back page and applied the entry stamp with a thump which made Houghton jump. He passed the documents back to Houghton without eye contact.

Houghton could feel the anxiety as he made his way to the baggage carousel. He wanted to wipe his face with his handkerchief but needed to give the impression he was relaxed and at ease. Eyes were everywhere.

Houghton was a natural choice for this mission, not just because of his expertise in the field, but also because of his looks. His mother was born in Syria, and he had inherited many of her Middle-Eastern traits, including a dark complexion and wavy black hair. With his short beard, he did not look out of place in Tehran and would not be easily recognisable as English unless he spoke. He was not a Farsi speaker, but he was fluent in Arabic.

The carousel started moving, and eventually, his luggage was disgorged from the bowels of the machine, and he grabbed the handle as it reached him. He looked across the arrivals hall and noted the number of armed police; there were security cameras everywhere. His glasses darkened in the glare of the internal lighting.

It was seven-thirty in the evening and dark outside, but pleasantly mild as he reached the exit. Numerous taxi-drivers were eagerly trying to attract fares. He looked along the mass of men holding their signs, then spotted one in a smart sports jacket and dark trousers holding up a white notice with 'Houghton' printed on it.

He approached the man. "Houghton, Gholhak Garden?"

"Yes, come," said the man, grabbing Houghton's suitcase.

Houghton tagged along behind with his cabin bag, as the man strode purposefully out of the exit.

They approached a black Jaguar, and the driver stowed the luggage in the boot and opened the back passenger door. It was eerily quiet as the car pulled away. The driver made no attempt at conversation, and Houghton had no intention of initiating any. He observed the passing buildings on the stop-start journey. People were going about their normal lives, but he noticed a significant military presence. Armed units were in evidence at regular intervals. They passed the impressive Azardi Tower, lit by arc-lights; an enormous construction which had, surprisingly, survived the Islamic revolution despite being commissioned by the reviled Shah. Houghton took it all in.

It took around forty-five minutes to reach the gates of the Gholhak compound. After a cursory glance from the guards, the barrier was raised, and they were waved through. There was a long drive leading to the accommodation area. It was dark, any external street-lighting was shielded by the towering trees.

The Jaguar pulled up outside the main building; an impressive colonial design which housed the diplomatic apartments.

A smartly dressed man appeared at the entrance and approached the car. He opened the door for the visitor to exit.

"Mr Houghton?"

"Yes."

"Come, I am Javad, the concierge, we have been expecting you. I will show you to your quarters."

Houghton thanked the driver who had retrieved the baggage from the boot of the car. The Jaguar pulled away to the vehicle compound at the back of the house; the driver's job was done for the day.

Houghton followed Javad into the building. The reception area was deathly quiet, but he could just make out the low sound of TVs coming from upstairs.

Javad explained that the diplomatic support staff were housed in the residential block, while the diplomats had their own private apartments which were separate from the main building and much larger. His English was excellent with only a hint of a local accent.

Houghton followed him up a wide staircase to the first floor.

"These are the staff apartments," said the concierge. "You

are number eight. It has been made ready for you."

"Thank you," said Houghton and they walked down a long corridor to the last door. Louder sounds of televisions could be heard as they passed other apartments.

The concierge unlocked the door at the end of the corridor and handed Houghton the key.

"This is yours; let me know if I can help with anything."

"Thanks," said Houghton. He walked into the room and closed the door.

He put his suitcase on the bed and looked around his temporary residence. 'Basic' would be the most appropriate word for it. There was a small lounge with a two-seater settee facing a portable TV, a breakfast bar and adjoining kitchenette. The flooring was parquet and looked as though it might have been a ballroom in years gone by. Well-worn rugs were placed in strategic places. A door at the back of the room led to a single bedroom and bathroom. There was no décor as such, just plain walls, although the architecture matched the colonial style; this was part of the original building judging by the coving and high ceiling. The conversion had been adequate rather than tasteful. It reminded Houghton of a bedsit he'd used in London in his university days, but without the rats. It would do while he was in Iran; he had no desire to stay any longer than was necessary.

He went into the bedroom, unpacked his suitcase and stowed his clothes in the small wardrobe; his shirts and suit had creased, but they would drop overnight. He opened his briefcase with his work documents, which were in line with what would be appropriate for a consular official. The pretence would need to be water-tight; there was bound to be a level of scrutiny of new arrivals.

Houghton was jolted by the sudden sound of a telephone ringing. On the bedside table, there was a cream-coloured, ancient-looking handset; the loud trill was a throw-back to the seventies.

"Houghton," he said, picking up the receiver. The attaching cord was twisted several times, restricting its length. Houghton pulled it, and the handset fell off the table. "Shit," he muttered as he tried to reposition the phone and rewind the cord.

"Nick, are you there? It's David Dexter; I heard you had arrived. Can you be ready for seven tomorrow morning? You can drive in with me; I'll meet you outside."

"Yeah, sure," said Houghton. There had been no pleasantries and Dexter dropped the call.

The local time was ten-thirty, but Houghton's body clock was three hours behind, and despite the journey, he did not feel particularly tired. He did feel hungry though; he had not eaten since the afternoon snack on the flight. He went into the kitchen area, an alcove off the lounge; there was a small fridge which he opened; it was empty.

"Great!" he said under his breath.

He popped his keys in his pocket and walked down the stairs to the reception. The office door was open.

"Hello," called Houghton. He looked around the reception area; it had been well-maintained, and again, the architecture was impressive.

The concierge appeared. "Mr Houghton, can I help you?"

"Yeah, is there anywhere I can get some food?"

"Let me see if there is anything in the refrigerator."

The man left and appeared again a few minutes later. "I

have found a sandwich, and I can make you a coffee or tea if you would like."

"A tea, please," said Houghton and once again the man retired to his office.

The following morning, Houghton was waiting at the front entrance of the accommodation block carrying a briefcase and a holdall. As the embassy car drew up, he could see a man in the back.

The driver got out and took Houghton's baggage, stowed it in the boot, then opened the rear passenger door for the agent to get in.

"Hi Nick. David Dexter," said the man and they shook hands in greeting.

"Good to meet you," acknowledged Houghton as the car pulled away and headed for the gated exit.

"How's the accommodation?" asked Dexter.

"I've had a lot worse," said Houghton and smiled.

"Have you eaten?"

"Not yet, there was no food in."

"If you speak to the concierge and let him know what you need, he'll see to it. You can charge it to the embassy account. We can have breakfast at the embassy."

The conversation was polite and mundane; the back of the car was no place to talk about operational issues. Houghton looked out of the window to familiarise himself with the route. It took just under half an hour to complete the three-mile journey.

The main building was protected by a wall about twelve or fourteen feet tall with metal spikes to deter potential break-ins. Either side of the blue gates were concrete plinths topped with sculptures of lions similar to those in Trafalgar Square.

The gate opened, and the car was confronted by a yellow barrier, which raised as the vehicle approached. Another barrier blocked the way to enable credentials to be examined. The main gates closed behind them.

There was a small building to the left, and a security guard came out and looked at the occupants. He recognised the diplomat and the second barrier raised.

"As you can see security is pretty tight," said Dexter as the car drew up outside the main embassy building.

The construction was impressive; like the Gholhak Garden property, its design was nineteenth-century colonial-style. For a moment, Houghton took in the splendour of the embassy. White stone with balconies and balustrades; it felt like a flash-back to the 'Empire', a long-gone era.

The driver opened the passenger doors in turn, and the two men exited and went inside.

"I'll show you where to sign in," said Dexter. "You'll get a security pass which you're encouraged to wear at all times while you're in the embassy."

"Cheers," said Houghton, who was looking around the magnificent reception area. There was a desk to the left; an officer sat behind it dressed in a smart business suit. Behind her on the wall was a large portrait of the Queen and the Coat of Arms.

'Honi soit qui mal y pense'.

Houghton considered the motto. There was no denying the evil which pervaded; it seemed to be everywhere. Even the embassy, with all its security, seemed far from a safe-haven.

Dexter led Houghton to the desk and made the introductions.

"I have your security pass and badge for you," said the officer and produced the said documents from a drawer.

Formalities completed; Dexter led Houghton to the canteen. "They do a very good breakfast here," said Dexter.

Breakfast was a very civilised affair and lasted over an hour. Houghton replenished his calories with a full-English and copious cups of coffee. The conversation was relaxed and convivial. David Dexter portrayed the very essence of a diplomat. Urbane, with a 'BBC' accent. At only thirty-seven, he was young for a senior diplomat. He was immaculately presented with a coloured handkerchief protruding from the top pocket of his suit jacket. Brown 'Church' brogues completed his ensemble.

Over the meal, he gave Houghton a full run-through of embassy procedures and history, then a brief career background. Houghton listened intently but did not share the same level of information; at no stage were operational matters mentioned.

Eventually, the meal was finished, and Dexter led Houghton out of the canteen back to the grand reception area. On the opposite side of the desk, to the right of the main entrance, there was a door with a security pad. Dexter punched in four numbers, and there was a click as the lock disengaged. There was a staircase leading up, a lift, and another set of stairs leading downward.

"That leads to the main admin area and the Ambassador's suite," said Dexter pointing to the ascending stairs. "You're down here." He walked past the lift and descended with Houghton following behind. "I've found you an office you can use."

"Cheers," said Houghton.

The corridor was narrow and claustrophobic; there were doors on either side labelled with numbers and letters. They reached B23.

"This is the Comms Centre," said Dexter. "Let me introduce you to one or two people, then I'll show you to your office." Dexter opened the door into a working office with several employees milling around, engaged in their respective duties. There was an impressive array of office equipment – computer terminals, monitors, fax machines and photocopiers.

The room was quite large but with a much lower ceiling than the upstairs rooms in the building. It reminded Houghton of the war rooms in London. Dexter introduced several people, but Houghton would probably forget their names. After a few minutes, he led Houghton out of the Comms Centre and back down the corridor to room B35.

"This is you," said Dexter, and he opened the door.

It was a functional office complete with keyboard and terminal. There was a desk with a chair on either side.

The pair made themselves comfortable. "Ok, now we can start the proper briefing," said Dexter. "Let me know if you have any questions as we go along."

"Sure," said Houghton.

"Ok, firstly, this room, and the whole of the basement, is a secure area, including internet traffic; it's continuously being swept for bugs and transmitters. It's lead-lined with a high-frequency wave baffler; that's the background hum you can hear; so there should be no eavesdropping. Any emails you send from here are automatically encrypted. You are quite safe if you need to contact Vauxhall."

"Good to know."

The diplomat leaned forward and addressed Houghton in an earnest fashion. "Ok, let me tell you about Tehran. The locals are ok, and if you get to know them, they make good friends; they are extremely generous with their hospitality. But, be careful who you trust, there are spies and informers everywhere; MOIS is extremely active."

"Ministry of Intelligence?" said Houghton recognising the acronym.

"Yes, they're brutal and have a very large network across the country. Fear tactics are a very powerful tool and very productive, as I'm sure you know."

"Yes, I'm aware of their reputation," said Houghton.

"Ok, down to business. I'll arrange for you to meet Mahabadi's wife, Afareen?"

"Excellent. Have you got any more information about the situation?" asked Houghton.

"Not a lot. She started working for us as a domestic a few weeks ago, a delightful lady and smart," said Dexter.

"And she just passed the note, out of the blue?"

"Yes, you've read it, I take it?"

"Yeah, it's caused quite a stir in Vauxhall and the F.O. Mother's all over it. It's gone right to the top this one, given the political sensitivity, but we've been given the green light."

"So, what do you think? Are we going to be able to spring Mahabadi?"

"That's what I'm here to find out, but it's not going to be easy, that's for sure."

"No, it's likely Afareen will be under a great deal of

scrutiny."

"Yes, and that did give us some concern. We were wondering back home if the authorities actually know who she is; I mean, allowing her to work at the British compound. We thought she would have been picked up by now," said Houghton.

"Yes, we had the same thought."

"Well, it could be they are monitoring her and just waiting to see what she's up to. Unless, of course, she's a plant," said Houghton.

"No, I really think she's genuine; you saw the note, but you can make your own mind up when you meet her," said Dexter.

"Yes, sure. So, how do we do this?"

"Ok, well, Afareen knows you're coming; she's very keen to meet you. The safest option will be for you to talk to her in the compound. It's her day-off today otherwise we could have arranged it for this morning."

"That's ok, I want to have a look around Tehran and get to know the place."

"Do you want a driver?" asked Dexter.

"No, I'm just going to slip out if I can."

"Ok, let me know if you need anything; I'll leave you to settle in. Ring me before you go; you'll need to sign out."

This did give Houghton a problem. Ideally, he needed to leave without attracting any attention.

"Hmm," said Houghton. "Is there any way I can slip out under the radar? Bearing in mind the security situation."

"Yes, ok, that can be arranged, you can sign out with me which means you just need to let me know when you leave and when you come back. I'll cover if there are any fire drills or emergencies. You don't have to tell me where you are."

"Yeah, ok, that's great, give me half an hour."

"Just ring me on the internal phone before you leave."

"Ok, got that," said Houghton.

"Oh, I'll get someone down from IT to log you onto our internal system. It's secure as far as we know but speak to them first if you need to email anything sensitive; they'll explain the encryption process."

"Yeah, ok, cheers. I'll call you when I get back."

Dexter left, leaving Houghton to sort out his office. He picked up his holdall and took out a change of clothing; a rather crumpled plum-coloured jacket, distinctive but not remarkable, grey slacks and a pair of well-worn trainers. He walked down the corridor to the gents' toilet and got changed.

Back at his desk, suitably clothed, he unlocked his briefcase. He peeled back the false bottom and took out an envelope that had been concealed there. He read the instructions again from Proctor.

'Tehran Grand Bazaar, Moslem Restaurant 12:00-13:00'.

That was all he had. Mayflower would be at the restaurant between those times for three days and would approach him. She had his description and would look out for the jacket.

Just before eleven o'clock, Houghton called Dexter as arranged, left the office and walked up the stairs to the main entrance. He left the embassy building and headed for the exit.

It was about two hundred yards to the front gate. It was peaceful inside the confines of the boundary walls, but traffic noise was audible from the neighbouring streets. There were not many people about; a car passed him in the opposite direction on the way to the main building. Another car was being checked as he approached the control gate. Houghton walked up to the officer monitoring foot traffic and showed his credentials; he was waved through.

He left the safety of the embassy, and immediately a feeling of threat engulfed him; he could feel the adrenaline rush. He was wearing his new glasses which, in the bright sunshine, were now dark and would disguise some of his facial features. He took his bearings and walked down the street to the nearest metro station, Sa'adi. He crossed the main road, dodging the bustling traffic; blue single-decker buses and yellow taxi cabs were everywhere. He approached the station.

It was a strange façade; it looked more like a cave entrance, a hole in the ground with marble surrounds. The blue gates were open, and people were coming and going like bees into a hive. The signage was in Farsi and English. There was a moped parked on a small patch of waste ground next to the entrance. Houghton took it all in. He walked down the steps and found the ticket machine on the platform.

He bought his ticket and checked the platform; there were around twenty people waiting, mainly mothers with pushchairs and old men. All looked normal, but he wasn't taking any chances.

It was just two stops to Panzdah-e-Khordad, which was the nearest station to the Bazaar. The seats were bench-type against the windows with occupants facing the centre of the carriage; it allowed Houghton to scan his fellow passengers. There was no-one he recognised as a potential tail, but he would not drop his guard.

It was only a short journey, and Houghton was soon above ground again and walking towards the Bazaar.

He wasn't prepared for the scene that greeted him, utter pandemonium. It reminded him of his first visit to a football match at Stamford Bridge to see his favourite team. It felt like thousands of people were milling about the entrance to the Emporia. To the right was the Shah Mosque with its distinctive minarets either side of the famous clock tower.

Street traders were out in force, hustling for sales; there were stalls piled high with dried fruit and herbs; a pomegranate seller shouted to attract buyers. Houghton passed cages full of budgerigars; their urgent chirping adding to the cacophony. He noticed some uniformed men in North-Korean style hats. He was unsure what they represented and would stay clear of them.

The Bazaar was over six miles long with over twenty-two miles of passages and malls, some specialising in goods, such as jewellery, perfume or carpets. Houghton consulted the notes he had gathered from his internet search. There were many entrances, but this was the one nearest the metro station. It had a typical Islamic-style entrance, shaped like the Ace of Spades in a pack of cards. He entered the chasm; it was difficult to imagine the sight and sounds, a cacophony of voices, music and footsteps, merged together into a distinctive backdrop. Smells of scented candles, incense, perfumes, coffee, and other things invigorated his senses as he walked.

The walls on both sides were festooned with hundreds of items, garments and household goods, all suspended from coat hangers. Stall proprietors, he noticed, would use a boat-hook to lift down an item for a potential buyer. Houghton continued to be vigilant, but without looking furtive; he needed to appear more relaxed than he was feeling. His glasses adjusted to the light.

He was being swept along in the throng like a twig in a stream. He came to a junction and stopped in a shop doorway to collect his bearings. He looked along each passageway, the horde was unabated. The shop proprietor immediately stepped out from behind his cash-desk and confronted the potential customer. He spoke in Farsi; Houghton replied in Arabic and then asked for directions to Moslem Restaurant.

"Moslem Restaurant?" repeated the shop-owner and pointed down an adjacent mall.

Houghton nodded to the man and followed the directions. He walked down the rows of stalls and shops for about ten minutes and suddenly noticed a queue of people ascending metal steps. The sign was in both Farsi and English, 'Moslem Restaurant'. He joined the back of the line and checked the time, eleven-fifty.

It took twenty minutes for him to make the entrance to the restaurant at the top of the stairs. The sight that awaited him was something to behold. It was like no restaurant he had ever seen, more a very large canteen; it was heaving with people. The seating was interesting, clearly designed for functionality, not for comfort or ambience. There were several rows of long, narrow bench-style tables in the centre of the room and further tables around the outside walls. Uncomfortable-looking chairs were stationed close together, ensuring maximum occupancy. None appeared to be conducive to any sort of conversation but, nevertheless, the sound of a hundred, maybe two-hundred, voices added to the clamour of the place. Every space appeared to be taken.

Houghton waited for another five minutes then noticed two women leaving, chatting away to each other. He moved for one of the vacant seats; the person behind him in the queue took the other. The array of food was impressive, local dishes, kebabs of every description and flavours; the house speciality was Tanchin, a savoury cake, which seemed to be in great demand.

It was almost twelve-fifteen before he was seated; a young man took his order, and a girl in an apron cleared the place-setting and wiped it down with a cloth. Houghton took off his glasses so he would be recognised, and ordered a salad, in English.

His food arrived, and he looked around his fellow diners trying to spot his contact. No-one appeared to be looking in his direction; they seemed to be too busy concentrating on their food or chatting. He checked the entrance; the queue was unabated. Then he noticed a woman at the front of the line. She was wearing a light top-coat, trousers, and a blue silk scarf. She seemed to be scanning the restaurant. She could have been looking for a spare seat, but then her eyes stopped at Houghton and appeared to nod. After a couple of minutes, she walked to a spare seat. It was on the same table as Houghton, about four spaces down on the opposite side. She sat down and made eye contact with Houghton again. He nodded back. Houghton's food arrived, and a few minutes later, she received a sandwich. The eye contact was repeated several times.

Having consumed her food, the woman vacated her seat and gesticulated discreetly with her head. It would have gone unnoticed by any casual observer, but Houghton spotted it. He left the rest of his meal, immediately vacated his seat and followed the woman. The blue scarf would be his guide.

They descended the stairs, passing the line of people waiting to get in. At the foot of the steps, the woman turned right; Houghton followed.

For about ten minutes, the woman led Houghton down different malls, occasionally doubling back on herself. Houghton followed at a discreet distance, not taking his eyes off the scarf; if he did, he would lose her in the throng.

She reached an alley and turned left. Houghton walked briskly; she was now out of sight. He reached the corner and looked around. She was about fifty yards away, looking into a shop window. She turned and saw him, then walked on. The alleyway was almost deserted; the woman stopped at another shop and waited. Houghton looked behind him; there was no-one there. He was as certain as he could be that they weren't being followed.

He went over and stood next to her, looking in the same window.

"Come with me," she said. Houghton complied, and they walked about fifty yards further to a traditional tea shop.

"In here," she said assertively.

They walked through the entrance door; in front of them was a flight of stairs which they ascended.

They entered a small room set out with about twenty tables; four of them in separate booths. It was quite dark, and Houghton's new eye-wear responded accordingly. She walked to one of the booths in the corner and gestured for Houghton to join her. They sat opposite each other, quite close. It was ideal for anyone wishing privacy.

A man approached with a menu and handed it to the woman. She spoke in Farsi, and the man left them.

"I have ordered two coffees," she said, looking into his eyes, studying his face.

"I am Eliz Bashi; I believe you wanted to see me."

Chapter Three

"I'm really pleased to meet you," said Houghton. "Yes, I think you could be very important to a project I'm involved with. I can't explain in detail right now, but I wanted to make contact."

Eliz looked at Houghton intensely; fully engaged, assessing her new acquaintance. Houghton was finding it unnerving.

"So, in what way can I help you?" She spoke with a local accent; her voice was low and breathy.

"I'm not sure yet, but I must warn you, it could be very dangerous."

"I knew, always, that one day I would be asked to help; I was expecting it. I am prepared."

She had striking features, high cheekbones, dark eyes; her makeup looked as though it had been applied by an expert; she could have been a Bollywood movie star. Her dark hair was completely covered by the scarf as required in Iran. Her coat was open, and Houghton could see the blue uniform of a nurse underneath.

"I understand you work at a hospital."

"Yes, at the Mardom, District Four, not far away."

The proprietor interrupted them to deliver their coffee. Eliz spoke to him in Farsi and dropped some notes in his tray in payment.

Eliz handed Houghton a small cup of espresso. On the tray, there was a small pewter jug filled with hot water. Eliz topped up her drink and passed it to Houghton.

"Thanks," said the agent, who did the same, then returned the vessel to the tray. The proprietor bowed slightly and left them to their conversation. The nurse put her cup to her lips and took the first sip. The process was slow and deliberate.

"It is ok; this is a safe place. I know that man – he is the owner; he was a friend of my father."

"Your father? He was killed, I heard. I'm sorry to hear that."

"Yes. He was killed by Khomeini's thugs." She looked down at her coffee.

"Sorry. You were talking about your work at the hospital."

"Yes, I work with the surgeons."

"That's a big responsibility," said Houghton.

"Yes, but it is something that I am trained to do. So, what will you want me to do?"

"I'm not certain yet. I'm still planning, and I need to make a lot more enquiries before I can go into detail. What I really wanted to do today was to meet you and work out some sort of way of contacting you when I need to. What would be the safest way for me to get in touch?"

"I can give you my phone number. You say what time, no more. We always meet here; it is safe."

"What about work?"

"If you can give me one day if possible, I can arrange my break: if I cannot do it, I will say."

"So, you will need a day's notice?"

"Yes, if it is possible or you will have to wait for me. This time of day, it is good."

"I can work with that."

They exchanged numbers.

"Do you have a family?" asked Houghton.

"It is best I do not say too much," replied Eliz.

She was holding her cup in her right hand. She looked around, wary of the two customers that had just entered the café; women, early-twenties, dressed casually, jeans and tops with headscarves. The proprietor escorted the new arrivals to another booth, away from where Eliz and Houghton were. Eliz watched the two women animatedly chatting to each other, breaking the silence of the café. She took a large gulp from her cup, finishing the last of her coffee. She looked around again, then stood up.

"I need to leave now. You wait five minutes, then you leave."

"Yes, ok," said Houghton, slightly taken aback. "I need to get to the metro station; which is the quickest way?"

"It is not far. If you go this way for one hundred metres, it is the finish of the Bazaar; then you go to the... er, right... two, three hundred metres across the road; you will see." She illustrated her directions with hand signals.

"Thanks, I'll be in touch very soon," said Houghton and he watched as Eliz moved towards the exit. She said something to the proprietor who looked at Houghton and nodded. Then she was gone. The sound of eager voices continued, uninterrupted by the nurse's departure.

Houghton ordered another coffee and reflected on his meeting. It had given him food for thought, but everything would hang on his meeting with Mahabadi's wife.

He waited fifteen minutes before he left the coffee shop. He thanked the proprietor, who nodded in acknowledgement.

He was once again wearing his glasses, but in the darkness of the bazaar, they would not significantly disguise his face. He stopped at the entrance to the coffee shop to get his bearings and check if there were any possible threats. He saw none.

He left the cafe, following Eliz's directions. He looked right and could see the exit; although it was not the one he had entered. As he left the cauldron of the Grand Bazaar, he made a note of landmarks so he could find their meeting place again. Across the road, there was a pharmacy, which would be his marker.

Once outside, he turned right and walked for about ten minutes before he recognised where he was. The metro station was about a hundred metres on the other side of the road; he could see the entrance.

Houghton made his way back to the embassy. At the gate, he showed his pass and was let through, then he made his way down to the basement and called David Dexter.

"David? It's Nick; just to let you know I'm back. I need to send some secure emails; you mentioned the tech guys could help...? Great, I'm in my office."

Houghton quickly changed back into his shirt and suit in his office; it was private enough.

A few minutes later, Ryan Hudson, the embassy's chief technician, arrived in Houghton's office and explained the procedures for sending encrypted emails. Houghton was impressed by the man, and an idea occurred to him.

"I have a problem which you may be able to help me with", said Houghton.

"Sure, shoot," said Hudson.

"Ok, say if I was in a sensitive installation here in Iran, and I wanted to get private messages out to someone, how would I do it?"

"Ok, so I presume this someone is under surveillance?"

"Twenty-four-hour monitoring," replied Houghton.

"Hmm, more difficult. So, I guess phones are going to be a problem."

"Yeah, no phones or computer, and only limited contact with the family."

"Wait, are you talking about the micro-message?"

"You know about it? I didn't realise," said Houghton.

"Yes, it was me who encrypted it and sent it through."

"You'll understand my problem then."

"Hmm, yeah."

Ryan was seated on the chair in front of Houghton's desk, deep in thought.

"So, you want to try and get him away?" said Ryan.

"Yeah, that's the general idea, but keep it to yourself, eh?" replied Houghton.

"Yes, of course, naturally." The tech thought for a moment. "A simple coding system would probably be the best way."

"That's a bit Elizabethan," said Houghton.

"Yes, but it works. The Russians and Germans used it extensively in the Second World War, and the terrorist groups still use it today. When are you seeing the wife?"

"Tomorrow," said Houghton. "The difficulty's going to be getting a message from her to him. I'm assuming he can use the micro-message again, but I need to speak to his wife."

"There is one thing in our favour, he speaks English, which will be easier for us. I assume his wife does too," said Ryan.

"She certainly speaks it; I'm not sure about writing

45

though," replied Houghton. "I'll check."

"Well, if you need anything on the tech side, let me know."

"Sure thing."

Ryan Hudson left with Houghton deep in thought, trying to piece together a workable plan; a lot depended on his meeting with Afareen Mahabadi.

He started composing his encrypted email; it was to Jordan Proctor, for the file, detailing his first meeting with Mayflower.

He then made a call to Vauxhall on the secure line. It was picked up straight away. "Fellows," came the assertive reply. It was just an update, but it was good to hear a familiar voice. The line was clear; it was as though Houghton was in the same room as his colleague. The conversation was suitably cryptic, Houghton was taking no chances.

"It's Nick… yeah, good, thanks. I met our friend this lunchtime, and I think we could definitely do business there. I'm meeting with our main supplier in the morning; I'll update you on their terms tomorrow. Can you pass on the update?"

"Yes, of course, pleased to hear sales are going well," replied Fellows.

"So far, so good. I'm hoping for a positive result tomorrow."

There was a brief catch up before Houghton dropped the call. He paused for a moment and steepled his fingers on his chin, deep in thought.

Dexter called on the internal phone just after five o'clock; he was about to leave and offered Houghton a lift back to the

Gholhak Garden compound.

Houghton packed away his laptop and locked it in one of the desk drawers, then walked up the stairs to the reception area. He also left the holdall containing his change of clothes in another drawer; he would need them again. Dexter was waiting.

The Jaguar was parked outside the front entrance; exhaust vapour puffed from the pipe at the rear as it idled. The uniformed driver got out and opened the door as the two men approached.

"Thank you, Darius," said Dexter as the pair buckled their seatbelts in the back of the car.

The journey back to the compound was slow; the rush-hour traffic crawling along the Modares Highway was incessant. Conversation in the car was mundane; nothing to alert the attentive Darius. As with all local embassy staff, he had been suitably vetted, but no chances would be taken. The gate of the compound opened as the Jaguar approached; they were expected, and after a cursory glance at their ID, the car was waved through with minimum fuss or delay.

As Houghton was about to exit the car at the main reception block, Dexter extended an invitation.

"What are you doing for dinner tonight?"

"Nothing planned," replied Houghton.

"Why don't you join us, say seven-fifteen; we're just over there, number four?" Dexter pointed to the more substantial accommodation properties reserved for senior diplomats.

"Yeah, ok, great, see you then, thanks," replied Houghton, and he left the car and entered the building.

Just before seven-fifteen, Houghton was walking through

the grounds to the Dexters' residence. It was a warm, dry evening, and birdsong reverberated through the trees. Houghton was dressed casually in jeans and a short-sleeved shirt. For the first time since his arrival in Iran, he felt a degree of peace and was starting to relax.

He reached Dexter's front door and knocked. The residence was by no means luxurious – more functional than anything. It resembled a large seaside holiday chalet, but brick-built, not wood.

"Hi Nick, come in," said Dexter, opening the door. "This is my wife, Sophie," he added as they were joined by his partner.

"Hello," said Sophie and shook hands with their guest.

Houghton looked around the room. It was much bigger than it appeared from the outside and the Dexters, presumably Sophie, had made it very comfortable and homely.

"Take a seat," said David. "Would you like a beer?"

"A beer? Thanks, yes please," said Houghton. "I thought alcohol was banned."

"Diplomatic privileges," said David, and walked through an adjoining door into the kitchen.

"So, David tells me you live in London; how are things there?" said Sophie.

"Oh, much the same," said Houghton, who was not being deliberately vague; he just couldn't think of anything worthwhile on which to comment.

"What about security? I hear the threat level is quite high."

Houghton was slightly taken aback at the question.

"Hmm, yes, that's still high; there are plenty of people with agendas out there," replied Houghton, as David brought in the drinks.

There was more polite conversation before Sophie retired to the kitchen to plate up the meals.

"Take a seat; I'll bring the dinner through," she shouted from the kitchen.

There was a four-seater dining table in the corner set for three with a bottle of wine and three glasses. David and Houghton took a seat as Sophie came into the room holding two plates with a tea-towel.

"Careful the plates are hot," she said as she put the food in front of the two men. Houghton looked at the meatballs and rice.

"It's Kufte, it's a traditional Iranian dish. Afareen brings them in from home; they are delicious. I had some in the freezer, so it was simple enough to do when David mentioned you were joining us."

"That's really good of you, I appreciate the invite; I'm still trying to get my bearings here," said Houghton.

The dinner was consumed with convivial conversation; there was no mention of the pending meeting with Hassan Mahabadi's wife. Sophie served Sholezard for dessert, a saffron-flavoured rice pudding, another Iranian dish which Houghton had never tried before.

After the meal, David turned to Houghton; "I expect you'll want to freshen up; let me show you the bathroom."

"Thanks," said Houghton, and while Sophie cleared the dishes into the kitchen, David escorted the guest to the bathroom.

"Just here," said David and opened the closet door. Houghton looked surprised when David entered with him and closed the door behind them.

"This room and the bedroom have been cleared for bugs, so it's safe to talk. I just wanted to let you know that Afareen will be here at about eight o'clock tomorrow. Sophie will give you a dish with some food before you leave, which you can return in the morning. That will be your excuse for the visit here. I'll be on a conference call from eight o'clock as far as anyone is concerned; I'll order the car for nine, then we can leave for the embassy together; it will look less suspicious."

"Yeah, ok, got it," said Houghton.

"If you get here about eight-fifteen, that will be about right. Sophie leaves about ten-to-nine for work. I'll hang on for you in any case; I have things I can be getting on with. You might want to mention to the concierge that you are returning something and that you'll be waiting for me to take you to the embassy."

"Yes, ok, no problem. You think the concierge might be an informer?"

"I think they could all be informers if the price is right; I don't trust anyone. It might be fine, but we just can't take any chances, people's lives are at stake."

"Yeah," said Houghton. David left the bathroom and returned to the lounge. Then Houghton flushed the toilet and re-joined his hosts.

It wasn't a late night; it had just turned nine-thirty when Houghton made his way back to the main building carrying a Pyrex dish. As he opened the door to the main entrance, he noticed the concierge come out of his office behind the desk to see who was there.

"Hello Javad," said Houghton, deliberately acknowledging the man's presence. "Just been to the Dexters, been trying some delicious meatballs, an Iranian dish."

"Ah, yes, Kufte," said the man taking an interest in the Pyrex dish.

Houghton looked at him. "Yes, that's it; I couldn't remember the name. See you in the morning."

The concierge returned to his office and Houghton continued to his apartment.

Gholhak Garden Compound – Wednesday, April 12th – 8:00 a.m.

The following morning, Houghton was in the lobby of the main building at eight o'clock carrying the empty Pyrex dish and his briefcase.

He walked to the reception desk where Javad was attending to a smartly-dressed woman, probably in her thirties, wearing a business suit and designer glasses. A black scarf was wrapped around her head and draped over her shoulders. She turned as Houghton approached the desk.

"Hello, you must be the new arrival," she said.

"Hello, yes, got here a couple of days ago," replied Houghton.

"I'm Dee, pleased to meet you," she replied, and they shook hands.

"Nick... Houghton."

"Are you going into town?"

"To the embassy? Yes, but later, I have a lift."

"That's a shame, you could have shared the minibus; there are a couple of others; they'll be down shortly."

Houghton noticed she had brown eyes, and there was dark hair protruding from the white shawl around her head and shoulders. She spoke with a distinctive Home-Counties

English accent; the kind you would hear on BBC Radio 4.

"What are you doing this evening?"

"Nothing special," said Houghton.

"Good, I'll invite a couple of the others around for some drinks and nibbles, say about eight. You can meet your neighbours."

Houghton hesitated for a minute, and Dee detected a reticence.

"It's ok if you're busy."

"Oh, no, no. Sorry, yes, I'll be glad to. What number are you?"

"Number one; first floor."

"Ok. Eight o'clock, I look forward to it."

"Great. Sorry, did you want Javad? I'm just waiting for the others," said Dee.

Javad was hovering at the desk watching the pair in polite conversation. Dee moved to one side to allow Houghton access to the concierge.

"Mr Houghton. How are you today? Can I help you with anything?"

Houghton was conspicuously holding the Pyrex dish, which Javad noticed. "Only to let you know, I'll be going in with Mr Dexter again. I'm returning this, and then we'll be leaving from his quarters."

"Yes, yes, of course. I will let the driver know. Have a nice day."

"Thanks," said Houghton and turned to Dee.

"Thanks again for the invite; I'll see you at eight."

"Great," said Dee, and Houghton walked towards the exit, trying to re-focus on his meeting with Afareen.

Houghton reached the Dexters' residence and knocked

on the door; it was David who answered.

"Nick, hi, come in. I hope you slept well."

"Yes, fine thanks," replied Houghton and went into the lounge where Sophie Dexter was gathering some paperwork from the table they had used for dinner the previous evening.

"Hello Sophie," said Houghton and handed her the Pyrex dish. "Thanks again for dinner last night, it was very good."

"Hello Nick," she replied and took the dish from him. "Glad you enjoyed it. Would you like some breakfast? David will be tied up for a little while."

"Yes, thank you," said Houghton.

"Just toast, I'm afraid, and a coffee?"

"That's perfect, thanks," said Houghton.

He noticed someone in the kitchen, which he assumed was Mrs Mahabadi.

"I'm just about to take a conference call," said David. "Why don't you take a seat."

"Thanks," said Houghton.

Sophie went into the kitchen with the dish and returned a few minutes later with a plate of toast and a coffee. Afareen was behind her pulling a vacuum cleaner. She plugged in the appliance and switched it on, making an almighty din. David beckoned Afareen and Houghton to follow him while Sophie started moving furniture and took over the appliance.

The pair followed David into the master bedroom and shut the door. The room was tidy, and the bed made.

"Nick, this is Afareen; Afareen, this is Nick."

Afareen put her arm across her chest and bowed her head slightly. "You are here to help my family, thank you."

David whispered. "I'll leave you to it, but don't be too long, twenty minutes only, ok."

He left and closed the door.

"Ok, Afareen, I'm Nick, and yes, I'm here to try to get you away, but it's not going to be easy. I'll need a lot of information from you."

He looked at her; she was attractive, but her face was lined from the traumas of life. Specs of grey mottled the wisps of hair that protruded from beneath her white scarf.

"Yes, I understand," said Afareen.

"Ok, I know you speak English, do you read it too?"

"Yes, we were taught at school."

"Ok, that's good. First, I need to know about contact with your husband. We'll need to be able to get messages to him without raising suspicion."

"Yes, we can do that. My husband is a scientist and mathematician; we use... er, a book sometimes."

"What do you mean?"

"We use words from it when we don't want them to know about what we are saying."

"Secret messages?"

"Yes," replied Afareen. "We use it for many years, even when we were at college."

"What about the micro-messages?"

Afareen looked confused.

"Sorry... the small writing. The one you gave to Mrs Dexter."

"Yes, yes, that was the first time."

"But you could use that to get a message back to him if necessary?"

"Yes, I can do that."

"Good, ok... Where is he based?"

"He is still at Natanz, but they move the scientists around

all the time in case of airstrikes."

"Hmm, yes I can understand that... So, do you see your husband at all?"

"Once a month, he visits our house and sees the children, but he is followed everywhere, even to the park. Our telephone is listened to, we are sure. He gave me the message that I gave to Mrs Dexter when he visited last time."

"How long does he stay?"

"Three days, that is all."

"Hmm... that doesn't give us long," said Houghton, thinking aloud. "When is he due to visit again?"

"Er... two weeks, he will come, I think, but who knows."

Houghton was jotting notes down on a small notepad.

"What about your job here? Did anyone say anything to you?"

"No, I have not seen anyone."

"But I mean, you working for the British Embassy, the wife of a prominent scientist?"

"No, they say nothing; my husband is too important; he has some very, how you say? Er, powerful friends in the Ministry."

"The Ministry?" repeated Houghton.

"Yes, the Ministry of Intelligence."

"I see. So, do you think you are being watched?"

"Yes, I am sure, but they do not bother me. I see them sometimes on the Metro. I recognise them; sometimes I want to wave to them." She smiled for the first time.

"What about searches?" said Houghton.

"They do not search me; they would not dare. As I said, my husband is a very important man."

"Ok, now I need some personal information from you.

We need to get you some new passports. What is your full name and date of birth, and your children?"

Afareen gave Houghton the information which he jotted down in his notebook.

"I managed to get a photograph from your husband's brother in England."

"Mehran? You have spoken to Mehran?"

"Yes, I needed to get some information."

"I have not spoken to him for two, maybe three years. It is as though he has abandoned us. You did not tell him we wish to leave Iran?"

"No, nothing at all."

"That is good. I have never liked him, and he doesn't like me. He disapproved of my marriage to Hassan. I do not trust him."

"Hmm, thanks for that, but don't worry, I haven't said anything about why I needed information."

"He may think something is wrong and tell the regime."

"You think he would betray you?"

"I do not know, but it is possible."

"Ok, I'll bear that in mind. What about photographs? The ones I have are ok, but if you have more recent ones, they will be better."

"Yes, I will bring tomorrow. I can give it to Mrs Dexter."

"Yes, that will be fine… Ok, we better leave it for now, but I'll contact you again very soon once I have something more. Is it just you and the children at home?"

"No, my mother also she is there. She looks after them while I work."

"You understand that we won't be able to take her too."

"Yes, of course."

"It could be dangerous for her if they find you are missing."

"She knows; she will help us."

"Ok, thanks Afareen, that's been very helpful. I'll be in touch soon."

Houghton put his notebook in his pocket, and they left the bedroom. The vacuum cleaner was stationary in the middle of the floor, unattended, but still making enough noise to make normal conversation virtually impossible. As Afareen returned to the lounge, Sophie switched off the appliance. David was reading some papers on the dining table.

"We better go," said David, as Houghton walked into the room. Sophie put on her scarf.

"I better go too," she said and picked up a hessian carrier bag containing books and papers.

"I think the car has arrived; I ordered it for nine," said David, looking at his watch.

The three left the residence together. Sophie continued walking towards the school, while the two men got in the waiting Jaguar.

"I met one of the staff in the lobby earlier," said Houghton, making conversation as the car endured the morning crawl to the embassy.

"Oh yes; who?" asked David.

"Dee, I think she said."

"Dee Wilson? She's on my floor. Bright girl."

The conversation was kept to a minimum for the rest of the journey, both of them deep in thought. They eventually arrived at their destination.

Once in his office, Houghton was quickly on his laptop, sending an encrypted message to Andy Fellows and the

Commander. He included the Mahabadis' personal details for the passports, then made some observations. First, he confirmed that he was satisfied the request was genuine, then his assessment of the project. There was no way they were going to be able to lift the scientist from any installation, even if they could find him. It would have to be from the apartment during his monthly visit; there was no other alternative.

Five minutes after sending it, Houghton's desk phone rang.

"Houghton."

"Nick? It's Andy."

"Hi Andy. You got my message?"

"Yes, it's the reason I'm calling. Things are moving fast; have you heard the latest?"

"What's that?"

"Did you hear Ahmadinejad's speech a couple of days ago?"

"No."

"Well, basically, he said that Iran was now a nuclear player and the world had better get used to it. I thought it would have been big news over there."

"It probably is, but I've not been watching any TV."

"I expect the embassy will have heard," said Fellows.

"Hmm, yes. Certainly, but as no-one officially knows why I'm here, no-one's thought to tell me. I'll speak to David."

"Well, that's not the main problem. Condoleezza Rice has just made a speech to the United Nations wanting the Security Council to take, and I quote, 'strong steps to get Tehran to change course in its nuclear ambition'. That's what she said."

"Hmm, that's going to stir things up a bit," said Houghton.

"That's for sure. Now the assessment here is that it's going to be more sanctions again, but we can't rule out some sort of airstrike by the Americans."

"Jesus," said Houghton.

"Yes, you can imagine what the response will be from the Iranians, but it would be fair to say, our job has just got a bit harder."

"That's putting it mildly. The Ministry will be going ape shit."

"No question. UK and US citizens are particularly vulnerable; they're going to be under a lot of scrutiny that's for sure, if not in downright danger. The Foreign Office has already announced a warning to UK citizens about travelling to Iran. You're going to have to be very careful, my friend."

"So, what does that mean for the project?"

"Ah, that's the good news; they want Hassan Mahabadi real bad; he's like gold dust. His defection could put their nuclear programme back by some time."

"Really? He's that good?"

"Apparently. It also means you get an unlimited budget, within reason, of course, and a code word."

"Code word?" said Houghton."

"Yes, the project is now officially Operation Tiger Lily."

"Tiger Lily? Why Tiger Lily?"

"Have no idea, probably someone's clue in the Times crossword puzzle."

"Oh, ok. What about the passports? Do you have all the information you need?"

"Yes, I think so. I'll let the tech guys know; they'll deal with them," said Fellows. "When they're ready we can ship them out in the diplomatic bag."

"I may have some better photographs; Mahabadi's wife said she can let me have some more recent ones."

"Ok, that's great, I'll ask them to leave the pictures for now; the team down there have plenty to get on with," said Fellows.

"Ok, thanks for the information; I'll call you tomorrow."

After a brief catch up on domestic matters, they dropped the call.

The phone conversation gave Houghton a great deal to think about, and he was in a contemplative state when David Dexter knocked on his door.

"Hi David, come in, just had Andy Fellows on the phone. Something about Condoleezza Rice stirring things up."

"Yes, I've just heard it myself. I was going to tell you about the President's TV broadcast, you won't have seen it."

"No, Andy told me."

"There have been some big anti-west demonstrations in the city; Ahmadinejad has got them really fired up."

"So, Condoleezza Rice's speech is not going down too well then?"

"You can say that again. We may need extra security; we're expecting demonstrations outside the embassy."

"Hmm, that's not going to help things."

"No, you'll need to be very careful if you go out again."

"Yes, I guessed as much, thanks. I'll let you know."

Houghton was in thought again; he needed to contact Mayflower."

Chapter Four

Once David Dexter had left, Houghton sent a text message. *'Today?'* was all it said.

Ten minutes later, there was a reply; *'2:30.'*

Houghton spent the morning working out possible scenarios and the logistics and feasibility of each option. The operation would need to be in two phases, extraction and exfil; getting the family out of Tehran and then out of the country and to the UK. The more he considered the operation; the more impossible it seemed. The recent political shenanigans had definitely exacerbated the situation.

During the morning, Houghton spent some time in the comms room. There had been a significant increase in communication activity, and the place was busy. About a dozen people were huddled over computer screens; two large TV monitors on the wall were showing pictures of the demonstrations outside several embassies that had supported US sanctions, including the German and French. A ribbon message at the bottom of the screen was displaying Farsi subtitles for the hard-of-hearing or for those watching in a bar or coffee shop. Every so often, the pictures would cut to the President who was addressing a raucous meeting somewhere. When he paused for effect, the baying mob would raise their fists in the air as in salute. Houghton watched the events with more than a passing interest. He could feel his adrenaline rise as the anxiety levels increased.

He was about to leave when a familiar face entered the

room.

"Hi," she said. "Fancy meeting you here."

"Oh, hi Dee," said Houghton. "Do you work down here?"

"No, but I spend a lot of time in here, particularly at the moment."

Houghton looked at her inquisitively.

"I'm a senior data analyst, but don't tell anybody," she said, putting her index finger to her lips and smiling. "We're expecting demonstrations here this morning. Ahmadinejad's got them really fired up; I'm just checking the latest traffic."

"Yes, I guess you'll be busy then."

"For sure. We still ok for tonight?" said Dee.

"Yes, of course. Eight o'clock. I'll be there."

"Great, see you later," said Dee and she walked towards one of the monitors as Houghton left the room, deep in thought. Demonstrations were all he needed.

He was at his desk considering his pending meeting with Mayflower. He made a quick call, and a few minutes later, Ryan joined him in his office.

"You wanted a word?"

"Yes. Thanks for coming down, I need a favour. Have you got a decent small camera?"

"Of course, can you tell me what it's for, I've got several."

"I have an idea for extracting the Mahabadis, but I'll need a pass for the Mardom Hospital. Is that doable?"

"Possibly, if we can get a real one to work with."

"That's why I need a camera. I don't think I can get hold of a pass, but I think I can get a picture of one. Do you think that will work?"

"Hmm, it depends on how sophisticated the passes are. If it's a straightforward bar-code swipe, then it should be ok."

"I'll know later. If you can let me have one, that'll be great, not too conspicuous… I don't want to look like a tourist."

"Yeah, sure. There are some great miniatures about now, fabulous detail. I'll bring one down in a few minutes. You'll need to sign for it; they're expensive," he said laughing, and he left the office.

Twenty minutes later, Ryan returned with the camera and gave Houghton a quick tutorial. It was ideal from a size perspective, no bigger than the palm of his hand; it would be easy enough to conceal.

At one-thirty, Houghton called David.

"David? It's Nick, just wanted to let you know, I'll be leaving the embassy shortly."

"Yes, ok but be careful, there are about a hundred of Ahmadinejad's rent-a-mob outside. At the moment, they're just shouting, but you don't want to be running the gauntlet."

"Hmm, is there another way out?"

"Well, there is a door in the wall at the side of the embassy, but it's alarmed and controlled."

"How do I get access?"

"That's not the problem, I can do that, but it's almost certainly being monitored by MOIS; there are CCTV's across the road pointing at it. There's nothing we can do about that, unfortunately."

"Hmm, so I'm going to have to risk being set-upon by the protestors, or being caught on camera, leaving the embassy's back door."

"Yeah, but there're also TV crews everywhere out front. You might get caught on camera leaving the embassy if the mob decide to make it uncomfortable for you. Is your excursion necessary?"

"I'm afraid it is; any suggestions?"

"There might be something. Meet me in the vehicle compound in ten minutes. Where do you want to go?"

"Just to the Metro station."

"Yes, ok. I'll see you in ten minutes."

They dropped the call, and Houghton changed into his casual gear and jacket. His photochromatic glasses were in the pocket, and he put them on. He checked the mirror; with his dark features and beard, he easily passed for an Iranian, a detail that would work in his favour.

As he got outside the main entrance, the sound of chanting was deafening; a great cacophony emanating from over the wall in front of the embassy's main entrance. It was spine-tingling, and the feeling of threat returned.

He turned right outside the embassy building, walked along the frontage to the end and turned right again. There was a small yard with six vehicles parked, all with 'CD' number plates. The two Jaguars were being cleaned; the Ambassador's Bentley was gleaming, having already been valeted; a minibus and two anonymous saloons were parked close by. David Dexter was waiting beside one of them, a Nissan Primera. There was a local man standing next to the diplomat.

As Houghton approached, Dexter introduced him. "Nick, this is Kazem Younesi, he's in charge of our vehicle pool. He'll drive you to the Metro station; it will be safer. Darius will sit in the front, and you can sit in the back. It will be less conspicuous. The windows are tinted, but not blacked out completely; it should give you some protection from prying eyes."

"Thanks David."

Houghton shook hands with the driver and Darius was called over from his car-washing duties. Houghton recognised him; he had driven him before. Kazem spoke to the man in Farsi, and the pair got in the Nissan. Dexter opened the rear door for Houghton to get in.

"If you call me half an hour before you need to get back, we can pick you up from the Metro station."

The Nissan pulled away and approached the outer gate of the security area. Houghton was in the back seat and could hear the shouting from the protestors quite clearly.

The barrier went up, and the main gates slowly opened towards them.

The scene outside was frightening. As Dexter had said, there were maybe two hundred people shouting and jostling towards the gates. They were mostly men, but there were plenty of women in niqabs too; many had placards with the usual anti-west rhetoric in English and Farsi depicted on them. It was not a large crowd by Iranian standards, not the half a million protestors seen in anti-American demonstrations in previous times, but, nevertheless, intimidating. A large Iranian flag was being waved. The throng was being held back by riot-police dressed in combat gear and black crash helmets with visors, resembling something from a sci-fi movie. There was a lot of fist-clenching, faces contorted in hatred and howling vitriol towards the embassy. Houghton was seated low in the seat; his glasses medium colour, responding to the luminosity of the car.

As the car drove out, the horde pushed forward,

becoming even more incensed; the police were having difficulty holding them back. One or two got close enough to hammer on the roof of the car before they were pushed away. A placard landed on the bonnet as the car eased past the protestors. Houghton was not easily fazed, but he feared for his life. It just needed one protestor to break through, and he would be torn limb from limb.

Finally, they were through, and the melee was behind them.

It was only a short distance to the Metro station. The Nissan pulled over to the kerb and Houghton exited while it was still moving and disappeared quickly down the steps into the bowels of the station, hoping he hadn't been spotted. The activity helped to dissipate the adrenaline he had experienced from the encounter with the protestors; he felt calm and focused again.

He reached the mezzanine at the top of the escalators. There was a destination board on the wall, and Houghton stopped abruptly, appearing as if he were checking directions. In reality, it gave him a moment to look behind him to see if anyone following had also stopped. There was no-one; just an old lady in a niqab struggling down the steps with two shopping bags. Houghton's immediate reaction was to help her, but he could not afford to let anything get in the way of the mission.

He turned and rode the escalators to the track before buying a ticket at the pay-station on the platform. Of the twenty or so other people waiting, most were standing close to the platform edge to be first on the train and get a seat. Houghton stood at the back and watched, away from the group. After the clamour of the demonstrations and the noise of the traffic above ground, it was remarkably calm, and Houghton started to feel easier.

He looked at his surroundings. Being less than seven-years-old, the station was modern and well-lit; the platform area was remarkably clean, well-maintained, and graffiti-free. The marble flooring glistened in the neon lighting. The walls were decorated with various artworks and engravings. The comparison with the more-familiar London Tube was favourable.

More passengers joined before the smart white and blue train approached. Houghton, ever-watchful, held back and waited for everyone to get on. The old lady was stood looking quite helpless next to him at the carriage door; this time, he took her bags and helped her onto the train. He couldn't see her face, but her eyes seemed to smile, and she nodded as she took her seat. Houghton decided to stand, holding onto one of the leather straps suspended from the ceiling.

Two stops later, the train eased into Panzdah-e-Khordad station, and Houghton joined the crowd being disgorged from the carriages. Being the closest station to the Grand Bazaar, it was a popular exit point on the Metro system. It seemed most of the passengers had also de-trained and were riding the escalators out of the station. Hundreds of people jostled for positions at the top of the three moving staircases; it quickly backed up at the bottle-neck. The good news for Houghton, it would be almost impossible for anyone to have tailed him successfully.

Eventually, Houghton reached the exit and stopped on the street for a moment to get his bearings. It was bright sunshine, and after the comparative darkness of the Metro station, his glasses soon darkened.

He checked his watch, then turned right and looked for the pharmacy. Two hundred yards later, he crossed the road at his check-point and reached the mall entrance. It was heaving with people.

Houghton entered the mall and was quickly hounded by vendors anxious for his custom. He rebuffed them in Arabic, which seemed to accord some respect. He'd been walking for a few minutes, then to his horror, realised he was lost. He had missed the alley to the coffee shop. He quickly retraced his steps and soon spotted his route; it looked different from this direction. He walked the fifty yards to the café and went inside. The proprietor recognised him and led him to the same booth he had used previously. There was no sign of Mayflower. Houghton sat down and looked around. It was busier than the last visit, with at least fifteen people taking refreshment. Most were women, but there were a couple of older men in their fifties sat chatting at an adjacent table. They appeared oblivious to Houghton's presence, but he was on his guard.

The proprietor returned with the coffee and sandwich that Houghton had ordered; there had been no time for lunch at the embassy.

He checked his watch, two thirty-eight. He started his sandwich and looked around the café again; all the customers appeared to be locked in conversation, and he felt reasonably secure. Eliz arrived at the door; she went straight across to Houghton and sat down.

"I am late, I think. I am sorry; it is very difficult, so many people," said the nurse as she sat down.

She was wearing a different headscarf, a grey one, Houghton noticed. She looked flustered.

"It's me that should apologise for not giving you more notice."

"It is ok," said Eliz, as the proprietor approached them and took her order. Once he left, Eliz turned her attention back to Houghton; "You wanted to see me?"

"Yes, I have a few questions." He looked around to ensure no-one was in hearing distance and dropped his voice to a whisper. "I don't want to say too much at this stage, but the project I am working on could be integral to world peace; it is that important."

"Ok," said the nurse, who had moved closer. From a distance, the pair resembled two lovers sharing intimate secrets.

"I need to be able to access the hospital; do you have your staff pass with you?"

"Yes," said Eliz and moved her jacket to one side revealing a lanyard around her neck with a photo ID attached to it.

"Can I borrow it for a moment?"

She pulled the cord over her head and handed Houghton the pass.

"I won't be a minute. Where are the toilets?" he said.

Eliz pointed to a corridor to the right of the serving counter, and Houghton got up and walked through the café.

The cubicles were empty. Houghton put the pass on top of the porcelain cistern and took out his camera. The light wasn't ideal, but he thought it would be good enough. He focussed and took two photographs; then turned the pass over and repeated. Most of the writing was in Farsi, and he had no idea what it said.

He replaced the camera in his pocket and examined the pass closely one more time, remembering the look and feel of the plastic.

He walked back through the café and returned to his seat. Eliz had been served with her coffee; Houghton's half-finished sandwich was on his plate.

He surreptitiously returned the pass. "Thanks, that's been very helpful. So, if I wanted to disguise myself as a doctor, what would I need?"

"You want to be a doctor?"

"Just pretend," reassured Houghton.

"It won't be easy, you will need a white coat, and possibly a… er…" she mimed something.

"A stethoscope?" queried Houghton

"Yes."

"Hmm, I don't know where I could get one of those. Is there a medical supply shop in the city?"

"I do not know; we have them at the hospital."

"Do you think you could get me one, and a coat?" asked Houghton.

"That will be difficult, a coat, yes, I think, but it will not be easy. If I am caught, I will be in big trouble."

"Yes, it's ok, I understand. I will see if I can get one through the embassy."

"Give me two days, I will see."

"I need to know the layout of the hospital and any access codes." He mimed 'access codes' with his fingers as if he were punching numbers.

She looked confused. "Layout? I do not understand."

"Sorry, er, a map to show how to get around the hospital."

"Yes, they have it for relatives of patients, I can get one. Will that be ok?"

"Possibly, I'll need to see it. What about the codes for

security?"

"Yes, security is very strict. They search without warning, but they do not bother me."

"But do you have numbers to get into rooms?" Houghton mimed the actions again.

"Yes, I understand. Only some rooms – where we have drugs and we do operations. They do not change for many years. I can give you those."

"Ok, thanks, leave it until nearer the time, in case they do decide to change."

"Yes, that will be ok."

"What about parking?"

"Yes, there is a big carpark there."

"What about close to the building?"

"Yes, for when they deliver the laundry and other things. I can show you when I get the map."

"Thank you," said Houghton. "For everything. Oh, I nearly forgot to mention. Can you get hold of any Rohypnol, by any chance?"

"Rohypnol?" She looked confused, then her face indicated recognition. "Ah, Flunitrazepam, you mean."

"Yes, I think it's also called that."

"No, it is impossible, the drugs in the hospital are very controlled since the sanctions; there is always someone in charge."

"Oh, ok, it's a pity; it could be very important."

"Ok, I will see, but I cannot promise. I will tell you when we meet next time." She looked at her watch. "I need to go now. We meet in two days, here at one-thirty?"

"Yes, ok, thank you again." Houghton was getting used to her apparent bluntness; it was almost refreshing after the feigned politeness he was more used to.

The nurse got up and walked to the door. The proprietor was pouring coffee at another table, and she acknowledged him as she passed. There was a polite exchange, and Eliz left the café.

Houghton watched for anyone observing her, but there was no movement from the clientele who all appeared to be absorbed in whatever conversations they were having. He had a lot to think about.

He finished the remnants of his lunch and ordered another coffee. Ten minutes later, he was outside retracing his steps to the Metro station. At the end of the mall, he took out his phone and made a call.

"David. It's Nick. Any chance of the ride, I should be there in about thirty minutes or so. That's great, cheers."

There were still hordes of people around the mall entrance, but once he had crossed the main road, it was less crowded, and in ten minutes he was walking down the steps into the Panzdah-e-Khordad station.

There was another ten-minute wait for the next train, and after the brief journey, he was walking up the steps to the Sa'adi station exit.

He reached the street and checked around, but there was no car. As the main thoroughfare, the road was busy with vehicles, bumper to bumper, crawling along in both directions. He could hear noises in the distance; the chanting of the demonstrators. It was a fearsome sound and Houghton could feel the anxiety levels rise; he was on high alert. He stood back away from the kerb, close to the station entrance. The moped he had noticed on his last visit was still parked in the same place, and he stood next to it away from the continuous foot-traffic heading for the trains.

He checked his watch again and then spotted the Nissan in a line of traffic crawling towards him.

He walked to the kerb, and the car pulled over just long enough for Houghton to open the back door and get in. Then it eased away; the driver cursing the car behind who had remonstrated the stop with a continuous honking of the horn.

"You are ok, Mr Houghton?" said Kazem, the same driver who had dropped him earlier.

"Yes," said Houghton. "Thanks for picking me up. How are the demonstrations?"

"Now, it is ok, many they leave, go to other embassies."

"Thank goodness for that," said Houghton.

The Nissan continued for another half a mile before there was a turning allowing Kazem to reverse the journey and head back to the embassy.

Reaching the gates, Houghton could see the crowd had dispersed considerably, and there were no more than thirty people, still chanting and waving placards. The police presence had also diminished, but it was still sufficient to hold back the angry mob to allow the car to enter the embassy. The heavy steel gates opened, the Nissan went through, and the gates immediately closed behind them. Houghton exhaled.

Kazem parked up outside the main entrance, got out of the car and opened the back door for Houghton to exit.

"Thanks Kazem," he acknowledged and walked into the embassy with a lot on his mind.

Back in his office, he changed back into his suit and checked in with David Dexter.

"I need a word," said Dexter. "Is it convenient now?"

"Sure, if you're passing the canteen can you bring a coffee down?"

"Yes, good idea. I'll be with you in a few minutes."

It gave Houghton enough time to send an email back to Andy Fellows in Vauxhall to update him. He would call later.

Shortly afterwards, Dexter walked into Houghton's office carrying two takeaway cups of coffee and handed one to Nick.

"Cheers," said Houghton. "You said you wanted a chat."

"Yes, just an update on the security situation. There's been another broadcast by Ahmadinejad; he's really stirring things up. The analysts are saying they've not seen such a high nationalist feeling since the Ayatollah came to power. The President's got them in the palm of his hand."

"Hmm," said Houghton. "What about the protests?"

"Us and the French have taken the brunt of the demonstrators today. It's all for show. They'll make the morning editions of Le Figaro, and the BBC will also be all over it. Great propaganda, the locals lap it up."

"It doesn't make our job any easier."

"No, that's for sure."

"I've been doing some thinking on the exfil; I'm going to need a car to get them away; a people carrier preferably, any thoughts?" said Houghton.

"Possibly, at a price."

"I have an unlimited budget," said Houghton and he smiled.

"Hmm, yeah, I heard," said Dexter. "The Ambassador's taken more than a passing interest; he's had calls from the Foreign Office to give you every support. Although he won't be told any details of the operation – plausible deniability."

"Ah, yes, I understand," said Houghton, recognising the terminology.

"We do have some contacts in the city. I'll put some feelers out and see what I can arrange."

"Great," said Houghton.

"I'll be leaving today about five-fifteen if you want a lift back to the compound," said Dexter.

"Yeah, cheers, see you in reception," said Houghton, and Dexter left the office.

Houghton was quickly on the phone again. "Ryan, it's Nick, can you spare a few minutes? Great, see you shortly."

A few minutes later, the tech guy knocked on Houghton's office door and came in.

"Hi Ryan," said Houghton. "I've got something for you." He handed Ryan the camera. "I've taken photos of the pass I mentioned, front and back. A lot of it is in Farsi, got no idea what it says. The passes are plastic, like a large credit card, if that helps, in a clear wallet. My contact had theirs on a lanyard."

Houghton realised that by photographing the pass he was ostensibly compromising Mayflower, but he had little choice in the matter.

"Yeah, ok, I'll get the team on it. Have you thought of a name?"

"A name?"

"Well, you said you wanted to be a doctor; I assume you won't be Nick Houghton."

"Ha, no, that's for sure. Wait a minute, let's think of something. It'll need to be Arabic; I don't speak a word of Farsi. What about Manzur Al-Fadhli; that was my uncle's name in Syria?"

"You'll have to write it down for me," said Ryan.

Houghton took out a piece of paper from the printer feed and wrote down the name.

"I'll need your photo too... Here, stand against the door."

Houghton complied, and Ryan took two headshots with the camera.

"Was there anything else?"

"No, that's all for now. Thanks for your help."

"No problem," said Ryan and left the office.

After he had left, Houghton made a call to Andy Fellows back in Vauxhall.

"I see you've had fun and games there with protestors," said Fellows, after a brief catch-up.

"Yeah, you can say that again, I had to run the gauntlet earlier, not a pleasant experience. What's the take of it in London?"

"It's been covered heavily in the media, Ahmadinejad's speeches are, and I quote, 'getting tiresome', according to one correspondent I talked to. The general consensus is that it's mostly rhetoric, galvanising his position in the country."

"Well, the opinion here is that he's succeeding; the popular support is as high as when the Ayatollah took over."

"Hmm, not sure if that's a good thing or not," said Fellows.

"It beats civil war, but it's not going to help our marketing effort."

"Yes, that's true. How did the meeting go with your representative?"

"Very positive, sales are going well. Please pass the news on."

"Will do," said Fellows and after further chit-chat, they dropped the call.

By five o'clock, the demonstrators had left the front of the embassy, their work done for the day. No-one knew if they would return tomorrow. Houghton locked his office and went up to the reception to wait for his ride. David Dexter joined him after a couple of minutes, and they walked toward the car.

"I think it will be better if you take the minibus tomorrow; it might seem a bit strange for an admin assistant to be using a diplomatic car and we don't want to draw attention. It may be fine, but I don't want to take any chances."

"No, you're right. I can do that, no problem; it makes sense."

It was after five-thirty before Houghton was back in his apartment in the Gholhak Gardens compound. His fridge had been stocked with some essentials by the housekeeping staff at his request. The remaining portion of Kufte that Sophie had given him was on a plate in the fridge; five minutes in the microwave and he would have his dinner. He had no idea what constituted as the 'nibbles' he had been promised at Dee's.

By seven-fifty, he had eaten, showered and changed and was ready for his get-together with his new neighbours. He would normally take a bottle of wine to such functions, but with the alcohol ban in Iran, there were no off-licenses.

It was a warm evening and quite stuffy as he walked down the long corridor to the first apartment. It was next to the stairs that led down to the reception. There was a large picture window at the top of the stairs, providing a nice view of the grounds. He could see the trees swaying in the breeze; the sun was in its final throws of daylight.

He reached the door and gently tapped. He could hear music coming from inside.

The door opened, and for a moment, Houghton couldn't believe his eyes. The business suit and shawl had been replaced by a floaty casual top and jeans; Dee's hair was down, nearly to her shoulders. She had also removed her glasses.

"Come in," she said and moved aside to allow Houghton to pass. The apartment was slightly larger than his and had been tastefully decorated. It was also very tidy.

There was a three-seater settee in the middle of the room with a coffee table in front of it where bowls of peanuts and assorted crackers were placed. A scented candle was burning, giving off a pleasant aroma of Jasmine from its dancing flame. There was a large window along the side, but the curtains had been drawn. Next to the settee was a small dining table with two chairs. There was also an ancient-looking TV on a table in the corner, below that a small music system. It was illuminated indicating the track playing: Celine Dion – 'My Heart Will Go On', from the film Titanic.

"Have a seat," said the host and Houghton complied. "Unfortunately, the others have been delayed at work – the demonstrations and all that. They won't be able to make it, so it's just you and me."

Houghton did not feel disappointed. He sat on the settee on the far end so he wouldn't invade Dee's personal space.

"Would you like a drink? I've got wine and a couple of cans of lager."

"Really? How did you manage that?"

"You can get alcohol if you know where to look. I've been here for six months, so I have my contacts."

"You must introduce me," said Houghton. "A lager would be great, thanks."

Dee went into an adjoining room which Houghton assumed was the kitchen; the layout was slightly different to his apartment. He could hear the opening of a refrigerator. Dee returned with the can of lager and a bottle of red wine with two chunky glasses that looked like they were originally a free gift from a garage.

"Sorry about the glasses; it's the best I could find."

"No problem, it all goes down the same way." Houghton pulled back the ring-pull and poured. Then lifted the can and looked at the label. "Belgian – my favourite, thank you."

"Ha, lucky guess, it's all they have."

Dee sat on the opposite end of the sofa; her legs curled underneath her. More Celine Dion emanated from the music system.

"So, you've been here six months, you say, how has it been?"

"Hmm, ok, I guess, but it's not easy if you're a woman on your own. Going out can be intimidating, so I tend to stay around the complex, but there's not much to do."

"What about getting home?"

"I get a long weekend once a month paid for by the UK tax-payer; Friday to Tuesday, otherwise I'm pretty much on twenty-four-hour call."

"That must be hard."

"Boring, mostly, but every now and then it gets interesting, like today."

"What about the others? The ones who were supposed to come tonight."

"They're career diplomatic staff and a lot older than me; we don't have that much in common."

"Hmm, yes, I understand."

She poured a measure of wine and took a large sip. "Ah, that's better, it's been full-on today."

"Yes, I noticed; do you think they'll be back tomorrow?"

"The demonstrators? Difficult to say, possibly; it depends on the American's response to Ahmadinejad's latest diatribe."

"Hmm, that'll be interesting."

"By the way in case you were worried, the apartments are clean. The tech guys sweep them regularly. The music is just for background." She took another sip and looked at Houghton; he was starting to feel warm.

Chapter Five

"So, what's your story? Are you married?" asked Dee.

Houghton took a sip of his lager. "Divorced, three years... You?"

"Relationships are difficult when you're living away from home. I was engaged, but I broke it off when I caught my ex in bed with my best friend – the bastard. Still, it was for the best, I am well over it now."

She passed Houghton a bowl of peanuts. "Help yourself to nibbles."

"Thanks," he said and took a handful.

"You live in London?" she asked.

"Yeah, you?"

"Henley, not far away."

"Ah, yes, the famous regatta. Do you row?"

"Ha, not these days, but I did for a while up in Cambridge."

"You went to Cambridge?"

"Yes, Clare College."

"Really? What did you study?"

"Politics and Middle-Eastern Studies."

"Hmm, very good. So, I guess the diplomatic corps was a natural fit career-wise?"

"Well, yes, it was always going to be likely; my father was UK Ambassador for Sweden for many years. I went to school there."

"That must have been interesting."

"Yes, it was. I love the place; Stockholm's such a liberated city."

"A bit different from Tehran, I guess."

"Like a different planet." She took a sip of her wine. "So, you're a bit of a mystery man; no-one knows anything about you. They just said you were covering for Leo Sinclair. His mother's sick apparently."

"Yes, I got asked to cover."

"How long for, do you know?"

"They didn't give an exact timescale, but at least a few weeks."

"I notice they've given you your own office; you are honoured. Leo works on the second floor in admin, processing visas and dealing with lost tourists mainly. You won't be doing that, I guess."

"No, that's not my remit," said Houghton. He was starting to feel uncomfortable with all the questions.

"So, how long have you been in the service?" said Dee realising that Houghton wasn't going to give much away.

"About three years."

"And before that? Let me guess, military service. It's ok, say no more, I get it, no more third degree, honest. I'm fascinated, that's all; it's ages since I've had a decent conversation with anyone remotely interesting."

"It's ok," said Houghton.

"Did David explain what I do?"

"Not in detail; a Data Analyst, he said."

"Hmm, yes, but a bit more. I get most of the intelligence reports and sift through them for anything that might be of interest to the Foreign Office. I also provide David with information that he can use in his role as Commercial Attaché." She looked at Houghton in a knowing way.

Houghton nodded.

"I know you can't discuss what you're here for, but if I can help in any way, let me know. I'm very resourceful."

"That's good to know; I'll certainly bear that in mind."

Dee noticed that Houghton had finished his lager.

"Let me get you another beer," she said and went to the kitchen before Houghton had time to answer.

"Cheers," said Houghton, although Dee might not have heard.

She returned and passed Houghton another can of lager, then topped up her glass with more wine. She sat back down on the settee but this time much closer to him. He refilled his glass; the atmosphere had suddenly changed. He felt his personal space being encroached, but he wasn't feeling uncomfortable.

Dee took a sip of her wine and looked at Houghton.

"So, what do you do for fun?" she asked, looking over the top of her glass as she drank. He could read the signs but was in a dilemma; lives were at risk, and he couldn't afford any distractions.

"Fun? Hmm, you'll need to define that for me; I don't recognise the concept," he said. "Let's just say it's been a while." He smiled.

She smiled back at him.

"Yes, me too, this place closes in on you after a while; it's like a prison. Sometimes you have to make your own fun."

They looked at each other, silently weighing up what the potential consequences of their next actions might be, but almost sensing it was inevitable.

Finally, Dee leaned forward and they kissed. Houghton could taste the wine on her lips and smell her perfume; it seemed to enhance the moment.

It started slowly but quickly gained in intensity. The kissing became more and more urgent. Dee started to unbutton Houghton's shirt. He found the zip at the back of her top and pulled it down. He lifted the garment over her head and placed it on the settee beside him as she unclipped her bra. His attention moved lower, and he traced his tongue slowly down Dee's neck to her breasts. He gently massaged them, feeling the softness of her skin in his hands. His tongue found her nipples and she tossed her head from side to side as he teased them one at a time.

His right hand moved to her jeans, and he unfastened the top button then the second, third, and the final one. Dee lifted her bottom, and Houghton pulled off her jeans. She lay down on the settee in just her panties. His hand moved under the fabric and went lower. He found her sensitive spot and caressed it with his fingers; Dee was in ecstasy. "Oh… oh… yes!"

She leaned forward and helped Houghton take off his shirt, then she unzipped his jeans and pushed them to the floor. She could see by the bulge in his shorts he was ready. Her fingers found the gap and his erection broke free. She wrapped her hand around it and gently moved it up and down. Houghton closed his eyes, taking in the sensations.

"Now! Now!" she begged, pulling down her knickers and opening her legs. She lay back on the settee and moaned as she felt his hardness slide into her; it was as though he was touching her very soul. She helped the rhythm by bucking her hips in time with his thrusts; her fingernails digging into his back.

There was a deep sigh, then a long groan, as Dee climaxed,

and Nick quickly followed.

For a moment, they both lay together; not saying anything.

"That was amazing," Dee said.

"Yes, it was," he said and kissed her. He was still panting from the exertion.

She was cradling Houghton's head on her chest. "I don't want you to get the wrong idea; I'm not usually this forward. It's just… Well, I don't know really."

"It's ok, I'm not judging. I think it's something we both needed; it's been a while."

"Yes, that's for sure," said Dee and gave Houghton a tender, loving kiss.

"Would you like a coffee?" she said, breaking the moment.

"Yes please," said Houghton.

"The bathroom's just through there," she added, pointing to a short corridor on the opposite side of the room.

Houghton picked up his clothes and padded along to the bathroom. Dee put on her knickers and went into the kitchen. A few minutes later, Houghton returned, fully dressed. Dee was seated on the settee in a dressing gown. Two mugs of steaming coffee were on the coffee table.

"I haven't sugared; I didn't know how you took it."

"That's fine, thanks."

He sat down next to her, she leaned towards him, and they kissed again.

"We'll need to be careful," she said. "They tend to frown on in-house relationships."

"Yes, don't worry, discretion is assured. Oh, forgot to mention, I'm on the minibus in the morning."

"Slumming it, eh?"

"Something like that," said Houghton and smiled. He picked up his coffee, blew across the surface, and took a sip.

Dee smiled at him. "I have a slight confession to make."

"Oh," said Houghton.

"I lied earlier. I didn't actually invite the others tonight. I was going to, but then I thought, no, I wanted you to myself. The other staff here, they're not the most interesting of people; we'd have ended up just talking shop all night. I hope you're not upset with me."

"No, of course not, how could I be?"

"That's good." She smiled and then her expression grew more serious. "Can I ask you a question,"

"Yeah, sure."

"Can I see you tomorrow in your office? I want to share some information with you, which may be helpful. I know whatever you're doing will be dangerous, and I want to keep you safe. Don't worry, I don't want to know any detail."

He looked at her, also reflecting the gravity. "Yes, ok. I should be free all morning."

Dee looked at him and held his hand. "Thanks for tonight, it's been special."

"Yes, it has," said Houghton as he finished his drink.

"I really want you to stay, but we don't want to get into any trouble."

"No, you're right." He checked his watch; "I best be going."

"I'll see you in the morning; eight o'clock. We normally get breakfast at the embassy."

"Sounds good."

He stood up, and Dee led him to the door where they engaged in a deep kiss.

"I hope we can do this again," said Dee.

"Yes, so do I," said Houghton.

He left Dee's apartment and walked along the corridor back to his own, deep in thought.

Gholhak Garden Compound – Friday April 14th – 8:00 a.m.

The following morning just before eight o'clock, Houghton walked along the corridor to the stairs. He'd endured a restless night; Dee had been on his mind a great deal. It was a pleasant distraction, but a distraction, nonetheless. As he passed her apartment, he considered knocking on the door but decided against it.

He was hovering around the reception area as Dee descended the stairs a couple of minutes later wearing her business suit and scarf. Thoughts of the previous evening flashed through his mind as she smiled at him. He smiled back.

"Good morning," he said as she approached. "I hope you slept well."

"Best night's sleep since I arrived. Can't think why," she replied, and smiled even more. Javad, the concierge, was behind the reception desk, paying no attention to their exchange.

They were soon joined by three more staff who would be taking advantage of the ride to the embassy. They were chatting animatedly as they walked down the stairs.

Dee greeted them. "John, Edward, Felicity, this is Nick Houghton, he's just joined us; he's Leo's temporary replacement."

They shook hands in turn. "Hi Nick, so you're the mystery

man? We've not seen you on the second floor," said Edward, a greying fifty-something with heavy glasses.

"No," said Nick, looking around to see if anyone else was in earshot. The concierge had returned to his office, leaving the desk unattended.

Dee could sense his unease. "The bus is waiting," she said, curtailing further discussion, and they made their way to their transport. The driver, who Houghton did not recognise, slid the door across allowing access to the three rows of seats. Houghton waited for the three elder staff to get in the back and then followed Dee into the seats in front. She caught his gaze for a moment as she sat down and smiled.

The journey was completed in silence for the most part. Being Friday, the road was quieter, the faithful had been called to prayer. There were occasional comments from the back row – merely some observation or another, not really a conversation.

The front of the embassy was busy as they approached. Television cameras were evident, but there were no signs of any organised protests yet. The gates opened and the minibus drove quickly into the security area. Passes were checked before the vehicle was allowed forward to the main building.

The five passengers walked into reception and signed in.

"Are you joining us for breakfast?" said Dee as they walked towards the stairway. The staff canteen was on the first floor.

"Yes, ok, but I can't stop long."

Dee led the way as Houghton followed; the three other passengers were a few steps behind.

The first floor was the main administration area. At the top of the stairs, there was a large mezzanine with marble columns and intricate stonework, another throwback to Colonial times. To the right was the public area, with several interview rooms and a reception desk for members of the public seeking Consular help or advice; to the left, the staff canteen. As Dee opened the door, the smell of cooking hit them; Houghton suddenly felt hungry. They went to the serving station where an array of fried food was laid out in heated trays. Dee picked up two trays and handed one to Houghton. The others were deep in conversation and had disengaged from the pair.

"What are you having?"

"Well, I was going to have just a tea and some toast, but seeing all this food, I'm feeling hungry."

"Been exercising have we?" said Dee and grinned.

"Yeah, you could say that," said Houghton.

After a few minutes, Houghton and Dee were sat at a table tucking into a full English.

"What time will be best for you?" said Dee. "For me to come down," she clarified.

"About ten-thirty, I guess, if that works for you."

"Yes, that's good for me. I'll bring a couple of coffees down with me; how does that sound?"

"Yeah, thanks, that will be good," said Houghton.

It was after nine o'clock when Houghton took the stairs down to the basement, his hunger suitably satiated by the breakfast. Dee walked up to the second floor. This morning was going to be busy.

Houghton was emailing Andy Fellows with an update when David Dexter knocked on the door and entered his office.

"Hi Nick," said Dexter.

Houghton looked up. "Hi, David, take a seat, I won't be a second." He hit send.

"What's the news?" asked Houghton, closing his laptop and giving Dexter his full attention.

His face looked grave. "I've just come off the phone to the F.O. They're getting a bit paranoid about the protests and, not to put too fine a point on it, concerned about the reaction if the Iranians discover that we have sprung one of their top scientists."

"Hmm, yes, but we knew all that before the protests."

"Yes, I think seeing them on the news has spooked one or two in high office; the Foreign Secretary is getting a particularly hard time in the press."

"Fucking politics," said Houghton. "So, what's happening then?"

"Well, there was a view that Tiger Lily should be pulled; but I strongly argued against that; anyway, it's an MI6 operation, so any decision will need to come from there."

"So, where are we?"

"We continue. Personally, I think things will calm down in a day or two once the mob have let off steam. There's nothing further from Ahmadinejad today and no protestors. Most of the press have left, so fingers crossed."

"Thank goodness for that; it was pretty hairy yesterday I don't mind telling you."

"Yes, I'm glad it was relatively quiet when we left. So, what's the latest?"

"I need your help. I've been thinking about chaos theory."

"Chaos theory?"

"Yes, we need to create some."

"Ok, what do you have in mind?"

"We need a distraction. We can be certain that the world and his dog are on high alert which means the Iranians will increase security, especially around their nuclear facilities, which, in turn, means our guy is going to be under even more supervision."

"Yes, I get that."

"Well, what if we leak some traffic that we're looking to turn someone else; one of the other technicians, perhaps a senior programme director or that sort of position? I was thinking, if we can find a suitable target, we can start some email traffic expressing an attempt to persuade them to leak information, that sort of thing. While MOIS are distracted with that, they won't be focusing attention on our real target."

"Yes, I get the idea. Mind you, blindsiding them is not going to be easy."

"We just have to generate the uncertainty. I'm hoping it will gain its own momentum."

"Ok. I'll make some enquiries. Oh, nearly forgot, Afareen brought some photographs of her and the children and a more recent one of her husband. I've given them to Ryan. He'll get them off to Vauxhall; said they should have the passports ready in the next week or so."

"Ok, that's great. Well, the clock's ticking; we don't have long if we're going to get them away on the next visit."

"If he gets another visit."

"What do you mean?"

"According to Dee, they're battening down the hatches on all the nuclear sites; leave among the technical and admin personnel has been cancelled; there's all sorts going on according to reports. It's the security situation."

"Can you find out from Afareen what the position is with her husband?"

"I'll ask her tomorrow, but the chances are she won't know anything."

Houghton looked concerned. "Timing's going to be crucial; we need to know what days he'll be home so we can arrange everything. Is there any news on transport?"

"No, not yet but we're working on it."

"Ok," said Houghton, and he rubbed his hands down his face, a sign of anxiety.

"Right, anything else you need?" asked Dexter.

"What? Er… no thanks, thank you, that's great. I'll call you if I need anything."

"Are you going out today?"

"No, I'm not planning to at the moment; maybe tomorrow."

"Ok, just let me know if you need any help."

"Cheers, thanks," said Houghton and Dexter left.

Houghton was contemplating Dexter's conversation when there was a knock on the door, and a friendly face appeared. "So, this is where you're hiding. I come bearing gifts."

Dee walked in the office carrying two takeout coffees and a paper bag. "I got you a pastry; I hope you like Danish."

"Yeah, great, come in, thanks," said Houghton, who was glad of the interruption.

Dee pulled back the chair recently vacated by David Dexter and sat down. "So, how's your morning?" she said as she handed the coffee and pastry to Houghton.

"Well, it's just improved a notch," he said.

"Hmm, bad as that?"

"Let's say there have been some challenges."

"Well let's see if I can help." Dee took a bite out of her Danish and washed it down with a mouthful of coffee. "As I said, I don't need to know the details of what you're here for, but I have signed the O.S.A. In any case, I want to do all I can to help."

"I appreciate that, thanks," said Houghton also making light work of his mid-morning snack.

Dee shuffled in her chair and took another slug of caffeine. "Ok, let me explain some more. As I told you last night, my role involves data gathering. You're familiar with System X, I take it?"

"Only the outputs," said Houghton.

"Well, basically, it's a digital switching system; GCHQ uses it for filtering data. We can programme keywords that will trigger an alert. It saves so much time in filtering information, the amount of data passing through Cheltenham is mind-blowing."

"Yes, I can imagine," said Houghton, who was now wiping his hands with a paper napkin having finished his pastry.

"Ok, so if I know a little more about what you are doing, I can search deeper for relevant information you may find useful."

Houghton thought for a moment. "Yes, ok, let's just say any traffic referencing the nuclear facilities would be extremely helpful."

"Natanz and Esfahan?"

"Hmm, you are well-informed."

"Not really, we've been monitoring those places for

ages, as well as the heavy-water production plant at Arak. I wondered if you might have an interest in that direction. I can certainly give you the latest intel."

"That's great, thanks."

Dee sat back in the chair and looked at Houghton. Just for a moment, memories of the previous evening flashed through her mind, but she quickly dispelled the thoughts.

"Well, as you might expect, there's a great deal of noise coming from the three plants; Natanz especially – daily air-raid drills, constant switching of personnel, the usual stuff. They've moved in anti-aircraft missile-launchers; they're all over the place – not easy sites if you were considering any infiltration."

"No, nothing like that, just the opposite as it happens."

"I see, so you're trying to get someone out?"

"Let's just say, I'm looking into the feasibility."

"Hmm, my advice? Forget it. Security is at their highest level; all leave has been cancelled, and technical personnel are being monitored closely."

This confirmed David Dexter's information.

"Yes, I'd heard. I don't propose going to the sites, but I do need to understand the climate out there. Do we know any more about the protests?"

"Nothing new today; Condoleezza Rice's speech is all over the newspapers as you can imagine. The press are having a field day. I've not known such a high a nationalist fervour; it's bordering on fanatical. Support for the President is unprecedented."

"Yes, a difficult mission has just got a whole lot harder."

"Well, anything I can do, you just have to ask."

"Do you have anything on what MOIS is up to?"

"We're keeping close tabs on things; there's been an increase in arrests over the last week or so; anyone dissenting is being rounded up, and of course, there's a lot of hysteria about what the Americans might be up to. Mind you, we don't even know what they're up to half the time. They keep us in the loop when it suits them, otherwise…" she shrugged her shoulders.

"I can understand that."

"You'll need to tread very carefully, Nick, Tehran is a very dangerous place at the moment."

"Thanks for your concern, I really appreciate it."

"Ok, well, I'll leave you to your work." Dee got up and looked at Houghton. "What are you doing tonight?" She was a little tentative; unsure how Houghton would respond.

"Nothing planned."

"Would you like to come over for dinner? I can cook us something. It's boring cooking for one."

Houghton thought for a moment. "Yes, ok, that would be great, thanks."

"About seven?"

"Sure, thanks, I'll see you then."

Dee left Houghton's office and went into the comms room. Houghton was left to his planning.

Mardom Hospital, Kerman Street, Tehran – 10:30 a.m.

Mardom Hospital is a private medical facility, catering for wealthy patients and members of the government. The main block is a large, austere building, resembling 1960's multi-storey car parks, but outside appearances contradict its modern interior with its excellent facilities. Operating theatres are situated on the first floor, with wards taking up the top three.

Senior Theatre Nurse, Eliz Bashi, yawned. She was very tired; sleep had not been easy the previous evening and, although she had only been working for two and a half hours, she felt drained. She was scrubbing down after assisting Consultant Surgeon, Professor Hossein Chehrazad, in an appendectomy. It was a fairly routine operation, but when it was being carried out on the son of a prominent politician, extreme attention was required to ensure the best possible care. There could be no mistakes.

The patient, a fourteen-year-old boy, was being taken up to the wards under sedation. The consultant was beside Eliz at the wash-station, applying povidone iodine to his hands as part of the hygiene routine. He was a busy man and revered in the hospital because of his experience and expertise. They spoke in Farsi.

"We'll need some drugs from the pharmacy for the patient; can you sign for them for me?" asked Eliz.

"Yes, ok, just the usual painkillers? Oh, and you better add some benzethonium to be on the safe side. They should have some in stock. We can't afford for him to die of sepsis. I don't want to take any chances."

"No, we don't," said the nurse, as she removed her plastic gown.

The consultant had finished and was putting on his jacket. "Ok, bring me the form; I'll be in my office," he said and walked purposefully out of the room.

It wasn't the operation on the son of a prominent politician that was causing the nurse her anxiety; it was what she was about to do next. Not only would she lose her job if she was caught, but in the present climate, she would almost certainly end up in the hands of MOIS.

Getting a doctor's white coat hadn't been a problem; the large laundry basket had plenty ready to be washed; nobody would notice one going missing from the unattended trolley. It was safely in her locker. The stethoscope would, however, be a problem, and she had yet to source that. It was the drug, though, that was going to be the major hurdle.

Eliz was familiar with using Flunitrazepam; she had administered it herself occasionally on the wards as a pre-anaesthetic sedative to calm anxious patients. Nevertheless, it wasn't in common use and not easy to obtain, particularly during the sanctions.

As a senior theatre nurse, she had a desk on the first floor, close to the operating theatres and surgeons. In front of her was the slip she would need to secure the drugs for the patient; painkillers and antiseptics. She stared at the document. She knew the consultant would normally just sign without too much notice, but if he challenged her she had no idea what she would say. Her hands were shaking as she compiled the list, and added Flunitrazepam and Flumazenil, to be used as an antidote.

She walked down the corridor to the consultant's office to get his signature, but stopped before she reached it and, instead, headed for the toilets. She washed her hands and took in some deep breaths, then returned to her task.

He was standing in front of his desk reading a memo as she reached the door to his office. He looked up as she approached and could see the chit in her hand.

"Put it on my desk; I'm late for a meeting," he ordered.

She thought quickly. "I need to go for them now... We

don't want there to be any delay with this patient, do we?"

"Here, give it me," he growled, impatiently.

Eliz handed him the form and held her breath. She watched as he put the docket on the table and signed it without paying it much attention.

"Here." He handed it back.

"I won't be long?" she said, putting the paper in her apron pocket.

"Wait, why are you going? Get one of the other nurses to go; it's not your job."

"They are inexperienced, and we can't afford any mistakes, can we?"

"Ok but be quick; we have another operation in thirty minutes, I will need you again." He looked at his watch.

"Yes, of course," she said and hurried out of the office. She wanted to be sick. She turned and watched the consultant leave his office and head in the opposite direction.

She quickly walked down the wide staircase to the ground floor and the large reception area, holding on to the chrome handrail to support herself.

Outside the building, she took more deep breaths. There was an angry hoot as she almost walked in front of an approaching ambulance. The warning startled her, giving her an adrenaline rush, and she waited for the vehicle to pass. The driver glared at her and muttered something under his breath. She continued to the pharmacy.

Like the rest of the complex, her destination was a functional concrete structure, mirroring the austere façade of the main building. It was the administration block; the pharmacy was in the basement. She reached the top of the steps that led down; her footsteps echoed around the stairwell as she descended. Here the investment in the main block had not been replicated, and forty years of neglect was starting to show. Layers of paint were peeling off and hanging down. Two medics were coming up the stone steps, and one of them nodded to her in acknowledgement. She appeared oblivious to the greeting. A bored security officer was pacing the corridor and took little notice as the nurse passed him and approached the pharmacy window.

The pharmacy was a secure unit; drugs were valuable and much sort after for exchange on the black market. The dispensing staff entrance was via a reinforced metal door at the side; access for medics was by a small sliding window which opened from the inside. She checked her watch and peered through the grimy glass. Two men in white coats were busy, appearing to be making up prescriptions. She tapped on the glass and one of them looked up, then continued whatever he was doing. Eliz was getting impatient, partly through nervousness.

She was hopping from one foot to another, then the window raised upwards; a strong unidentifiable smell emerged from within. "Yes," barked the pharmacist.

Eliz handed him the docket. "Wait," he said, and the window dropped.

Five minutes later, the window opened, and the pharmacist handed through a paper bag containing small boxes of tablets. He was holding two packets in his hand.

"Why do you want these?"

"What?" asked Eliz.

"Flunitrazepam and Flumazenil. It is unusual."

"We have just finished operating on the son of Mohammad Hossein Modarresi. Taken out his appendix; do you want him to suffer? You can call Professor Chehrazad; if you wish, although he is busy at the moment; I'm not sure how he will react to being questioned."

"Professor Chehrazad? Sorry, I didn't recognise the signature. Of course."

The pharmacist passed the rest of the medicines and closed the hatch.

The nurse retraced her steps and reached the fresh air. She suddenly felt nauseous and quickly rushed to the side of the building before disgorging her breakfast. She held onto the wall and coughed as the bile stung her throat.

She put the two small boxes she would need in her pocket and carried the paper bag with the remainder of the drugs up to the ward where the patient was recuperating, then went to the ladies toilets, took a drink of water and splashed her face. Her immediate mission had been accomplished.

Chapter Six

Back at the embassy, Houghton was unaware of the risks being taken by Mayflower. He was in his office working on several scenarios, all emphasising the enormity of his mission. Over the days since his arrival, he had become used to the hum of the high-frequency wave-baffler that was protecting the embassy from eavesdroppers; it was ambient, but for some reason, this afternoon, it was intrusive, eating into his mind as he tried to get his thoughts into some sort of a cohesive plan.

He was disturbed by a knock on the door, and David Dexter walked in carrying a laptop computer under his arm. He had an excited look on his face.

"I think we've found our man."

"Sorry," said Houghton, not immediately making the connection.

"Your chaos theory. We've found someone who fits the bill."

Dexter put the laptop down on Houghton's desk and opened it. There was a man's face on the screen.

"Saleh Amadi Aziz Al Rajhi; he's a Project Director in charge of some of the construction work for the Uranium enrichment plant at Esfahan. Still there, as far as we know. He's Egyptian, but trained in Europe, studied in Switzerland initially, then France. He was involved in building one of their nuclear facilities at Saint-Alban; an important guy, been in Iran since the mid-nineties."

"You seem to know a lot about him."

"Well, we know some. He was targeted by the Americans as a possible recruit two, maybe three, years ago. They were desperate to have someone in Esfahan, and with his background, he was an ideal candidate. If I remember rightly, someone actually met him, but it seems the guy wasn't interested – too worried about his family and told them where to go; I don't blame him."

"Were we involved?"

"No, not directly, but we were briefed at the time, unusually; it was purely an American enterprise."

"He sounds ideal. So, how do we do this? We can't just start announcing his name all over the place. MOIS are no fools, and they'll spot it's a ruse straightaway."

"Yes, you're right there, and I've been giving it some thought. First, we can give him a code name; 'The Egyptian' seems appropriate; it will give MOIS a clue. Then we can drop in oblique references in emails and even in conversation. There's one of the drivers we know feeds information back to MOIS."

"Really? Why is he still here?"

"Simple – misinformation. Sometimes we deliberately let something slip, nothing too obvious or too damaging. Just enough to give him some credibility. Once we start, we can get Dee to give GCHQ a keyword and monitor traffic. We will soon know if they've taken the bait," said Dexter.

"Sure, ok, but don't mention to her, or anyone else, that we're using him as a decoy. I want to keep it between us. I'll have to tell Andy in Vauxhall, but that's all."

"Yes, ok," said Dexter.

"Luckily, Mahabadi's not due on leave for another

couple of weeks, so that should give us enough time," said Houghton.

"Well, I'll start the ball rolling upstairs. Why don't you join me in the car this evening for the journey back and we can discuss the Egyptian, nothing too obvious, just enough to get them interested; their driver is on this evening."

"Sure. Five o'clock? Oh, and I'll give Vauxhall a call on the open line about our friend."

"Good idea! Ok, I'll meet you in reception."

Dexter left, leaving Houghton to write an encrypted email to Andy Fellows."

'Be advised, I will be calling in twenty minutes on the open line and will make reference to 'the Egyptian'. Please respond accordingly. Tiger Lily says hi.'

Shortly after sending his email, Houghton was on the phone to his colleague in MI6 Headquarters. The call was on the open line.

"Hi Andy. How are things?"

"Good, thanks, how are things with you?"

"Not too bad thanks. Is there any news from our Egyptian friend at Esfahan?"

Fellows knew straight away what to say.

"Nothing new since the last report?"

"Hmm, what about our American cousins? I believe they're also interested in him."

"Yeah, I'm sure they are. I'll let you know if I hear anything."

"Ok, thanks. I'll make further enquiries from here; I hope we can get him on board before the Americans get to him. Signs are looking hopeful."

"That's great news; I'll let you know if I get any more

information."

"Cheers, we can chat tomorrow."

Houghton rang off; the deception had started.

Later that afternoon, as arranged, Houghton met Dexter in reception, and they walked to the waiting Jaguar together. Houghton had emailed Dee to let her know he wouldn't be on the minibus and would see her later.

The driver courteously opened the doors for his passengers, ensuring they were safely seated before closing them. He climbed in, started the engine and steered the vehicle toward the main gate. Once the car was through security and onto the freeway that would take them to the compound, Dexter turned to Houghton and spoke in what was a barely audible whisper.

"Have you heard the latest about our Egyptian friend?"

"Not since that email from Vauxhall."

"Well, according to my sources, he seems very keen to come over to us."

"That's great; that would be a result – someone with the Egyptian's experience would be very valuable to us, and the Americans – they're bound to be interested."

"Well, to get someone from Esfahan would be a real bonus."

Although the bulk of the conversation was in a whisper, the volume increased slightly for some keywords which would be audible to the driver. 'Egyptian', 'Vauxhall', 'Americans' and 'Esfahan' would have been recognised by the chauffeur. The idea was to create confusion with the Iranian secret police once the message had been relayed back to them. Enough to start a mild panic; that was the hope.

Just before seven o'clock, Houghton left his apartment and walked the short distance down the corridor for his dinner date. Having been tied up in work most of the day, he hadn't had much time to consider his date but, every now and again, his thoughts did stray, and it gave him a twinge of excitement. He tapped lightly on the door.

Dee answered, wearing a white tee-shirt with a gold motif across the front, pale blue jeans and leather slip-on shoes.

"Hi, come in, dinner's nearly ready."

"Thanks," said Houghton and followed Dee into the living area. There was a pleasant aroma of herbs and spices.

"Have a seat. Would you like a glass of wine?"

"Yes, thanks. I feel my manners are lacking here. I would have brought a bottle, but I haven't been able to get away."

"Don't be silly, it's fine. I keep a couple for special occasions."

"Thanks, something smells good," said Houghton.

"I hope you like it," said Dee. She went to the kitchenette and returned with a bottle and two glasses.

"This one's Bulgarian," she said, presenting the bottle to Houghton for examination. "Don't know what it's like, but we can't be too choosey, I'm afraid."

"Bulgarian is fine," said Houghton.

She sat down next to Houghton and put the bottle and glasses on the coffee table.

"I've been thinking about you today," she said and leaned in to kiss him on the lips.

"I've been trying not to," said Houghton and smiled. He could smell her perfume and could see her nipples protruding from her tee shirt.

"Yes, it's easy to get side-tracked. You pour the drinks; I'll dish up," said Dee.

She got up and returned to the kitchen.

There was a small table in the corner of the apartment set out for two people. Houghton poured the wine and placed a glass either side of the table adjacent to the placemats.

Dee returned carrying two plates using a pair of oven-gloves to protect her hands and set them down on the table.

"Careful, the plates are hot," she warned.

She placed the oven gloves on the back of the chair and sat down.

Houghton looked at the food in front of him. "This looks good."

"It's Kotlet, a local dish… minced beef, mash potato and onions."

"Sounds great; thanks for going to this trouble."

"Don't mention it, but I do have a confession; I didn't cook it." Dee laughed. "One of the staff does the cooking for the compound on a takeout basis. You just put the order in with the concierge. It's brilliant, and the food's great. It's also paid for by the embassy."

"No one told me that; I must remember to use it."

"Yes, it's fantastic, you just put it in the microwave; there's a menu in reception. If you place your order when you leave in the morning, you can pick it up when you get back at night."

Houghton blew on the hot food and took a mouthful.

"Hmm, I see what you mean; this is good."

Dee looked at Houghton. "So, what's the news?"

"I've been thinking about what you said, and I might need your help," said Houghton as he took another mouthful of food.

"Go on," said Dee.

"Ok, let me give you some more information," he dropped his voice to a whisper. "One of the senior programme directors on the Esfahan project wants to defect."

"Hmm, that's not going to be easy, and you've been sent to get him out."

"To facilitate it, yes."

"Based in Esfahan?" she confirmed. "How can I help?"

"I'll need you to flag any traffic that mentions the Egyptian – that's the codename we're using."

"Yes, ok, I can do that. I'll get onto Cheltenham tomorrow."

"Thanks."

There were two reasons for Houghton's disclosure. He was not entirely convinced of the integrity of the apartment block. He also did not want to reveal the real target to anyone. It wasn't that he didn't trust Dee, but the less anyone knew about the Mahabadis, the better.

"This is good," said Houghton again as he cleared his plate. He took a sip of wine and looked at Dee; her tee-shirt struggling to hold in its contents. He could feel himself becoming aroused.

She looked into his eyes; she had not finished her dinner, but she put down her knife and fork, took a large gulp of wine, then grabbed Houghton's hand.

"I'm not hungry; let's go to bed."

It was almost two hours before Dee and Houghton returned to the living room. Dee's half-finished meal was on her plate, cold and unappetising.

"I'll help you clear the stuff," said Houghton, gathering up his cutlery and crockery.

"It's ok, I'll just put them in the dishwasher. Would you like a coffee?"

"Yeah, cheers, thanks," said Houghton, following Dee into the kitchenette. She was wearing a dressing gown.

"I've got some dessert as well – saffron ice cream."

"Yeah? Thanks," said Houghton.

"Go and sit down, I'll bring everything through; it's a bit crowded in here with two," said Dee, as she filled a kettle with water.

Houghton complied and sat down on the settee, deep in contemplation. He was starting to have feelings for Dee, but he couldn't afford any distractions; lives depended on it.

A few minutes later, Dee walked in with two bowls of white ice-cream, which she placed on the coffee table, then returned for the coffees.

She sat next to him as he started eating his dessert.

"You're quiet," said Dee.

"Sorry," said Houghton. "Got a lot on my mind."

"Come on then spill it; I'm a big girl," she said and looked at him. Her brown eyes were wide, her dark hair glistened reflecting the light from the two wall lamps.

Houghton said nothing, trying to pick the right words. They continued eating ice-cream; the atmosphere had changed.

"Look, I think I know what you want to say," said Dee, taking the initiative. "It's all been a bit quick, too soon to be involved, it's been fun, etcetera, etcetera. I've heard it all before."

Houghton looked at her. "No, you've got that wrong.

I really have got feelings for you, but I can't afford any distractions."

"Is that what I am? A distraction," she said sharply.

"I didn't mean it to sound that way, sorry. No, you know the situation; the mission I'm on is dangerous; many people's lives are at stake."

"Yes, it's ok, you're right, but I do care about you."

"Yes, and that's the thing, I'm starting to care too," said Houghton.

She held his hand. "It's ok, I just want you safe." There was a long pause. "So, what do you want to do?"

"For the moment, I need to concentrate on putting a plan together; my timescales are tight."

"Well, maybe I can help; I've got to know Tehran pretty well, and I've made some friends who I trust. If there's anything you want me to do, you just have to ask."

"Thanks, I appreciate that," said Houghton. Dee leant forward and kissed him. He could taste Saffron ice-cream and coffee.

Dee's wristwatch was on the table where she had left it; Houghton noticed the time.

"Hey, I better get going. It's getting late," he said as they disengaged.

"Yes," said Dee. She looked at him again. "You will tell me if there is anything I can do; anything," she repeated.

"Yes, of course. For the moment, just let me know about the Egyptian."

"Yes, I'll speak to Cheltenham tomorrow."

Houghton got up and kissed Dee again. "See you in the morning, I think I'll be back on the minibus."

"I see, slumming it again."

"Yeah," said Houghton and smiled.

Next morning, Houghton was in reception just before eight o'clock waiting to ride the minibus to the embassy. Dee walked down the stairs a few minutes later and greeted Houghton warmly but professionally.

"You ok?"

"Yeah, good, thanks," said Houghton.

Any further discussion was curtailed as the final passengers joined them.

The journey in was uneventful; it seemed like just a normal day, no signs of protests or demonstrators. There was relief among the embassy staff that there had been no further inflammatory rhetoric from the Americans that was likely to aggravate the situation. The traffic crawled, and there was little conversation among the minibus commuters. Houghton was seated next to Dee, and occasionally there was eye-contact and smiles.

Once at the embassy, they entered reception; Dee turned to Houghton. "Are you stopping by the canteen for breakfast?"

"Yeah, but it will need to be a grab and go, I've got a lot on."

"Yeah, me too; I'll join you."

A few minutes later, Houghton was heading to his office in the basement, carrying his takeout breakfast and a cup of coffee. Dee had returned to the second floor.

He opened his laptop and accessed his emails. There was one from Vauxhall concerning news about 'the Egyptian', just a couple of lines saying that someone was trying to make contact with him at Esfahan. Houghton smiled.

At ten o'clock, there was a knock on Houghton's door,

and David Dexter walked in.

"Hi David," said Houghton, looking up from his computer screen.

"Hi Nick, I've got an update. Just been speaking to Dee and it seems the ruse is working, there have been numerous messages referencing 'the Egyptian' from MOIS, but that's not the best news. I've just come off the phone with someone from the Canadian Embassy."

Houghton raised his eyebrows.

"Apparently they've got a vacancy for a senior construction engineer and are looking to recruit."

"What's that supposed to mean?"

"It's all code. It seems our guy is on their radar; it's got Langley written all over it."

"CIA?"

"Yeah. It's an open secret they've got two or three agents holed up there at the embassy. They want to arrange a meet."

"Really? Now that is interesting."

"Yeah, they wouldn't go into details over the phone, but asked if someone could meet with them this afternoon, said it was urgent."

"And you want me to meet them?"

"Yes, it would make more sense. I've given them your name; they want you to meet someone called…" he checked the piece of paper he was holding; "Antonio Alvarez."

"Ok, where? What time?"

"City Park. There's a bench by the Park-E-Shahr Library. They want you to be there at three-thirty. Alvarez will make contact."

"Ok, I'll be there. I'm going out earlier anyway, around twelve-thirty. Any news from Mrs Mahabadi?"

"No, which is a bit worrying; she's had no contact from her husband for two days. She doesn't know what's happening."

"Hmm, that's going to be a real problem; if there's no contact, it's going to make planning anything virtually impossible. Can you keep me updated? I may need to speak to her again."

"Yes, of course," said Dexter. "You mentioned you were going out later, do you need me to sign you out again?"

"Yes, I'll give you a call around twelve-thirty. I'll let you know how I get on with Mr Alvarez when I get back."

"Good but be careful with Alvarez; my guess is he'll be a field agent. Just play along and see what they want."

"Yeah, ok," said Houghton. "I'll catch you later."

Dexter left the office. With no contact from Mahabadi, there was little more Houghton could do. The logistics were going to be complex, and the list of items he would need was growing.

At eleven o'clock, he had another visitor; it was Dee with another offering of coffee and pastries.

"Hi, hope you don't mind me coming down. I just wanted to give you an update. I come bearing gifts."

"Gratefully received," said Houghton. "Take a seat. What's the latest?"

Dee sat down and took the lids off the two cardboard mugs; the smell of coffee permeated the room. She passed Houghton a pastry and a napkin.

"Cheers," said Houghton and took a bite.

"Looks like there is some interest in your Egyptian. There's been a lot of traffic going out of MOIS headquarters to Esfahan, which in itself is not unusual, but reference to 'the Egyptian' has appeared in four messages today. We don't know, of course, what's happening at the facility or what action, if any, has been taken. It may be that he's just being put under increased scrutiny; that would be my best estimate; it's consistent with their modus operandum. I think they'll keep an eye on him in the hope they can catch whoever is trying to make contact with him. You need to be very careful, Nick, these guys are hardcore; I mean real bad. If you get caught, you can forget about human rights and the Geneva Convention. Not many come out of their interrogations without some life-changing injuries, and that's if they survive at all. Some of the stories my Iranian friends tell are hideous."

Part of him wanted to put her mind at rest and disclose the ruse, but for the moment, he would let things play out. He looked at her as he took another swig of coffee.

"Thanks for your concern, I promise I'll be very careful."

"Don't forget, if there's anything I can do, you just have to say," said Dee with a look of concern.

"Yes, I will... and thank you."

They finished their mid-morning break, and Dee returned to the second floor. Houghton had been glad of the interruption; it had eased the sense of frustration he felt at not being able to contact Mahabadi. Without knowing when he was due to return to Tehran, it was difficult to move into the final planning phase. There was, however, the forthcoming meeting with Mayflower which might change things.

At twelve-thirty, he left the embassy wearing his casual clothes and sunglasses. Dexter had signed him out. Everything was much quieter than on his last outing when he had to run the gauntlet of the mob. Today, it was deserted outside the embassy, no sign of demonstrators or press; just the constant flow of vehicles going about their daily lives. He passed through the security gates, as surreptitiously as possible.

He retraced his journey to the mall, adopting the same routine as previous meetings to ensure he was not being followed; he even allowed for one Metro train to pass without boarding. He watched the passengers from the back of the station; everyone waiting got on.

By twenty-past one, Houghton was in the coffee shop drinking coffee. He'd ordered another sandwich and was taking his lunch when he saw Mayflower enter. She nodded at the proprietor and walked over to Houghton's booth.

Straightaway he noticed her demeanour. Her face was etched with worry; her eyes looked as though she hadn't slept for a week.

She sat down without any greeting, and the proprietor came across and took her order.

"Are you ok?" said Houghton.

She looked down at her hands. Her fingers were linking, then unlinking; Houghton could see her shaking.

"It has been difficult," she said without eye contact.

There was more silence. The proprietor brought the nurse her drink, and Houghton continued to eat his lunch, not wanting to rush her. He looked at her, the anxiety palpable.

"Look, if it's too much for you, please say. I don't want to put you in danger."

"I am already in danger. I have got what you asked, but if it is discovered, then I am a dead person."

"I don't know what to say; I have no desire, or right, to put you in danger. You asked to help; we both knew it was dangerous."

"Yes, but I did not know I would feel like this. I am just a nurse; I care for my patients."

"Yes, I know. I'm sorry. You told me it was for your father and to help to bring better lives for you and the people here."

"But stealing drugs. How will that help?"

"I can't tell you just yet, but I will nearer the time. Let me say this, if this mission is successful, it may prevent a nuclear war."

Houghton was measured in his delivery, grave in his message. Mayflower considered the remark.

"It is that important?"

"It could be, yes."

Eliz sat and said nothing as she drank her coffee. Meeting Houghton had helped to lessen the isolation she had felt. She put her hands in her nurse's uniform pocket and pulled out the two small packets and reached across the table. Houghton took her hand like a lover might do, and he enveloped it with his hand. He quickly retrieved the packages from her fingers and put them in his jacket pocket. No-one would have spotted the transaction.

Houghton could see her visibly relax. She looked up for the first time and met his eyes.

"They are labelled," she whispered. "I have also got the coat for the doctor, but I cannot get a…er… the stethoscope." She mimed to clarify. "Each doctor has his own; they are very expensive here."

"Ok, I will try and get one myself, please don't worry. I won't need the doctor's coat just yet; I'll let you know."

"You want me to meet you again?"

"Yes, but not for a while; I will let you know when."

"Ok, send me a message," she said and reached out a hand to Houghton's. He held it for a moment and then she got up and walked to the door without a backward glance.

Houghton fiddled with the packages in his pocket; he knew the danger that the nurse was in. He just hoped she would be safe.

He finished his lunch and ordered another coffee. His next meeting intrigued him. The rendezvous point was about a twenty-minute walk from the bazaar. He checked his watch; he had some time to kill.

He considered a stroll around the mall but discounted that; bazaar shop proprietors were aggressive in their sales approach, and he had no desire to risk any confrontation. He looked around the café; lunchtime, and it was not particularly busy. Houghton wondered how it was paying for itself.

He finished his coffee, and the proprietor walked over to collect his cup.

"Is there anything else I can get you," said the man.

"No, thanks, I have another meeting."

"You will not put Eliz in any danger will you?"

Houghton was taken aback by the question and the force in which it was delivered. It seemed more like a threat.

"Danger? No, of course not; we are friends, that is all."

The proprietor did not look convinced and continued to clear the table and wipe it down with a dishcloth.

"That is good, I would not wish to see her hurt in any way. She is a precious and gifted person."

"Yes, I understand."

"That is good. Will we see you again here?"

"Yes, I would think so," said Houghton.

"Please be careful my friend; there are many unseen dangers. The bazaar can be a bad place."

"Thanks for the warning. I will be careful."

"Good, good. Until next time then."

"Yes," said Houghton and gave the man some notes. "That is for Eliz as well."

The man bowed in reverence. "My pleasure."

Houghton walked out of the coffee shop, thinking about the exchange with the proprietor. It disturbed him.

He had an hour before his meeting with the CIA agent but decided not to hang around the Bazaar. The exit was swarming with people, some entering, some exiting, all creating a great deal of jostling. Houghton kept close to the wall to avoid the worst of the human maelstrom.

Houghton's journey to City Park meant retracing his steps back towards the Panzdah-e-Khordad Metro station, then turning right. After about half a mile, the park was in front of him. On the right, as he approached the entrance, he could see the Tehran Judicial Palace and Supreme Court with its impressive Greek-influenced frontage. He hoped that was as close as he would ever get to the Iranian seat of justice.

The Park-e-Shahr, to give its local name, is the oldest park in Tehran and is in the central area, providing a welcome oasis of green in the urban sprawl. It is traversed by impressive cross-hatched stone footpaths. The meeting point by the library was on the south side.

By three-fifteen, Houghton was seated on the bench as instructed. There were, in fact, several benches along the walkway; he hoped he had chosen the correct one. It was the closest to the library entrance.

It was a warm afternoon, and Houghton took an interest in the passers-by. He checked his surroundings more than once; there seemed to be no-one nearby that might be watching or eavesdropping. It was a good place for a discreet meeting.

Antonio Alvarez was an engineer and senior project manager working for a large German construction company, Brechtel GMBH. At least that's what it said on his visa. He had worked for the company for over ten years, but for the last five, was engaged on major construction projects in Iran. Before that, he had been based in Cairo, working on one of the new dams.

His present venture was managing the building of a large industrial complex in the city of Arak, home to one of the country's top-secret nuclear facilities. Known as IR-40, the Arak facility was a 40-megawatt heavy-water reactor and, in 2006, was nearing completion just outside the city in the district of Khondab.

The employment was a cover; Alvarez was one of the CIA's most important field-agents in Iran. A competent, rather than fluent, Farsi speaker, his main activity was to pass information about the Arak facility to Langley via his station chief at the Canadian Embassy. During his time there, he had cultivated several 'friends' who were working on the IR-40 project, and he had been able to supply valuable intel on the construction progress.

That morning, Alvarez received a call from his boss in Tehran; he needed a meet. This was a fairly regular occurrence and the main process for transferring information, but this sounded different.

It was two-fifteen by the time Alvarez had completed the hundred and eighty-mile journey; it had taken him just over five hours. The rendezvous with his station chief was in a nondescript coffee shop, close to one of the new shopping malls. There was a list of five meeting points they used, numbered one to five. Today was number four; Alvarez knew the destinations by heart.

Head of station, Jo Podesta, was waiting in one of the booths as Alvarez walked in.

"Tony," acknowledged Podesta, and the pair shook hands. Alvarez sat down, and an attendant was quick to take their order. There was an exchange of pleasantries while they waited for their beverages.

"How was the drive?" asked Podesta after their drinks had been delivered.

"Not so bad? So, what's the beef about?" said Alvarez.

Podesta looked at the agent with concern. "You ever heard the name Saleh Amadi?"

"Yeah, sure. He's that construction guy over in Esfahan. Didn't you try to recruit him?"

"Yeah, about two years ago when I was in the field...."

"So why's he come up again now?"

"We got a message this morning from Langley..." Podesta leaned forward, looked around and whispered. "The Brits are trying to spring him."

"What?"

"Yeah, there are some angry people back home, I can tell you."

"I bet."

"If Amadi's changed his mind and wants to defect, then we want him; we can't have him going over to the Brits with what he knows," said Podesta.

"What do you need me to do?"

"I've spoken to Dexter, my contact at their embassy, and told him we need a discussion."

"So, you want me to meet this Dexter?"

"No, there's a new guy there." He took out a piece of paper from his pocket. "Houghton. I've told Dexter you'll meet him in the park at three-thirty. You know, the usual spot."

"Ok." He looked at his watch; it was two forty-five. "I better make a move then."

Podesta looked at him; the stress was etched over his face. "Just shake a few trees. See if you can find out what they're up to. Then we can meet back here, and you can let me know what you find out."

City Park, outside The Park-E-Shahr Library – 3.:15 p.m.

Houghton was basking in the warm sunshine; his reactive glasses were now dark. He was still thinking about his liaison with Mayflower; she was an integral part of his plan, and he hoped she would have the courage to carry it through; there was no feasible plan B. In that event, the mission might have to be aborted.

He noticed someone walking up the path in his direction. Ray-ban sunglasses with black frames; fit-looking and slim, as though he had run one-too-many marathons. He was dressed casually in jeans and a short-sleeved white shirt; he was carrying a jacket in the crook of his arm. At first, Houghton did not take a great deal of notice. He looked Iranian and did not appear out of place among the local population.

Then the man approached the bench.

"Houghton?"

"Mr Alvarez, I presume?"

He deliberately spoke in a quintessentially English way, cultivated from his private school upbringing.

"Well, it's Doctor Alvarez if you wanna be precise." He sat down next to Houghton.

There were no handshakes; the atmosphere felt frosty.

"You wanted a meet, I understand," said Houghton.

"Yes, it appears you guys have really pissed off some people."

"Really? Why's that?" said Houghton nonchalantly. Alvarez looked ahead, avoiding eye content.

"Come on Houghton, don't play the innocent. You know very well why – Saleh Amadi."

"Ah, the Egyptian?"

This time Alvarez did make eye contact; or as much as was possible through his sunglasses. He had a dark complexion, and there was a hint of a Hispanic accent. Houghton did a quick assessment, Puerto Rican or Mexican origins, he thought.

"Yeah, the fucking Egyptian. We don't like people who tread on our toes."

"We're not treading on anyone's toes."

"Sure! So, what's your interest in him?"

"We have none, officially anyway. We got a message that he was looking for a new employment opportunity. We've not done anything about it; we thought you guys were interested. We just flagged it up to Vauxhall."

"What message?"

"That's not for disclosure, my friend."

"Now listen, we've been nurturing him for the best part of two years."

"Yes, I heard, which is why we've done nothing about it."

"And I'm not your friend."

"Sorry, point taken."

Alvarez was in a hole with nowhere to go. He could not disclose the CIA had been monitoring messages from the British Embassy, but they both knew they had been. That was part of Houghton's deception plan.

"So, you're not going to try to get him out?" said Alvarez.

"We don't have the resources at our disposal."

Alvarez thought that was probably true; he assessed the information.

"Vauxhall doesn't want to pursue it," continued Houghton. "Probably concerned about your reaction... It looks like they were right."

"Ok, yeah, sorry, we seem to have got off on the wrong foot."

"Yeah, you could say that. You Americans always jump in with both feet."

"I guess, that's one of our more endearing features," Alvarez said and smiled for the first time.

"So, is that it then?"

"I guess."

"If there's anything we can do to help our American colleagues, you only have to ask."

"Thanks," said Alvarez.

They both looked ahead.

It was Alvarez who turned to speak first. "How long are

you going to be in town?"

Houghton faced him. "Not sure yet, I'm just covering for a sick colleague."

"Maybe we can share a beer while you're here, give us a chance to exchange ideas."

"Yeah, ok, why not," replied Houghton.

The agent got up. "Take care Houghton. I'll be in touch." He handed him a business card, 'Dr Antonio Alvarez, Senior Project Manager, Brechtel GMBH, Dusseldorf', and his mobile phone number.

Houghton looked at it. "You're a long way from home, Doctor Alvarez."

"Yeah, you could say that," said Alvarez.

Houghton took out a small notepad from his jacket pocket, tore off a page and wrote his number on it. He handed it to the agent.

"Thanks," he said, holding up the paper and then putting it in his pocket.

"You take care and have a nice day," replied Houghton, somewhat sarcastically. Alvarez ignored the comment and turned around. Houghton stayed seated on the bench and watched him walk away down the pathway to the park exit. His plan was working even better than expected.

British Embassy, Ferdowsi Avenue, Central Tehran – 4:50 p.m.

Houghton was back in his office before five o'clock and immediately called Dexter, who dropped what he was doing and headed to the basement. Houghton, meanwhile, had placed the drugs he had got from the nurse in his desk drawer.

Moments later, Dexter walked in.

"So, a good meeting?" said Dexter as he walked into Houghton's office.

"Yeah, you could say that. They've bought it hook, line and sinker," said Houghton.

"Well, that should keep MOIS occupied for the foreseeable future."

"Yeah, the Americans will be trying to make contact with Saleh Amadi by any means possible which will almost certainly be picked up by MOIS," said Houghton.

"Which means we don't have to do a thing," interrupted Dexter. "Now, that's what I call a result."

"Chaos theory," said Houghton.

"This calls for a celebration. Why don't you join Sophie and me for dinner?"

"Yeah, cheers, that sounds great."

Chapter Seven

Iran's Ministry of Intelligence and Security (MOIS) has unlimited financial resources and uses all means at its disposal to protect the Islamic Revolution of Iran. To achieve its ends, it utilises such methods as; infiltrating internal opposition groups; monitoring domestic threats and expatriate dissent; arresting alleged spies and dissidents; exposing conspiracies deemed threatening; and maintaining liaison with other foreign intelligence agencies as well as with organisations that protect the Islamic Republic's interests around the world.

Its background can be traced back to the 1950s. The secret police organisation was established by Iran's Mohammad Reza Shah in 1957, with the help of the U.S. Central Intelligence Agency and, ironically, the Israeli Mossad, ostensibly to protect the Pahlavi dynasty. SAVAK, as it was initially known, operated until the Iranian Revolution of 1979. It was a hated and feared organisation, with a reputation for brutality, and was closed down with the coming to power of Ayatollah Khomeini.

Following the departure of the Shah in January 1979, SAVAK's central staff and its agents were targeted for reprisals; however, the value of the organisation in maintaining civilian control was quickly recognised, and many ex-SAVAK's staff were recruited to the new organisation.

By 2006, MOIS was the most powerful organisation in

Iran, with an estimated thirty thousand employees and agents, many trained by Russian secret service personnel; in fact, all other ministries were required by law to share information with it. The ministry oversees all covert operations; it even has its own Department of Misinformation, which is in charge of creating and waging psychological warfare against the enemies of the Islamic Republic. It is the largest individual department within MOIS.

Although its technical surveillance capability was far less sophisticated than the US, UK or Israel, its network of informants and agents was second-to-none and its prime source of intelligence. There was even a three-digit telephone number (113) which members of the public were encouraged to use to report any instances of anti-government activity.

With the country's nuclear programme coming under increased international scrutiny, MOIS had become obsessed with preventing foreign intelligence activities. The creation of a special counterintelligence unit resulted in the capture of several alleged spies which, in turn, increased the pressure on Iran's adversaries.

At this time, however, the organisation was facing a significant number of challenges internally. Two years earlier, General Ali Reza Asgari, a senior member of the Islamic Revolutionary Guard Corps, (the military wing of MOIS), defected. He was reported to have provided significant information to the Israelis, including the intelligence Mossad used in Operation Orchard to strike Syria's nuclear reactor.

Earlier, in another damaging setback, the United States managed to successfully stall Iran's uranium-enrichment programme by intentionally providing defective tools, machines, and blueprints.

It was against this backdrop that, in 2005, Tehran changed the director in its Security Division and appointed Saeed Hajjarian as section head. He had a ruthless reputation and a history of being able to get things done.

One of the early actions taken by Hajjarian was to establish a new intelligence force called 'Oghab 2' or 'Eagle 2'. This unit was put together under the counterintelligence bureau, exclusively responsible for protecting all Iran's nuclear programmes, nuclear facilities, and the scientists working there, against threats; this included threats from domestic opposition groups and foreign intelligence agencies. It was widely believed that Mossad agents had assassinated a number of Iran's nuclear scientists.

With the world's attention being drawn to Iran's nuclear activity, Eagle 2 was going to be very busy.

MOIS Headquarters, Central Tehran – Sunday April 16th

MOIS has several buildings in Tehran; the counterintelligence bureau is in one of the old colonial buildings with an impressive circular colonnade entrance. Head of Eagle 2, General Gholam Reza Moghrabi, was in a morning conference with his team of personnel. The room, in a basement area of the main building, was oppressively hot and stuffy with no natural daylight. Several of the all-male audience were smoking, and a blue fog hung in the air. The atmosphere for the ten agents facing a podium where the head of section was speaking, was a mix of anticipation and anxiety; the General was a fearsome leader and a renowned bully.

Standing at six-foot-two, with a stocky frame, he had an

imposing presence. His black wavy hair was greasy and in need of a wash; beads of sweat glistened at the margins of his hairline and dark stains discoloured the underarms of his uniform. There was a laptop and, behind him, a screen which had the MOIS emblem illuminated as a backdrop.

They spoke in Farsi.

"First, gentlemen, an update. We have been analysing video footage from the demonstrations on Thursday, and the security division have made several arrests. At the moment, there is nothing to concern us; unless of course, anything is found in the interrogation."

He pressed the forward button on the laptop, and photographs of the demonstrators outside the different embassies appeared on the screen.

"What about airstrikes? Has there been any news?" asked a concerned team member. Others looked on expectantly for the answer.

"I think we can discount airstrikes. The intelligence we have suggests the Americans will press for more economic sanctions. They are too busy in Iraq and Afghanistan to start a war with us. But that is not why you are here today."

He forwarded the next slide, a photograph of the Esfahan Nuclear establishment.

"We have had some new intelligence from our contact at the British Embassy."

There were expectant looks around the room. The General lit up a cigarette. Smoke billowed across the room in front of the projector, casting shadows on the screen. He coughed and continued his briefing.

"Two days ago, our man was driving two diplomats back to the compound in Gholhak." The General pulled on his cigarette. "He overheard their conversation. He was unable to hear all the words clearly, but he heard enough to be concerned. They talked about Esfahan, which alerted our agent, and someone called the Egyptian."

"The Egyptian?" asked an agent in the front row.

"From what our man could understand, someone at a high level at Esfahan wants to defect to the British."

There were sharp intakes of breath.

"Do we know who this person is?" asked the same agent.

"We have spent the night searching through the personnel files and we believe it is this man. Saleh Amadi Aziz Al Rajhi." A grainy photograph, which looked like it had been taken from a security pass, appeared on the screen. "He's the only senior person from Egypt, and he has connections in France, so it makes sense."

He pulled on the cigarette again.

"Our communications people have also picked up messages from the British Embassy, referring to the Egyptian, but there is more. Two hours ago, there was a message from the Canadian Embassy, which also mentioned the Egyptian."

"Why would the Canadians be interested?" asked another agent.

"They probably aren't," said the General. Smoke billowed from his nostrils. "We know for a fact that there are CIA agents based there. It was in one of their messages to Langley."

There were looks of concern among the team.

"Do you want to arrest this man?" asked the inquisitive agent.

"Not at the moment, but I want him watched twenty-four

hours a day – his house, his phone, his office, his family. I want every move he makes monitored. If he sneezes, I want to know about it. We do not want another General Asgari situation." He spat the name of the formal General and slammed his fist down on the podium, making several agents jump. The computer mouse, which was close to the impact, rose in the air and fell towards the floor, then hung in mid-air with its lead still attached to the computer.

The room went quiet. Everyone in the room was aware of the former General's defection and the damage it caused.

An agent put his hand up.

"Yes?" barked the General.

"You said there were two diplomats in the car; do we know who they were?"

The General picked up a plastic bottle of water, removed the top and took a slug.

"We know one of them – Dexter; we know he is MI6. The other is new, arrived this week according to the driver."

"Do you think it's a new agent?"

"Possibly," rasped the General.

"Maybe he's been sent to get the Egyptian out."

The General thought for a few moments. He took the last drag of his cigarette, stubbed it out in an ashtray and immediately lit up another.

"That could be possible," he said, adding more smoke to the increasing haze in the room.

"Can the driver find out?" asked the agent.

"I don't know, but there may be a better way," said the General. "Afareen Mahabadi works at the British compound. Do we still have someone watching her?"

"Sir, we have been watching her, but not every day

because of her connections."

"Ah yes, General Khatami. Do not worry, I will speak with our head of security and explain our interest."

The General paused for thought; he was almost hidden in a blue haze.

"I think we need to speak with Mrs Mahabadi and test her loyalty; maybe she can get us the information we want."

He took another long pull on his cigarette, which appeared to aid his thinking process.

"Right, this is what we will do. Commander Fallahian?"

"Yes sir," said a younger man, who stood to attention. He was immaculately dressed, swarthy-looking and sporting a trimmed beard.

"I want you to take a small team to her house, no more than three or four. Go in uniform and make it late, about ten o'clock tonight. Be courteous but firm. She is not to be arrested. Tell her we need her help on a matter of national security."

"I will be here to question her at ten-thirty, don't keep me waiting. Any questions?"

"No, sir," said Fallahian.

The Mahabadi Residence, Bahar District, Tehran – 9:45 p.m.

Afareen Mahabadi lived with her mother and two children in the Bahar District of Tehran, a ten-minute walk from the Shohada-ye Haftom-e Tir Metro Station where she caught the train each day to Gholhak Garden, just seven stops away. It was a large apartment, befitting of a senior nuclear scientist and his family.

She was on the sofa watching TV in the lounge; her

mother was dozing in one of the two armchairs, trying to stay awake and keep her daughter company. They spoke in Farsi.

"Would you like a drink, mama?" said Afareen, which startled her mother into consciousness.

"What? Sorry; what time is it?"

"It's after nine-thirty. I'm making a hot drink; would you like one?"

"Just a tisane, please dear," said her mother.

"Would you like some ginger in it?"

"Yes please," said her mother and Afareen went into the kitchen. While the kettle was boiling, she went into the children's bedroom; they were both asleep.

A few minutes later, Afareen returned to the lounge with a tray holding two steaming cups of the herbal tea and a sugar bowl full of cubes.

"Thank you dear. I'll drink this, then go to bed. You have been very quiet tonight; are you still worried about Hassan?"

"Yes, it's been four days since I've heard from him. I have no idea how he is. I am so worried when I see all the problems on the TV. They are even saying the Americans might use missiles to destroy the place where Hassan is working; it was on the news."

Afareen's mother held her hand in an attempt to comfort her.

"Please do not worry, my dear. I am sure he will be fine."

The words of comfort had little effect. The worry was starting to affect Afareen's health; she had eaten very little for two days and was existing on water and herbal tea. At the compound, Sophie Dexter had tried to reassure her that everything would be ok; but the lack of contact was not only a concern for Afareen. The communication blackout threatened the very success of Operation Tiger Lily. It had been the topic of much discussion between Sophie and her husband, and of course, Nick Houghton.

Afareen had just taken her first sip of tea when there was a sharp rap on the door; not a polite knock that a neighbour might apply at this late hour, but an urgent, authoritative thump which had Afareen jumping off her seat and spilling her drink in shock. Adrenaline coursed through her body; she started to shake uncontrollably.

"Who is that at this hour?" said her mother, not sharing the same concern. She sipped her drink as Afareen got up and went to answer the enquiry. There was a short hallway that led to the entrance to the apartment.

A chain secured the front door with a spy hole in the middle. She peered through and froze as she saw four uniformed officers. The front one approached the door and knocked again; this time more loudly. Afareen recoiled for a moment, then opened the door as far as the chain would allow.

"Mrs Mahabadi? Can you open the door please? Police."

An ID card was shoved through the gap. She saw the words, Ministry of Intelligence. Afareen felt as if her legs would give away. She pushed the door closed, removed the chain and opened it. Four men pushed passed her.

"I am Commander Fallahian, Ministry of Intelligence," he showed his identity card again.

Afareen was visibly shaking. "Why are you here at this time of night? Don't you know who I am? Just wait until General Khatami hears about this intrusion."

"The General is aware of our visit. Do not concern

yourself; you are not under arrest. We just need your help; it's in the interests of national security."

Afareen's mother was seated in her chair watching events, appearing oblivious to the danger.

"Who lives here?" asked the Commander.

"Just my mother and my children, and my husband when he is allowed home."

"Ah, yes, Professor Mahabadi? A very important man and a great servant to Iran. But I'm sure you understand the way things are at the moment. We live in difficult times; the country is in a state of emergency."

Afareen was beginning to feel physically sick now. The three other officers were surveying the apartment, looking into each room in turn.

"Have you spoken to him recently?" continued the Commander.

"No, I have not heard from him for several days now."

"Hmm, that's not good. He will be worried about you, I expect."

"Yes, yes, he will be very worried," replied Afareen.

"Ok, well, General Moghrabi would like to talk to you; he is waiting for you at headquarters. I need to take you there."

"Now?"

"Yes, now," said the Commander assertively.

"But what about my mother? I can't leave her."

"You leave her when you work for the British?"

"Yes, but this is different. It's late; she will worry."

"I'm sorry; I have my orders. You must come with me now."

"It is alright my dear; I will be fine. You must do what the officer wants," interjected her mother, seeing her daughter's anxiety.

The other three officers were back in the room, and the small troupe waited while Afareen collected a jacket and headscarf.

Afareen kissed her mother, not knowing whether she would see her again. A myriad of thoughts ran through her mind. Her biggest fear was that their escape plan had been discovered. It would possibly mean the death of her and her family.

"I will take my keys mama. Please go to bed; everything will be fine," said Afareen, not very convincingly.

"I will not be able to sleep until you return," said her mother. "I will wait."

"Come now," ordered the Commander.

He ushered Afareen to the front door, and they left the apartment.

Afareen felt as though she was having an out-of-body experience, watching herself going through the motions. It was as though she was sleep-walking through her worst nightmare.

She would never remember following the three officers or the close attention of the Commander who was behind her, as they descended the stairs to the street. But she would remember the smell; male sweat, an unpleasant stale odour. She felt sick again and retched, but with little food for several days, it was no more than a dry gag.

A new black eight-seater SUV was waiting outside the apartment block. The streetlights cast ghostly shadows as one of the men slid open the door and helped Afareen to climb inside. She sat in the middle row with an officer either side. The Commander got in the front next to the driver. She stared straight ahead; the side windows had been blackened out. She heard the click of the door locks.

MOIS Headquarters – 10:23 p.m.

It took just over twenty minutes to reach the MOIS compound where General Moghrabi would be waiting. The journey had been made in complete silence. The Commander checked his gold Rolex watch as the vehicle stopped at the security checkpoint. It was ten twenty-three. He would make the General's deadline.

They were hastily waved through, and moments later, the vehicle drew up outside the central block. The driver got out and slid open the side door. There was a rush of cold air which caused Afareen to shiver. The officer next to Afareen helped her from the vehicle. Her legs gave way and she stumbled, but the officer caught her before she could hit the floor. She staggered, more than walked, towards the main block flanked by two officers. The Commander moved to the front of the group and opened the entrance door.

Afareen could not take in the austere surroundings; it was as though the décor, or lack of it, had been deliberately created to enhance the feeling of menace. The atrium was large with a domed roof. There was just one desk at the back attended by a uniformed guard; behind it, pinned on the wall, a large Iranian flag.

The footsteps of the group echoed on the stone floor as they walked towards the man. He stood to attention as the Commander approached. They exchanged salutes, and the guard escorted them to one of the five doors leading from the entrance lobby.

There was a security pad to the side, and the Commander

used a swipe card to disengage the lock. Afareen was ushered through and down some steep steps towards the basement.

"I need the toilet," she said to the Commander.

"Come with me," he directed and tutted.

They continued walking down a long corridor, past the room where the General's earlier briefing had taken place and stopped at a closed door with the word 'Toilet' stencilled on it in English. The commander pushed it open.

"Here," said the Commander. There was an old-fashioned pull-cord cistern and a single toilet bowl, significantly stained. Afareen entered and tried to shut the door.

"No, sorry," said the Commander.

"I need privacy."

"Sorry, do what you have to do. I will not look, but the door remains open."

"You wait till General Khatami hears about the way I have been treated, taking away my dignity like this."

She quickly completed her toilet requirements and pulled on the chain.

"Where is the wash basin?" she exclaimed as the Commander turned around on hearing the flush.

The Commander shrugged his shoulders. "Come," he ordered again, and Afareen followed him to the last room at the end of the corridor.

The officer knocked and opened it.

It was a small room with just a bare wooden table in the middle and two chairs either side. A single light bulb hung from the ceiling illumining the area. Two other seats were positioned against the wall. There was a heavy presence of tobacco smoke. General Moghrabi was seated on one of the chairs and turned as the Commander entered the room.

"Ah, Commander Fallahian." He looked at Afareen; "And you must be Mrs Mahabadi. Please come in and take a seat. I am General Moghrabi."

The General got up and ushered Afareen to the vacant chair in front of him. Afareen sat down. On the table was an ashtray with a burning cigarette, a pack of twenty cigarettes and a green transparent plastic lighter, the kind you would buy from a kiosk.

"Why am I here?" snapped Afareen. "You wait until General Khatami hears about this travesty. You will be nothing more than a private by the time he has finished with you."

"On the contrary," said the General, picking up his half-smoked cigarette and taking a long drag. "He is aware of our discussion this evening and fully supports our actions. We are living in difficult times and sometimes we have to make tough decisions for the good of the country."

Afareen could see she was not going to get anywhere using her well-placed contact and was now very worried.

"But you haven't answered my question. Why have I been brought here in the middle of the night?" said Afareen trying to maintain some element of control.

"All in good time, all in good time," said the General. "I want to talk about your work at the British compound."

"What about it?"

The Commander sat on one of the vacant chairs behind Afareen and took out a small note pad from his top pocket.

"How long have you worked there?"

"About four months," replied Afareen.

"And where do you work on the compound – which building?"

His beady eyes seemed to penetrate Afareen; she was feeling faint.

"I work in one of the chalets. I do the cleaning. Can I have a drink of water please?"

The General looked past Afareen to his colleague.

"Commander Fallahian, can you get Mrs Mahabadi a drink please?"

The Commander got up and left the room. The General sat there, smoking his cigarette, not relaxing his stare for a moment. It was eerie. There were strange noises coming from outside, and a high-pitched scream sounded from an adjoining room. The General stubbed out his cigarette.

"Sorry about that. Some of our officers can get a little, shall we say, over-enthusiastic with their interrogations."

He reached down and opened his packet of cigarettes and lit up another. The smoke billowed outwards, causing Afareen to cough. A minute later, the Commander returned with a bottle of water and handed it to Afareen. She unscrewed the top and took a long gulp. Despite her recent toilet visit, she wanted to pee again.

The Commander took his seat and picked up his notebook.

The General continued. "You were saying you worked in one of the chalets. For one of the diplomats?"

"Yes,"

"Which one?"

She hesitated for a moment, not wishing to disclose the information.

"I said, which one?" the General's voiced was raised and more threatening.

"For Mr and Mrs Dexter."

The General became animated. "The Dexters? You work

for the Dexters?"

"Yes," replied Afareen.

"Commander Fallahian, why did we not know this?"

"I do not know General," said the Commander, squirming at the implied criticism.

"Find out who has been monitoring the compound and let me know," said the General.

"Do you meet Mr Dexter at all?"

"I have seen him a few times, but mostly he has left before I start work."

"What do you talk about?"

"Nothing, my English is not good. I just clean and sometimes cook. Mrs Dexter works, so I am mostly on my own."

"Where does Mrs Dexter work?"

Afareen was in a dilemma; she was concerned about giving away any information that might put her escape at jeopardy but, on the other hand, she needed to placate the General.

"She works at the school in the compound."

"I see," said the General but not in a pleasant way. Every comment felt like a threat to Afareen.

He stopped for a moment to digest the information and stubbed out his latest smoke. Then immediately lit up another.

"Tell me, has there been any new people you have seen recently?"

Afareen knew exactly who they were referring to, but this time she decided to bluff it.

She looked down and involuntarily touched the side of her face. "I have not seen anyone. I do not go to the main building. I am in the chalets."

"But you must see what's going on there?"

"No. I go to the chalet, clean, and then I go home."

"Hmm," said the General and pulled on his cigarette again. His eyes continued to scrutinise Afareen. She took another swig from her water bottle.

"And your husband; how is he?" said the General, the deliberate change of direction completely throwing Afareen.

"What?"

"Your husband, Professor Mahabadi. How is he?"

"I haven't heard from him for many days."

"Yes, these are difficult times. All our nuclear facilities are in lockdown at the moment because of the security situation, you understand. You have seen the news I expect."

"Yes," said Afareen. His menacing expression changed, and he looked at her in a fatherly way.

"It is possible, of course, that we might be able to make things easier for you; if you can help us, that is. Perhaps we can arrange some leave for your husband. Even give him access to a phone, so you can speak together. How does that sound?"

"That is good, but you will want something in return, no doubt."

"Well, nothing that will be hard for you. We just want some information. There is a new person who has started at the British Embassy – last week we think. He has been working with Mr Dexter. We want to know who he is, his name and anything else you can find out about him for us."

"How can I do that?"

"I don't know, you will have to think of something; I'm sure you will, you are an intelligent woman. If you can find out the information we need, then I have a feeling communication between you and your husband will greatly improve. Unfortunately, if you do not want to help us, then it could be some time before you will see your husband again. Remember, it is in the national interest; that is why General Khatami was happy for us to have this discussion."

"No, no, it's ok, of course I want to help if it is in the national interest."

"That is good. How are your children by the way?"

"They are fine, thank you." Afareen went white; her need to pee was getting desperate.

"And how old are they?"

"Ten and six," replied Afareen.

"Ah, a nice age; what are their names?"

"Afshin and Kiana."

"Nice names. And they are doing well at school, I expect. I mean, with such gifted parents."

"Yes," replied Afareen weakly.

"Good. Well, that's all for the moment. I will pass on your good wishes to General Khatami; I am having lunch with him tomorrow. I will tell him you are going to assist us. Commander Fallahian here will arrange a way of contacting you."

The General stubbed out his latest cigarette and stood up. He was about to leave when he suddenly turned to Afareen.

"Wait, there was one more thing. While you have been working for Mr Dexter, have you heard anyone mention the Egyptian?"

"The Egyptian?" replied Afareen, genuinely confused.

"Yes, do you recognise that word at all? Maybe you overheard it somewhere, maybe Mr Dexter."

"No, no, I have not heard this word 'Egyptian' at all. I told you I do not understand the language too well."

The General looked at her; for some reason, he wasn't entirely convinced.

"Ok, our meeting is concluded," he said in a snarl and headed for the door.

The Commander hastened to the door to open it for his boss. The General whispered something to the Commander as he left but made no acknowledgement to Afareen.

Afareen was about to stand up.

"No, wait there," he ordered. "I just need a couple of things before you go."

"Can I use the toilet again please?" said Afareen.

"Come," said the Commander, looking irritated, and he led Afareen back to the communal facilities. It was the same procedure, with Fallahian keeping guard.

Having completed her ablutions, they returned to the room. It was oppressive; the cigarette smoke hung in layers in the air. Just then another scream echoed from somewhere in the building. The Commander ignored it and ushered Afareen to sit down. She wanted to vomit.

"Thank you for agreeing to help us; I need to make a contact arrangement with you."

Afareen nodded.

"Wait here, I will be a few minutes."

The Commander got up and left the room; he needed to visit a different department, Counter-Espionage, which was on the first floor. Afareen could see another officer stood outside, and the Commander said something to him. The door remained open.

The break gave Afareen a chance to gather her thoughts.

In some ways, the opportunity to have better contact with her husband could actually benefit them. She needed to speak to David Dexter.

More screams echoed around the building, sending shivers down Afareen's spine. It was the house of horrors.

Five minutes later, the Commander returned and closed the door sharply; the slam made Afareen jump.

He moved the over-flowing ashtray to one side and sat down. He was holding a box, which he opened, pulling out a mobile phone. To the untrained eye, it looked like any other Nokia which every Iranian seemed to own.

"This is just to be used to contact the Ministry. If you press here twice," he indicated the zero button, "it will immediately ring me or, if I am not available, it will divert to one of my team. It is quite secure, and no-one will be able to listen to your conversation."

He handed over the phone, and Afareen put it in her pocket.

He looked at his watch. It was after midnight. "I need the information quickly. I will expect something later today, or tomorrow at the latest."

Afareen was almost paralysed with fear; she just nodded in acknowledgement.

"Don't look so worried, soon you will be speaking to your husband and telling him how much you love him."

Afareen just looked down to the table, unable to make eye contact with the officer.

"Ok, you can go now. I will get one of my officers to drive you home."

The Commander walked towards the door. As Afareen got up, he addressed her; there was a menace in his voice.

"Just one more thing. You must tell no-one about your visit here today. The consequences will be severe for you and your family. Do you understand?"

"Yes."

"This officer will drive you home," said the Commander nodding to the guard who had been stationed outside the door. The officer escorted Afareen out of the building. The SUV was still parked where they had left it.

Afareen sat next to the driver, but she would never be able to recall the return journey.

The vehicle stopped outside the apartment block, and Afareen got out. She watched as the vehicle pulled away and disappeared into the distance. She exhaled audibly and spent a moment clearing her head. All she could smell was cigarettes. She desperately needed to shower and change into fresh clothes.

Chapter Eight

Sleep was impossible for Afareen after her ordeal.

The night was filled with demons; every time she closed her eyes, she could picture the General's gaze. She tossed and turned, trying to make sense of everything. Her husband would have been a great sounding board at this moment; having an analytical mind meant he was always practical. She wondered what he would do.

One thing it had confirmed was her resolve to escape. She could not bring up her children in such an environment. She needed to speak to Mr Dexter and tell him what had happened; she was sure he would help.

Afareen was still feeling the effects of the trauma the next morning; deep down, she was exhausted, but the adrenaline was keeping the fatigue at bay. She prepared her children for school; they were blissfully unaware of their mother's torment. Their grandmother would escort them to school as normal; it was important they maintained the routine. Afareen left the apartment at the usual time.

The walk to the Metro helped clear her head; as she descended the steps into the station, her confidence began to return. She stood patiently waiting for the train and looked around the packed platform. She recognised two men she had seen before. She felt like waving to them; they had obviously been instructed to follow her but were clearly not experienced operatives.

The intrusion did not unduly concern Afareen; she knew

she had been under surveillance on previous occasions. In some respects, she found it amusing; they had an extremely boring job to do.

The train was heaving with rush-hour travellers, and she had to stand for the twenty-minute journey, holding onto the straps from the ceiling. She swayed with the movement of the carriage and, every now and then, lurched as the train braked or cornered.

She left the Metro at her usual stop and walked the two-hundred yards to the compound. She noticed a car with blacked-out windows parked opposite the entrance to the gates. She could almost feel their presence, but she was undaunted; they were in for a long wait. She reached the security check and showed her identity card. She was asked to open her bag, but after a cursory glance, she was waved through without further scrutiny.

It was a pleasantly warm morning, bright and dry; birdsong echoed around the trees as she walked to the Dexters' chalet. In different circumstances, it would be a perfect day, but this would never be so while she remained in Tehran.

Sophie Dexter was in the kitchen and, seeing Afareen walking towards the door, went to greet her.

"Good morning Afareen," she said and allowed her to pass before closing the door.

Afareen put the bag containing her work clothes and cleaning materials on the table.

She looked at Sophie; her face was etched with worry.

"Are you ok?" said Sophie.

Afareen shook her head and put her fingers to her lips. She indicated that Sophie should follow her and walked towards the bedroom. Sophie complied.

They went inside and Sophie closed the door. Afareen started sobbing as the tension of the previous night surfaced.

"What is it, Afareen? What has happened?"

She gradually composed herself and revealed her ordeal at the hands of the secret police.

"I need to speak to Mr Dexter. It is very urgent."

"Oh that's a pity, you've just missed him. He left about ten minutes ago."

Sophie could sense Afareen's anxiety. "Just a minute, let me see what I can do," she said, and went back into the lounge, picked up her mobile phone from the table and dialled a number.

"Darling, can you return home? You've left some papers on the table; you said they were important."

This was a code agreed between the Dexters.

"Yes, dear, straightaway. Thank you for telling me."

David alerted the driver. "I'm sorry, we need to return to Gholhak; I've left some papers I need."

The driver took the next junction and made the turn to take them back.

David was too busy wondering why Sophie had called him back to notice the surveillance car outside the compound. There were two MOIS agents inside, watching; one was using a camera with a telephoto lens as Dexter's Jaguar returned. He took several shots.

"I am sure there was someone inside the car," he said. "It can't have gone to the embassy and back in that time."

"How long was it gone?" said the second agent.

The first agent checked his notebook. "Twenty-five minutes. That is not enough time to go to the embassy and return."

"So, should we report it?"

"No, it's ok, we will tell the Commander when we call in. There's no need to disturb him now."

The Jaguar pulled up outside the Dexter residence, and David spoke to the driver; "I'll work from home for a while to save going back through the traffic again. I'll call you when I'm ready."

The driver acknowledged him and pulled away to return to the car compound.

It was almost eight-thirty as David entered the residence; Sophie greeted him. She indicated toward the bedroom, and he followed her there.

Afareen was seated on the end of the bed, still recovering from her emotional outburst. She was shaking, and every few seconds, dry sobs convulsed her body.

"I need to get to work," said Sophie. "Will you be ok?"

"Yes, we'll be fine. Have a good day," replied David.

They kissed. Sophie went back to the lounge and put on her jacket and scarf.

"Bye," she shouted as she left the house and closed the door.

David Dexter tried to calm Afareen.

"You better tell me what's happened," he said, once she was more composed.

Afareen looked at him; her faced lined, eyes red and swollen from crying.

"Last night, the secret police came for me. They took me to their headquarters," she managed to say.

"What?" exclaimed Dexter. "When was this?"

"It was late, maybe ten o'clock. They knocked on the

door. There were four of them, including a Commander."

"A Commander? What was his name, can you remember?"

"Hmm, no… wait, let me think a minute. Yes, it was, er, Fall…something; Fallahian, I think. It was something like that." Dexter took out a pen from his pocket, picked up a writing pad from the bedside table and jotted down the name.

"Did they arrest you?"

"No, no, he said they wanted my help. Then, I had to go with them; it was terrible. I had to leave my mother. She is not very well; she gets confused."

Afareen started to become upset again. She wiped away her tears with a handkerchief which was now quite wet.

"It's ok, take your time," said Dexter, and allowed Afareen to compose herself again.

"So, you went with them. Can you remember which building?"

"It was white, with a big entrance, and…er… columns." She used her hands to give a visual representation of the word 'columns'.

"So, where did they take you when you got there?" David was using his interrogation experience trying to get her to relive the trauma so she would recall detail; it might prove useful later.

"We went downstairs, it was terrible and the smell…" She held her nose. "And the screaming." She put her head in her hands.

"Who did you meet? Did he give you his name?"

"Yes, it was General Moghrabi; a dreadful man."

"Hmm, Moghrabi. I've heard of him. So, what happened?"

"I needed the toilet, but they made me keep open the door. It was so… er… humiliating."

"Really? That's terrible. And Moghrabi? What did he want?"

"He wanted to know about the new person that joined last week. I think he was talking about Mr Houghton."

"What did you tell him?"

"I told him I did not know any new person. I told him I only worked here in this house."

"And he accepted that?"

"Yes, I think so, but that is not the end of it. They want me to be their spy and find out more. They even gave me a special phone… wait."

She got up from the chair, opened the door and went back to the living room. She rustled about in her bag, then returned to the bedroom.

"This," she said, handing the phone to Dexter.

He examined it carefully.

"I have to press here, two times," she said, pointing to the zero button.

"Ok, that's fine, but be careful, there will almost certainly be a tracking device inside."

"Tracking… what is tracking, I do not understand?"

"They will be able to tell where you are."

"Really?" said Afareen and looked down.

"Yes, I've seen these before." He continued to examine the device closely. "But don't worry; as long as you keep to your normal routine, it won't be a problem."

Afareen looked back up at him.

"So, when do they want you to contact them again?"

"Today, I must call them today." She put her head in her hands in exasperation.

"It's ok, don't worry, we will help you."

"Thank you," said Afareen.

"Was there anything else, can you remember?"

"Er, no… I don't think so." Afareen looked down as if thinking. "Wait… yes, yes, he asked me a question I did not understand, something about an Egyptian."

"Egyptian?" said Dexter animatedly. "Are you sure?"

"Yes, certainly, as I said, I did not understand it. He asked me if I had heard anyone say this word."

"Excellent," said Dexter, but more to himself.

Afareen looked at Dexter, her eyes still puffed and red. "They told me that if I help them, they will let my husband go on leave and maybe give him a telephone so we can speak."

"Well, that's great news. This might be just what we needed. If we can get in contact with your husband we can start making plans to get you and your family away."

"Really?"

"Yes. Look, why don't you carry on with your work and I'll make a phone call."

"Yes, ok. Oh, I forgot to tell you. I was followed here today; there were men on the Metro, and there is a car outside watching."

"Ok, yes, I guess that was to be expected, but don't worry, everything is going to be fine; leave it to me."

Afareen got up and went back to the lounge and unpacked her cleaning materials. She felt like a weight had been lifted from her shoulders.

Dexter called Houghton on a secure line from his bedroom. The vacuum cleaner in the lounge would ensure there was no danger of anyone overhearing.

"Nick, it's David. I've got some news."

Dexter outlined Afareen's story. "Ironically, I think this could be what we were looking for. Oh, and it seems they've bought the Egyptian story." He recounted the question Afareen was asked.

"Hmm, now that is interesting. How do you want to play it?" said Houghton.

"Well, we need to give Afareen something to go back to them with. Personally, I can't see any problem in revealing your name. The driver that feeds them information would be able to confirm it in any case; it's not a secret. They could always check with immigration. I've also been thinking about the Egyptian. I think I know how we can confuse them even more."

"What do you have in mind?"

"I'll let you know when I've worked it through. Why don't you come for dinner again tonight? I can update you then."

"Sounds good; what time?"

"Around seven?"

"Ok, great, see you then," replied Houghton, and they dropped the call.

Dexter went to the kitchen and made a coffee. Afareen was still using the vacuum cleaner. He went to her and whispered. "Leave that running and come to the bedroom."

She complied and followed the diplomat. Dexter closed the door, then addressed Afareen.

"Do you go to the main house at all?"

"Sometimes, to get cleaning stuff."

"Ok, we need this to look convincing. I want you to go there and speak to the concierge. Do you know him?"

"Yes, of course, he always says hello."

"Good. He sees everything that goes on there. I want you to ask him about the new person, just say you had seen him around at the house here. See if he will tell you his name and what he does at the embassy. Make it look casual. Can you do that?"

"Yes, I… I think so."

"Good, well, go now and let me know what he says, ok?" Afareen nodded. She looked nervous.

"Don't worry Afareen. This is what they expect you to do," David reassured her.

Afareen picked up her coat and left the chalet. She was running through what she would say in her mind.

She reached the main building and looked around; it was almost deserted. There were a couple of cleaners working but no residents; they would be at the embassy. Afareen spoke to one of her colleagues and collected a plastic bottle of disinfectant. The concierge emerged from his office. He'd seen her arrive.

"Afareen, how lovely. How are you today?" he gushed as she walked towards his desk.

"Hello," replied Afareen. "I'm well, thank you, just collecting some stuff."

She held up the disinfectant.

"That's good. How are things down at the chalet?"

"Yes, good thank you, they are nice people."

"Ah, yes, Mr Dexter is a fine man."

Afareen moved closer. "There was another man there last week I had not seen before."

"Ah, yes that would be Mr Houghton, I think. He's new. He arrived last week."

"And he also works at the embassy?"

"Yes, but I don't know what he does. They don't tell me. Why did you want to know?"

"Oh, just wondered, that's all. I saw him with Mr Dexter. Anyway, I better go."

"Yes, ok, nice to see you. Have a nice day."

Afareen's legs were shaking. She hoped she had done enough.

She walked back to the chalet, the exercise helping her to regain her composure. Dexter was waiting for her when she returned; he indicated toward the bedroom with his head.

They closed the bedroom door. "So, how did it go?"

"He told me it was Mr Houghton, but that's all. He doesn't know why he is here."

"No, don't worry, that's good. I wasn't expecting him to say much. He probably doesn't know anything anyway, but I don't know if that will be enough to keep them from wanting more."

He thought for a moment and decided they would have to play it out. "I've been speaking to Mr Houghton, and this is what we need you to do. I will give you precise instructions and then I want you to repeat them."

Afareen nodded. "Ok."

"Ok, first, tell them about Mr Houghton. Say that you found out his name from the concierge. You can say that he is just here for a short time while someone is sick, but no-one knows any more about him. That should keep them busy for a while. Secondly, and this is important, tell them that while you were cleaning, you heard me speaking to someone on the telephone. You thought you heard the words 'Egyptian' and 'Americans'. Tell them you don't speak English very well so you couldn't understand everything I said."

Afareen was taking in the instructions. "Yes, I told them already that my English is bad."

"Good," said Dexter. "Now repeat what I have just said."

Afareen repeated the instructions to Dexter's satisfaction.

"The important thing is to try to act as normally as possible, we don't want them to think you are being used."

"Yes, I will do that," said Afareen.

"That's good; I just hope it will be enough to get you some access to your husband. Don't forget to ask about it."

"No, I won't forget."

"Right, I'm going back to the embassy now; call them later this afternoon. It won't hurt to keep them waiting."

"Yes, I will, and thank you for your help for my family and me."

"Well, we are not there yet, there's a long way to go, but I'm hoping this could be the break we need."

Dexter ordered the car and ten minutes later, was heading back to the embassy.

Canadian Embassy, Ostad-Motahari Avenue, Tehran – 10:00 a.m.

The American Embassy in Tehran was closed in 1979 following the hostage crisis. When diplomatic relations were broken, the United States appointed Switzerland to be its protecting power in Iran. Informal relations were carried out through the United States Interests Section of the Swiss Embassy. Services for American citizens are limited, and there are no immigration facilities there.

Without a permanent base in Tehran, the CIA was using the Canadian Embassy as a quasi-residence. Such was the intensity of anti-American feeling in the country, travel to Iran was discouraged. American citizens were not allowed to work there; it was considered too dangerous. The risk of kidnap and being held to ransom for political capital was high. All the U.S. personnel at the Canadian Embassy, therefore, had foreign passports.

Canada's relationship with Iran, however, was also fractious.

Following their help in the escape of six U.S diplomats in 1980, Canada closed their Embassy through fear of reprisals, though relations were not formally severed. For several years, the Canadian government was reluctant to reopen an embassy, both because of the history, and the Iranian government's Human Rights record, particularly the kidnapping and torturing of diplomats. However, in 1988, the two governments agreed to resume diplomatic relations at a low level, and the Canadian embassy in Tehran was re-opened in Shahid Sarafaz Street.

Although never officially acknowledging direct assistance with the U.S. government in accommodating secret service personnel, Canada had an 'arrangement' whereby a small number of agents could use the embassy in order to 'support U.S interests'.

The office they had been allocated, at a significant rent, was large, filling most of the lower ground floor. It was not the most comfortable of working spaces and, being in the basement, had no natural lighting. Thankfully, it did have air-conditioning, and the environment was manageable. Over the years, a significant amount of hi-tech equipment had been installed, although their messaging service and Internet was routed through the embassy's system and its security was not guaranteed.

The floor had been divided into four separate work areas, so each agent had their own space, plus a spare for the occasional visitor. The computer hardware, including the servers, were stacked against the back wall; wires ran in all directions. There was a low hum of a cooling system. A small area had been sectioned off into a kitchenette with coffee-making facilities, a refrigerator and a water cooler. Toilet facilities and the canteen were upstairs.

There was a team of three based there; the section head, Jo Podesta, an Italian national, from Fort Meade, Maryland; Javi Rao, an IT expert of Indian heritage from Sacramento; and Jim Blasic, a Canadian from New York State.

Doctor Antonio Alvarez, the field agent based in Arak, had a Mexican passport, but his home was in Dover, Delaware.

The team had been specially selected to work in Iran, and each brought their own unique skills. Although Alvarez was the only acting field agent, Podesta had served with distinction in neighbouring Iraq and had also been active as an agent in Iran before Alvarez's appointment.

On Monday morning, while Dexter and Afareen were having their discussion elsewhere, the atmosphere in the basement of the Canadian Embassy was tense. The station chief put out a call.

"Alvarez," was the response.

"I've had a message from Cherokee?" said Podesta. "Can you make a meeting?"

'Cherokee' was the codename for the Director of Operations at Langley.

Alvarez was in his office in Arak concentrating on his computer monitor and the interruption disturbed him.

"Sorry, Jo, just give me a second." He finished typing something then took the call.

"This about our friend?"

"Yeah," replied Podesta. "When can you get here?"

"Hmm, it's gonna take me five hours, give or take." He checked his watch. "Mid-afternoon, I guess. Can we do this over the phone?"

"Prefer not to," said Podesta. "You can stay over; I'll buy you dinner."

"Yeah, ok, copy that. How can I refuse?" said Alvarez.

It was gone three-thirty before Alvarez arrived at venue number two, another coffee shop in one of the malls. It was busy. The two exchanged greetings and Podesta waited for the two coffees to be delivered before getting down to business.

"Your meeting with that Houghton guy has pressed a few buttons back home. I told them what he said, and they think it's all bullshit."

"Houghton seemed on the level."

"Hmm, that's not the opinion back home."

"Cherokee wants Amadi," said Podesta, lifting his cup and taking the first sip of his beverage.

"Yeah, ok, and how are we going to do that?"

"Well, we know where he lives…"

"Used to live," interjected Alvarez.

"Used to live, yeah," corrected Podesta.

"How long since we had any contact with the guy?" asked Alvarez.

"Not since my meeting with him in '04," said Podesta. He looked around the café. It was still busy, but no-one appeared to be in earshot.

"That's two years," replied Alvarez.

"Yeah."

"So, what happened back then; I'm interested?"

"I had a couple of meetings with him, but, you know, I've never seen anyone so wound up. Couldn't keep still for a second, kept looking over his shoulder the whole time."

"Did he contact us?"

"No, we had him on our list; we were desperate to get someone into Esfahan. He ticked a lot of boxes; worked in France in '98. We thought he might help us, you know, slip us the odd bit of information. We tracked him for a while, and we eventually found out where he lived. One afternoon, I followed him to the market and just casually invited him for a coffee."

"That simple?"

"Yeah, we went to a café but, as I said, the guy was real scared."

"What happened?"

"Nothing, but I told him I would meet him the same time the following day. I didn't think he would turn up, but he did. He told me in no uncertain terms to get lost; threatened to dial 113 if I didn't leave him alone."

"And that was it?"

"Yep, pretty much, he just got up and walked away. Not heard from him since."

"Hmm, so why now… and why the Brits?" asked Alvarez.

"That's what we want to know. We need to get to him and find out what he's up to before the Brits. If he does want to defect, we need to make sure it's to good old Uncle Sam. We can't have him going over to the Brits with what he knows."

"Yeah, that's for sure."

There was a pause while they finished their coffee; each deep in thought.

"I think it might be worth another chat with our friend again," said the Station Chief.

"Houghton, you mean?"

"Yeah," said Podesta.

"Hmm, yeah, ok. Though, I thought he was ok. He was adamant they weren't pursuing the approach; said they'd got no interest."

"But they would say that, wouldn't they?" countered Podesta.

"I guess," replied Alvarez.

"It would be good to know where the contact came from," said Podesta and looked at Alvarez in a quizzical way.

"I did ask him," said Alvarez, slightly defensively; "but he wouldn't disclose his sources."

"Maybe we can lean on him a bit more, see what he can give us," said Podesta.

"Yeah, we can do that, I guess."

"Why don't you call him? Maybe he can meet you while you're up here, save another trip."

"Yeah, it's worth a try."

"Then we can work out some sort of strategy to get Amadi away if that's what he wants. Tell you what; let's invite this Houghton guy to dinner.".

"Yeah, ok... good idea," said Alvarez, finishing the last dregs of his coffee.

"Invite him to Dizi's. He won't be able to resist that," said Podesta.

"Do you think we'll get in?"

"Sure, I know the owner. You ring Houghton, I'll call the restaurant."

Both accessed their mobiles and made calls.

Houghton was sending a message to Andy Fellows, giving him the daily update. His ring-tone made him jump; it was unusual to get a call on his mobile phone. Phone signals were routed through the embassy's security system enabling him to get a connection. He dropped what he was doing and picked up the phone from his office desk. He looked at the screen but didn't recognise the number.

"Houghton."

"Hi, Houghton, it's Tony Alvarez. I want to invite you to dinner tonight to say sorry for being rude at our meeting the other day. Can you make it?"

Houghton was momentarily caught unawares. "Er, hmm, er, yeah… ok. What time?"

"Shall we say seven-thirty."

"Yeah, ok, where?"

Alvarez looked across at Podesta who put his thumb up and nodded.

"You know Dizi's on Mousa Kalantari Street?"

"No, I'm new here."

"Best place in town. Can you find it ok?"

"Yeah, sure."

"Ok, that's great. See you at seven-thirty."

Alvarez dropped the call. Houghton looked at his phone for a moment, then dialled Dexter's number on the internal phone.

"David? It's Nick. I'm going to have to pass on the dinner invite tonight. The Yanks have just called; they want another meet… Yeah, seven-thirty. Do you know a place called Dizi's?"

The Dexter Residence, Gholhak Garden – 4:00 p.m.

Afareen had finished her cleaning and was starting to feel the effects of the previous evening; she was now exhausted, but there was still another task she needed to do which was causing her great anxiety.

Several times she had taken the phone out of her bag and looked at it before putting it back. It was now four o'clock and Sophie Dexter would be home very soon; she couldn't put it off any longer. She took a deep breath and took out the phone again. Her hands were having difficulty in holding it and, despite only having two digits to press, her fingers were not corresponding to her commands.

She took another breath and rehearsed her story. She pressed the zero button twice and held the phone to her ear. She could hear it ringing; a voice answered in Farsi.

"Ah, Mrs Mahabadi, I have been waiting for you. You have some news, I hope."

It was the Commander and he sounded even more menacing over the phone.

"Yes. I… I think so."

"Go on then, tell me."

"I went to the main house and saw the concierge. He said… er… the new man that arrived… he is called Mr Houghton."

"The new man?"

"Yes."

"What does he do at the embassy?"

Afareen was starting to relax. "He did not know for certain, but he has seen him with Mr Dexter. He said Mr

Houghton was just here for a short time… while someone is sick, he said."

"Anything else about this Mr Houghton."

"No; no-one knows anything."

"Hmm, that's not much help."

"I am sorry, I did what you told me to do. Please let me see my husband."

"We may need your help again."

"Of course, anything. Wait, wait, there was something else."

"Go on?"

"Last night you asked me if I had heard anyone speak about the Egyptian, yes?"

"Yes, yes, I did. Why? Have you heard something?" said the Commander, becoming animated.

"Yes, today. Mr Dexter came back to collect some work, and I heard him on the telephone. I heard him say er… 'the Egyptian' and he also said 'Americans'… I heard that."

"Americans? Are you sure?"

"Yes, I am certain."

"What else did you hear?"

"I did not understand; they speak very quickly."

"Hmm, ok thank you, that is very helpful."

"When can I see my husband?"

"I will speak to the General," said the Commander. "I will call you on this phone when we need your help again."

The Commander dropped the call, and Afareen almost collapsed onto the sofa with relief. Just then, the door opened as Sophie Dexter returned from work.

"Afareen, why are you still here? Are you ok?"

She looked up. "Yes, I am ok. Please tell Mr Dexter, I

have done what he asked."

"Yes, I'll pass on the message. Sit there and let me get you a drink."

"No, no, I am ok, I need to get back for my children."

"Yes, ok, I understand," said Sophie, and she watched as Afareen gathered her stuff together and left the chalet.

Chapter Nine

Houghton left the Embassy at just after six-thirty to give himself plenty of time to get to the restaurant.

Dizi's, he'd discovered, was around three miles north of the embassy and the nearest Metro stop was at least three-quarters of a mile away. Houghton had already decided that walking through the back streets of central Tehran was not a good idea, so he would take a taxi. Dexter had been on hand to give him some advice on using them.

It would have been more straightforward to order one to pick him up from outside the embassy, but Houghton needed to take some diversionary tactics to shake off any possible MOIS operatives who might be following. Given the recent discussion with Afareen, the embassy would be under increased surveillance.

It was time to put his plan into action.

Sure enough, as he passed through the security gates, a blacked-out SUV was parked in the bus stop lay-by, directly opposite the entrance; it was a bit obvious and Houghton noticed it straight away. He knew there could be others; he would expect them to have more than one vehicle on watch, considering the manpower they had at their disposal. He would be vigilant.

He did not want to appear furtive by behaving unnaturally, but, as he left the embassy, he kept to the shadows of the perimeter wall. It was quite busy with foot traffic, and the passers-by would help shield his departure.

He walked towards the Metro station at Sa'adi and rode the escalators to the concourse. The ticket machine was halfway along, and he walked down the platform and stood behind it, out of sight from the other travellers. Three minutes later, the next train pulled in, and he watched as the waiting passengers boarded. The train left. Houghton peered around the ticket machine; the station was deserted.

He went back up the escalator and immediately turned left out of the exit. He was on a busy junction, and he waited for a moment watching the traffic go by. He felt vulnerable now, but he had little choice.

Taxis in Tehran are everywhere, mostly yellow, green or orange. It was an orange one that Houghton spotted first. It had signage on its roof, 'Tehran Taxis', which was unlit.

Houghton went to the side of the road and shouted, "taxi". He looked around, there was no way of knowing if he had been spotted by a surveillance team, but it was a chance he was going to have to take. The cab driver saw him and immediately cut across two lanes of traffic, causing much honking of horns. He pulled up alongside his fare. Houghton got in and spoke to the driver in Arabic. "Dizi Restaurant, please… Darbast."

Dexter had advised him to use the word 'darbast' which would ensure the driver did not pick up any other passengers on the way; it would be reflected in the fare.

The driver acknowledged and filtered back into the traffic.

Houghton repeatedly looked back through the rear-view window to see if they were being followed, but, with the amount of traffic, it was impossible to be certain. It took nearly half an hour before the cab meandered through a number of side streets and pulled up outside his destination.

He paid the driver and got out.

Before going inside, Houghton held back and surveyed the surroundings; he removed his glasses to get a better view and put them in his pocket. The street was double-parked for its whole length, making it difficult for two cars to pass each other. He checked both ways; there were no other vehicles in sight.

From the outside, the restaurant didn't meet the build-up Dexter had given it. A non-descript double wooden door, painted in a bluey-turquoise colour with matching trellis work instead of glass windows. The name was written in large white Farsi script. Only one of the doors was open, making it quite narrow to walk through.

Houghton went in and was greeted by the smartly-dressed maître d'. This time Houghton spoke in English.

"Doctor Alvarez?"

"Ah, yes, he is waiting," said the man in a heavy local accent. "Please follow."

Houghton took in his surroundings. The floor area was a reasonable size and would comfortably seat fifty people. It was divided into two; separated by a large arch. The tables were long, like you would find at a medieval banquet, with benches either side instead of chairs. The walls were tiled halfway up in a strange green colour; Houghton thought it resembled a public urinal. Above the tiles the walls were adorned with typical Persian art; large Qajar-style paintings showing very romantic Qajars holding birds and flowers in dancing poses.

A large fan whirred above them, suspended from the ceiling.

It was busy, mostly businessmen engaged in urgent

chatter; one or two were smoking from shisha pipes. Houghton followed the man through the archway into the second section. Here, it was less noisy and more conducive to discussion. There were two men in the corner opposite the service hatch who were deep in conversation. Houghton recognised one of them. Alvarez looked up and saw Houghton approach and immediately got up from the bench. He held out his hand in greeting.

"Houghton, good to see you; glad you could make it. Let me introduce you to one of my colleagues, Jo Podesta... here, take a seat."

Houghton had to cock his leg over the bench to sit down. He sat next to Alvarez and opposite Podesta. There was no-one in the immediate vicinity.

He shook hands with the station chief.

"What do you think of the place?" asked Alvarez.

Houghton looked around. "Different."

"You wait until you taste the food. It's the best in Tehran, I guarantee."

Having seen Houghton settled on his bench, the maître d' left them for a moment and returned with a menu. With the alcohol ban in Iran, there was only a soft-drink section.

"What would you like to drink?" asked Alvarez.

"In the absence of a twelve-year Malt, I'll have an orange juice," responded Houghton.

"Three," said Alvarez to the attentive waiter and held up three fingers. The man nodded and left to fetch the beverages.

"So, what's good?" said Houghton scanning the menu.

"All of it," replied Alvarez, who had taken the role of sponsor very seriously. "But you gotta try their Dizi."

"Dizi?"

"Yeah, it's where they get the restaurant name from. It's a lamb dish; they cook it over a fire, and it comes with… what do they call that stuff, Jo? You know all about it."

"Sangak," said Jo.

"Yeah, it's a kind of bread… tastes real good," said Alvarez.

"Yeah, ok, I'll go with that," said Houghton.

After further deliberation and numerous other recommendations from Alvarez, the food was ordered, and the drinks arrived.

Alvarez looked around to ensure no-one was in ear-shot and kicked off the discussions. Houghton turned and leaned back slightly to maintain eye contact.

"Well, we appreciate you joining us tonight, and at short notice. I was in town and thought we should pick up from our meeting in the park."

"Yeah, sure, no problem," said Houghton. Podesta took over.

"Tell me what you told Tony. How come our guy contacted you?"

"I've no idea," said Houghton.

"How did he make contact?" Houghton was expecting this question and had discussed a possible answer with Dexter.

"I can't disclose our source, as I'm sure you will appreciate, I'm sorry." This was an opening gambit; Houghton wanted to see what the Americans would do.

"Ok, yeah, I get that. Look, we're not looking for names, we just want to know the methodology, that's all. How did he get in contact?"

Houghton picked up his drink and took a deliberate sip.

Podesta was getting impatient with Houghton's stalling tactics.

"Look, we need a little co-operation here. I'm sure there could be some kind of quid-pro-quo; your back might need scratching one of these days."

"Yeah, true… ok, I'll give what I can." He took another sip of his drink as if thinking. "We got the tip-off from one of our drivers. His brother's a construction engineer in Esfahan. He knows several of the guys working at the nuclear plant there. The driver said that one night, someone approached his brother… looked like one of the managers, not an engineer, and said he was looking for a new job."

"So?" said Podesta.

"Well, this guy says he was particularly interested in working in Britain. I guess he must have known about the connection."

Podesta looked at Alvarez.

Houghton picked up the glance. "Yeah, that's what we thought, but then he said to the brother… tell them it's the Egyptian."

This was the story Houghton had agreed with Dexter. It was on the thin side, but they thought it would stand up to modest scrutiny.

"The Egyptian? You sure?"

"Yeah, as I said to Doctor Alvarez here."

"Call me Tony," interjected Alvarez.

"We made one or two enquiries and thought it might be the guy you were interested in."

"How do you know about that?"

"Dexter knew about him; apparently, we were briefed by your people at the time."

"Ok, but why did he contact you? He knew we wanted to use him?"

"I have no idea. Probably thought it was safer... and you don't have an embassy here. Maybe he didn't know how to make contact and just saw this opportunity, I don't know."

Podesta looked at Alvarez with a thin smile. Houghton was convincing.

"So, how are you gonna get him out?" asked Podesta.

"We're not. We don't have the resources. It's what I told Tony here," said Houghton looking at Alvarez. "We assume he'll get back in touch with us when he's got something more. We don't have his number," he said sarcastically.

The starters arrived which broke the conversation and an array of nibbles, dips and flat-breads were placed on the table. It had come at a good time for Houghton who was becoming concerned that his story might not add up under too much more enquiry; he could not afford to be caught in a lie.

The two waitresses returned to other customers.

"So, what's his story, anyway?" said Houghton, trying to turn the conversation around. "Why is he so important?"

"You don't know?" said Podesta, with a surprised look.

"No, I just got here."

"Our friend Amadi virtually built the place over at Esfahan."

"Hmm, I see," said Houghton. "No wonder you want him."

"Yeah, but that's the point; we didn't want to get him out in '04. We just needed someone on the inside," said Podesta. "It was me who met him. We thought with his background, he might play ball, you know, give us the heads up every now and then – construction progress and stuff. But these MOIS guys are scary people; they've got a lot of spies in the nuclear complexes."

"I see," said Houghton, helping himself to more bread, but the thought registered.

"That's why we were confused. If he'd wanted out, we could have got him away two years ago."

Houghton needed to think quickly.

"Yeah, but they weren't worried about being fucked over by an American missile back then."

Podesta looked at Alvarez. "Yeah, there is that," said Podesta and smiled.

"I don't know what more I can say. If he gets in touch again, I'll be sure to let you know, trust me. We don't have the budget, personnel or inclination, for that matter, to get him out. Vauxhall have washed their hands of it; it would cause all kinds of political fallout. He's all yours if you want him," said Houghton.

"Fair enough," said Podesta. "So, when do you think he'll get in touch again? Have you spoken to your driver?"

"Yes, of course, but he's not heard from his brother for a few days now. In fact, he's worried about him... but, as I said, we're not chasing it." Houghton seemed very plausible.

There was a long pause. "So, what do you think of the food?" said Podesta. The topic was finished.

"Very good," said Houghton.

The main course arrived, and they sampled the famous house speciality, 'Dizi', a lamb dish with potatoes and tomatoes; Houghton was impressed. Finally, a waiter brought them some Persian tea and a kind of confectionery. "Bamieh," said Podesta as Houghton examined it. The station chief was clearly up on his Iranian cuisine.

Conversation continued for the rest of the evening, convivially swapping stories and anecdotes. Houghton began to change his opinion of the agents; he quite liked them. Although, what their reaction would be if they discovered that the Egyptian story was a ruse was now concerning him. It could even lead to a diplomatic incident.

As Podesta was paying the bill, he turned to Houghton. "How are you getting back to Gholhak; I assume that's where you're heading?"

"Yeah, was just going to call a cab," replied Houghton.

"No, don't do that. We can drop you off; Tony won't mind, will you Tony?" he said, turning to his colleague.

"No problem," said Alvarez.

They left the restaurant, turned left and walked down the street about twenty yards. "We're just here," said Alvarez, flicking his key fob towards a large black Mercedes. The automatic lock disengaged.

There was little conversation on the return journey back to the compound. Houghton asked to be dropped off at the Metro stop, in case of surveillance. There were farewells with a promise of reciprocity as he left the Mercedes. He watched it drive off and wondered what chain of events he had started.

In the Mercedes, an immediate debrief of the evening took place.

"So, do you believe this guy?" said Podesta as they headed back to his apartment.

"It makes sense."

"Yeah, I guess," said Podesta. "But... I don't know, I

mean, I met Amadi and he was scared, I mean real scared. If Houghton's right, he's certainly changed his mind big time. Call it a gut-feel."

"Yeah, but as Houghton said, it's been a couple of years and a lot can happen," countered Alvarez.

"Well, there's only one way to find out. We need to find him. How do you fancy a trip to Esfahan?"

"Yeah, ok, sure, I can get over there tomorrow; Arak's in good hands."

The Mahabadi Residence - 9:00 p.m.

Earlier that evening, Afareen was seated with her mother watching TV. She was still on edge and feared another visit from the police any moment. Any extraneous noise spooked her. The children were in bed and, as usual, her mother was asleep in the armchair. It was around nine o'clock when the telephone rang. Afareen nearly jumped out of her skin. The noise startled her mother.

"Who is that at this hour?" said her mother, drowsily, wakened from her slumber.

Afareen slowly got out of the chair and lifted the receiver.

"Hello," she said hesitantly.

There was a muffled voice on the other end. Then the line cleared.

"Hassan? Is that you?"

"Afareen?" came the reply. Afareen let out a huge sigh of relief; it was so good to hear her husband's voice. She was fighting back tears, not wanting to upset her husband.

There was a catch-up, the usual things; how was mother, how were the children, how was work; then she dropped the message she'd been longing to tell him. "Your uncle has arrived and sends his wishes. When will you be back home? He wants to take you out."

Afareen knew her husband would understand.

"Soon, I hope my dear. They said they would try and arrange some leave for next week. I will call again when I can to let you know."

Afareen felt a twinge of excitement. There was more domestic chat and then the line dropped as if it had been cut off. Afareen looked at the phone. There had been connection problems; that would be the cause. She felt a wave of disappointment; she missed her husband so much and wanted to speak to him for longer than the five minutes they had had.

MOIS Headquarters – 9:00 p.m.

It had been a hectic day.

About the same time as Afareen was talking to her husband, General Moghrabi, Head of Eagle 2, was in his basement briefing room with his key personnel and about twenty agents being apprised on the day's events. He was seated at a table in front of the group. A cigarette was burning in an ashtray, and to his right were two full packets.

"Commander Fallahian, tell me about your conversation with Mrs Mahabadi," the General opened, seeing everyone was seated.

"Yes sir," replied the Commander. "She called this afternoon at about four o'clock. She has found out the name of the new diplomat. His name is," he checked a piece of paper, "Houghton. Our driver has confirmed he believes that was who was with Dexter when they mentioned the Egyptian."

The General nodded with approval. "I have arranged for her to speak to her husband. I thought you would have no objection. We may need her help again," added the Commander.

"No, no, that's fine," said the General, but not really taking in the comment. He was thinking about the connotations of the message.

"Do we know what he looks like, this Houghton?"

"Not definitely, but we think it is this person." The Commander handed the General a grainy picture of Houghton walking away from the compound. "It was taken by our surveillance people earlier this evening. It has just come through."

Houghton's head was bowed away from the camera and his dark glasses prevented any meaningful identification.

"Is this the best we can do?" ranted the General.

"They have just sent it through. Maybe the original pictures will be clearer. They will be off-duty at ten, sir," said the Commander. "I have asked them to bring the photographs straight here."

"Ok. Did anyone follow him?" asked the General.

"Yes sir, agents Gerami and Taherian," replied the Commander. "They have just got here."

The General looked around the room and recognised them in the middle of the group. They were both sweating, as though they had been running.

"Where did he go?" the General asked them.

The agents looked at each other nervously.

"Unfortunately, we lost him in the Metro," said Gerami. "We have been looking for him."

"Lost him? How can that be? Don't they train you how to

follow someone at the academy?"

"Yes sir," replied the agent.

"Well, you're clearly in need of more training," he bellowed. "You're relieved of your surveillance duties; you clearly cannot be trusted to do your job. Report tomorrow for guard duty at zero five-hundred. You are dismissed; go, leave now, you two are a disgrace."

The two agents got up and walked out. Neither mentioned the morning's premature return of Dexter's car, in case it irritated the General further. The room was deathly silent.

The General took a long drag on his cigarette. "Is that it?" he said, looking at Commander Fallahian.

"No, General, there was something else. In her phone call, Mrs Mahabadi mentioned she overheard a telephone conversation between Dexter and someone else. She said she heard him say the words 'Egyptian' and 'American'."

The General blew a long stream of smoke from his mouth. "Hmm, really? Are you sure?"

"That's what she said."

"Did she say anything else? She must have heard more," he challenged, his nostrils flared. Smoke billowed from everywhere, masking his face in a blue haze.

"No sir, she said they spoke quickly, she doesn't speak very good English."

"Hmm, I wonder what they are up to?"

"Who?"

"The British, the Americans… someone is planning something, I am certain. Do we have any more information from the Canadian Embassy?"

"Yes sir, we intercepted another message last night which mentioned the Egyptian," said the Commander.

"Hmm, I think they're trying to get Saleh Amadi away – the British and the Americans, that must be it. What are we doing about him?" said the General.

"I've sent three of my best agents to co-ordinate surveillance over there. They will link up with our people on site."

"Good, let's hope they are better than those clowns keeping watch on the British."

"Yes," countered the Commander. "They are very experienced. I have put Lieutenant Modarresi in charge; he's very capable."

"Good, good. Yes, a good man. So, what's the plan?" said the General, as he stubbed out a cigarette and opened a new pack.

"I have asked them to meet with the agents in the plant."

"How many have we got there?" asked the General.

"There are five in the construction area and one in the processing centre."

"And Amadi is where?"

"He's the Project Director, he has his own office in the main control room."

"Hmm, I see. No wonder the Americans want him."

"The information I have is that he returns home every night to his apartment in town. The construction workers are not in lock-down like the scientists."

"So, we can track his movements? You are confident?"

"Yes, my agents are already working on that."

"Good," said the General.

"What about the British?" asked the Commander.

"No, they do not have the means to get him out, but the Americans… now, they certainly do. I think the British may be helping them, and the Canadians. How many CIA are there in their embassy, do we know?" added the General.

"Not for certain, sir, but we think there are at least two, maybe three; they change," replied the Commander.

"Hmm, we need to keep a careful watch there. I want you to step up surveillance. Have we got anyone inside?"

"Just one of the cleaning staff," said the Commander. "It is she who tells us about the CIA. There is a large room downstairs which she is not allowed in. This is where she thinks they are. She has seen people go in."

"Ok, I hope you have thanked her for her help. We must always show our appreciation."

"Yes, General, she has been rewarded."

The General thought for a moment. He picked up his cigarette and took another pull.

"Good, good. But why don't we encourage her some more? Let's see if she can get into the room and find out what's going on there."

"I think she has tried, sir."

"Well, ask her to try harder. I want to know what's going on in that room."

"Yes sir, I will call her as soon as we have finished," replied the Commander.

"Ok, good. In the meantime, I want Amadi monitored closely, twenty-four hours. What about his family?"

"He has two daughters, they are both at school," replied the Commander.

The other agents were making notes.

"And they are being watched?"

"No sir, not at the moment."

"Why not? We need to watch the whole family. He's not

going to leave without them." He looked around the agents who were present and chose two. "Right, you and you," he pointed. "I want you two to go to Esfahan first thing, report to Lieutenant Modarresi, and find out where the school is. I want them watched, is that clear?"

"Yes General," replied the agents.

"What about his wife, does she work?" asked the General.

"No, she's at home," replied the Commander.

"And the apartment is under surveillance?"

"Yes," replied the Commander. We have managed to put a listening device in their living room this afternoon. One of our agents called and told them their telephone was faulty."

"Excellent, excellent," said the General and took a long drag on his cigarette, looking pleased with himself. "Let's see what happens."

Canadian Embassy, Tehran – Tuesday April 18th– 5:00 a.m.

Zhila Ghorbani was waiting for her colleagues outside the gates to the Canadian Embassy on Ostad-Motahari Avenue. The building is unremarkable and lacks the colonial-grandeur of the British and former U.S. Embassies, status symbols of a forgotten era.

It was a cool morning, but dry; the sun had not yet risen, although a hint of lightness over the distant mountains heralded the approaching dawn.

Moments later, three other ancillary workers joined her, and she rang the buzzer at the entrance to be allowed access.

As supervisor, she was responsible for allocating work rotas and duties within the embassy; today, she needed to make a couple of changes.

The door clicked open and the women entered the embassy and signed the attendance register on the desk.

She called the women together and reallocated the duties. Today, she would be looking after the ground-floor and basement areas, which, as well as the CIA quarters, contained the public toilets. Normally, exercising her seniority, she would assign this work to one of the others. Her colleagues looked at each other in surprise when she announced the rosters.

There was only a skeleton staff on duty in the embassy, including the night porter, an IT and communications officer on the first floor, and two diplomatic staff on the second. The women grouped around the store cupboard next to the toilets and Zhila unlocked the door. They went inside and collected their aprons and materials, then dispersed to their duties.

The Commander had called her the previous evening and explained the new priority, and she had formulated a plan which she thought might work. The hundred dollar reward for the information was more than an incentive to take the odd risk; it exceeded a month's wages.

She waited for her colleagues to go to the upper floors before starting to polish the marble flooring with an industrial cleaner. She was watching for anyone going in and out, but it was quiet.

At ten-to-six, Zhila was dusting the reception desk; the night porter was in his office when a man walked in through the front entrance. He was dressed in jeans and a denim jacket and looked more like a janitor, she thought. He had used a security pass and not called reception for access. She watched as he walked purposefully across the newly-cleaned floor. His sneakers made a squeaking noise as he strode to the basement entrance and headed down the marble steps.

Quickly, she picked up her basket of cleaning materials and followed the man. She reached the lower floor and could see him keying in numbers on a security pad along the corridor.

Her English was limited but, as she approached the man, she called out, "Hello."

The man looked at her.

"Today, clean, yes?" she said, more in hope than anything.

It was Javi Rao, the IT and communications expert. He was totally unaware of the cleaning regime and thought nothing of opening the door and politely waiting until she had passed.

"Sure, go right ahead," said Rao. He closed the door, and Zhila took out her polish and started dusting the desks. She made a mental note of everything she could see, the number of workstations, the equipment. She was trying to work out how many staff it would accommodate; this was one of her objectives. She needed to be quick; she was in an area they were expressly forbidden from entering.

She concentrated on her dusting and then went into the kitchenette and washed the coffee cups and wiped down the sink. It took less than half an hour; more than enough time to complete her mission and do a passable job of cleaning. Rao was on his computer, downloading the numerous emails which had come in overnight from Langley. As she passed his desk, she recognised the CIA logo on the monitor. She had seen it enough times in the briefing room at MOIS headquarters. This was the evidence the Commander had wanted.

She walked towards the exit and waved to Rao.

"Tomorrow?" she mimed the motion of a vacuum cleaner and mimicked the sound. It distracted the techie, but he smiled and waved back.

"Yeah, sure," he replied, and Zhila pushed down on the heavy metal handle, opened the door and left the room. She stopped outside and breathed deeply; next stop, the ladies toilet.

Gholhak Garden Compound – 7:30 a.m.

Afareen arrived for work having slept well for the first time in days. Her brief chat with her husband had lessened her feeling of isolation and gave her some much-needed motivation. She was looking forward to telling Mr Dexter her news. It was a warm, bright morning as she walked through the avenue of trees to the chalets. The omnipresent birdsong reverberated among the branches, and this morning, it seemed louder.

She approached the door and knocked. Sophie was in the kitchen; David was in the bedroom, getting ready for work.

Sophie left her chores and opened the door. "Afareen, come in; how are you today?"

"Good, I am very good, thank you. My husband called me last night."

They walked through to the bedroom where David was just putting on his suit jacket.

"Hello Afareen," he said as she came into the room. He could see an excited look on her face.

"You've heard from your husband?" he proffered.

"Yes, last night; only for a short time."

"That's good, it sounds like they believed your story."

"Yes, I think, but I do not want to talk to them again. It

was very hard."

"Yes, I'm sure. So, what did he say, your husband? Were you able to find out when he is coming back to Tehran?"

"Yes, he said he hopes next week."

"Next week? Hmm, that doesn't give us much time. Ok, let me know when he contacts you again. It's important we know exactly when he's coming back."

"Yes, of course. I hope he will call again tonight."

Just then there was the sound of the diplomatic Jaguar pulling up outside the chalet.

"Right, that's my lift; I'd better go. Thanks Afareen, I'll speak to Mr Houghton and let him know."

David kissed his wife. "See you later darling; have a good day," he said and left the house.

British Embassy, Tehran – 10:00 a.m.

Houghton had taken the minibus to the Embassy and was in his office. Dee was just about to leave having debriefed him on the overnight communications traffic from GCHQ when Dexter knocked on his door and walked in.

"Hi Nick, I've got some news," said Dexter.

"I was just leaving," said Dee. "Would you like me to get some coffees for you?"

"Yes, thanks," said Dexter.

Houghton nodded. "Cheers."

"Ok, I'll be right back," said Dee. Dexter waited until she had closed the door.

"Afareen's spoken to her husband."

"Really? Thank goodness for that. So, what's happening?"

David relayed what Afareen had told him. "It seems that not only has Mahabadi been given a phone, but the Iranians have definitely bought into the Egyptian story."

"That's great. Mind you, if he's going to be on leave next week, it doesn't give us much time."

"No, it doesn't. I said the same thing to Afareen," said Dexter.

"I need to speak to you about my plan," said Houghton. "I've been going over it again and I'm short on personnel. I'm going to need two more people to get him away. I can't do it on my own; there are just too many pieces to fit together."

"Can you get someone else out from Vauxhall?"

"There's not enough time to bring them up to speed if we're going next week and, to be quite honest, I don't want to go down that route."

"Yes, I can understand that."

"I really need someone who knows Tehran. I do have one suggestion."

"Go on," said Dexter.

"Dee?"

Houghton waited for the response.

"Dee?" repeated Dexter, not sounding convinced.

"Yes. I think she'll be ideal. I've been really impressed with her. She's smart, resourceful, and she knows Tehran."

"I'm not sure the Ambassador will go for that… or Vauxhall for that matter."

"I'm not going to tell them," replied Dexter. "I just need some logistical support."

"Ok. It's your call, but be careful; whatever you do, don't get caught. There will be hell to pay."

"I know. But that does still leave me one short."

Dexter could see where this was leading.

"Hmm, well, as you know, I can't really be involved with

the actual operation. I mean, given my diplomatic status."

"But you are field-trained?"

There was a delay. Houghton could see Dexter was giving it serious consideration.

Dexter looked at Houghton. "What would you need me to do?"

Chapter Ten

Canadian Embassy, Tehran – 9:00 a.m.

The embassy was busy with all the diplomats and support staff. Zhila Ghorbani was discreetly observing traffic to the basement office. She had counted three people going in, and one of them leaving again within an hour. She noted everything. It was time to take her break and make a call.

The usual receptionist was on duty, and one or two members of the public were queuing for attention. With the front door now open, Zhila slipped out. She walked for about ten minutes, away from any possible observers in the embassy. It was pleasantly warm, the sun bright, glistening on the white tops of the mountains in the distance. She reached a small park. There was a children's playground, and several mothers were pushing young children on swings, others were on small roundabouts; everybody seemed to be having fun.

Zhila sat down on one of the benches that surrounded the play area and took out her phone. She pressed two digits and waited for the call to connect.

"Mrs Ghorbani," came the distinctive voice on the other end.

"Commander Fallahian? I have some information for you."

The cleaner disclosed her detailed observations regarding the basement. The Commander was impressed and confirmed that her reward was assured.

Canadian Embassy, Tehran – 8:30 a.m.

Tony Alvarez had stayed the night at Jo Podesta's apartment in the centre of town, a twenty-minute journey from the embassy. They had driven in together in his Mercedes. As he was not officially attached to the embassy, Alvarez did not have a space in the underground carpark and had to leave the car in an adjoining street. Ironically, it was opposite the park where Zhila would shortly be filing her report. The two men chatted as they made the walk. The exercise would do them good, Alvarez joked. The previous evening, on their return from the restaurant, he and Podesta had stayed up for several hours sharing a bottle of Jim Beam.

Their mood was upbeat as they entered the embassy and descended the marble steps into the basement.

They did not notice one of the cleaning operatives taking a special interest in their arrival. She noted the time and memorised their appearance and features. Both were wearing expensive clothes; one of them was short, early-forties, slim and muscular; he looked as though he could have been Iranian judging by his complexion. He had a bright-coloured shirt, brown Chinos and a light-blue sports jacket. The other man was older and wearing a smart light-weight grey suit with a white shirt.

Alvarez joined Podesta at his workstation, and they were enjoying a morning coffee and discussing the mission when Javi Rao joined them. He was holding several print-outs.

"Jo, thought you might wanna take a look at last night's messages from Langley."

"Yeah, great, take a seat, have you met Tony?"

"No," said Javi and shook hands with Alvarez.

"Javi joined us a couple of weeks ago. Looks after all our IT and comms – been a great asset," Jo told Alvarez.

"Thanks," said Rao, humbly.

"So, what have we got? Anything interesting."

"Nothing much on the Egyptian; it's been quiet from the Brits for a couple of days now."

"Well that's not surprising, we're taking over that baby. What about the Iranians – any noise from them?"

"Not referring to the Egyptian specifically, but it seems they are stepping up their security at Esfahan."

"Should we read anything into that? What do you think Tony?" asked Podesta.

"If there's no reference to Amadi, then my guess is they're doing the same thing they did at Natanz. They've certainly beefed things up there."

"Yes, that's possible," said Rao. "It's still in lock-down, and they've brought in some serious hardware. The place is bristling with anti-aircraft missile launchers – Scuds everywhere. I've got some satellite photos I can show you."

"Yeah, great Rao; do that."

Rao got up and went to his pod.

Podesta turned to Alvarez. "So, you still ok to go down to Esfahan?"

"Yeah, sure, the sooner we get in touch with this guy, the sooner we know what's happening," said Alvarez.

"What time are you planning on getting away?" he said, moving forward in his seat and folding his arms.

Alvarez looked at his watch. "As soon as I've finished this," he replied, lifting his coffee mug and taking another mouthful. "It'll be mad trying to get out of Tehran."

"How long will it take?"

"I checked the map, it's about two-eighty miles, so five hours and then some, I guess. Depends on the road; they get a lot of traffic heading that way. I'll be glad when they get that new freeway open."

"Well, you take care, you hear. Where are you staying?"

"The Safir, it looks ok and it's fairly central. I got my assistant in Arak to book me a room for three nights."

"And you've got your cover story?"

"Yeah it's good, I mean one project manager visiting another's not unusual. I'd guess the day job is not dissimilar, but he probably gets twice my paycheque."

"Yeah, that's true," said Podesta and chuckled.

Rao returned; his face etched with concern.

"What's up, Javi?" said Podesta recognising the worried look.

"Just got a message from Langley. They've picked up some noise that a couple of high-ranking Russians have been talking to Iran's top brass. Some kind of enrichment deal, they reckon; a possible joint venture. Langley thinks they'll be announcing something in the next couple of days."

Podesta looked at Alvarez. "Jeez, this could up the stakes a bit; that's all we need, the Russians in the mix."

"Hmm, yeah that's for sure. What do you reckon, are we still going ahead?" said Alvarez, who was also looking concerned.

"Yeah, I guess. Tell you what, I'll speak to Cherokee, you get down to Esfahan, and I'll call you later this afternoon with an update. If you want my honest assessment, the sooner we get this guy out, the better."

"Yeah, I get that," said Alvarez. He knocked back the last of his coffee and stood up.

Podesta also got up. "You take care, you hear," he said and shook Alvarez's hands warmly as good friends would do. Rao followed suit.

Alvarez picked up his jacket from the back of his chair, left the room and walked along the corridor.

Upstairs, Zhila was still cleaning. She noticed Alvarez leaving.

Alvarez reached the embassy entrance and stopped at the top of the steps to put on his sunglasses. There was an anonymous delivery van opposite. He didn't hear the sound of a motor-driven Nikon camera coming from inside where three MOIS agents were watching, armed with an embassy brochure that had photographs of all the Canadian diplomats.

Alvarez's departure was of interest. They had seen him enter the building with Podesta before the embassy was open to the public. Podesta had used a pass-key, they observed, but his picture was not in the brochure; neither was Alvarez's.

"He is leaving," said Agent Dabiri. "I will follow him. Let the Commander know."

Dabiri left the van while one of the others reported in what was happening.

The MOIS Agent turned the corner and saw Alvarez climbing into a Mercedes. He quickly went back to the van to retrieve his crash-helmet and black leather jacket. His motorcycle was parked just behind. He started it up, turned around and slowly drove towards Alvarez's parking spot. There was no sign of the Mercedes. He peered into the distance and opened up the throttle; it couldn't have gone far.

Sure enough, he spotted Alvarez about two-hundred yards away, caught in slow-moving traffic. The motorcycle reduced speed; Dabiri could afford to stay back; the Mercedes was not going to get away from him in this traffic.

MOIS Headquarters – 9:20 a.m.

Commander Fallahian was outside General Moghrabi's office, waiting for him to finish a meeting with the MOIS director of security. He could see a blue haze coming from the keyhole; any time spent in the General's office was a potential health hazard.

Ten minutes later, the door opened and General Khatami, the Head of Security appeared. The Commander sprang to attention, which the departing General acknowledged with a salute. There was no conversation.

The Commander knocked on Moghrabi's office door and entered. The General was seated behind his desk, lighting another cigarette. Fallahian coughed as his nasal passages came under attack from the smoke-filled atmosphere.

"Ah, Commander, come in," said the General. "I was going to call you; I have been discussing the Amadi situation with General Khatami."

"Yes, General. I too have some news. What have you decided?"

"We are both of the same opinion. We are certain that the Americans are going to try to get Saleh Amadi away, probably with the help of the British. We have considered this carefully and it makes absolute sense. The Egyptian's knowledge in building nuclear plants would be important to the Americans but, more than that, he knows everything about our installation at Esfahan. We can't let that happen; if necessary, he must be eliminated, but that is not our goal. I want to know who he is in contact with."

"Why don't we just arrest him? He will talk, surely."

"Yes, of course we can do that, but if we can catch the people who are helping him, think of the political opportunities; especially if it is CIA. According to General Khatami, the Ministry of Counterintelligence believes it could even help us with the United Nations. We will be in a strong bargaining position; we can rightfully express our anger at America's intervention in Iran's affairs."

The General looked at the Commander and blew another stream of smoke into the room. "This mission has the utmost priority over anything else you are doing. If you need any more resources, you just have to say." The General looked at the Commander with steely eyes. "You said you had some news."

"Yes General, I have heard from our agent in the Canadian Embassy."

"Good, that's very good, what did she have to say?"

"She was able to get into the secret room in the basement, and it is as you had thought, CIA."

"Are you sure?"

"Yes, she saw the CIA insignia on one of their computers."

"Hmm, now that is interesting."

"She said there were four desks and a kitchen. There was a lot of computer equipment against the back wall. I asked her about it, but she could not identify what it was, just lots of black boxes, she said. One of their agents was in there, working on them."

"Hmm," said the General. "Well, that certainly gives us the proof we need. How many agents – do we know?"

"Yes, she said she saw another three men go down the stairs towards the room, one about eight o'clock and two more came in together less than an hour ago, so that is four that we know of. One of them left again just before nine o'clock. She gave us some very good descriptions."

"Excellent, so that's four. I wonder if we can identify them. Do we have pictures of the diplomats there?"

"Yes sir, they provide a very helpful booklet with pictures. Here, I have a copy."

The Commander handed over the official handbook of the Canadian Embassy. The inside page had the names of the various diplomats, their role and a picture, starting with the Ambassador.

"That is very useful. Do we have surveillance on the embassy?"

"Yes sir, we have three agents on watch. They have been ordered to photograph anyone going in and out, but that is not all. They saw two people enter before the embassy opened, and one of them had a pass-key, but neither of them are pictured in the brochure. When they saw one of them leave, Agent Dabiri followed him. His arrival and departure match the timings of the men our operative saw going into the basement office. I am confident the man Dabiri is following is a CIA agent."

"Excellent, excellent. That is wonderful news." Another pall of smoke contaminated the air; Fallahian coughed. The General stubbed out his cigarette and immediately lit up another.

"Can our operative in the embassy find out anything else?"

"I would counsel against it, sir. The cleaning staff are forbidden from entering the room; she was very lucky to get in today. She thinks the person in there was new. If she were to try again, then she might be compromised, and then we would have no-one inside."

"I take your point. You have rewarded this lady?"

"Yes sir, one hundred dollars."

"Good, double it, and give her my personal thanks; she has done the country a great service."

"I will, thank you," said the Commander.

"So, what is happening in Esfahan?" asked the General.

"We have many agents there now. I have authorised motorcycles; it will make them more mobile. There are many places to cover."

"But we know which one Amadi is in?" asked the General.

"Yes, he is in the main processing plant."

"Good, good… and the school, where the daughters are?"

"Yes, the agents are in place sir."

"What about inside the facility?"

"Yes, we have people watching him there."

"Excellent, excellent; now we wait."

Outskirts of Tehran – 10:00 a.m.

It took over three-quarters of an hour for Alvarez to escape the urban sprawl of Tehran and reach the open road. He'd consulted his directions and watched for signs for Route 65. The journey was going to be long and, without the benefit of the yet-to-be-constructed freeway, was not conducive to high speed. Way behind him, a motorbike was having no difficulty in keeping pace, but Alvarez had no idea he was being tailed.

He was running through his plan, such as it was. His first challenge was to contact Saleh Amadi; Podesta had given him the address, but there was no knowing if he was still living there. Calling on him at home, in any case, was fraught with danger. A more detailed plan would follow once the exfil was confirmed. Resources were not an issue.

After about two hours, Alvarez made his first stop as he reached the village of Aveh. It was just a smattering of dwellings, little else, but there was a truck-stop, so he pulled in for some refreshment. He got out and stretched. There was a gas station with a solitary pump; behind that, a kiosk where a bored youth was reading a comic. To the right, was a larger building. The place looked run-down; paint was peeling, and the wood was rotten. It looked in danger of collapsing at any moment. There were three trucks parked on the gravel waste-ground in front. Alvarez went inside and found the toilets, then ordered a coffee and some food to go. Speaking Farsi and having dark features, a casual observer would easily mistake him for being local. His visit would be unremarkable. He looked around as he waited for his order. It was World Cup year and posters of the Iranian soccer team were posted on every available wall space. The eating area was thick with cigarette smoke; a group of truckers were chatting animatedly. Alvarez would not stay longer than was necessary to collect his food.

Dabiri had seen the Mercedes pull in. He stopped at the side of the road and waited, out of sight of the ramshackle building.

Ten minutes later, Alvarez walked to his car and sat inside, eating his lunch with the window wound down for some fresh air. The temperature in the car was climbing with the warming sun. He tossed the empty sandwich wrapping out of the car and pulled away. His follower immediately kick-started his Suzuki and re-joined the road two hundred yards behind.

During Alvarez's refreshment break, Dabiri had attempted to call the Commander, but there was no signal. He would try later; he was certain now where Alvarez was heading.

Esfahan, also known as Isfahan, is Iran's third-largest city with a population of over one and a half million people. It has an ancient history and was once the country's capital.

Despite Alvarez's time in Iran, this was his first visit and he was amazed as he reached the city. Traffic was almost as dense as Tehran, but there was a different feel about the place. Wide-open parks and high-rise tenements are overlooked by Mount Soffeh to the south; it is an industrial centre and home to several facilities supporting the nuclear industry as well as the uranium processing plant that was making all the news. This was where Saleh Amadi was based.

Alvarez passed the impressive Naghsh-e-Jahan Square, one of the many tourist attractions in the city, surrounded on three sides by walls with typical Islamic arches. Tall minarets rose from the corners. With traffic almost at walking pace, he was able to take in its grandeur.

It took another twenty minutes to locate his hotel. He parked outside at the drop-off point and a porter took his car keys; he would drive it to the underground lot. Alvarez took out his baggage and went inside. He waited in line at the reception desk and looked around. The lobby area was modern with classy decoration and beautiful paintings; a wide spiral staircase snaked upwards to the Mezzanine. He made a note to thank his assistant in Arak for her choice.

He reached the check-in desk and presented his Mexican

passport. The receptionist explained he would have to leave it with them for a couple of hours, for security reasons.

For the first time since his departure from the embassy, he suddenly felt vulnerable. He knew it was routine, but the process still made him uncomfortable.

A porter came to assist with his luggage and the pair walked to the lifts, then rode up to his room on the sixth floor. Alvarez tipped the man and settled in. He went to his briefcase and took out his scanning device which would sweep the room for bugs. It was a routine which he took seriously, particularly in Iran. Satisfied it was clear, he called Podesta. It was almost three p.m.

"Hi, Jo, just got in. How're things?"

"Yeah, good. You got there ok?"

"Yeah, hey this Esfahan's a great place, I don't mind stopping here for a few days, and the hotel's the deal."

"Glad you're comfortable. Ok, listen up, I've had the latest from Cherokee and we're good to go with the project. In fact, with the present situation, he wants it to take priority."

"Copy that. I'm on it."

Down in reception, Alvarez's details were logged into the computer. Outside the hotel, Agent Dabiri was calling the Commander.

MOIS Headquarters – 6:00 p.m.

Commander Fallahian had spent the day pulling together the pieces of information received from the surveillance teams and was briefing the General.

"We have identified the man who was at the Canadian Embassy this morning."

"Excellent, excellent," said the General. "So, who is he?"

"He is this man," replied the Commander who handed him an excellent A4 size picture of Alvarez.

"Agent Dabiri has followed him to Esfahan; he is staying at the Hotel Safir. I have spoken to them and they have faxed through a copy of his passport. His name is Antonio Alvarez, and he is using Mexican documents."

"Mexican?" queried the General.

"According to his papers, he is a construction engineer based at Arak."

"Arak!" exclaimed the General.

"Yes, but not on the heavy-water plant; he's in charge of building one of the new industrial complexes. Been in Iran for eight years."

"Eight years. Hmm, he will have been watching the nuclear plant; that's why he is there." The General slammed his fist down in frustration. "Eight years! Why have we not discovered him before?"

"I am checking with the company he works for, it's Brechtel."

"Hmm, Brechtel, I might have known; they get everywhere. Ok, find out what you can, and keep him under surveillance in Esfahan, but be careful, we don't want to alarm him. I want to see if he makes contact with Amadi. If he does, then we can arrest both of them."

British Embassy, Tehran

Completely unaware of the chain of events that he had set in motion elsewhere, Houghton was in his office working on his plan to exfil the Mahabadi family. He needed to speak to Dee.

It was after eleven-thirty before she was able to leave her

office and meet up with him. She knocked on his door and walked in.

Houghton had just come off the secure phone to Vauxhall having updated Andy Fellows.

"Ah, Dee," he said, as his colleague entered carrying two coffees and pastries.

"I've brought you some sustenance," she said and passed him the goodies.

"Hey, thanks, that's great. Take a seat, I need a chat."

Dee sat down and started eating her pastry, which she had wrapped in a serviette. "Of course, anything."

Houghton took a drink of coffee. "So, what's the latest upstairs?"

"Not a great deal on the political front, things are still tense here in Tehran, but there's been a lot more traffic on the Russians. Vauxhall and Langley are going crazy, as you can imagine. The White House doesn't want to rock the boat just yet; they're waiting to see the next move. There's still been no official confirmation about any tie-up."

"Hmm, that's all we need," said Houghton. "Still, we can't do a great deal about it."

He took a bite of his pastry, then sat back in his chair and looked at Dee with a serious expression.

"There was something else?" said Dee, noticing his change in demeanour.

"Yes… yes, there is. I've been talking to David and I want to take up your offer of help."

"Ok," said Dee, leaning forward in her chair.

"First, I need to tell you something that must not go outside this room; people's lives are at risk."

Dee looked at him. "Of course."

"I haven't been able to give you the full background on why I'm here, it's classified, but I've spoken to David and he's agreed to reallocate your duties for a short time so you can come and work for me."

Dee's eyes widened. "Sure, wow, great, anything."

Houghton fiddled with a pen on his desk.

"Ok. I'm here to try and exfil someone from Natanz."

"Natanz? How will you do that? They're in lock-down."

"Yes, I know, but I'm not going to get him away from the plant. I want to spring him and his family when he's on leave."

Dee looked at him. "Hmm, no wonder you wanted to keep it secret. How long have we got?"

"I'm not entirely sure, and that's the least of the problems. The target is one of their leading nuclear scientists and, as you can imagine, he'll be under significant surveillance in the present climate."

"So, what about the Egyptian we've been monitoring?"

"Let's just say that was a diversionary tactic."

"Ah, I see. So, how did we get involved?"

Houghton outlined the original contact and the meetings with Afareen, then briefed her on his strategy to get them away.

"Hmm, that's going to be tough."

"Yes, but I think with your help, we can do it."

"Ok, so what will you need me to do?"

"Nothing for the time being. I need you to continue what you're doing and not arouse any suspicion; I don't want anyone else to know of your involvement, and that includes the Ambassador. I'll let you know what's happening on a daily basis; when I know the date, I'll brief you." He paused for a drink, then continued. "The priority I have at the moment is transport. David was looking into it, but he's drawn a blank. Do you know where I can get an old ambulance, by any chance?"

"An ambulance?" Dee started to laugh. "You serious?"

He looked at her. "Yeah."

"Hmm, not off-hand, but I can make some enquiries."

"Yeah, ok, but be discreet."

"Discretion is my middle name," said Dee and smiled. "I can do a few searches in the ads, you never know."

"Failing that, a van that we can make look like an ambulance," said Houghton.

"That might be a better bet."

"Ok, great, let me know."

"Is there anything else you want me to do?" asked Dee, still pondering over the ambulance request.

"No, but I'll keep you up to speed."

Dee went to get up. "Do you fancy joining me for dinner tonight at mine?"

Houghton thought for a moment. "Yeah, ok, that will be great."

"Fantastic, seven ok?"

"Sure, I'll see you at seven."

Dee left the office. Houghton felt a degree of relief at having someone with whom he could bounce ideas off. Her local knowledge would be invaluable in the final stages of preparation.

Hotel Safir, Esfahan – 6:00 p.m.

What had supposed to be a quick nap for Alvarez had turned into three-quarters of an hour and his head felt heavy as he woke from his slumber. He took a shower to revive himself and made a coffee. As he took his drink, he stared out of the window and studied the vista. The view across the city to the mountains beyond was stunning. He could see the surrounding high rise tenements, and the myriad of cranes gave away the volume of construction work that was going on. In the distance, towers, spheres and chimneys rose incongruously. Below him, brake lights illuminated the streets as busy commuters struggled with their homeward journey.

He took out his map and checked his bearings. The nuclear facilities were not shown on any town atlases; in fact, Langley had had difficulty in locating the exact position. For some time, satellite images were the only source of reference. This was the primary reason for trying to get Saleh Amadi on board two years earlier; his information would have been extremely valuable. In the present climate, however, with his detailed knowledge of the nuclear plant and its associated facilities, his stock had risen considerably.

Alvarez took out his laptop; there would be no hotel Wi-Fi, in fact, internet connection outside the Embassy was almost impossible. The room phone was next to his bed; he traced the wire to the input socket in the wall and pulled it out. Then he inserted a lead attached to a modem which was plugged into the side of his laptop and dialled in. The familiar beeps indicated a connection. After the satellite connection in the embassy, it was frustratingly slow, but after fifteen minutes, he had downloaded his emails from the server. Not the most secure communication, but the text would be in code; he was not unduly concerned.

There was an email from Podesta. *'Cherokee anxious that*

holiday plans are expedited in the light of pending news'.

Alvarez replied. *'Copy that. Hopeful of meeting client tomorrow'.*

He pressed 'send' and watched the email disappear into the ether.

He checked his watch. He would eat at the hotel restaurant and then drive around for a while to familiarise himself with the locality. He would not make any move to contact Saleh Amadi this evening, but he did want to take a look at the industrial complexes.

The importance of The Uranium Conversion Facility at Esfahan for the Iranian nuclear industry cannot be overstated. As well as converting material into weapons-grade uranium hexafluoride, there is also a Zirconium Production Plant (ZPP) located nearby that produces the necessary ingredients and alloys for nuclear reactors. Construction of the Conversion Facility was started in 1999 with considerable help from China and completed in 2004, although production of nuclear material did not start until the following year.

The Nuclear Technology/Research Centre is Iran's largest research centre and is said to employ as many as three-thousand scientists. According to Alvarez's information, the Uranium conversion facility, which was the subject of the present international tension, was about three miles outside the city between the villages of Shahrida and Fulashans. This was where Amadi was based.

Over dinner, Alvarez checked the map and found the road he would need to take.

Outside the hotel, MOIS agent Dabiri had been relieved

by three more officers and had to face the gruelling five-hour trek back to Tehran, but with the praises of his commander ringing in his ears, the journey would be made in good spirit.

The surveillance team were parked outside the hotel's main entrance, not immediately in front of the doors, but behind a row of orange taxis in an anonymous three-year-old BMW. They would not be disturbed by the hotel porters who were only too aware of their presence. The two in the car were backed up by a motorcyclist dressed in the same outfit as Dabiri; black leather jacket, crash helmet with a black visor.

It was eight o'clock by the time Alvarez left the hotel. He was dressed in jeans, a shirt and a light jacket. There was still a few minutes of daylight left, the traffic mercifully lighter, which would make his exploration much easier.

The surveillance team had been supplied with Alvarez's photograph and spotted him straight away, causing a great deal of excitement.

As Alvarez stood on the hotel steps waiting for his car to be retrieved from the underground parking lot, he surveyed the scene. He looked up at the exterior of the building and beyond to the stars just starting to make their presence visible in the darkening sky. He saw the line of taxis waiting for fares, some of the drivers reading newspapers. Others further down the queue had got out and were chatting. He didn't take much notice of the BMW at the back of the line. From his vantage point, he could not see the activity inside. One of the passengers started taking photographs using a telephoto lens.

The motorcyclist was alerted. He put on his helmet and

watched as the porter got out of the Mercedes and handed the keys to Alvarez. He kick-started his machine and saw the Mexican slowly pull away down the exit ramp. The motorcyclist, slowly followed by the BMW, headed out onto the main road, about five car-lengths behind. The traffic was lighter at this time of night, but it was still busy. The streetlights cast shadows across the highway as Alvarez drove east towards the industrial centre. He could see the outline of the nuclear installations against the twilight sky in the distance.

In the BMW, the passenger was on the phone to the Commander. "He is heading for the nuclear processing plant."

Chapter Eleven

Hotel Safir, Esfahan – Wednesday April 19th – 9:00 a.m.
Alvarez had breakfast in the hotel dining room and reflected on the previous evenings trip to the nuclear installation; it had given him a useful perspective.

The plant and ancillary buildings took up a wide area. It was heavily protected by double barbed-wire fencing; armed guards patrolled the perimeter, and there were cameras everywhere. There was just one entrance gate, set back about one hundred yards off the main road, with a security post. As he drove by, he noticed a vehicle being scrutinised by three security personnel. Then he spotted something more sinister; a Scud missile launcher, then another. He counted six more as he skirted the installation boundary; there would be many more on the other side, he was certain.

Alvarez felt tense; this was no ordinary mission.

He checked his rear-view mirror several times; it was instinctive, but in the darkness, it was difficult to spot if anyone was following. There was little car traffic, mostly trucks delivering to the various industrial complexes in the vicinity. If he was stopped, he believed his cover story would prevail.

It was after eleven by the time he returned to the hotel. The BMW did not follow him up the entrance road but drove past and parked about half a mile away. The motorcyclist, however, did follow him and, from the end of the line of taxis, he watched as Alvarez got out of the Mercedes and handed his car keys to the duty porter.

As soon as he had finished his breakfast the following morning, Alvarez went to reception to get a copy of the Esfahan area phone book, which he took back to his room.

He scanned the directory. It was in Farsi and, although he spoke the language, he did not read it that well. Luckily, company names were also displayed in English. He was not certain how the facility would be listed, so he started from the beginning and worked his way through. Then he spotted something; Esfahan Nuclear Technology Center; that would be his first calling point.

He dialled the number using the hotel's telephone; his mobile phone signal was still weak, and he did not want his connection to drop.

"ENTC, how can I help?" answered a woman in English.

Alvarez replied in Farsi.

"I would like to make an appointment to see Doctor Saleh Amadi, please. He works in the Process Centre."

The switchboard operator replied in Farsi.

"Please hold sir, I will transfer your call."

There was a delay before he was reconnected.

"Hello, can I help you?" came another voice, this time in Farsi.

"I would like to make an appointment to see Doctor Amadi, please. My name is Doctor Antonio Alvarez, project director with Brechtel GMBH in Arak."

"One moment."

The line went quiet; One minute, two minutes; Alvarez was tapping his pen on the desk.

"Hello sir, Doctor Amadi is busy at the moment. Can he

call you back?"

"Yes, of course." Alvarez had no choice, but it meant he had to provide his mobile phone number. He couldn't risk any calls going through the hotel switchboard.

The call dropped. On the plus side, at least he had made indirect contact with Amadi; on the minus, he had no control over the call-back.

He sat on the sofa and went over his story again in his mind; when Amadi eventually did return the call, he would be prepared.

The original idea was to try to contact Amadi at his house as Podesta had done two years earlier. However, they soon realised this was not a realistic option. In the present climate, there was a strong likelihood that Amadi would be being watched. Also, they didn't know for certain if he was at the same address and Alvarez could not afford to go knocking on doors; it was far too dangerous. There was another problem; Alvarez had no real idea of what Amadi looked like. The photo he had was at least two years old and not particularly clear.

So, it would have to be a different plan. It was bold, but it had a reasonable chance of working. Everything depended on the phone call.

Alvarez was restless. He didn't want to leave the hotel room in case he lost the phone signal. He also did not want anyone eavesdropping.

He tried reading a book but couldn't concentrate. A knock on the door at eleven o'clock made him jump. He went to check the enquirer, but the door opened before he got there, and he froze.

"Oh, I am sorry, I have come to do your room," said a

woman, dressed in the uniform of the cleaning staff.

"Oh, er, yes… sorry," said Alvarez, momentarily flustered, and he held the door while she brought in her cleaning materials.

"You go or stay?" said the woman. "Only ten minutes."

Alvarez was in a dilemma. If Amadi called while his room was being made up, he would have a problem. He needed to be on his own.

"It's ok, I will leave," he said, making what he thought was the right decision.

He picked up his keys. "Ten minutes?" he confirmed with the cleaner, holding both hands open to indicate ten digits.

"Yes," she said, "That is all."

Alvarez went down the corridor and took the lift to the ground floor. He would have a coffee while he waited. He checked his phone. There was no signal. "Shit!" he exclaimed to himself.

He ordered a drink and sat in the lounge area.

Meanwhile, with Alvarez out of the room, the cleaning operative took out a gadget from her overall pocket. She remembered the instructions from the agent who had briefed her and went to the telephone. Compared to American standards, the bug wasn't particularly sophisticated, a simple microphone and transmitter, but it would do what was necessary. The hotel telephone was also fairly ancient. She lifted the bulky handset off the cradle and turned over the receiver. She peeled off the self-adhesive tape from the bug and removed the contact strip which would activate the device, then pressed it to the bottom of the phone. She replaced the receiver, quickly completed her cleaning and left the room.

Alvarez checked his watch; it had been over a quarter of an hour. He finished his coffee and headed back to the room.

He was an experienced agent and careful with security, but he didn't think to scan the room again; he had already carried out a sweep the previous evening, and his mind was on the pending call from Amadi.

Another hour went by, and Alvarez was considering alternative options. He paced the room; there was nothing he could do. He was feeling frustrated and bored; he was not used to inactivity. His laptop was on the table, and he decided to check his emails again. He went through the tedious routine of unplugging the phone lead and connecting his modem to dial in. There was just one routine message from Brechtel in Arak. He closed down the laptop and reconnected the hotel phone.

In pulling the lead, the phone fell from the bedside table. He swore, picked it up and returned it to its rightful position, not spotting the bug.

The agent in the van outside the hotel cursed as the static attacked his ears through his headphones.

"What's the problem?" said his colleague, who sat beside him holding a camera with a zoom lens.

"It sounded as if the telephone fell."

"Do you think he spotted the device?"

"I don't know; it's still working as far as I can tell." The discussion was interrupted by the sound of a Nokia ringtone coming from the headphones. "Shh," said the listening agent; his pen was poised over a piece of paper.

Back in the room, Alvarez was making himself another coffee when the familiar ringtone of his mobile reverberated from the table top where it had been charging. He grabbed the handset, composed himself and pressed the green button. He spoke in Farsi.

"Doctor Alvarez speaking, hello."

"Doctor Alvarez, this is Doctor Amadi. I understand you called earlier wanting an appointment. I am very busy; what is this about?"

"Yes, Doctor, and I am sorry to disturb you. I'll come straight to the point. I'd like to see you if you can spare me a few minutes. I am the Project Director at one of the new commercial ventures in Arak. I work for Brechtel. I want to get the opinion of a fellow engineer on a construction matter."

"Ah, yes, Brechtel. I know them, from Germany, yes?"

"Yes."

"And what's the problem?"

"We're experiencing issues with the drainage system of the whole complex and I could do with the benefit of your experience; engineer to engineer, so to speak. I will not take up much of your time. I'm sure you are like me; it's a lonely job being in charge with no-one to discuss issues, would you agree?"

"Yes, that is true. Hmm, I don't know. How did you get my name?"

"One of my engineers... er Maher... er El-Beheiry? Worked here in Esfahan and knew your reputation. Do you remember him? He said you were an expert."

"No. I don't think so."

Given that Alvarez had just made the name up, he wasn't expecting a positive answer. There was a pause; Alvarez held his breath.

"Yes, ok, I can see you tomorrow at eight-thirty."

"Eight-thirty, yes. How do I get in?"

"Do you have your passport?"

"Yes,"

"Good, it saves many problems. Can you send through a copy to my secretary and she will arrange a pass for you? It will be at the gate waiting." Doctor Amadi recited the fax number.

"Where are you staying?"

"At the Safir."

"Ah, nice, you will be comfortable there."

"Yes, it's very good," said Alvarez.

"Goodbye, Doctor Alvarez, until tomorrow."

Before Alvarez could respond, the line went dead.

In the surveillance van, there was a great deal of excitement as the headphone agent recounted the conversation to his colleague.

"I must pass this information to the Commander immediately."

Back in his room, Alvarez sat for a moment and reflected on the conversation with Amadi. He felt disappointed at the fairly cold reception; he was expecting a more positive response. He tried to put himself in Amadi's position. Surely he would have expected some sort of contact given his exfil request; but then, maybe he was just being cautious; that was probably it.

He picked up his phone again and dialled Podesta's number.

"Hi, Jo, some good news. I've spoken to the client and he's agreed to meet me tomorrow at eight-thirty."

MOIS Headquarters – 2:00 p.m.

Commander Fallahian was anxious to bring the General the latest news from Esfahan and was pacing up and down outside his office. He'd knocked on the door, but there was no reply. The smell of stale cigarettes and sweat permeated the whole of the basement area; it was not pleasant. Five minutes later, the General appeared at the bottom of the stairs and was walking towards him. His footsteps on the stone floor echoed along the corridor.

"Ah, Commander Fallahian, I was going to call you. You have some news? The director wants to know the latest."

"Yes, General, some interesting news."

The General unlocked his office door and the pair entered. The Commander stood to attention and waited for the General to be seated.

"Sit down," ordered the General. "Well?"

"The CIA agent has made contact with Amadi."

"He has?"

"Yes, about an hour ago. We managed to install a listening device in his hotel room, and he received a phone call from him."

"So, Amadi actually phoned the agent. Now that is interesting. He must have had his number. Do you think they are planning something?"

"Well, it's possible. The agent is going to the installation tomorrow to meet Amadi at eight-thirty."

The General opened a new packet of cigarettes and lit one up; he took a long drag and sat thinking for a moment.

"The agent is an engineer from Arak yes?"

"Yes sir."

"I wonder what they're up to."

"The surveillance officer said it was to discuss a construction issue, problems with drainage at Arak."

"What problems? Do we know about this?"

"It's not at the facility; it will be at the construction site Brechtel are developing."

"Hmm, I wonder how many more foreign agents are working there." The General took another long drag of his smoke. "I want you to send someone over there tomorrow; get all their personnel records and bring them here on my orders. I want every foreign worker checked."

"That will take some time, there are over two-thousand men working on that project."

"I don't care. It's the security of this country we're talking about. Get those records and do it. Today's Tuesday, I want it completed by Friday. Anyone you suspect, bring them in for questioning."

"Does that include labourers? We have many from Afghanistan."

"Hmm, no, no, not the Afghans, they will not be a problem, but anyone with a European passport, or from the Americas or Canada."

"And Egypt?"

"Hmm, yes, especially Egypt," said the General.

"Yes sir," said the Commander. "What about Amadi?"

"Hmm, that is more difficult."

"They could be discussing how the Americans intend on getting him out," said the Commander.

"There is only one way to find out. Get someone to put a listening device in his office. I want you to personally oversee this. Go down to Esfahan this afternoon, I need you on the ground. Ring me when you are there. Then tomorrow

I want you to call me and tell me what you heard."

"Do you want them arrested?" asked the Commander.

"Not yet, let's see what they say. I want to make sure we have enough evidence to put them on trial."

"But we will have both of them together; they could not get away."

"No, that is true," replied the General.

"And if we let the American leave, we could lose him."

"Then we must make sure that we don't. He will go back to his hotel," said the General.

"Or back to Arak."

"Yes, or back to Arak, possibly. But, think about it; if the Americans are going to get him out, Amadi will not leave without his family and that will take a great deal of organising. No, I think the American will stay there to make arrangements. Are Amadi's apartment and family still being watched?"

"Yes sir"

"Good, then let's see what happens tomorrow. I will decide when we have more information. Was there anything else?"

"Yes sir, what do we do about the British?"

"Ah, yes, a good question, what about the British?"

"There's been nothing about the Egyptian for two days, just routine messages."

"Hmm," said the General. "I wonder what their role in all this is. Is there anything on that new agent?"

"No, nothing, he's not been out of the embassy that we know of. He goes to and from the compound in the bus with the other diplomats. We are keeping a close watch."

"And we have someone in Gholhak?"

"Yes sir, Taherian, he's one of the drivers; he's been very helpful."

"What about monitoring inside the compound; how is that?"

"It is not very good; the reception is not reliable. We can never hear clearly what is going on; the static is very bad."

"What about the new bugs? They are much better. Have you tried those?"

"No General."

"I think we need to get Mrs Mahabadi to help again. Yes, get someone over to her apartment with two of the new listening devices tonight and tell her to place one in Dexter's house and one in the new man's apartment too. What's his name?"

"Houghton, sir," replied the Commander.

"Yes, Houghton, and get someone to show her what to do. Get it arranged before you go to Esfahan."

"Yes sir, it will be Lieutenant Mishdar; he will be in charge here while I am in Esfahan."

"Good, good, see to it." The General stubbed out his cigarette. "Ok, that's all for now. Let me know when you get to Esfahan. Wait, I have an idea, why don't you stay at the same hotel as the American, undercover; you can watch him. We will cover the cost."

"Yes sir, I can do that."

The Commander walked down the corridor, up the stairs to the ground floor and left the building to get some fresh air and consider the conversation.

He made a call to his deputy. "Mishdar? I have General Moghrabi's orders. Two things, I am going to Esfahan later so you will be in charge here until I return. I need someone to go to Arak and visit Brechtel's office first thing tomorrow morning. I want their personnel records bringing back here; there will be much work to do. Choose someone reliable – Sergeant Daribi. Tell him to go tonight; he can take two men with him in uniform; this is official. Let me know tomorrow when you have them; I will tell you what to do. The other thing I need you to do is to go back to Mrs Mahabadi with two of the new listening devices. The General wants one in the Dexters' residence in the British Embassy compound where she works and one in the apartment of the new diplomat, Houghton. Show her how to put them on the bottom of the telephone. It should not be difficult for her to do. You understand?"

The lieutenant repeated the orders.

"Good, I will call you tonight when I get to Esfahan for an update. Oh, and book me a room at the Hotel Safir in Esfahan. Two nights, for now."

The Commander dropped the call and went home to pack some clothes for the long trip south.

Gholhak Garden Compound – 6:55 p.m.

Nick Houghton was adding the final touches to his wardrobe before his dinner with Dee. His mind was still totally immersed in the mission and, with Dee now on board, he felt an added responsibility to ensure her safety.

Earlier, he had taken the minibus from the Embassy to the compound and noticed that the driver was once again Habib Taherian, the MOIS agent who had so obligingly passed on the false information about the Egyptian. Houghton observed from the back seats and could see the driver looking at him in his rear-view mirror at every opportunity; it made Houghton feel uncomfortable and left him in no doubt that he had become a person of interest to the Ministry of Intelligence.

That wasn't a particular problem at the moment, all diplomats would be under scrutiny and any new addition to the Embassy personnel would be the subject of curiosity. The difficulty would arise when he had to visit Mayflower again, some deception would be necessary.

He had sat next to Dee in the minibus, opposite the two other regular diplomats, and conversation, such as there was, was polite; Houghton appeared to have been accepted as part of the team.

Outside the compound, the latest surveillance team noted the return of the bus and its occupants.

Houghton left his apartment just before seven and, as he walked down the corridor, he thought about his relationship with Dee. Since they had had their 'chat', they had been completely professional, although every now and again there was the knowing look that said more. Houghton could not afford any distractions or personal attachments that would affect his judgement.

He knocked on the door and could hear music coming from inside.

"Hi, come in," said Dee as she opened the door.

"Mmm, something smells good," said Houghton as he walked past her. There was no kiss.

"Thanks, but it's not mine, another from reception. I just don't get the time to cook these days. Would you like a glass of wine? It's Bulgarian again," she said and laughed.

"Bulgarian's fine," said Houghton.

Dee went to the kitchen and returned a couple of minutes later with two glasses of the said wine and sat down next to Houghton. She passed him a glass.

"Cheers," she said, and they clinked glasses.

"Thanks for the invitation," said Houghton.

"It's ok, it's been so full-on at the moment. I just want to unwind, but I would prefer to do it with company."

"Yeah, I get that,"

"It's ok to talk, by the way. One of the IT team came in this afternoon and swept the apartments. They're all clean."

"Well, that's good news, but I still think we need to be careful."

"Sure," said Dee.

Houghton took another sip of wine and looked at her. Her hair was tied back; she was using makeup, but not too much. He could smell her perfume. Her blouse was undone to her cleavage and her wardrobe completed by a pair of beige leggings cropped halfway up her calf.

"So, how was your day?" he asked, and they both started laughing loudly.

"Where do you want me to start? No, don't answer that. I'll get dinner and we can talk while we eat."

She got up, put her glass on the small dining room table and went to the kitchen. "You can sit up, the food's ready," she shouted.

Houghton picked up his glass and sat at the table just as Dee was bringing in the food.

"Barbery rice with chicken," she said as she put down the plates. "It's got pomegranate seeds and all sorts in it according to the concierge. It was his recommendation."

Houghton cut off a piece of chicken. "Mmm, this tastes

really good. I've been living on take-outs from the embassy."

"Pleased you like it." She finished a mouthful of food and looked at Houghton. "I was glad you could come over tonight," Dee whispered as she started eating again. "I could do with some more info about what you need me to do. I feel a bit in the dark and I don't do uncertainty."

"Well as I said this afternoon, my main priority at the moment is the transport. Without it, the plan won't work."

"The ambulance?"

"Yeah. Did you get anywhere, by any chance, with your search?" he whispered back.

"Yes, I've been giving it a lot of thought, and I do know someone whose father owns a garage. I don't know why I didn't think about it earlier."

"Really? And you trust them?"

"Yes, I do, completely, her parents supported the Shah, back in the day. She hates the regime, especially being told what to wear."

"This person, how did you meet her?"

"She has a small shop next to the Bazaar selling tapestries, really beautiful they are. I stopped to look at them one day and we started talking. She went to the University of Tehran and speaks very good English."

"And you approached her. Not the other way around?"

"No, it was completely at random. I know what you're saying, but I really do trust her. We go for coffee quite regularly; I take a long lunch hour. She was quite outspoken at university."

"Hmm, that's not necessarily a good sign. They'll probably have her on a watch list."

"She says not; she's had no contact with the Ministry.

Why don't we meet her for coffee tomorrow together, you can make up your own mind?"

"Yeah, ok, but we'll need to be careful, the embassy and the compound are being watched."

"What?"

"Don't sound so surprised. With the way things have been over the last week or so, most western embassies will be under scrutiny."

"Yes, of course. It's ok, I was being a bit naïve. I don't think like a spy," she said and smiled.

"No, don't worry, but you will need to be vigilant; you could get killed, or worse."

"Worse?"

"There are good deaths and bad deaths."

"Jesus, I'm glad you don't run my advertising campaigns."

They finished eating their food in silence, both locked in their thoughts.

"It's just ice cream for dessert."

"That's great, thanks," said Houghton.

As she went to pick up his plate, he grabbed her arm and pulled her towards him, and they became locked in a deep kiss. They broke away and she looked at him.

"I think we can leave the ice cream for later."

"Yeah, I'm not that hungry," said Houghton as Dee took his hand and led him to the bedroom.

Later, as they relaxed in each other's arms, Dee turned to Houghton. "Can you stay? I'd like you near me tonight."

"Yeah, I'd like that," said Houghton and they kissed. It was against his better judgement, but for now, it felt right.

The Mahabadi Residence – 8:30 p.m.

Afareen kept looking at her watch, hoping the phone would ring. The previous evening's call had been so brief; she needed to talk with her husband again.

Suddenly there was an authoritative thump on the door.

Afareen looked at her mother, who was in her favourite chair watching the TV. "Who's that dear?" she said.

Afareen knew exactly who it would be; she momentarily froze. There was another bang on the door which spurred her into action. She walked towards the front door and looked through the spy-hole. Three uniformed officers.

"Open up, Mrs Mahabadi. Lieutenant Javad Mishdar, Ministry of Intelligence." He held his identity card where she could see.

She opened the door, and the two men with the Lieutenant barged in. Afreen went into the lounge and confronted them.

"Why are you here? What do you want? I have already done what you have asked of me."

The Lieutenant stood square-on in a very authoritative fashion while his two colleagues started looking around. It was deliberately designed to be intimidating.

"Yes, and we are grateful, as we have demonstrated. I understand you were able to speak with your husband last night; but not tonight, I think. Maybe tomorrow, maybe he will spend some time here in Tehran soon, who knows?"

"What do you want?" said Afareen.

"We have a small task we need you to do tomorrow, early, as soon as you can."

"What task?"

The Lieutenant took out the new bug devices and displayed them in the palm of his hand. "Do you know what these are?"

"No," said Afareen. "I do not."

"They are what they call 'bugs'. They enable us to listen to conversation."

"Yes, I have heard of them."

"We need you to put them in the house where you work at the compound, Mr Dexter's, and also in the apartment of Mr Houghton."

"But I do not know Mr Houghton's apartment."

"Then I expect you to find out; it shouldn't be difficult."

"But I don't know what to do."

"I will show you." The officer lifted up the telephone from the table and turned it over.

"It is simple; you just pull off this strip of paper, stick it to the bottom of the telephone and then pull this piece of plastic. That will activate it. Can you do that? It is simple."

"Yes, I think so."

The Lieutenant watched as she practised with a spare device. Her hands were shaking so much she had difficulty in controlling them. "It's ok, take your time," said the officer.

She had another go.

"Yes, that is excellent," he said when she had demonstrated competence.

"Now remember, you must do this as soon as you can tomorrow and you must tell no-one, is that clear? The consequences otherwise will be severe."

"I understand."

"Good, now when we have the devices working, you will be able to speak to your husband again and there could be some news of some leave for him. I understand he has been under a lot of pressure. The rest will do him good."

The officer gave Afareen the two devices and left with his companions. Afareen collapsed onto the settee.

"Are you alright dear?" said her mother.

Chapter Twelve

Hotel Safir, Esfahan – 7:00 p.m.

Commander Fallahian arrived outside the hotel and his car was parked by one of the waiting porters. Before going to register, he walked to the surveillance van and spoke to the occupants. They were expecting him and listened intently to his orders. He handed over two of the new listening devices. Only one was needed this time, but there was a spare just in case.

As soon as the Commander left, one of them telephoned an agent in the Nuclear plant control centre and gave instructions to meet him at the entrance of the installation. He would hand over the listening device for Amadi's office. The surveillance agent picked up his leather jacket, put on his crash helmet and roared off down the exit ramp to the main road.

The Commander checked in and before going to his room, made a call to the General to confirm his arrival. The lobby area was quiet, just a few baggage porters waiting for new arrivals. Fallahian waited until the reception desk was empty and approached the attending assistant. She was smartly dressed in the hotel uniform complete with black headscarf, neatly in place. He showed her his identity card and a look of fear covered her face.

"You have a guest here called Alvarez. What is his room number, please?"

"One moment," said the girl. She checked her system.

"It's number 614."

"Thank you," said the Commander. "Do not speak of this."

"No sir, of course," replied the girl; she breathed a sigh of relief as he walked towards the lift with his luggage.

Meanwhile, Sergeant Daribi was making the long trek from Tehran to Arak. He would be meeting with two other agents ready for the visit to the local Brechtel Headquarters the following day.

Esfahan Nuclear Technology Center – 8:30 p.m.

A man in janitor's overalls swept the corridor outside the main operations control room. He had been polishing the same area for several minutes and it was spotless; not a speck of dust would be found in any inspection.

Every now and then he looked up; he could see the programme director in his office, still working at his desk. He had been told Doctor Amadi was a workaholic; it appeared to be a correct assessment.

Finally, at just after eight forty-five, he noticed movement. The janitor picked up the wastepaper bin and walked to the door just as Doctor Amadi opened it.

"You're not allowed in there," barked Amadi.

"But I have to; it's my job. Don't worry, I will lock the door when I leave."

The cleaner held up a set of keys for Amadi to see. "I won't be long," he added.

Doctor Amadi had been working since six a.m. and was past caring.

"Very well, but make sure it is locked," he muttered and walked down the corridor to the exit.

The janitor walked into the room, picked up the telephone and applied the listening device to the underside, then emptied the bin.

Ten minutes later, he too was walking towards the exit with a mobile phone pressed to his ear. The centre had its own telecommunications mast and the signal was good.

"Commander Fallahian? It is done."

Gholhak Garden Compound – Thursday April 20th – 7:30 a.m.

Houghton walked along the corridor from Dee's apartment to his; he would just have time for a shower and change before meeting up again in reception for the minibus ride to the embassy. His mind was now firmly tuned to his task, refreshed from the welcome distraction.

Elsewhere in the compound, Afareen was walking through the gardens to the Dexters' residence, filled with dread at the task she had been given by the secret police. The warning about telling anyone was ringing in her head. She was fearful for her safety and that of her children; it had kept her awake most of the night, but she had concluded that she was making the right decision. She trusted the Dexters.

Sophie Dexter saw her coming up the path and opened the door before Afareen had chance to knock.

"Hello Afareen, how are you today?"

"Is Mr Dexter here?"

"Yes, let me get him, he's in the bedroom," said Sophie, sensing Afareen's distress.

David Dexter came into the living quarters.

"Morning Afareen. Everything ok?"

"The secret police came again last night," she said, her

voice cracking slightly as she struggled to stay composed.

Dexter looked concerned. "Do you want to come into the other room?"

"No, it is not necessary, they told me their listening things, they do not work."

Dexter smiled at the irony.

Afareen described the police visit and her mission. She showed Dexter the new devices. He picked one of them up and looked at it expertly.

"Hmm, Chinese, about four years old, not that good, but it will do the job. Don't worry, Afareen, it's fine. In fact, it could be helpful. Hopefully, they will let you speak to your husband again and allow him to visit. I'll let Mr Houghton know and you can go there later. Here, let me do it for you."

Dexter picked up the telephone and fixed the device to the underside, then put his fingers to his lips and mouthed "Shh."

Hotel Safir, Esfahan – 9:00 a.m.

Commander Fallahian was having his breakfast in the hotel restaurant and saw CIA agent Tony Alvarez walk in. He was dressed in a suit with an open-necked shirt and looked ready for a business meeting. The Commander was pretending to read a newspaper while keeping a close eye on the new arrival. The restaurant was busy with only a few tables vacant, mostly businessmen with meetings at the various industrial establishments.

At seven twenty-five, the Commander noticed Alvarez walk towards the restaurant exit. He would also leave, but not to follow his quarry; he knew where he was going. He joined his fellow agents in the surveillance van, although there wasn't a great deal of room. There were three others; the motorcyclist, dressed in his leathers; the driver, who was carrying a camera with a telephoto lens; and a third, who was in the back sat in front of some fairly ancient electronic equipment wearing a pair of headphones. The Commander got into the passenger seat, put on a pair of sunglasses and briefed the team.

"We'll wait for the American; he will be here soon. Hashemi, you follow him. We'll leave after he has gone; we do not want him to see us. We'll meet you at Shahrida." This was the site of the main control centre for the complex where Amadi was based.

Alvarez collected his car from outside the hotel just before seven-forty, prompting activity in the surveillance vehicle. Agent Hashemi exited via the rear door and started up his bike. Within moments, he was a few car lengths behind Alverez's Mercedes, safely out of sight of the rear-view mirror.

The surveillance van followed with the Commander directing operations from the passenger seat.

As he approached, Alvarez could see the scale of the complex. In the dark, it had been difficult to get a clear picture. As a piece of engineering, it was impressive. There was more evidence of high-security levels and he could see the missile launchers and their operatives in a state of readiness.

He reached the facility entrance and waited behind a truck which was being investigated by several uniformed men. He felt anxious and kept checking his watch; eight-sixteen. He did not want to be late for his appointment. He would not get another opportunity; he was sure of that.

The truck moved on and he was called forward. One of the guards approached the driver's side window; he was carrying a clipboard and spoke in Farsi.

"Identity," he ordered. Alvarez handed over his passport and the guard disappeared into the adjacent building.

"Come on, come on," whispered Alvarez to himself as the time ticked on. He realised he hadn't factored in the security check when he left the hotel and cursed himself for his stupidity.

Then the guard reappeared. He returned the passport and handed Alvarez his pass, then pointed to the building he would need. Alvarez pulled away and followed the directions.

The guard went back into the perimeter control centre and made a phone call. The Commander in the surveillance vehicle picked up the call. A few moments later, the van arrived at the gate. The barrier was raised, and it was immediately waved through. The guard saluted.

Alvarez found the car park and checked his watch, eight twenty-six. He got out and walked briskly towards the main reception area. He could feel the sweat dripping down his temple into his eyes. His shirt was sticking to his body under his suit jacket.

He reached the reception desk, took off his sunglasses and wiped his face with his handkerchief.

"Can I help you," said the receptionist in English.

He gave her his passport. "Doctor Alvarez, for Doctor Amadi. I have an appointment."

She checked her manifest and picked up her phone.

Alvarez took a moment to compose himself; he looked around. The entrance area was impressive; it was bright with large picture windows and gave an excellent impression to any visitor; it was also air-conditioned. Several people, some wearing white coats, were milling about. Around the perimeter, there were room dividers with aerial pictures of the facility pinned to them. All the signs were in English.

"Doctor Amadi is expecting you. He's on the first floor. Can you sign in?" she said and pointed to the next space on the register. "You will need to sign out and return your pass when you leave."

She watched while Alvarez signed. "Take a seat over there and someone will come down and meet you."

The receptionist pointed to a waiting area to the right of the desk. There were four ancient-looking leather chairs against the wall with a coffee table in front. Pamphlets and magazines in Farsi and English were scattered on the table for the interested visitor. Alvarez wasn't interested; he was concentrating on his cover story.

Five minutes later, Alvarez spotted a young man walking down the stairs. He was in his late twenties and wearing a white coat. He turned and headed toward Alvarez. Alvarez stood up.

"Doctor Alvarez? I am Doctor Mir Sasani, Doctor Amadi's assistant. Would you like to follow me, please?" He spoke in English.

Alvarez complied and followed the assistant up the stairs. He took in his surroundings; to any outsider, this was an impressive place. The first floor mirrored the reception area in its cleanliness; he noticed a male cleaner polishing the handrails. Alvarez thought he felt his gaze following him along the corridor, but he could have been mistaken.

They passed several offices on the right; to the left were

picture windows with extensive views across the complex. The industrial landscape of stove-like chimneys, huge spherical containers and pipes of all shapes and sizes gave way to the sight of mountains in the distance.

They reached a door with a nameplate attached. 'Doctor Saleh Amadi Aziz Al Rajhi, MA, PhD, C.Eng. Project Director.'

The assistant knocked and waited for the reply.

"Come in," came a voice from within, again in English.

The assistant opened the door for Alvarez and stood to one side, closing it behind Alvarez and leaving the two men alone.

The room was large but functional; there was a desk with a computer monitor to the right and a white phone to the left; in the middle, a blotter and pen set. There were two chairs in front of the desk.

Amadi got up to greet his guest.

"Doctor Alvarez? Doctor Amadi, please, have a seat."

He spoke English, which was interesting; he had spoken in Farsi on the telephone. He ushered Alvarez to the seats in front of the desk; Alvarez sat down and looked at the man. He was not what he was expecting. About five feet, ten inches tall, late forties, greying hair, thinning; he looked weary, care-worn and his grey suit jacket was hanging to his frame, as though he had lost a lot of weight and not visited a tailor for a while.

"You wanted my opinion on a construction matter, I understand. You speak English, I presume?"

"Yes, English is fine. My Farsi is not perfect."

"No, I detected that," replied Amadi.

Outside, the surveillance van was parked in the same car park as the Mercedes but closer to the building. The headphone agent had switched to speaker mode so the Commander could also listen. They had heard the greeting loud and clear. The Commander was taking notes; the General would want a detailed report.

"I appreciate your time, I know you are a busy man, thank you for seeing me."

"I was a little intrigued. You work for Brechtel, you mentioned… in Arak."

"Yes," replied Alvarez.

"Well, I have to admit some surprise at this call, with the resources Brechtel has at its disposal, I would have thought they were well-placed to answer your drainage issue."

Alvarez was on the back foot.

"Yeah, I guess, but, you know, it's always good to meet another professional and exchange ideas. Outside the box thinking, I think they call it."

"Hmm," said Amadi in a non-committal way.

"Well, I'll come straight to the point. The complex we're working on used to be a factory. The drainage is a real pain in the ass. I've had to halt the project until I can find a solution, which is when one of my assistants suggested I contact you."

"Yes, you mentioned; what was his name again?"

Alvarez had to think quickly trying to remember the name he had used previously. "Er… Maher… El-Beheiry." He hoped the uncertainty wouldn't be obvious.

"Hmm, as I said, I cannot recall that name. It sounds Egyptian."

"Yeah," said Alvarez.

In the surveillance van, the Commander was writing furiously; he circled the man's name.

Inside the complex, the conversation continued.

"Have you taken drainage surveys?"

"Yeah, pretty much."

"And drilled bore-holes."

"Yeah, the usual."

"In which case, you should be able to resolve the problem. I'm not sure what else I can tell you."

"Yeah, ok, that's great. That's been helpful."

"Was that it? It seems a long way to come for that information. It's basic construction protocols. We could have dealt with it over the telephone."

"That's ok, no sweat. Brechtel's picking up the tab; they can afford it. I wanted to meet you in person, put a face to a name, you know, do some networking."

Amadi looked confused and was about to say something when Alvarez continued.

"There was something else before I go. Have you considered a career change? Maybe moving to somewhere else – outside Iran perhaps?"

Alvarez had tossed the metaphorical grenade into the room and waited for the explosion.

"Career change? What are you saying? What are you talking about? Of course not, I am committed here."

"It's ok, I've heard you might want to move away."

"Move away? Whoever told you that?"

Alvarez was feeling uncomfortable; he had not got the reaction he was hoping for. He was going to have to expand the conversation.

"Well, I've got a friend; he's British, works in Tehran. He told me you were looking for a new vocation."

"British? I don't know any British people. I have no idea where you got this information."

The penny was beginning to drop. Alvarez suddenly felt uneasy; something wasn't right. Perspiration was dripping down his face again, despite the air conditioning.

"Wait. You're American? You are, aren't you? Why are you here? You could get me killed just for speaking to you. No, no, I told you people I wasn't interested two years ago. Now leave before I call security. Go on... get out!"

Alvarez stood up and went to the door. "You're making a big mistake. We can get you and your family away, get you to the States, nice house, schools for the kids, great salary."

"Get out," said Amadi and he picked up his phone as if to dial.

"Ok, ok, I get it. I'm out of here."

Alvarez was worried; he was beginning to wonder if he had been set up. But by the British? That didn't make any sense. He quickened his steps and descended the stairs two at a time. He wouldn't be signing out; he needed to get away.

He almost sprinted to his car. He didn't look around; if he had, he would have seen Amadi watching him from an upstairs window. The Egyptian, too, was very concerned. He turned and headed to the men's room.

Alvarez started the Mercedes and swung it around, causing dirt and grit to fly from its wheels as it picked up speed. He reached the long straight road to the perimeter exit about three-hundred yards away. Guards were everywhere. His mind was mush, so many thoughts running through his head. Had Amadi called security? If he had, he was in big trouble.

He pulled up at the exit gate behind a truck. To the left, he could see the security control centre with two armed guards stood outside; one was smoking, seemingly taking a break. For Alvarez, eyes seemed to be everywhere. Three more guards were checking the lorry. He tapped his steering wheel.

It moved on and he was waved forward. Sweat poured down his face. He wiped it away, put on his sunglasses and edged toward the barrier. He activated the window control. A guard moved closer and spoke in Farsi. Alvarez could smell stale garlic on his breath.

"Papers," barked the man.

Alvarez handed over his site-pass and passport.

"Pass, you hand in at reception." He pointed back to where Alvarez had come from.

Just then another truck arrived and parked close behind the Mercedes, blocking his path backwards.

Alvarez turned his hands over in a gesture of helplessness. "I cannot move."

The guard uttered a curse in Farsi. "Give it to me," he ordered. Then handed back Alvarez's passport.

The guard waved to the person operating the barrier and it slowly raised. Alvarez watched in frustration; it wasn't moving quickly enough.

As soon as it was past the height of the Mercedes, Alvarez accelerated away.

He continued towards town, going over the conversation in his head. It didn't make any sense; he'd given Amadi the chance that he allegedly wanted. Why had he turned it down? He seemed genuinely surprised at the suggestion – horrified even. Amadi's fear of the secret police was still very much alive. But why had he contacted the British?

His thoughts turned to his immediate situation. He could be in grave danger if Amadi had reported the approach to the authorities, and there was a strong possibility he would do that just to cover himself. As he headed back towards Esfahan city, Alvarez was considering his options. The sweat started to roll down his forehead again and into his eyes; he blinked at the stinging moisture. He took out his handkerchief, removed his sunglasses and wiped his face. He had to get as far away from Esfahan as possible; back to Arak would be the safest bet; he needed to stay well away from Tehran.

He cursed his stupidity. He'd hidden his laptop under the bed in his hotel room, which meant he would need to return to collect it; he hadn't considered this outcome. He could have managed without his clothes, but not his laptop. He also needed to call Podesta and let him know what had happened.

The surveillance van was also heading out of the site and, again, it was waved through by the guard who saluted the departure. The Commander was calling the General as they drove back into Esfahan. In front of them, the motorcyclist was keeping pace with the Mercedes.

Alvarez reached the hotel and parked outside the front entrance. As usual, one of the porters approached him to park it in the underground lot.

"No, it's ok; I'm leaving in a minute," said Alvarez.

The porter walked away, looking crestfallen at having

missed the opportunity to drive such a prestigious car and receiving the possible tip that followed.

Reception was quiet; there was no-one on duty. Alvarez walked past the desk and along the corridor to the lifts. All three elevator cars were on higher floors. He pressed the call button; for a moment, there was no response.

"Come on, come on," he whispered to himself and started pacing up and down.

The third lift started to descend but then stopped on floor four. Alvarez wiped his face again. It was taking too long.

In reception, the desk-clerk had seen Alvarez walk through the atrium from the security window in the back office. She picked up her phone and dialled.

"Sir, I thought you should know that room 614 has returned."

The line was crackly. "Repeat, please."

The receptionist repeated.

"Is he leaving?"

"I don't know; he has just gone to his room, I think," said the receptionist.

"If he comes back down, keep him there; we will be with you very soon."

The surveillance van had been delayed in traffic but was now only three minutes away from the hotel. On their way back, the Commander had apprised the General of events. The biker was waiting next to the line of taxis outside the hotel but, without communication, he had no orders; he would just wait for the Commander to arrive.

Upstairs on the sixth floor, Alvarez changed into fresh clothes, bundled up his dirty washing and toiletries, then threw them into his suitcase and locked it. He retrieved the laptop from under the bed and put it in the briefcase, took one last look around and left. He walked down the carpeted corridor to the lift and passed the housekeeper with her trolley of cleaning equipment and toiletries. He made no acknowledgement; she could be an informer. He reached the lift and pressed the call button.

All three lifts were on the ground floor. The middle one slowly climbed but stopped on the second floor. Alvarez punched the call button again.

"Fucking come on," he shouted.

He looked down the corridor at the cleaning lady; she was staring at him.

The lift arrived, and the doors slowly opened. Another cleaning operative was standing there with a large trolley.

"Floor seven," she said in Farsi.

There was not much room in the elevator, so he decided to wait while the lift continued its upward journey. He pressed the call button again. He would catch it on the way down.

It seemed to take an inordinate amount of time, but a minute later, Alvarez was on the ground floor and about to head for the exit. He wasn't going to waste time checking out; the hotel had his credit card details.

He was halfway across the reception area when the desk clerk spotted him heading for the exit.

She shouted. "Sir, Doctor Alvarez, are you leaving? Your account, sir."

"Just putting these in the car," he shouted back.

Moments earlier, the surveillance van had arrived at the hotel. Agent Hashemi was waiting for them and joined the others in the vehicle. There was a great deal of activity.

"You, and you, come with me. We are going to arrest the American. You, stay here and listen for any messages."

The driver and Agent Hashemi, who was still in his leathers, followed the Commander to the hotel. All three were wearing side-arms. The Commander took off his sunglasses and spotted Alvarez approaching the door, pulling his suitcase along with one hand and carrying his briefcase in the other. Alvarez hadn't seen the men, having been distracted by the receptionist. He was starting to feel really anxious now; he needed to get away.

As he approached the exit, the doors opened automatically. Just as Alvarez was about to walk through, the Commander stepped in front of him.

"Doctor Alvarez?" said the officer. He spoke in English.

Alvarez began to panic; the two other agents were now behind him. He had nowhere to go.

"What's this all about? Move please, I am late for an appointment."

"Then, you will be even later," said the officer. "I am Commander Fallahian, Ministry of Intelligence. I need you to come with us. I will take that."

Fallahian seized Alvarez's briefcase, then spoke to the other agent who grabbed Alvarez's suitcase.

Before he could move, Agent Hashemi had taken out a pair of handcuffs and secured Alvarez's wrists.

"What is this? You can't do this; I have important work to do here."

"Yes, I'm sure you have, you can tell me all about it. Car keys?"

"In my pocket," said Alvarez and the Commander took them out and gave them to Hashemi. He also found Alvarez's passport and took it.

The Commander directed Alvarez toward the van. Alvarez walked slowly, trying to work out a plan. He couldn't see a way out.

The driver opened the door and pushed Alvarez into the back, behind the front seats. Hashemi produced a canvas bag and put it over Alvarez's head.

Alvarez was a trained and skilled field agent, but no amount of simulation could have replicated the fear he was feeling now. He wanted to be sick and was in danger of losing control of his bowels, but just about managed to hold himself together. Meanwhile, the driver and the comms agent were struggling with Hashemi to push his motorcycle into the back of the van next to the electrical equipment. Alvarez's two bags were alongside.

They managed the manoeuvre and Hashemi walked towards the Mercedes. In the van, there was a smell of petrol from the motorcycle. Ahead, was a five-hour journey.

British Embassy, Tehran – 9:30 a.m.

Houghton was in his office, having finished his breakfast in the embassy canteen and caught up with his emails. He had also called Andy Fellows and given him an update. Mother was apparently happy with the progress.

He had arranged to meet Dee at ten-thirty for a discussion on the plan he was putting together; she was now part of the team.

There was a knock on the door and Dexter walked in.

"Nick, I've got some news. Afareen's had another visit from our friends at the Ministry."

"Shit!" said Houghton. "We could do without them on

our case."

"Well, it might not be as bad as you think."

Houghton explained about the bug planting. "It seems that they've not been able to hear a thing."

"Ha, now that is ironic," said Houghton.

"Yes, you can say that again. If we'd known that, it would have saved many an unscheduled visit to the bathroom."

"Well, they won't find my apartment very interesting. I hope they like my taste in TV."

"Yes, we can bore them into complacency. But, this is the really good news, they've promised her a call from Mahabadi, and some leave for him if she completes her mission."

"Hmm, now that's interesting. Did they say when the leave would be?"

"Possibly next week," said Dexter.

"Ok, that's great," said Houghton pensively. "I think we can go with that. I've got to sort out some transport, but Dee says she has a contact."

There was a knock on the door and Dee walked in carrying three paper cups of coffee in a plastic receptacle.

"I thought I would find you here, David, saves me an extra trip. Do you mind if I join you? I've got some news."

"Of course, take a seat, what have you got?" said Houghton.

She handed out the drinks.

"Just came through on CNN; Iran has just formally announced the tie-up with Russia with this enrichment deal. Details are a bit sketchy at the moment, but they say the development will be in Russia somewhere."

"Yeah, that figures," said Dexter.

It went quiet while they were trying to work out the consequences. It was Dexter who made the first comment.

"Well, as I see it, politically, it's a really clever move by the Iranians; it means they will now be linked with Russia, so that definitely rules out any airstrikes or military action. Come to think of it, it won't help Condoleezza Rice's sanctions motion at the UN either. What's the American's response, do we know?"

"Ha, they're going ape-shit, as you can imagine," said Dee. "Traffic at Langley's been non-stop, and the White House doesn't really know how to respond. If they go in too hard, it will upset the Russians; too soft and they will lose authority. They are between a rock and a hard place."

"What about our project?" said Houghton.

"Well, my assessment is, it will have a neutral effect. Security levels have already been relaxed, so the nuclear facilities are out of lock-down, but they are still on high alert," said Dee.

"Any news from MOIS?"

"Not really, although there has been a lot of chatter between Tehran and Esfahan, possibly about the military threat."

"Hmm, ok, thanks for the heads-up," said Dexter. "I'll leave you two to it. Nick, you can bring Dee up-to-date with the surveillance situation."

He got up and left the room.

"What's this about the surveillance?" said Dee.

Houghton explained Afareen's mission and the fallibility of the MOIS's listening devices. "Hmm, after all that, I could have been much louder," said Dee and started to laugh. Houghton smiled.

"So, are we still ok to meet your contact today?"

"Yes, I called her a few minutes ago and I've said we'll meet her at her shop about one o'clock. The Bazaar will be heaving by then."

"I'll let David know; he'll sign us both out, save having to go via reception. We need to think about how we're going to get out without being spotted. MOIS is all over this place. There are at least two surveillance vehicles outside."

"Really?"

"Yeah, leave it with me, I'll speak to transport, see if we can get a car. But we need to be careful, one of the drivers is a MOIS agent."

"What? Which one?"

"Taherian."

"Oh, yes, I know the one you mean, a right creepy bastard. You can feel his eyes all over you, urgh." Dee shivered.

"Ok, I'll go and speak to them when we've finished. Can we meet in reception about twelve-fifteen?

"Yeah, ok, no problem."

Just after mid-day, Houghton changed into his casual gear and walked up to reception. Dee was waiting, dressed in black trousers, black long-sleeved cardigan and a light-grey scarf which was draped over her head and down to her waist.

"You look good," said Houghton.

"Thanks, you too," said Dee.

"Some good news, Taherian is not in today. Kazem will drive; he's reliable. We won't be going far anyway, just to the Metro stop."

"Is that all? We could walk."

"No, we'd be spotted straight away. We'll get in the back and lie flat. It's ok; I've done it before; the driver knows what to do."

The pair went outside where one of the staff cars was waiting. Kazem Younesi, head of the carpool, was driving and he opened the back door for them to get in. Houghton had also briefed the security gate and as the car approached, the barrier raised, and the front gate opened. Houghton and Dee were lay flat on the back seat, out of sight from any prying eyes.

"You didn't say we would be in this position again," said Dee and smiled.

"Stay focused," said Houghton.

"Copy that," whispered Dee.

The car pulled up outside the Metro stop, and Houghton opened the door and quickly got out, Dee followed. The car pulled away.

"Down here," said Houghton, and they hurried down the stairs into the Sa'adi Metro station. When they reached the platform, Houghton walked along to the ticket machine.

"Follow me, I'm going to give you a lesson in anti-surveillance techniques… Quick, behind the ticket machine," said Houghton, and Dee joined him out of sight from the other passengers.

An elderly woman, holding the hand of a five-year-old boy, walked up to the machine and fed in some coins, then collected her ticket. She took little notice of the pair against the wall and walked back along the platform to wait for the next train.

Moments later, the train pulled in, and the waiting passengers got on. Dee went to approach the train.

"No, wait," whispered Houghton and Dee stopped.

The train left. "What's happening?" whispered Dee.

"Take a look," said Houghton.

Dee peered around the ticket machine. "There's no-one there."

"Exactly, everyone has got on, which means we have no-one tailing us."

"Ah, yes, I get it. How many trains do we have to wait for?"

"We'll get the next one; it will be fine, but we'll stay here until it arrives to be on the safe side."

It was another ten minutes before the next train arrived. Just as the doors were about to close, they jumped on board and found a seat.

Chapter Thirteen

Houghton and Dee left the Metro at Panzdah-e-Khordad station and headed for the Grand Bazaar.

He was starting to recognise landmarks automatically now; the route becoming more familiar. As he walked, he was silently going over his to-do list. As soon as they knew the dates of Mahabadi's leave, he would need another meeting with Mayflower. She would have a big part to play in the success of the project.

"It's down here," said Dee as she crossed over the road and entered one of the many openings that seemed to disappear into the Bazaar.

Houghton was keeping close to Dee to give the appearance of tourists, but they refrained from holding hands. Although some couples were doing so, it was generally frowned upon, and Houghton did not want to do anything that would draw attention to them.

After negotiating various alleyways, they eventually arrived at the tapestry shop. Houghton noticed a woman taking down display items from outside the shop. She had her back to the couple.

Dee walked up to the woman. "Hi Leila."

Leila turned around and smiled warmly. "Hello, Dee, I won't be a minute, just getting these rugs inside."

Houghton assessed the woman's appearance; mid to late-thirties, dark hair, olive skin, striking eyes, carefully made up. She was wearing calf-length pinkish-white trousers with turn-ups, white deck-shoes, white V-neck blouse with a light-weight pink jacket and matching scarf. She was a picture of elegance; a woman who could easily have inspired a song.

"Come in," she said as she took down the last of the rugs.

Inside, there was a distinct 'new carpet' smell. Houghton looked around the walls which were covered in the most exquisite Persian rugs.

"Wow," said Houghton. "This is amazing."

"Thank you," said Leila. "They are all hand-made from Qom, many hours work. I only buy the best. They are nearly all silk, but those over there, are wool. I choose only the best-grade highland wool from the Zagros Mountains." The name meant nothing to Houghton, but it sounded impressive.

"They really are beautiful," said Houghton.

"I can ship them to the UK. They start around five hundred dollars; the larger ones, two, three thousand. That one, ten thousand," she said, pointing at a striking piece that covered most of the side wall.

Houghton could see she wasn't joking and was tempted to buy one, but he needed to complete his mission before considering any retail purchases.

"I'll certainly bear that in mind," said Houghton.

Dee was also looking around. Leila went into the back room and returned carrying a handbag.

"Ok, we can go to a place I know; it is quite safe."

The three left the emporium and Leila locked the door.

"Down here," she said and walked down an adjacent lane. It was narrow with grey pitted concrete. The whole bazaar felt like one giant maze; it would be easy for the unfamiliar to get totally lost. There were shops on either side with owners outside trying to entice trade. After a few minutes, Houghton could see they were approaching a café on the left-hand side. There was a wrought-iron sign of a black metal kettle hanging over the entrance.

"Here," said Leila and she pushed open the door. It was small, with probably only twenty or so seats downstairs. It had dark grey wooden flooring with matching tables and chairs. A man was standing by a till in front of a serving hatch. The kitchen was visible, and two people were preparing food.

Leila spoke to the man in Farsi.

Houghton looked around. There were about a dozen customers seated at tables engrossed in conversation; none were taking any interest in the new arrivals.

In the corner, there was a flight of narrow wooden stairs. Leila led the way. The stairs creaked under their weight. Upstairs, the decor replicated the minimalism of the ground floor but with a few more settings.

It was empty, and they made themselves comfortable on a table at the far end next to a window which over-looked the alleyway. Houghton looked down and could see one or two people walk by, but it was nowhere near as busy as the main malls. A dog trotted past and cocked its leg against a parked bicycle. It did its business and continued to wherever it was going.

They made themselves comfortable with the two women sitting together and Houghton opposite. The proprietor trudged up the stairs, his footsteps echoing across the room. Leila addressed him in Farsi, and he took their orders. As it was lunchtime, the three ordered some food to go with their coffees.

Leila looked at Houghton. "Dee tells me you need my

help."

"Yes, but I must warn you now, it could be dangerous; so, I understand if you don't want to be involved."

"No, it is ok, I understand. What do I need to do?"

"Dee says you may be able to get us some transport, a van. I understand your father has a garage?"

"Yes, for many years. It could be possible. What kind do you want?"

Houghton shuffled, he needed to give more information than he would have really liked.

"Ideally, I need an ambulance, or at least something that we could make look like an ambulance."

"An ambulance?"

"Ideally, but if not, as I said, something that we can make look like one. I can't go into details, but it's very important, and I must ask you to be discreet; it could cost lives."

Leila looked at Houghton, her expression reflected the seriousness of the situation.

"It is ok, I understand, and you can trust us."

She looked around; there was no one in earshot, the floor was still empty.

"Let me tell you something." She looked down at her fingers in reflection. "My parents suffered a great deal after the Shah was deposed; my father was a supporter and a prominent businessman. We had a large house in the country. I was only very young, but I still remember it now. One night, a mob turned up; my mother was screaming; my baby brother, he was crying. They had guns and forced us onto a bus. There were others on the bus too, I can still remember their faces... frightened... terrified. My mother told me afterwards they thought we were going to be shot. We were taken into the city and put in a squalid apartment. We had lost everything; later we heard that the house was looted and set on fire. My father, when he left school, trained as a mechanic and he managed to build up a large motor business from nothing; but, of course, that was all taken away from him. So, he started again, mending cars in a back street for just a few dollars. Now we are ok. Business is good and my parents have a good living, but they still resent how all their hard work was taken away from them."

"I can't imagine what it must have been like," said Dee. Leila looked at her then at Houghton.

"It was difficult, but I studied hard and I was able to go to university to learn about business and management. I met many students there who were opposed to the government, but there were informers there also; they were paid by the secret police, so, we had to be very careful who we trusted. I still have some of those friends, but we never talk about politics. When I left university, my father gave me some money and I started my own tapestry business; that was ten years ago. I have been lucky; it has been very successful."

"What about the police?" asked Houghton.

"We have not been troubled by the police; we keep ourselves to ourselves. But I hate this regime and I could get hanged for just saying that, you know."

Dee looked at Houghton with an expression of concern. Leila shrugged her shoulders.

"The police are just thugs and psychopaths. I am smarter than most of them." She smiled.

"Well, I'm glad that Dee has introduced us," said Houghton.

Leila looked at Dee. "Yes, Dee has been a special friend."

The echoing footsteps of the proprietor returned, and he walked over to them carrying a tray with their order, then left.

"He is the owner here; he's also been kind. He is a friend of my father. You will always be safe here; the police don't come," said Leila.

"That's good to know," said Houghton as they started eating.

"When do you need the ambulance?" asked Leila.

"Soon, possibly next week. I'll have to let you know," said Houghton.

"Hmm, that doesn't give us much time. I will speak to my father tonight."

"Thanks. Oh, just one thing, if you're talking to your father, please don't use phones. The police could be listening."

"Do not worry, we are used to it; we know how to communicate."

"Yes, I'm sorry, of course, just habit; oh, and don't worry about cost. I'll pay whatever's necessary; I can pay in dollars if you prefer, just let me know. The most important thing is it must be reliable, please tell him."

"Of course. How should I contact you?"

"You have Dee's number?"

"Yes."

"Ok, it should be fine; use that." He paused momentarily, working out the best way to proceed. "If you can get the vehicle, just say the tapestry has arrived or will arrive. If there's a problem, say that it's been delayed and say a date when you think your father can get it. Oh, and let me know the cost, I'll bring the money when we collect it. How does that sound?"

"Yes, ok. I will visit my father tonight and let you know."

"Good. When everything is ready, we can meet here again, and I'll make arrangements to collect it."

The three finished their lunch and went their separate ways. Leila gave Dee and Houghton directions out of the maze of alleyways and back to the Metro station. Houghton was taking no chances and observed the same routine as before. Dexter had arranged for a car to be waiting for them outside Sa'adi station; the surveillance team had not noticed anything amiss.

Gholhak Garden Compound – 12:30 p.m.

It was lunchtime, and Afareen was considering the next stage of her mission. With Dexter's reassurance, she was feeling more confident, but she still needed to access Houghton's apartment without raising any suspicion.

She left the Dexters' chalet and made her way to the main building. She walked through reception and up the flight of stairs to the first floor. The concierge was at lunch, and one of the cleaning staff was vacuuming around the desk. She noticed Afareen go by but thought nothing of her visit.

Afareen walked along the corridor and noticed a cleaning trolley positioned outside Houghton's neighbour's apartment. The cleaner was inside washing down the shower and Afareen attracted her attention.

"I need to get in this room; can you let me in, please?" she pointed towards Houghton's apartment.

The cleaner left her work; Afareen was waiting anxiously.

"Why do you need to go in?" asked the cleaner.

Afareen looked at her sternly. "Police business, say

nothing, ok?"

The cleaner opened the door for Afareen and went back to her duties; she was curious about Afareen's task but knew better than to say anything.

The rest was straightforward. Afareen attached the bug to the bottom of the phone and left.

She returned to the chalet and took a breather, then took out her MOIS phone and dialled. It was a different voice; the Commander was away, she was told.

She spoke hesitantly. "I have done what you asked. When can I see my husband?"

"When I have had confirmation that the devices are working, I will speak with the Commander. We will contact you when we need you again."

MOIS Headquarters – 15:33 p.m.

The van containing the Commander and the surveillance team pulled into the Secret Police headquarters at just after three-thirty. It had been a gruelling journey, not least for their terrified passenger. Alvarez felt the vehicle stop and the engine shut down. They had reached their destination, and, despite being hooded for the journey, he had a pretty good idea where he was.

There had been one stop on the way, around eleven-thirty, when Alvarez was desperate to relieve himself. Under the circumstances, it had taken a significant effort to last that long.

Eventually, the Commander acceded to his complaints and the van pulled off the road; they were miles from anywhere. Alvarez was considering some sort of escape plan in his mind. He was confident in his fitness and speed of thought; if he was given an opportunity to get away, he would take it.

As it happened, he was disappointed. After he was bundled out of the van, he prepared himself mentally for the moment his hood was removed, and his handcuffs unlocked. Instead, he felt fingers pulling at his zip and then manipulating his penis from its confines. He could feel fresh air around his nether regions.

"Ok, you pee," said the Commander.

Alvarez had no choice but to suffer the indignity and humiliation. Whoever was conducting the exercise even gave it a shake after Alvarez had finished, much to the amusement of the watching officers.

His trousers were unceremoniously zipped back up, and for a moment Alvarez thought he was going to be shot. Instead, he was bundled back into the van and it pulled away. The whole exercise had been incredibly traumatic for Alvarez; he felt vulnerable and very much alone.

When they arrived at their final destination, Alvarez was frog-marched into the building and his hood removed. The sudden light caused him to blink. His stomach growled; he'd had no food since breakfast, but that was the least of his worries. His eyes became accustomed to the light, and he looked around the austere surroundings. The building seemed to have been designed to create the maximum amount of fear. No soft furnishings or fine art; just drab walls and Iranian flags, with slogans in Farsi which Alvarez couldn't read.

He was still handcuffed and accompanied by armed guards on either side. The Commander led them down a flight of stairs to the basement. It was the same journey that Afareen had made a few days earlier.

They reached the basement corridor and the nauseating smell of cigarettes and sweat was overpowering. They passed several doors; Alvarez could hear noises, then a high-pitched scream; a blood-curdling scream, a scream indicating incredible pain. He couldn't precisely pinpoint its origin, but he could feel the sweat dripping down his temple and into his eyes again.

They reached the end of the corridor, and one of the guards opened the door. It was a bare room with just a heavy metal table in the middle which had been crudely bolted to the floor. There were two chairs on one side and one opposite. Two manacles about eighteen inches apart were set in the table. The lighting was one neon strip which was blinking intermittently.

The Commander ordered Alvarez inside.

"Sit there." He pointed at the solitary chair.

Alvarez complied. His handcuffs were removed, but before he could massage some circulation back to his wrists and hands, they were secured to the table. One of the guards locked the shackles.

"I will return," said the Commander and he walked out, leaving the two guards standing either side of the room.

The Commander walked down the corridor and up two flights of stairs to the General's headquarters. A large suite comprising of his office and a small admin area that was overseen by an adjutant. The Commander walked in and spoke to the officer situated at the desk just outside the General's room. The officer picked up a phone and tapped in two numbers. The Commander waited.

"Please go in; the General is expecting you," said the adjutant.

The Commander walked in and was confronted by a thick fog of cigarette smoke.

"Ah, Commander Fallahian, come in; you have apprehended the American, yes?"

"Yes sir, he is in the interview room."

"Good, good, and how does he appear?"

"He has not spoken, apart from complaining about wanting to piss."

"Yes, that is to be expected. Would you like a coffee after your journey?"

"Thank you sir."

The General picked up his phone and ordered two coffees.

"Do you want to speak to the American, General?" asked the Commander.

"Most definitely, but we will wait, thirty minutes at least. I find that fear is a powerful ingredient in interrogation," said the General. "You have his papers?"

"Yes sir," said the Commander and handed over Alvarez's passport. The General flicked through the pages, then looked at the front.

"Mexican? What is a Mexican doing working for the CIA?"

"It's probably a cover," said the Commander.

"Of course it's a cover, Americans are not allowed to work here. What's the news from Arak, did you get the personnel records?"

"Yes General, they have them, they are due to arrive here in about an hour, maybe two."

"Good, good, we must find out if there are any more

foreign agents working over there; we have been very careless. It must not happen again."

"No sir," said the Commander, just as the adjutant entered the room with two coffees.

The General lit up another cigarette.

For Alvarez, the General's strategy was proving correct. The delay merely increased his anxiety. More screams could be heard; the whole building seemed to be consumed with pain. Gradually, his anxiety was replaced by fatigue; he felt overcome with tiredness. His eyelids dropped and he could feel himself starting to drift off to sleep.

He was just in the zone between wake and sleep when he was abruptly disturbed by the opening of the door; not a gentle opening but a deliberate barge-in to make a statement.

Alvarez jumped; adrenaline coursed through his body, alerting his senses. He had been schooled in the art of withstanding interrogation, but it was not possible to replicate 'real-life' scenarios or predict how individuals would react in such situations, however good the instruction was.

The two officers sat down and faced Alvarez, who was desperately trying to look calm.

The senior officer introduced himself, speaking in English.

"Mr Alvarez?"

"It's Doctor Alvarez," corrected the American.

The General deliberately scanned each page of Alvarez's passport; then looked at him again. As he spoke, the smell of stale tobacco on his breath caused the American to grimace instinctively.

"Ah, yes, it says here... Doctor Alvarez. I am General

Moghrabi, and you know my colleague here, I think. Do you know why you are here?"

"No idea," said Alvarez.

"Hmm," the General continued to scan the passport. "It says here you are Mexican."

"Yes," said Alvarez. "And I want to see a consular official. I want to protest most strongly at my treatment. You have no right to kidnap me and bring me here."

"Your request is noted. Tell me, what is a Mexican doing working for the CIA?"

Alvarez felt sick. He wondered how much they knew and how much was guesswork.

"CIA? What are you talking about? I'm a project director working on an important project for your country."

"And which project is that?" The General was testing him; he already knew the answer.

"In Arak, the new commercial and retail centre; I work for Brechtel."

"Ah, yes, Brechtel. German, yes?"

"Yes," said Alvarez.

"Hmm, I see. Arak, now that is very convenient."

"What do you mean?" said Alvarez.

The General slammed his fist down on the desk, which made both the Commander and Alvarez jump.

"Do not treat me as a fool; I have studied in your country, in Boston, a very fine city."

"I don't know Boston, I'm Mexican."

"Ah, yes, so you say. But there are other facilities in Arak that would be of great interest to President Bush and his minions in Langley."

"Langley? I don't know any Langley."

"Why were you visiting Doctor Amadi today?"

"I wanted to get some advice from him on a construction issue."

"So, you drove all the way from Arak, just to ask his advice. This is nonsense, you could have just called him on the telephone," the General's voice was raised again.

"Yes, but I wanted to meet the guy. He's a legend in the construction business."

"So I understand, a very important man. Someone of interest to the CIA, yes?"

"I don't know what you are talking about. I just went to meet the guy and get his advice on a construction issue."

"Yes, drainage, I believe."

Alvarez's worst fears had been realised; Amadi's office had been bugged.

"Yes," replied Alvarez.

"I see. And you drove all the way from Arak?" said the General.

His packet of cigarettes was to his right on top of an A4 size manila folder. He picked it up and lit one, blowing the smoke in Alvarez's direction. His actions were slow and deliberate. He put the twenty-pack down and picked up the folder, leant back in his seat and started to flick through the contents. Alvarez was sweating again, although it wasn't caused by the temperature in the basement.

The General pulled out a photograph and threw it onto the desk; it skidded across the surface of the table, swivelled around three hundred and sixty degrees, and stopped at the edge right in front of Alvarez.

Alvarez looked at it.

"This is... what do you American's call it? Bullshit,

right? You didn't drive from Arak."

"It's where I work," said Alvarez.

"Yes, it is, so what were you doing in Tehran?"

"I stopped by to see a buddy."

The General went back to his folder and pulled out another picture. He tried the same trick, but the photo careered off the table onto the floor. The Commander leaned down, picked it up and put it on top of the first one.

"This person?"

It was a good quality picture of Podesta.

"Yes," replied Alvarez.

"Hmm, works at the Canadian Embassy."

"Yes."

"It's strange that he does not appear on their list of employees."

"What can I say?" said Alvarez. "I don't have their personnel records."

"I see. And how long have you known this man?"

"Years, we go way back."

The General slammed his fist on the table again, causing both photographs to fall on the floor. Once again, the Commander picked them up.

"He is CIA, we know this."

"No, he's not, he's Italian."

The General looked at him with scorn.

"Do not treat me as a fool; you will regret it."

Alvarez was desperate to pee despite having had nothing to drink for several hours.

"How did you meet this man?"

"I can't remember… at a dinner somewhere, I guess."

"Hmm, I don't believe a word of it. You are lying." The

General stubbed his cigarette and lit another. "This man is CIA; he has an office in the basement of the Canadian Embassy. What do you call it? A nest of vipers, yes?"

"No, I swear, I know nothing about that," said Alvarez, who was beginning to turn white.

"When did you go to Esfahan?"

"The day before yesterday, but I guess you know that already?"

"The Hotel Safir, yes? A nice hotel, ordinary Iranian's can't afford to stay there. And then you went to spy on our facility there."

"No, no, you've got it all wrong. I just wanted to see where I had to go for my meeting."

"But this is a lie, you say you drove down to Esfahan to see Doctor Amadi, but you did not have a meeting arranged, did you? So, why did you go to the facility if it was not to spy."

Alvarez was in a mess; his cover was starting to unravel. He had totally underestimated the resources of the secret police.

"No, I told you, I wanted to see where Doctor Amadi worked. I was confident he would see me."

"And why were you confident?"

"I'm a fellow engineer, I was sure he would see me."

"Perhaps he was expecting you."

"What do you mean? How could he?"

"You tell me. Maybe he had already been in contact with you, or maybe your British friends?"

"This is ridiculous. I don't know what you are talking about."

"I don't believe you. Do you, Commander?" said the

General looking at Fallahian.

"Not a word," said the Commander.

"Hmm, ok, let's move on."

The General's voice was quiet, almost soothing. Smoke continued to billow into the room from his cigarette.

"Let's talk about your meeting with Doctor Amadi. The Commander tells me you talked about drainage problems."

"Yes," said Alvarez.

"For about one minute," interjected the Commander.

"And then you suggested… how did he say it, Commander Fallahian?"

"A change of career," replied Fallahian.

"Yes, a change of career. You were trying to recruit him."

"Er, yes, we have a vacancy in Brechtel at a senior level. I thought Doctor Amadi would be an ideal candidate."

"Bullshit," said the General, his voice getting louder. "You wanted him to spy for the CIA. Or, maybe you wanted to get him out of the country to the USA, perhaps?"

"This is nonsense," said Alvarez.

"You were going to get him out of the country with the help of your British friends, we know this," retorted the General, his voice loud and threatening. He banged down his fist again.

"That's crap, we don't need their help." Alvarez slipped up under the pressure of the interrogation. He immediately realised his mistake.

It went quiet. The General looked at him and took another long drag of his cigarette.

"I mean…" Alvarez struggled for a way to backtrack.

"What *do* you mean?" said the General.

"Nothing, this is all nonsense. All of it. I just went to visit a business colleague to get his advice, that's all." Alvarez was flustered.

"Hmm, as you say, Doctor Alvarez." The General looked at Alvarez with a menacing stare. "So, let's see what we have. You drove all the way from Arak for a meeting you hadn't arranged, stopped off to see a friend at the Canadian Embassy in Tehran, who we know works for the CIA; you drive down to Esfahan to spy on our nuclear facility; then you call one of our top engineers to arrange a meeting to try to recruit him?"

Alvarez was not making eye-contact and remained silent, but inside he knew he was in trouble.

The General got up from his chair.

"That is all for now. Commander, arrange for the arrest of Doctor Amadi for spying, and bring him and his family here to our headquarters, I want to see what he has to say."

"Yes General," said the Commander. He stood to attention as the General picked up his cigarettes and left the room.

When he returned to his office suite, Moghrabi called General Khatami, Head of Security, outlining progress with the interrogation.

Canadian Embassy, Tehran – 5:00 p.m.

Jo Podesta was pacing up and down his basement office wondering what was happening. He was really concerned; it had been almost nine hours since Alvarez's meeting with Amadi. It was not like him not to report in on time. He made a secure call on the scrambled line.

"Cherokee," he said when the call was answered. There was a wait for a couple of minutes, then a voice.

"Yeah?"

"It's Corn Bow. We've lost contact with Mexico, request check on any traffic with said reference."

"Copy that."

"You may want to check with our cousins and GCHQ, they may have an interest."

"Copy that."

Podesta dropped the call; there was nothing he could do.

The Mahabadi Residence – 8:00 p.m.

The children were in bed. Afareen had skipped the dinner that her mother had prepared; her appetite had almost disappeared since the visit from the secret police. She was on edge, expecting a rap on the door any minute.

She was in her armchair watching the TV with her mother. She felt exhausted after the trauma of the day; her eyes felt heavy, but it was not a restful feel; more the body shutting down by way of protection.

She was jolted by the ring of the telephone.

She got up from her seat, and managed to stagger across the room and pick up the phone before the call dropped.

"Hello?" The line was crackly with static, then recognition. "Hassan, my darling. It is wonderful to hear your voice."

There was the usual domestic catch-up and then the news Afareen had been waiting for.

"Next Wednesday? For how long? Three days? That is wonderful; I will tell your uncle; he can't wait to see you. He said he would take us all out. Yes, it certainly will be exciting."

Canadian Embassy, Tehran – 9:00 p.m.

Podesta had barely moved away from his phone all day. Occasionally, he would stand up and pace the room. His colleague, Javi Rao, had been monitoring communications from Langley, but there was still no news. Jim Blasic seemed to be existing on a diet of caffeine; no one had the appetite for work or food. The whereabouts of Tony Alvarez was on everybody's mind.

The red telephone receiver which handled scrambled calls rang; shaking up the three agents.

"Yeah?" said Podesta picking up the phone; he listened for a minute. "Jeezus… when? Fuck!"

He processed the rest of the conversation.

He dropped the call after about ten minutes. Jim and Javi were waiting anxiously for the news; they could tell by Podesta's face; it was not good.

"Langley picked up a message from MOIS headquarters a couple of hours ago. They've arrested a Mexican; he's at the interrogation centre."

"Jeez," said Blasic. Rao just looked on in disbelief.

"It gets worse. There's been a meeting with the Chiefs of Staff. They're hanging Tony out to dry."

"What?"

"Yeah, too politically sensitive. As he said, we aren't going to admit that Tony's CIA; in the present climate that would cause all kind of problems with the Iranians, and probably the Russians too, especially after today's announcement. Washington says it's a Mexican issue."

"But what are we going to do? We can't let Tony just rot in a MOIS cell somewhere."

"He won't be rotting anywhere. There'll be a show trial and then a public execution. That's how they do things here."

Jim sat down, trying to process the information. "But we've got to do something."

"I'm all ears," said Podesta.

Chapter Fourteen

Gholhak Garden Compound – Friday April 21st

Afareen felt different this morning as she walked through the gardens towards the Dexters' residence. The birds seemed to be singing louder and the sun was brighter as its rays permeated the tree canopy. Her husband's telephone call had lifted her spirits.

She was greeted as usual by Sophie Dexter.

Afareen put her fingers to her lips. Sophie recognised the sign and led the cleaner to the bedroom where David was going through some papers while he waited for his car. Sophie went back into the kitchen, retrieved the vacuum cleaner and switched it on next to the telephone. There was no danger of any conversation being heard.

Dexter greeted Afareen; he could tell by her expression that she had good news.

"You've heard from your husband?" said Dexter.

"Yes, he called last night; he said he has been given some time to come home," she whispered.

"When?" said Dexter.

"Next Wednesday, for three days."

"That doesn't give us very much time. I must let Nick know. I will tell you what you will need to do when we have worked everything out."

"Yes, I understand. But you will help us to leave?"

"That's why Nick's here," said Dexter and Afareen's face lit up.

"I don't want to spend another day here in this country," she said.

British Embassy, Tehran – 8:30 a.m.

Dexter called Houghton as soon as he arrived at the embassy to arrange a meeting. "I'll ask Dee to join us too," he said.

Houghton had taken an early minibus with Dee and one of the other diplomatic staff and he was finishing his email update to Vauxhall when the pair knocked on his door and walked in.

Dee was carrying three take-out cups of coffee in a receptacle; Dexter, a paper bag with some pastries from the canteen.

"Hi, David, Dee, come in, take a seat, I won't be a sec," said Houghton.

Dee distributed the drinks and pastries while Houghton closed down his laptop.

"Ok, some news, I gather."

"Yes," said Dexter. "Spoke to Afareen earlier, her husband is being given some leave."

"That's great news. When?" said Houghton.

"Next Wednesday, for three days."

"Hmm, that doesn't give us much time." Houghton looked at Dee. "Have you heard anything from Leila yet?"

"No, not yet, although I'm sure she'll be in touch sometime today."

"Ok, I've been going through my plan again and I think we may need another car; a four-by-four, preferably. Can you ask Leila if her father can get hold of one? Japanese if possible, three or four years old."

"That might not be as easy as it sounds. The sanctions have hit hard here; certainly, there have been no new Japanese cars imported for some time. Most of them are local, Iranian or Russian, and you know what they're like for reliability."

"Shit! Ok, whatever she can get, but it will need to hold five people."

"Yes, ok, I'll ask her."

"Has there been anything on the wires we need to know about?" asked Houghton.

"Nothing that I think will interest us; security is still high. Ahmadinejad is still keeping up the rhetoric."

"What about the Russians?" asked Houghton.

"Nothing since the news yesterday. I think they are waiting to see what response they get from the West. Israel has taken more than a passing interest; there's stuff coming out of Tel Aviv but nothing that should concern us. There was something that we picked up last night from the Ministry about a Mexican being arrested, picked up in Esfahan apparently."

"Hmm," said Houghton; he felt a twinge of concern but didn't visibly show it.

Just then, Dee's phone indicated a text message. "Excuse me," she said and accessed her screen. "It's from Leila, she thinks they may have something for us."

"That's great, can you arrange to meet her today sometime and get the details? We need to ask her about the second car as well; I don't want to do it over the phone," said Houghton.

"Sure," said Dee and sent a message back. *'Can we meet today, 1:30?'*

Moments later, there was a positive reply.

"That's great." Houghton looked at Dexter. "David, how

are the new passports and my hospital pass? Will they be ready for next week?"

"I'll speak to Ryan and let him know the deadline. I'll make sure they're ready for next Wednesday; Vauxhall can send the passports in the diplomatic bag; they've got the photographs. The comms team are looking after your hospital pass."

"Thanks," said Houghton.

There was another meeting Houghton needed to arrange; he sent a message to Mayflower. *'Today, 1:30?'*. It was another half an hour before he received a reply, but again, the response confirmed the meeting.

MOIS Headquarters – 9:30 a.m.

Alvarez had endured a miserable night. Racked with fear he'd hardly slept. The noises didn't help – hideous screams, rattling of cell doors, clanking of keys, loud footsteps.

After his interrogation, he had been moved to another part of the complex. Once more, he'd been hooded for the transfer, so he had no idea exactly where he was. He was helped down some steps before his head-cover was removed. He was faced with a stark grey-metal door, flanked by two armed guards. There was no sign of the officers who had interrogated him.

One of the officers opened the door. Inside was a bare room with a bed, mattress and bucket. He was pushed inside, and the door locked. He looked at the bed; the mattress was covered in all manner of stains, including blood. The smell was nauseating. With little option, Alvarez lay down and tried to sleep. He had no concept of time; there were no windows to indicate daylight – just a single lightbulb set in the wall above the door, protected by a metal grill. They had confiscated his CIA-issue Breitling watch.

He had no idea how long he had been there when he heard the rattling of keys. He was on full alert. The door opened, and an armed guard entered carrying a metal tray with a bowl of unrecognisable food and a plastic bottle of water. Another guard looked on with his rifle pointing at Alvarez.

The tray was put on the floor. The guard examined the bucket, which was still empty, then left and locked up.

Alvarez hadn't eaten or taken on any liquid for over twelve hours, and while he didn't feel hungry, he was desperately thirsty. He consumed the water in one go, then realised he should have saved some for later; he had no idea when it would be replenished. He picked up the bowl. It was almost like a stew with a roughly cut slab of bread. He sniffed the food; it smelt ok, so with no alternative, he dipped in his bread and started to eat, this time more slowly. There were no utensils; knives and forks could be used as weapons. He finished the stew by putting the tray to his mouth and tipping back the contents until they had all gone.

He thought it was probably early morning when he received another visit. This time the bucket was changed, and some more food handed to him. He spoke to the guard in Farsi.

"I want to speak to the Mexican Ambassador and a lawyer."

The guard looked at him and laughed. Then left without responding.

"You can't do this! You can't do this!" Alvarez shouted as the door was locked.

In another part of the complex, another interview was ongoing.

Not long after Alvarez was interrogated, a small team entered the Esfahan nuclear facility control centre and arrested Doctor Saleh Amadi in his office. He too was hooded, put into a car and driven to Tehran. Unbeknown to him at the time, his wife and two children had also been taken into custody and were in a separate vehicle heading north, utterly petrified and shocked at their treatment.

On reaching MOIS headquarters, Amadi was put into a detaining cell, his family were in slightly more comfortable accommodation but still locked and guarded.

It was early morning, around six-thirty, when Amadi was eventually taken from his cell and taken to an interrogation room. He had remonstrated vehemently with his captors, as he had done in his office at the nuclear facility, but he was met with a wall of silence and a loaded Kalashnikov.

He was still in a belligerent mood as he was shackled to the table. Two guards stood at the back of the room; Amadi sat there a lonely and frightened figure. Time passed slowly; it was twenty minutes before the interrogators walked in. The guards stood to attention.

"At ease," said the General, in Farsi.

The usual smell of stale cigarettes heralded the arrival of General Moghrabi and his deputy, Commander Fallahian. The General looked at the prisoner, put his pack of twenty cigarettes to his right and sat down. Fallahian had a note pad and was starting to write.

"I understand you speak Farsi," said the General in his native tongue.

"Yes," replied Amadi.

"Do you know why you are here?"

"No, I don't, and I want to protest most strongly," replied Amadi trying to remain calm but feeling far from it.

"Your protest is noted. I will get straight to the point. Why did you contact Doctor Alvarez?"

"Alvarez? Is that what this is all about? I didn't contact him. He contacted me."

"But you phoned him, on his private phone."

"Yes, he called me, and I returned his call."

"Hmm, I see." The General lit his first cigarette of the interrogation; it wouldn't be his last. "So, he called you, and you called him back?"

"Yes, I have told you."

"Why did he call you?"

"He wanted to discuss a construction problem."

"And you believed him?"

"Yes, of course, why wouldn't I?"

"But that's not the real reason, is it? You wanted to arrange passage out of Iran?"

"That's ridiculous, I don't need anyone to arrange passage, I can leave at any time; I'm not a prisoner here."

This was not strictly true. The head of the nuclear agency had Amadi's passport, and there would have been stringent conditions applied to any overseas travel, including his family remaining in Iran.

"I see," said the General.

"I have a good life here; why would I want to leave?"

"Who knows why people turn their backs on the country that has rewarded them very well for their work? You are rewarded well, Doctor Amadi?"

"Of course, I have just said so."

"Yes, you are; a nice house, family, children at good schools, medical fees all taken care of."

"Yes."

"So, let me ask you again, Doctor Amadi, why did you contact Alvarez?"

"You are not listening. I told you, he called me. How many more times?" Amadi's voice was raised.

"Hmm, so you say. So, when did he call you?"

"I don't know, in the morning sometime, I was in a meeting. The switchboard gave me a message and I called him back; that was all."

"What time did he call?"

"I just told you; I don't know. I was in a meeting; the switchboard will know."

The General turned to his deputy. "Get someone to check that, Commander."

"Yes sir," said Fallahian and wrote on his pad.

"Ok, let's leave that for now. Tell me about the meeting; what did he want?"

"To discuss some problems at his construction site in Arak."

"And you believed that?"

"Of course, he was a fellow engineer."

"How long did you discuss these problems?"

"Not very long, a few minutes."

"Didn't you think it was a bit strange, an experienced engineer coming here to ask you some basic questions?"

"No, not at first."

"No, because then you discovered he wanted to recruit you."

"No, no, that's wrong; he offered me a new career."

"Ah, I see, and what was this new career?"

"I don't know, we didn't discuss it; I thought he wanted me to work with Brechtel."

"Ah, yes, Brechtel, German, I believe."

"Yes," said Amadi. "I believe so."

The Commander interjected. "When did you realise he was CIA?"

Amadi hesitated. "I didn't."

"But you did, you told him you weren't interested."

"Yes, I didn't realise it at first," said Amadi, recognising that the conversation had been bugged. "And I told him to leave."

The Commander scanned a piece of paper. "Yes, you did. But then, why didn't you report him? It was your duty."

Amadi was starting to panic now.

"I was not thinking straight and then we had an issue to deal with at the plant. Look, I didn't want to get involved; I haven't got the time; I am working fourteen hours a day; I thought that would be the end of it. I was busy."

The General slammed his fist on the table. "You were busy? You were busy? What can be more important than the security of the State? You were approached by a CIA agent and you were too busy to report it!" the General bellowed.

"No, no, you are right; I should have done. What can I say?"

The General lit up another cigarette and moved closer to Amadi. You could cut the tension with a knife.

"Well, it is ok, we have arrested the spy Alvarez," he said quietly.

"Good, it is he that is the traitor, not me."

"Hmm, but we still have a problem. I'll ask again; why didn't you report it?"

"I told you," said Amadi, his faced etched with anxiety.

"Yes, you did, and I want to believe you. What does your wife say about living here? Maybe she was putting pressure on you to leave. Is that it? Maybe she wants to return to France, or Switzerland, perhaps."

"No, no, she is happy here, we have made some good friends."

"Is she happy? We'll have to ask her. We have taken the liberty of bringing her here."

Amadi went white and started to shake.

"It's ok, your children are with her. They are comfortable for now."

"No, no, you can't do that. Why are they here? They have done nothing. Look, I have served this country loyally. My work is good, I have been praised by senior government officials; they appreciate how much I have given to the Esfahan project."

"Yes, it is a pity you have tarnished your reputation by protecting a spy."

The General stubbed out his latest smoke and stood up. The surrounding officers immediately stood to attention.

"Well, Doctor Amadi, it is out of my hands now. It will be up to the judiciary to decide what to do." He turned to the guards. "Take him back to the cells."

Canadian Embassy, Tehran

Jo Podesta couldn't sleep; he had decided to return to the embassy to monitor the communications traffic with Javi Rao. He had been in his office since six a.m., and there had been no fresh news regarding their colleague. The lack of information was proving difficult to take. Langley was not about to budge on the issue and options appeared very limited.

Finally, another intercepted message came through; it was nine forty-five.

"Jo, you'll want to see this," said Rao, holding a piece of paper. "It looks like the Iranians have picked up the Egyptian."

Rao showed Podesta the message.

"Hmm, I wonder what that means," said Podesta. "Do we know why?"

"No, nothing, but we can't rule out a link. I mean, if they picked up Tony after the meeting and they were monitoring everything, then that was always going to happen."

"Yeah, I guess," said Podesta. "I wonder what they'll do next."

"If their past record's anything to go by, they'll round up anyone who they think may have had a connection."

"Hmm," said Podesta. He drew his hands down his face in frustration.

Podesta returned to his workstation and re-read the message over and over, trying to work out how they had found themselves in this situation.

He picked up the secure phone and dialled a number.

British Embassy, Tehran – 9:50 a.m.

Nick Houghton was in his office. He'd finished his briefing with Dee and Dexter and his meeting with Mayflower had been confirmed. Dee would also be leaving the Embassy later to visit Leila.

It was just turned nine-fifty when he heard the distinct Nokia ringtone of his mobile phone. He looked at the number on the screen; it was Tehran, but he didn't recognise the caller.

"Yeah?" he said when he accepted the call.

"Nick? It's Jo Podesta. Can you make a meeting later today?"

"Yeah, I think so, where?"

"Same place you met Tony?"

"Yeah, sure, ok. What time?"

"What's your diary looking like?"

"How about three-thirty? I can get there by then."

"Sure, ok, yeah. See you at three-thirty."

He dropped the call and was deep in thought. He had a good idea what it would be about; he needed to cover some bases. He called Dexter.

Ten minutes later, they were discussing tactics for the Podesta meeting; they realised the implication of Alvarez's arrest. Houghton's chaos theory had backfired, and there was some damage limitation required.

Grand Bazaar, Central Tehran – 1:25 p.m.

Houghton was waiting in the usual café for Mayflower. As it was prayer day, it was fairly quiet, but there were still about twelve customers taking their lunch. He had again used his avoidance procedure to confuse any surveillance teams. Dee was taking similar precautions for her meeting with Leila.

It was just after one-thirty when Mayflower appeared. She was carrying a large leather shoulder bag.

She seemed pleased to see Houghton and smiled warmly

as she joined him in one of the booths. They both ordered food and drinks. "You wanted to see me?" said Mayflower, once the food had been served.

"Yes, I have some news. I will need your help next Thursday. Will you be ready?"

She considered the question for a moment. "Yes, I think so; what will you need me to do?"

"I will explain more next week. I just wanted to check you will be on duty."

"I'm always on duty," she said and smiled.

"I think it will be evening, about eight, nine o'clock."

"Yes, ok, I can be available then."

"Ok, I need to finalise one or two things, but can we meet next Tuesday, and I should be able to confirm everything then?"

"Yes, ok." She looked around the café. The other customers were all engrossed in conversation and oblivious to Houghton and his guest. "I have something for you," she said and opened her bag.

She took out a stethoscope and quickly passed it to Houghton under the table.

"Hey, that's great, thank you." He quickly pushed the item under his shirt. "How did you manage that?"

"One of the doctors moved to another hospital and he left it behind."

"Well, that was lucky, thank you."

"Yes, it will cost him much money for a new one. I also got this," she said and gave Houghton a map of the hospital. It was in Farsi, but he was confident he could make out the names of the various departments from the layout. "And this… you will need it for the drug." It was a syringe.

"That's great, thanks, I don't know what to say," said Houghton. "I really appreciate the risks you've taken to get these. I owe you big time. If I think of any questions about the layout, I'll let you know on Tuesday." He pointed to the brochure.

"Yes, of course, I will tell you what you need to know."

He looked at her; her eyes were tired and there was a weariness reflected in her face brought about by long hours and insufficient sleep.

"I can't tell you how valuable your contribution has been," Houghton said, unable to fully articulate his gratitude.

"It is what I wanted to do," she replied.

They finished their food. "I need to go," said Mayflower. "Next Tuesday, same time?"

"Yes," said Houghton. "Thanks."

She left the café without a backward glance.

Houghton, as he had done on his previous meetings, ordered another coffee and checked his watch. He had some time before he would need to leave for his meeting with Podesta.

City Park, The Park-E-Shahr Library – 3:15 p.m.

Houghton was in good time for his meeting. It was the same place he had met Alvarez less than a week earlier, just across from the library entrance. He checked his surroundings; there was nothing he could see that would cause a threat. No cars were allowed in the park, so any surveillance would have to be carried out manually. There was no-one in the immediate vicinity. He hoped that Podesta was as fastidious with his security as he was.

As it happened, Podesta was also a few minutes early.

Houghton spotted him walking along the pathway towards him but, instead of approaching the bench, he walked past. Houghton knew the drill and watched. He checked the library, but it appeared deserted; the coast was clear. Houghton stood up and followed; he could see Podesta pause and look back every so often.

They were in a different part of the park, towards the centre, well away from any parked cars, when Podesta stopped and sat down at a bench.

Houghton joined him and shook hands.

"Hi Jo, good to see you again, but I guess this is not a social occasion."

"Yeah, you could say that," said Podesta. "Look, I'll get straight to the point, have you heard about Tony?

"What about Tony?" replied Houghton.

"You've not heard then?"

"Heard what?"

"He's been picked up by the Ministry."

"Jeez, no, when?" Houghton feigned disbelief. Podesta wasn't entirely convinced, but he let any doubts pass.

"We don't have any details; we just heard they picked up a Mexican yesterday, and Tony hasn't called in for over twenty-four hours. He'd been down to Esfahan to speak to our friend, the Egyptian."

"And you think he was arrested while he was there?"

"Yeah, well, we don't know for sure, but it would make sense. We've made some enquiries and it seems our friend has also been arrested."

"The Egyptian?"

"Yeah."

"Jeez, that's bad, but I'm not sure why that concerns us."

"Well it might, and it might not, but given our discussion on Monday, I thought it was worth a shot, see if you had gotten any more information."

"No, as I said, we've not heard anything; although it can sometimes take a couple of days before we get anything from Vauxhall… you know the drill."

"Yeah, I guess. So, can you throw any light on the situation?"

"Well, no, after our meeting, I closed the file."

"Hmm, any chance we could take a look at that file?"

"Sorry, restricted I'm afraid, but there's nothing in there that would be of any interest, it was pretty much what I told you; we were happy for you guys to take over."

Podesta looked ahead. It was a warm day and the sun was starting to penetrate his skin; he could feel his face beginning to tingle.

"What about this driver who gave you the original tip-off?"

"Well, it's interesting you should ask; he's not been at work for three days. He seems to have disappeared."

"Yeah?"

"No-one knows where he is, but there's been an increase in the level of surveillance on the embassy and the compound recently, so it's possible it could be connected. It's quite laughable really, they aren't the most discreet of operators. They must be bored out of their brains. We play games with them; you know, walk to the supermarket and stuff, just to give them something to keep them occupied."

Podesta had nowhere to go with his enquiries. He wasn't sure whether he was being played or not but decided to give Houghton the benefit of the doubt.

"Yeah, ok. We'll leave it there, but if the driver guy turns up or you get any more information, be sure to let me know, yeah?"

"Yes, of course, sure thing. Sorry I can't be of more help. I just hope Tony's ok. I liked him; he seems like a good bloke."

"Yeah, he is a good bloke," said Podesta in a feigned English accent. He shook hands with Houghton. "You take care."

"Sure thing," said Houghton and the pair walked off in different directions.

Both were reflecting on the conversation. Podesta was trying to think what, if anything, he could do next. Houghton was breathing a little easier.

British Embassy, Tehran – 5:00 p.m.

Back at the embassy, Houghton gave Dexter an update following his conversation with the Americans.

"It sounds like we're off the hook," said Dexter.

"Yeah, pity about Alvarez though; I liked him," replied Houghton.

"Yes, that's the job though," said Dexter.

"Hmm."

Houghton rang off just as Dee knocked on the door and came in. He smiled and her face lit up.

"So, how did it go?" asked Houghton.

"Well, not bad. Leila went to see her father last night and he's more than happy to help. She said he has a van in stock which he thinks he could convert to an ambulance, but he'll need a couple of days to paint it. He's willing to do that for us. The four-by-four might be a little more problematical, as we thought, but he is going to ask around discreetly."

"What about the cost, did she say? Only I'll need to ask David to arrange some dollars for me from Vauxhall."

"No, but she said she would let me know."

"Ok, that's great. There's nothing more we can do for the moment; I guess we'll just have to wait."

"How do you fancy a night away from the bugs again?" Dee winked.

"Do you know, that sounds like an excellent idea."

"Ok, dinner at seven?"

"That's great, see you then."

Dee blew Houghton a kiss and left the office.

MOIS Headquarters – 6:00 p.m.

Alvarez was in despair. He was still stuck in his stinky cell with just his bucket for company which hadn't been emptied all day. He had been given another bowl of unidentifiable slop masquerading as food a few hours earlier, but without any reference to time, he had no idea when it was; he just felt hungry and very thirsty.

He was alone with his thoughts when he finally heard the rattling of keys again. He was on high alert. Two armed guards walked in, then handcuffed and hooded him.

He was man-handled back to the interrogation suite to be greeted by the General, his cigarettes, and the Commander. His cuffs and hood were removed, and he was shackled to the table again. The fear was immense; he was starting to shake, and he was in danger of losing his bladder.

The General lit up again, causing Alvarez to cough involuntarily.

"We've been going through your story, and I have

discussed your situation with the Head of Security. To put it bluntly, as you Americans prefer, it is bullshit; we don't believe a word of it. However, we do want to make things a little easier for you. I have had this document drawn up which we would like you to sign. It is ok, it is in English, but I can have it translated into Spanish if you prefer."

"English is fine," replied Alvarez.

A sheet of A4 was placed in front of him to read. Alvarez scanned the statement and then read it more slowly.

"I can't sign this; it says I'm a spy working for the American Government."

"But that is the fact of the matter isn't it? You *are* a spy; you are CIA,"

"That's ridiculous, I told you I'm just an engineer. I work for Brechtel; you can check."

"I assure you we have, Doctor Alvarez, and we are checking some of your colleagues too; it seems we have uncovered other operatives who are interested in our nuclear facilities at Arak. Don't worry, they will be questioned in due course."

"I am an engineer; I help build things. I am not a spy."

"Well, it seems Doctor Amadi disagrees; he has been most helpful in our discussions. So, you will sign the paper, yes?"

"No, I won't. It is not true, and if I do, I will be signing my own death sentence."

"Hmm," said the General. "Not necessarily. I have spoken to General Khatami; I expect you know him; he is Head of our Homeland Security. We are reasonable people; if you sign the document, we will not insist on the death penalty at your trial. You will serve a few years in prison until the incident is forgotten and then you will go home. Of course, your CIA may want to make a deal; in which case, you could go home a lot earlier. It is in your hands."

Alvarez was in a bad way; he'd had little sleep, less food, and just about adequate water. He hadn't washed or shaved for nearly two days and there was no toilet paper in his cell. He could smell himself.

"Ok, let me help you here. If you don't sign, your trial will take place next week and we will insist on the death penalty. General Khatami says you will be convicted, and in the present circumstances, our judges tend to carry out our recommendations."

Alvarez was staring at the General, but his face was expressionless, his eyes were dead.

"Have you seen any of our public executions, Doctor Alvarez?"

"What?" said Alvarez, who hadn't processed the question.

"I asked if you had seen any of our public executions. They are very popular with the people here; they draw large crowds. Usually, we hang traitors. When I say hang, we don't use gallows. We like to use a crane; it saves the expense of a carpenter. The rope is placed around the prisoner's neck, and they are gently lifted off the ground. It means death is not so quick. I have seen a prisoner hanging for twenty minutes with their legs still thrashing around. It's quite a spectacle." He looked at the Commander and smiled, but in an evil way.

Alvarez couldn't hold himself any longer and he vomited over the table and down the front of his clothes. The document was covered in sick.

The General avoided the disgorging.

"No matter, we have another copy. Ok, we need to clean

this up." He shouted an order to one of the guards and Alvarez was unshackled, cuffed and hooded again.

"We will meet again in one hour when I hope you have reconsidered your position. Take him away," he instructed one of the guards. "You, clear up this mess," he barked at the other.

Chapter Fifteen

British Embassy, Tehran – Saturday April 22nd – 9:30 a.m.

Houghton was in his office, working on his plan to exfil Mahabadi and his family. He looked at the schematic of the hospital trying to place where he would need to be. The more he looked at the fairly basic direction finder, the more he recognised he would need to make a visit. It was difficult to estimate the scale of the area from the brochure.

A visit to the hospital was potentially a risky venture, but this was one he could not avoid. He was still trying to work out a suitable scenario when Dee arrived with coffee and cakes.

"Hi," said Dee. "Brought you these. I've got some news."

"That's great, thanks."

He looked at her and, for a moment, reflected on the previous evening. He shook himself out of the recollection; he couldn't afford the distraction.

"So, what's the news?"

"It's just been on TV; it was pretty harrowing to watch actually. The Iranians have caught a CIA spy."

Houghton had never mentioned Alvarez to Dee, and she was unaware of the association.

"Really? What happened?"

"Apparently, according to the newsfeed, they picked him up at Esfahan. They didn't go into detail, but it seems he's signed a confession. I have to say, he looked in a real bad way. The press are all over it, as you can imagine. CNN have just picked it up; they're relaying footage live to the States as we speak. Langley will be going nuts that's for sure." She paused for a moment and took a sip of coffee. "It'll be interesting to see if Bush says anything about it. One thing's for certain, it's going to be very embarrassing for the Americans at the U.N. It definitely won't help their cause for sanctions."

"No, I guess it won't," said Houghton. "Did they say what's going to happen?"

"Not in detail, but the likely scenario is, he's done a deal. He'll be put before a judge, probably today or tomorrow, and sentenced. As he's signed a confession, there won't be a trial. If past experience is anything to go by, he'll probably get life. Then after a few months or a year, when the dust has settled, he'll be used as part of some bargaining chip and deported back to the States… unless of course, the CIA don't want him back."

"Hmm, let me know how it pans out. At least it should keep their eyes off our operation."

"Ha, yes, that's for sure. It seems to be the only topic of conversation coming out of MOIS; there's a lot of back-slapping going on."

"That's good news. Actually, Dee, I need your help; I want to take a look at the hospital in more detail."

"Sure, how do you want to do that?"

"Well, I've got this rather nasty stomach bug that might need some attention. How do you fancy a trip to hospital? You can be my concerned other. We can get one of the drivers to take us, it will look less suspicious."

"Yes, ok, sure."

"I need you to study the place too; keep an eye out for entrances and exits. I want to find one that is not covered by CCTV, if possible." He showed her the map. "This one would be ideal."

He pointed to a corridor that led off the main reception area. There was nothing on the map to indicate what it was used for, but halfway along, there was a fire-door that led to a service road that ran around the side of the hospital building.

Twenty minutes later, one of the official diplomatic cars had been drafted to drive Houghton and Dee to the Mardom Hospital. Both were dressed in their business attire; Dee had conformed to local requirements and had added a scarf to her apparel; something she did for any external excursions. The pair sat in the back and, with slightly tinted windows, the surveillance team were unable to positively identify the passengers. Not that they were taking a great deal of interest. With the capture of the CIA operative, the mood was upbeat within the organisation. The agents in the two vehicles outside the British Embassy were joking and laughing; they had taken their collective eyes off the ball.

In the morning traffic, it took over half an hour for the car to reach the destination. Houghton had deliberately not said anything to Mayflower; he didn't want to attract any attention to her.

They pulled up outside the main entrance and the pair got out. He would call the embassy when they needed to return. One or two people looked at the Jaguar as it drove away, merely out of curiosity; it was a rare sight in Tehran.

They followed the signs to reception. "I hope you're not going to tell them it was my cooking," said Dee. Houghton laughed.

"Ok, now when we go in, try and remember as much as you can, layout, cameras, guards, corridors; it could prove very important."

"Yes, sure," said Dee as they reached the doorway. "I'm quite enjoying this undercover stuff."

Inside, it was like all hospitals; chaotic with no discernible sense of order; people milling about, some with bandages being held to their heads, children in distress; nurses flitting from one area to another. Houghton could see three armed guards patrolling the area.

He approached the enquiries desk.

The receptionist was dressed in a white nurse's uniform with a white headscarf; she spoke in Farsi.

"Hello," said Houghton. "Do you speak English?"

"Yes, of course," said the woman. "What is your name?"

"Franklin. Dominic Franklin; I need to see someone; I have terrible pains in my stomach."

"You are a tourist, yes?"

"Yes." He looked at Dee. "We have been touring here in Iran."

"Where are you from?"

"Australia."

"You have a passport?"

"No, it's in the hotel."

"I will need to see your passport. You have travel insurance?"

"Yes, but I don't have the details. Don't worry, I can pay cash for any drugs."

The woman was taking notes and adding them to a rather ancient computer.

"Ok, Mr Franklin, take a seat; I will get someone to see you. There is a wait, it will be about one hour."

"Thank you, can you direct me to the toilet please?"

"Sure, it's over there." She pointed toward a corridor to the right of the desk. "You will see the signs."

Houghton and Dee went to sit down. The chairs were plastic and attached to the floor in rows and not very comfortable. There were maybe fifty people in the waiting area, leaving very few vacant seats.

"I want to check that corridor, see if there are any exits; keep an eye out for guards," he said and walked towards the toilet.

Houghton had been gone for about ten minutes. Dee was looking around anxiously. The guards had wandered down another corridor, but she could see them returning.

They spoke to the receptionist who handed them a clipboard which they scanned with interest and then started to look around the waiting area. She wasn't sure what to do, but her instincts told her to move. She got up and headed towards the corridor Houghton had gone down.

It was about fifty yards long, and at the end, there was the external wall. Several other doors led off the corridor. She saw the sign for the toilets and stood outside the men's facility. "Nick, Nick, are you ok," she called.

The door opened and a man exited the washroom. He looked at Dee with a puzzled expression and walked towards the reception area.

"Nick, are you there?"

Just then, she saw Houghton enter the corridor from another passageway about halfway down to the left.

She walked toward him. "Nick, I think we need to get out of here. I just saw the guards chatting to the receptionist and then looking at the names of patients. I've got a bad feeling."

"Ok, let's go and check."

The pair walked towards the reception area, but Dee suddenly stopped and pulled Houghton back. The man she had met outside the toilet was talking to one of the guards and pointing towards the corridor.

"Is there another exit?"

"That's what I've been trying to find out. Quick, down here."

They returned to the adjacent passageway that Nick had been investigating.

They walked further into the building; it was like a maze. There were various rooms on either side for specialist treatment. Signs were in Farsi and English. They passed Gynaecology, Paediatrics; the sound of children crying echoed down the corridor. Then, on the right-hand side, they came to a fire door.

Houghton checked it over. There were no CCTV cameras that he could see; the door was a simple push-bar and didn't appear to be alarmed. They were now on the opposite side of the hospital.

"Come on, we need to get out of here," said Houghton. He hit the bar and pushed the door.

It opened onto a service road. Houghton realised that this was the exit he had identified on the map earlier. Whether he could find it again was another matter.

They were close to the laundry and a large delivery vehicle went past them and pulled up about thirty feet away.

"Come on, this way," said Houghton following the route

the vehicle had come in from. "This must lead to a main road."

To the right, the austere, sixties building rose upwards to its seven stories. The verges were filled with shrubs and greenery; another service van went past them in the same direction.

The road veered left and Houghton could see the main road; the van turned right; it was a one-way street. It would be Kerman Street, he quickly realised, which would go past the main entrance.

"Come on, down here," said Houghton.

They reached the main road and turned left and waited under the lee of a tall fir tree; the flow of traffic headed right. Houghton took stock. "We need a cab."

The traffic was moving fairly quickly, and cars were passing at over twenty-miles-an-hour. "Keep an eye out," said Houghton.

It didn't take long before Houghton spotted an orange cab in the distance; it was unoccupied. He came out of the shadows and raised his arm, prompting an emergency stop by the driver.

"Sa'adi Metro Station," said Houghton. They got in and the car pulled away. After only about two hundred yards, the cab slowed as the traffic backed up, and by the time it was passing the front entrance of the hospital, they were travelling at walking pace. They could see guards patrolling the front of the hospital; one or two had their rifles poised at the ready as if they were searching.

Houghton moved down in the seat; Dee followed suit. He was fairly sure they couldn't be seen by anyone, but he didn't want to take any chances. The driver noticed their behaviour in the rear-view mirror and thought it strange. Then they were away, and, for the moment anyway, out of immediate danger.

It took another twenty minutes to reach the Metro stop. Houghton gave the driver some notes and a tip to cover the fare and opened the door. They both got out and ran down the station steps out of sight.

Houghton took out his phone and called Dexter. "David, it's Nick, can you send the car to the Metro stop at Sa'adi; we're waiting out of sight. I'll explain later."

They were at the usual station, close to the embassy; Houghton did not want to risk walking back, given the level of surveillance.

It was another fifteen minutes before Houghton spotted the car and called Dee to the pavement. He opened the door almost before the car had stopped and Dee jumped in; Houghton quickly followed.

Canadian Embassy, Tehran – 9:00 a.m.

The mood in the basement was dire. Podesta was frantically trying to think of a way to help the luckless Tony Alvarez; there was little chance of any intervention from Washington. More problematical though, with Alvarez's confession, the integrity of the unit was now a real concern.

It was clear that their operation had been compromised and, if Alvarez was to talk, which was possible, then it could make their situation not just awkward but downright dangerous. Just then, the red phone rang.

"Podesta," he responded. "Yeah." He listened while the Director of Operations gave his assessment of the situation.

"It's like this, Jo, with Alvarez's confession, it seems

like we've got a wolf by the ears here. If we confirm his status, we will lose a lot of credibility, you know what I'm saying? And, if we do nothing, then he's going to be doing a lot of time kissing the Ayatollah's ass. I've just come back from the Chief of Staff and he's concerned that the Canadian Embassy operation might not be sustainable now. We can't afford for any more of you guys to be taken, and I'm getting a lot of heat from Washington about why we got involved with this Egyptian guy in the first place. But I guess that's for another day."

"Yeah, I get that, sir. What do you want us to do?"

"Langley and GCHQ have been picking up a lot of chatter from the Iranians referring to the embassy. We think you might already be in danger. As you know, the Iranians have a history of not respecting diplomatic niceties, particularly if the mob get stirred up again like last week. If they find out the Canadians have been hiding CIA agents again like in 1980, God knows what will happen. You know what I'm saying?"

"Yeah, for sure," said Podesta.

"We've been talking to the Canadians and we need to get you out of there, fast."

"Yeah, ok. So, how do we do that? We can't just get a cab to the airport."

"Well, there's some good news. Now listen close, we don't have too much time. There's a flight from Tehran to Montreal this afternoon. You need to be on it, but you'll need to travel light, I'm afraid."

Podesta checked his watch; it was nine twenty-seven. "That doesn't give us much time."

"No, you'll want to be at the airport for eleven-thirty,

given their security checks. I hope you've all got your passports with you; if not, we're fucked."

"I'll check, but I don't think that'll be a problem."

"Well, if you need to go back to your apartments for anything, that's your call, but the place is going to be surrounded by surveillance teams. You'll need to be damn careful. Someone is speaking to the Canadian Ambassador there to get some transport sorted out as we speak."

"What about the equipment?"

"Yeah, that's the real bummer; you got a lot of dollars there. Still, it can't be helped. We're going to be donating it to the Canadians for their help."

"Yeah, ok, got that."

"Good. In the meantime, we need to get rid of any paper, printouts and files. Make sure you empty all the cabinets; you know the drill. Shred, or if you've got an incinerator, burn everything. Destroy all the computer hard drives, and I mean in bits. The rest of the kit you can leave for the Canadians. Any questions?"

"No, we'll get on it right away."

"Ok, and good luck."

"Thanks."

Podesta hung up and called his two colleagues over.

"Ok, Javi, Jim, listen up. We've been ordered out of here and we don't have much time. We need to get rid of all the files; Jim, you start over there." He pointed to a row of cabinets. "Javi, I need you to wreck the computers, make sure the hard drives are totally useless ok?"

"Sure," said the pair in unison and went to work. "I hope you've both got your passports."

The next hour was frantic, and by the time they'd finished,

the basement looked like a tornado had hit it. There was a knock on the door.

"Hi Tod," said Podesta, addressing Tod Blaine, one of the senior Canadian diplomats.

"Are you guys ready? We've got a car waiting, but we're starting to see some activity outside, and if we don't go now, you may not get another chance."

"Ok," said Podesta. "Javi, Jim, we need to go."

They grabbed what personal stuff they had from their desk drawers. "Don't forget your passports whatever you do."

They took one last look around and joined the diplomat carrying small holdalls with their personal belongings.

They took the stairs to the ground floor and, already, the distant chanting of protestors could be heard. The diplomat took a look through the main entrance.

It's not too bad at the moment, probably twenty or thirty, but we need to leave the back way to be on the safe side.

The group followed Blaine through a security-controlled door. There was a long corridor which led to an emergency exit. "We put this in after 1980," said Blaine.

"I'm glad you did," said Podesta.

The diplomat punched numbers into a keypad and pushed open the door. An official embassy car, complete with CD number plates, was waiting. The liveried driver was holding the door open.

"Ok guys, this is it," said the diplomat and shook hands with his guests. "Good luck."

The three got in the car and hunkered down. The rear external exit was controlled by a barrier and metal gates. As the car approached, the barrier raised, and the gates opened into a tree-lined thoroughfare with large houses on either side. The Indonesian Embassy was opposite. The sound of chanting could be heard in the distance, but this side was thankfully quiet.

The car sped away towards the airport.

Traffic was an issue and delayed the journey; they arrived at the airport terminal just before eleven forty-five. They grabbed their bags and walked through the main entrance. All three were wearing sunglasses which, if anything, made them look more suspicious and Podesta recognised that. "Ok, guys, nice and easy, let's find the airline desk."

The Canadian Airlines' check-in area was situated in the far end of the terminal, which was packed with armed soldiers and security police. Podesta felt as if he were running a gauntlet but was desperately trying to act naturally.

A few people were waiting, but within ten minutes, they had reached the front. Podesta handed in the three passports. "Ah, yes," said the girl. "We've been expecting you. I have your tickets; you can use our lounge until the flight is called."

The bags were stowed, and the boarding cards issued; just security and passport control to negotiate.

The departure process was very bureaucratic. Podesta sighed in despair when he saw a queue of maybe fifty people waiting in line. Each passenger's details were being checked rigorously by customs officers, flanked by armed guards, who were also taking an interest in the passengers. The line shuffled forward and there was a commotion at the front the queue. A middle-aged man was remonstrating with a customs official. Suddenly, one of the guards smashed his rifle butt against the side of the man's head and he went down. Two guards picked him up and dragged him to an adjacent office with blood pouring down the side of his face.

Podesta looked at Jim, who had also witnessed the scene. He raised his eyebrows. As they got closer to the checkpoint, Podesta's heartbeat increased; his palms felt clammy and he could feel sweat forming in his armpits and staining his shirt.

He reached the desk. The uniformed man looked at him with suspicion. "Passport," he barked.

Podesta handed over his documents. The officer opened it and studied it carefully. He held the picture in his outstretched arm and compared it to the real Podesta. Satisfied with the match, he scoured the rest of the passport checking for the entry stamp and any other country stamp.

Podesta held his breath. The back page was open and for a moment the clerk hesitated before bringing the indelible stamp down with a thump. He handed back the document to Podesta. The armed guards who were in attendance moved to one side and let him through.

Rao and Blasic were subjected to the same nerve-wracking treatment but, after ten minutes, all three were heading to the Canada Airlines' Lounge ending CIA operations in Iran for the immediate future. Next stop, Montreal.

MOIS Headquarters – 11:30 a.m.

Just before midday, the General and his deputy were in the interrogation suite waiting for the arrival of Tony Alvarez. The General had spent much of the morning with two judges from the judiciary discussing Alvarez's case, and he had some news; it was not good.

A few minutes later, two guards escorted Alvarez into the room, hooded and cuffed. The hood was removed and again he was shackled to the table.

The General looked at him. He still hadn't washed and had been existing on one dish of gruel and two bottles of water a day. His chin showed the start of a beard and his face was white; his eyes sunken into their sockets. He'd hardly slept.

Earlier, around six-thirty a.m., he'd been woken from his already broken sleep by rattling keys. The door to his cell swung open. This time he wasn't hooded, just dragged down the corridor to another room. He was still half asleep and not able to focus properly. When he got inside, he was almost blinded by TV arc-lights. He was placed in a chair, and then a commentator walked into the room, wearing a smart suit, and speaking to the camera. Then the lens turned to Alvarez. It scanned him up and down, zoomed in on his face, then returned to the presenter who finished his broadcast. Alvarez had no idea what was happening. Minutes later, he was picked up from the chair and frog-marched back to his cell.

Moghrabi lit up a cigarette. "Doctor Alvarez, I have some news about your sentence. I have been speaking all morning with the judges. I must tell you that, despite my pleading, they are going to apply the death sentence. You will appear before them this afternoon to be told officially."

Alvarez looked at the General in disbelief. "What? But you said…"

"Yes, I know, but we can only recommend. It is not my decision. Unfortunately, with the way the United States are treating Iran at the moment, the judges are not inclined to give their spies any leniency. I'm sorry, but there it is."

Alvarez was in deep despair. The General looked at him in an almost paternal way. "Do not worry, my friend, there may still be a chance; the decision has to be confirmed by the Ayatollah. It is possible that he will take pity on you and offer clemency, but…"

Alvarez's head was on his chest; he could feel water dripping down the inside of his trousers.

"There may be a way – something I could give to the judges to advise our Supreme Leader to consider a pardon."

"What's that?" asked Alvarez, clinging on to hope.

"I have been talking to General Khatami since we heard the news of the sentence, and he thinks, as do I, that if you could just provide us with a little more information, it will help your cause."

"I don't have any information," said Alvarez weakly.

"Of course you do!" shouted the General, causing more smoke to billow from his mouth and nose. "We know you have been using the Canadian Embassy as a base. We know this. Our contacts tell me three or four more agents are there. What do you say to that?"

"I can't say," replied Alvarez.

"But you are not denying it, are you?"

"You seem to know what's going on."

"So, you admit it? There are others involved here."

"I never said that."

"No, but you didn't deny it." The Commander was taking notes again and had completed a side of A4.

Suddenly, a piercing scream echoed around the building. Alvarez shuddered; the General did not bat an eyelid.

"It's ok, do not worry, we are already taking action. Our Government has made a formal complaint to the Canadian Prime Minister about the misuse of diplomatic facilities, and of course, it is impossible to keep this sort of news away from the press. I understand that you met one of our broadcasters this morning."

Alvarez just looked at him.

"Yes, the whole world will soon know about the treacherous workings of President Bush and the American Government. I mean, if our enemies are using spies against us, then we must defend ourselves? If they expect us to take no action, they are wrong. The Iranian people will raise their voices, you will see."

The General was getting carried away with his presidential-style remarks, which were taken almost word-by-word from a recent broadcast by Mahmoud Ahmadinejad. The General's voice dropped.

"So, let's go through this again, you don't deny that the CIA has agents in the Canadian Embassy. How many? Three or four?"

"You seem to know all the answers," said Alvarez.

"Hmm, what about Brechtel? You worked there, spying at Arak. How many more agents worked there?"

"I don't know," said Alvarez.

"But there were others?" pressed the General.

"Not to my knowledge," said Alvarez, who was, by now, almost totally compliant.

"So, just you?"

"As far as I know," said Alvarez.

The General checked his watch.

"Ok, that will do for the moment; I will report our discussion to General Khatami and see if he will speak favourably to the judges. You will need to be ready for two o'clock to attend the court. I will authorise a shower for you."

Alvarez felt dazed; if he were able to stand, it would resemble sleepwalking. The General and Commander stood up and left the room; Moghrabi spoke to one of the guards on the way out. Alvarez was released from his shackles and helped to an adjacent room. It was a toilet, with washing and shower facilities, provided for the guards.

He was taken to the shower area and one of the officers gestured for him to remove his clothes. He was given a block of soap and a towel. While the guards watched on with their Kalashnikovs primed, Alvarez washed himself down in the tepid water. It did have a reviving effect, but there was so little energy left in the agent.

Having completed his washing, Alvarez dressed again. He winced at the smell of his clothes and the various stains.

He was returned to his cell to await his appearance in court.

The Judicial Palace and Supreme Court, Khayyam Street, Tehran

Alvarez was taken by car, hooded and cuffed again, to the Supreme Court, arriving about one forty-five. He was taken to the cells, given a bottle of water and allowed to use the toilet.

Just before two o'clock, three armed guards led him up a flight of stairs and into a courtroom. He wasn't hooded but was seated with his hands cuffed in front of him. This was the biggest courtroom of the three in the building, probably seating a hundred people on church-like pews. Most of them were empty. At the opposite end of the courtroom was a large wooden rostrum which would hold eight people. In front of the seating area was a space filled with a phalanx of news reporters. Alvarez took in the scene; there must have been twenty or thirty journalists and an array of cameras and microphones pointing in his direction.

A court official walked in and cleared the newshounds to one side; then shouted something in Farsi. Alvarez was lifted to his feet as three men walked in, dressed in black ceremonial robes and turbans.

One of them read from a prepared script and then the three sat down. The whole process lasted about twenty minutes and was conducted entirely in Farsi; despite his reasonable understanding of the language, Alvarez had no idea what was happening. The judges appeared to be in conversation for most of the time, referring to pieces of paper every now and again. Having signed a confession, there was no requirement for a defence lawyer.

At the end of the proceedings, the senior judge appeared to sum up. There was a gasp from one or two of the reporters and then the cameras started up again.

One of the reporters shouted at him. "You are going to die, American spy." A couple of others joined in shaking their fists at the Mexican; their faces twisted with hate.

British Embassy, Tehran – 5:00 p.m.

Dee and Houghton had spent the early part of the afternoon discussing their hospital visit and Houghton had drawn a more detailed map on a sheet of A4 based on their observations and the hospital brochure. There were still many loose ends, and everything would depend on perfect timing.

There was a knock on the door and Dee returned.

"Hi, just thought you would want to know, that CIA guy's

got the death penalty. It's just been on CNN."

"What?"

"Yeah, his name's Alvarez, a Mexican apparently."

"What's the response from Langley?"

"Nothing, not officially anyway. They won't admit to any activity in Iran, despite the confession, not in the present climate. They're just repeating that it's a Mexican issue."

Houghton was deep in thought; he had expected another call from Jo Podesta, but it hadn't materialised.

"The Mexican President's been in touch with Tehran, according to Fox News, to appeal for clemency."

"What are your thoughts?" asked Houghton.

"Well the decision's still got to be ratified by Ayatollah Khamenei, but it does give Iran a great deal of power in the present political climate. My assessment would be, they'll do nothing for a while and make the Americans sweat until there's an opportunity to use the situation to their advantage. I could be wrong, mind. There is a view that if the people start getting angry, and that's a distinct possibility, they may just give him a show execution to keep the mob quiet; it would also send a message to the Americans. There was a demonstration outside the Canadian Embassy this afternoon, which is almost certainly linked to this."

"Hmm, neither scenario's particularly pleasant."

"You don't think it was anything to do with that Egyptian we were monitoring, do you?"

"I don't know; it's possible, I guess."

"Well, if you ask me, with the present security situation, they would be stupid to take any risks."

Houghton looked at Dee; he recognised the irony. Then the penny dropped.

"I guess that puts us in the same situation," she said, and the room went quiet, just the hum of the high-frequency wave baffler rumbling away in the background.

"Are you on the minibus?" she said, breaking the silence.

"Yeah, what time?"

"There's another run at six, we've missed the five o'clock."

"Yes, ok. I'll be with you."

"What would you like for dinner?" she asked and smiled.

Chapter Sixteen

British Embassy, Tehran – Sunday April 23rd – 10:00 a.m.
Nick Houghton was in his office when the internal phone rang. It was David Dexter.

"Oh, hi, David. You have some news?"

"Yes, everything's looking promising for next week. I spoke to Afareen this morning and she's still getting a nightly call from her husband, but the really good news is, she said he's been given a three-day pass for Wednesday. He needs to get back on Saturday for the evening shift."

"That's great news," replied Houghton. "You heard the latest on Alvarez, I guess?"

"Yes, sad news," said Dexter.

"I was expecting a call from Jo Podesta, but it never happened."

"Yes, and I know why. They've gone. We heard this morning that the Americans have pulled out."

"Really? That explains the silence then."

"Yes, and it's just as well. The Iranians have already lodged a complaint to the Canadian Ambassador; it could have sparked more unrest. There were a few hardcore protestors out yesterday, but it seems to have gone quiet this morning, thank goodness. There was a worry we were looking at a 1980 scenario."

"Jeez, now that was scary." Houghton reflected for a moment and there was silence on the line.

Dexter resumed the conversation. "Oh, by the way, the

Mahabadis' passports arrived in the diplomatic bag this morning. I've had a look at them; they look fine, and your hospital pass is also ready; Ryan and his team have done a great job; I think you'll be happy with the result."

"Thanks David, that's great."

"No problem, I'll ask Dee to pop them down."

They finished the call and Houghton went back to his planning.

A little later, Dee knocked on Houghton's door and brought in the usual coffee and pastries; it was part of the routine now.

"Hi," said Houghton, accepting the coffee and snack. "Cheers, have a seat. I'm glad you called. Is there any more news on that CIA guy?"

"The Mexican?"

"Yeah."

"No, not really; the Americans are still denying any involvement; although they're now saying the guy was probably tortured into confessing. That's got one or two human rights groups interested. Washington has promised to give support to their 'Mexican friends'." Dee made the inverted comma sign with her fingers.

"Hmm, that doesn't sound good."

"No, it isn't. What's your interest in this guy anyway? You haven't said," asked Dee.

"Oh, um, nothing really, we probably had similar missions. I need to make sure mine doesn't go the same way; it just goes to prove there's no room for any complacency."

His facial expression reflected the gravity of the situation; but, inside, he was also racked with guilt.

"Yes, it certainly does. So, what's on the agenda for today," said Dee, oblivious to Houghton's torment.

Houghton refocussed. "I've been thinking about our hospital visit yesterday and I need to meet a contact."

"I didn't know you had another contact."

"No, I thought it best not to say anything; it protects you, and the contact. In fact, no-one here knows about her, not even David, but she does have a crucial part to play in the project."

"It's a she?" commented Dee.

"Yes, she works at the hospital. She was the one who got me the brochure. I'll tell you more on Thursday."

"Ok, so, we're definitely going for it on Thursday?"

"Yes, I spoke to David earlier, and Afareen's still in contact with her husband. He's due back in Tehran sometime Wednesday, but it all depends if we can get the transport arranged in time. Is there any news?"

"Not since yesterday. I'll send Leila a text and get an update."

"Thanks, and I need to know the cost if you can find out. I'll have to arrange for the dollars from London and that'll take a day to arrive."

"Yes, ok, I'll ask her."

"We do have an additional day's window, if necessary, but Mahabadi's due back in Natanz on Saturday and we've got no idea when, or if, he'll get anymore leave in the short-term." He took a drink of his coffee. "Some good news; David tells me he's got the passports and my hospital pass; so that's one thing crossed off the to-do list. Can you pick them up for me, if you're passing; David has them?"

"Sure, I'll drop them down later."

They finished their coffees and Dee returned to the comms room. Houghton picked up his mobile phone and sent a text. *'2:30?'*

Ten minutes later came a reply; *'Yes'*.

By one-fifteen, Houghton had changed for his trip to see Mayflower. He made his way to the carpool for his usual ride to the Sa'adi Metro station. David would sign him out.

It was another routine exercise, with Kazem driving, and he reached the Panzdah-e-Khordad stop in good time for his meeting. He climbed the stairs from the platform, reached the exit and turned left towards the entrance to the Bazaar.

He didn't notice someone else taking more than a passing interest in the stranger with the maroon jacket. For Houghton, it was a case of being in the wrong place at the wrong time.

Agent Gerami was one of the guards summarily relieved of his duties by the General for failing to track Houghton on an earlier excursion. He was on a boring routine patrol, still sore at being removed from surveillance activities, particularly on such a high-profile target. As luck would have it, he just happened to be passing the Metro stop as Houghton emerged from the exit; he recognised him immediately. He unclipped his walkie-talkie from his belt and called his partner, agent Taherian, who was inside the station.

"Quick, I have seen him, the man from the British Embassy that we lost. He is here," said Gerami animatedly.

Taherian rushed up the stairs and into the bright sunshine, where Gerami was anxiously waiting. He was peering into the distance keeping Houghton in sight; he was not going to lose him again.

"Quick, hurry, before he goes into the Bazaar."

The pair started running and Gerami radioed for assistance. Houghton was early for his meeting and taking his time.

The Grand Bazaar was, as usual, teeming with people; but within the throng, there were numerous MOIS personnel, some on uniform patrol, others in plain clothes, watching out for any anti-government activity. The message, and Houghton's description, was soon being relayed around the various malls. Gerami was giving a walking commentary as he watched Houghton cross the road by the pharmacy towards the entrance. "Maroon-colour jacket, grey trousers, and sunglasses. He is entering the Bazaar at the Reza entrance; all patrols be alert; he is to be apprehended and taken into custody for questioning."

Gerami received several acknowledgements as the MOIS agents were put on alert.

Houghton, unaware of the activity around him, took a few moments to look up at the ornate stain-glass window; artistic mosaics reflecting the sun in a myriad of colours across the interior brickwork.

Then Houghton spotted a man on a walkie-talkie. He appeared to be staring at him.

Houghton had developed a sixth sense when it came to personal security. Something felt very wrong; the person's body language said 'threat'.

Houghton applied his experience, no sudden movements, avoid eye-contact. He was now on high alert and quickened his step. Then another man came towards him and Houghton dodged left into a smaller mall. The two agents started to give chase and were soon joined by Gerami and Taherian. With four MOIS agents on his tail, Houghton's heart rate had increased significantly. He was deploying standard avoidance tactics in an attempt to evade his pursuers.

Twenty yards further down the mall, he turned left out of sight and ran through the crowd until he came to another junction. He turned right and ran again for about fifty yards, then slowed, went into a jewellery shop and looked behind him. He couldn't see anyone, but the area was still packed with people and it was not easy for him to identify who was friendly and who was not. The shopkeeper, spotting a potential customer, approached him.

He ignored the vendor, much to the man's displeasure, left the shop and took the next left. He was in one of the specialist malls where every shop was a perfumery. The aromas wafted across the walkway, in normal times, the aroma would be fragrant and pleasant, but at this moment for Houghton, it was sickly-sweet and nauseating.

He dodged into another shop. This time, the emporium had a double entrance. He stopped for a moment, took off his jacket and turned it inside out. There was a powder-blue lining which he hoped would confuse his pursuers, at least from a distance, and give him the time he needed to escape. He took off his glasses and put them in his pocket. A small transition, but he hoped it would be enough.

The lady proprietor looked bemused at his behaviour; Houghton just smiled at her and nodded. He walked through the shop and out the other side.

He was now in another busy mall. He could see two uniformed officers about fifty yards in front of him; one of them was speaking on a walkie-talkie. Houghton ducked down. He looked again just as the other officer grabbed a passer-by who happened to be wearing a maroon jacket and pinned him to the floor. There was a scuffle and a considerable commotion which enabled Houghton to reach another turn.

With over twenty-two miles of alleyways and passages, the Grand Bazaar is rightly named. Unfortunately, Houghton was now totally lost; he knew he had to find an exit, any exit. They would be guarded; it's what he would do if he was in charge, but there was little option. He would cross that hurdle when it came to it.

He continued dodging, checking behind him over his shoulder, not looking where he was going. Suddenly, he crashed into a display outside a fruit stall and went sprawling, sending apples rolling in all directions. The proprietor came out from behind the stall and started remonstrating with Houghton while trying to pick up stray apples before he lost any more. The greengrocer shouted at a couple of youths who had helped themselves and were now running away.

Houghton picked himself up and held his hand up in apology, then continued. He made another turn into a narrow alley and peered around the wall back to the greengrocer's stall to see what was happening. One or two people had started helping the stallholder retrieve the fruit and put them back on the display. Then Houghton noticed a muscular-looking man approach the proprietor. There was a discussion and he saw the vendor point in Houghton's direction. Houghton turned around and quickly walked away, then took another right.

He felt a sense of recognition. The shops seemed familiar; he'd been here before. Then he saw the hanging kettle sign. It was the café he had visited with Dee and Leila. He had no idea how he had got there.

He reached the entrance and, taking a chance, walked inside. It was busier than his previous visit with probably thirty customers. He looked anxiously over his shoulder through the glass window behind him; for the moment, it was all clear.

He caught the eye of the proprietor who was serving a table not far from the doorway. There was no immediate recognition.

The man called one of the waiting staff over, handed her an order slip and pointed to the appropriate table. Then he went over to greet Houghton who was still in the doorway, sweat dripping down the side of his face, reddened from the exertion.

"Do you speak English?" Houghton asked.

"A little," replied the café-owner.

"Do you remember me…? I was here with Leila from the tapestry store two days ago."

The man looked at Houghton trying to place him; there was a familiarity.

"Yes," he said but still uncertain.

"I need to get away; people are after me… From the ministry," he added, hoping the man really could be trusted as Leila had said.

The man froze for a moment, then made his decision.

"Yes. Ok, come."

The man walked through the café and into the kitchen. Two other assistants were preparing food. He said something to one of them, then turned to Houghton.

"This way."

Houghton followed him.

There was a back door to the kitchen with a key in the lock. The man unlocked it and led Houghton into a small yard surrounded by a lattice fencing and a gate. There was an over-flowing dumpster in the corner; rubbish was strewn across the stone floor. Wasps were gorging on food waste; there were flies everywhere. In the corner of the yard, there was a small, ancient Vespa moped, probably the proprietor's pride and joy.

There was a crash-helmet on the seat which the man passed to Houghton. Then he pulled open the wooden gate and used a brick to keep it in place.

Houghton mounted the Italian scooter behind the café-man and held on. The weight of the combined riders strained the bike's suspension to breaking point. At least the headgear would go some way to preventing any facial recognition as long as Houghton kept looking straight ahead. His jacket was now folded on the pillion between him and the man; he was as anonymous as was possible. Everything was resting on the next few minutes.

"Where do you want to go?" asked the man.

"The Metro Station, at Sa'adi, thank you."

The man kick-started the scooter. It didn't fire; he tried again, and again; the engine just coughed. He leaned down, pressed something and tried again. This time the engine roared into life, prompting a plume of blue smoke from the exhaust. The noise echoed around the yard. The man twisted the throttle again and put it into gear; the bike jumped forward as the man released the brake.

He guided the bike slowly into the mall. It was still full with people and the man was weaving in and out trying to avoid pedestrians. It took several minutes before they reached the exit, a period of extreme anguish for Houghton. He leaned closer to the rider and held his breath. The man eased forward slowly into the daylight, but then stopped.

This was it, thought Houghton; there was no escape.

The café-owner started speaking to someone; Houghton could not make eye-contact. He was trying to decide whether he should leap off the bike and take his chances, but then the bike moved forward, and they were in traffic on the main road, heading away from the bazaar.

Houghton felt sick and was shaking. Sweat was pouring into his eyes and he lifted his hands to clear his vision. He did not want to make any sudden movements in case it caused the scooter to over-balance.

It took another fifteen minutes to reach the Metro stop. The man slowly pulled to the side of the road and Houghton dismounted, removed the crash helmet and passed it to him.

"Thank you, you saved my life," said Houghton.

The man just nodded and drove off. Houghton disappeared into the station and called Dexter.

Twenty minutes later, Houghton was in his office changing back into his suit with a lot of thinking to do. Then he remembered Mayflower, she would be waiting at the café. He sent a text.

'Sorry, could not see you, friends turned up will contact you again soon. Different place, ideas?'

It was over an hour before she replied.

'It's ok, give me new time, I will find somewhere.'

Houghton called Dee and a few minutes later she knocked on the door.

"Are you ok?" she asked, seeing Houghton looking serious and still recovering from his ordeal. Sweat was glistening on his brow.

"Take a seat; we have a problem."

Houghton described his near-miss. "I need to think of a way of getting about, my description will have been circulated, and the surveillance teams outside will be on the lookout too."

"Hmm, yes, have you got anything in mind?"

"Not yet, but I'll need a new jacket."

He smiled, but inside, he knew he'd been lucky today.

"I do have some better news," said Dee. "I had a message from Leila and her dad's managed to get a car he thinks would be ok."

"That's great; what is it?"

Dee checked a piece of paper she was holding. "I had to write it down. It's a Khodro Peykan, five-seater."

"A Khodro? Jeez. I've seen more of those parked up with their bonnets open than anything else since I've been here."

"Come on, Nick, that's the pride of the Iranian car industry you're talking about," she said and laughed.

"How old?"

"Two years,"

"Well, that's something… as long as it didn't belong to a taxi driver."

"Do you want me to tell her to find anything else?"

"No, no, we'll manage, thank you. Did she say how much?"

"For the van as well, he wants fifteen thousand," said Dee.

"Dollars?"

"Yes," said Dee.

"Hmm, ok, I'll get David to send a chit, we should get it by Tuesday. I wouldn't mind going to check them over.

Can you see if you can arrange a meeting Tuesday morning sometime?"

"Yes, ok, where?"

"Do you know where their garage is?"

"No, but I can find out from Leila."

"Great, do that, and if that's not safe, see if she's got any other suggestions about where to meet. In the meantime, I'll see what I can do about changing my appearance a little."

"I can always apply some makeup if that would help," said Dee and smiled.

Houghton smiled back; it had lightened the mood.

Dee left, having invited Houghton to dinner again; it would be another wasted night for the surveillance teams listening in on any conversations.

Houghton had another problem. He called David Dexter for a discussion.

A few minutes later, Dexter was with Houghton in the office. The agent described his near-miss. "I'm going to need to be very careful over the next few days."

"Well, if there's anything I can do to help, just let me know."

"Sure, cheers. There is something I need your thoughts on. I need to brief Afareen; she's going to be crucial to the success of this mission. The problem is, I don't want to speak to her at your place, given the bugging; I don't want to take any chances."

"No, I can understand that. Have you got something in mind?"

"Yes. I don't know why I hadn't thought about it before. Can we get her in here for a day? You know, to do some cleaning. We can say there is a special reception or something."

"Yes, I don't see why not; when will you need to do it?"

"Well, if we go Thursday, then I think we need her Wednesday morning. She's going to want Thursday to arrange things at home."

"Yes, that makes sense; I'll speak to her in the morning. She'll probably have to clear it with her supervisor, mind."

"Hmm, I hope that won't raise any questions," said Houghton.

"Well, she could just call in sick, I suppose," countered Dexter.

"Yeah, but what if she's spotted coming into the embassy? That would really cause problems."

"Hmm," said Dexter.

"No, we'll go with the original idea. We'll just have to hope that her supervisor is not MOIS. Oh, by the way, I need some money to pay for the vehicles – fifteen thousand dollars."

"I don't think we carry that amount here."

"No, I wasn't expecting you to. I need you to put a chit into Vauxhall. They are expecting it. How long will it take?"

"I'll get it in today; you should get it in the bag by Tuesday."

"Cheers," said Houghton.

Dexter stood up to leave, then put his hands in his jacket pocket. "Oh, I nearly forgot." He handed Houghton four passports and his hospital credentials.

"Cheers," said Houghton and flicked the pages. "Hey, these are really good. I must tell the Mahabadis to remember their new names."

He checked his hospital pass; it was a close match to Mayflower's. "They've even made you a lanyard," said Dexter as he watched Houghton examine the ID.

"Yes, this is fantastic," said Houghton and looked at the name; 'Doctor Manzur Al-Fadhli'. He would need to remember his new name too.

Gholhak Garden Compound– 7:30 p.m.

Dee and Houghton were eating their evening meal in an air of domesticity, at least that is how it would be viewed by a casual observer. There was, though, an underlying tension; not in any way to do with their bourgeoning relationship, but solely caused by the mission. Operation Tiger Lily hung over them like a shroud. It was the only topic of conversation.

"I've been thinking about the car situation," said Dee.

Houghton finished a mouthful of salad.

"What's your thoughts?"

"Well, after your experience today, I don't think you should be going out before Thursday. If you get caught, then it's all over... and worse."

"Yes, ideally, but I've got no option."

"Well, I can see to the cars and pay the money. I know my way around, and I'm certainly capable of checking out a couple of motors. Besides, if you want me to do the driving, I could do with some practice."

He thought for a moment. "That could work. When were you thinking of?"

"When will you get the money?"

"Tuesday, in the diplomatic bags."

"Ok, I'll call Leila tomorrow and arrange it."

MOIS Headquarters – 8:00 p.m.

General Moghrabi and his number two, Commander Fallahian, were in the interrogation room waiting for their interviewee. There was a manila folder in front of the commander and a fresh pack of smokes in front of the General.

The atmosphere was still triumphant following the capture and conviction of the CIA agent; both men had been commended by the Head of the Ministry for their investigative work. There was, however, an embarrassing loose end which they were about to close.

The door opened and a hooded and manacled man was pushed into the room by two armed guards. He was wearing a shirt and trousers, which were heavily stained with blood and other bodily fluids. The hood was removed and Doctor Amadi, now former, Project Director at the Esfahan nuclear complex stood in front of them, head bowed. His face was bruised and swollen, his right eye, almost closed, his left ear seemed to be connected to his head by congealed blood. He blinked as the luminesce of the room irritated his eyes. He was pushed onto the chair and shackled to the table.

The General opened the pack of cigarettes and lit up; then blew out a stream of smoke and stared at the man in front of him.

"Hmm, Doctor Amadi, I must apologise for the behaviour of one or two of my guards; they do get a little enthusiastic at times, particularly with people they believe have been acting against the State."

Amadi looked back at the General, not really taking in the remark.

The General continued. "Ok, well, the reason why I need

a further discussion with you was just to clarify your story again, to make sure I have my facts correct before I present your case to the judiciary and close my file. I don't like loose ends."

"I've done nothing wrong. I've already told you everything I know," replied the Egyptian, his voice shaking with fear.

"Well, that's what you say, but the Commander, here, and myself, we have been discussing your statement with General Khatami and he feels, how can I put this? Well, not to put too fine a point on it, we think you are lying."

"I swear, on my children's life that I have told you the truth."

"Ah, yes, your children, and your wife, too; very pretty, if I might say. She's very young for someone your age. She must give you much pleasure; several of the guards have already said how attractive she is. They all want to guard her." He turned to his number two and started to laugh.

Amadi was beside himself with rage and pulled at his shackles, causing his wrist to snag on the metal constraints and start to bleed; he wanted to kill the General.

The General stared at Amadi with those penetrating eyes.

"It's ok, don't worry, they are safe, for now, and in good spirits, I understand. Well, I say good; I mean as well as can be expected, under the circumstance, finding out her husband has been colluding with spies. It must have come as quite a shock to her."

"Why are you doing this? I have told you everything. I have not been colluding with anyone, I told you already."

"Well, you say that, but you discovered this man, Alvarez, was a CIA spy; he was in your operations centre, in an important nuclear facility, probably gathering useful information for our enemies, and yet you DID NOTHING!"

The General shouted his last word and banged his fist down on the table, causing the ashtray to fall on the floor and spill its contents.

He dropped his voice to a menacing whisper. "We can't ignore that, can we Commander?" He looked at his deputy.

"No, sir," replied Fallahian.

"But I explained that," pleaded Amadi.

"Yes, you did, but it was your duty to report him; he was an enemy of the State."

Amadi looked down, then looked at the General.

"I have done everything and more for this country," he said weakly. "I have served the State loyally, I have been working fifteen, twenty hours a day, designing and building the best nuclear facility in the world. I have always done my duty."

"Not always, it seems. Commander Fallahian, have you got the document?"

The commander opened the manila folder and produced a sheet of paper. There was a narrative written in Farsi.

"I just need you to sign this and then we can see about releasing your family."

"What is it?" said Amadi, squinting his eyes. "I can't see it without my glasses."

"Not a problem; I will tell you what it says. It's a summary of the statement you have given us; that is all."

"But what does it say?"

"It says that you are Doctor Saleh Amadi Aziz Al Rajhi, Project Director at Esfahan Nuclear Facility. That you met the spy, Alvarez, and recognised him to be a CIA agent. That is correct, is it not?"

"Yes, that is correct."

"Good, then I just need you to sign it. I can then speak to my superiors and see if I can arrange for your family to return home."

"And if I don't?"

"Well, as I said, many of the guards are hoping to be able to make your wife's acquaintance. I am sure they will be disappointed not to have that pleasure. It's your choice."

Amadi was in deep despair, realising he was probably signing his own death warrant. He took the pen being offered to him by the General and signed.

"Thank you Doctor Amadi. You will hear the court's decision very soon."

"Take him away," barked the General at one of the guards.

The shackles were undone, he was hooded again and dragged back to his cell with blood oozing from the wound to his wrist.

Later that evening a meeting took place between General Khatami, Head of Security and three judges. With the signed 'confession' obviating the need for a formal trial, Amadi would be paraded before them and the media the following day.

British Embassy, Tehran – Monday April 24th – 10:00 a.m.

Houghton had just finished his morning telephone call with London. He had been briefing Jordan Proctor in the absence of Andy Fellows who was on his way to Baku, the Azerbaijan capital, as part of the exfil plan.

Dee knocked on the door and presented Houghton with his morning coffee.

"I've got some news about that Egyptian guy we were monitoring."

Houghton looked at her. "What about him?"

"It was just on the local TV news. He's been sentenced to death for colluding with the enemy."

"Hmm, the same as Alvarez?"

"Well, no, not exactly. Alvarez still has some value if he's kept alive; unfortunately, with relations between Egypt and Iran being what they are, this is more likely to go ahead, to send a message."

"Shit!" said Houghton under his breath. This was all on him and he recognised that.

"It's just the way things are under the present climate."

"Yes, we need to be very careful over the next few days," said Houghton.

"Which is why I don't think you should be going out, certainly not today. Look, I've been thinking, I can go into town and get you a new jacket if you like. I know a place that sells men's clothes; it's quite safe. It's in one of the new malls; many ex-pats shop there. It's only a couple of stops on the Metro. I'll need some money though."

"Well, ok, if you're sure. What will you need, local or dollars?"

"Dollars are always good; you get more respect from the vendors."

Houghton opened the drawer of his desk and took out an envelope. "Here's a hundred," he said, passing her a note. "That should do it."

"Ok, I'll bring you the change. I'll take your old jacket

and make sure I get the right size."

"No, wait. That jacket's a bit too distinctive. Take the size from the label, just in case."

"Yes, ok," Dee took Houghton's jacket and jotted down the size on a slip of paper. "Is there anything else you need while I'm out?"

"Not that I can think of at the moment. Actually, I could do with a holdall or something to put my stuff in. I don't want to take my suitcase."

"Yes, ok, I'll see what I can find."

Dee left Houghton's office, and a few minutes later, David Dexter came in with more news.

"Hi Nick, just wanted to let you know I've spoken to Afareen this morning and she's going to speak to her supervisor about spending a day here, but she doesn't think it'll present a problem."

"Hmm, I hope not. I was thinking, it's possible the Ministry are monitoring her movements. That phone they gave her could well be a tracker," said Houghton, looking pensively.

"Yes, it almost certainly is, but that's ok; if she's cleared it with her supervisor, they can always check. As I see it, it's the lesser of two evils," replied Dexter.

"Yes, I'd sooner she was here for the briefing, there's a lot to go through with her and timing is going to be crucial if we're going to pull this off. I need to make sure she knows exactly what to do. Oh, by the way, do you know Andy Fellows?"

"Hmm, I don't think I've met him."

"He's working for the Commander at the moment, but

he's been seconded to me for this mission. He's been my main liaison at Vauxhall."

"Ok," said Dexter.

"Well, he was keen to get some field experience, so he's on his way to Baku. He's going to get me a boat."

"Hmm, I hope he knows what he's doing," said Dexter.

"Yes, he's quite resourceful. I've been very impressed with him. I don't think he'll let us down."

Chapter Seventeen

Heydar Aliyev International Airport, Baku, Azerbaijan – Monday April 24ᵗʰ – 5:00 p.m.

Acting MI6 agent, Andy Fellows stared at the approaching landscape as his plane began its descent into Baku. From the air, it looked just like any other city, a mix of apartment blocks and more modern office accommodation, and, surprisingly, green spaces, not something Fellows had considered. For some reason, he had thought of it as some far-flung outpost. From his window seat, he could see the shoreline of the Caspian Sea and ships making their way to the port.

The Azerbaijan capital had undergone a considerable makeover since the fall of the Soviet era and was now trying to seek its own individual identity. The airport terminal reflected this new confidence and, as Fellows waited at the customs check, he took in his new surroundings with a mixture of excitement and anxiety.

It took about twenty-five minutes by taxi to his hotel and, after getting something to eat, he made a call.

Tural Aliyev had been an MI6 asset for over twenty years and had provided useful information back to London, especially on Russian naval activity in the area. With Russia continuing to exercise its presence in the region, he was still an active participant in information gathering.

Fellows had made contact via the Balkan desk in Vauxhall, so Aliyev was expecting the call. Armenian by birth, Aliyev was a fisherman by profession and knew the local waters as well as anyone. He was an ideal contact for Operation Tiger Lily.

Fellows listened as the call rang out.

"Hello." It was a gruff voice as if someone had been woken from a deep slumber.

"It's Pettigrew." This was the code name Fellows had arranged.

"Where are you staying?"

"The Hyatt Regency."

"Ha, very nice, too much money for me, I think," replied the man.

"I need to meet you; can you suggest somewhere?"

"Yes, of course, no problem. Fountains Square – the taxi drivers call it Parapet. There is a bar – Le Chateau Music Bar – they will know it. It is ten minutes only by taxi; be there in twenty minutes, dress smart. I will be at the bar; order a bottle of Dutch lager."

The line went dead; Fellows stared at the phone for a moment; welcome to Azerbaijan, he thought.

Fellows had travelled light and had no idea what the definition of 'smart' might be. With limited options, he dressed in the jacket and slacks he had travelled in, with a change of shirt.

He was starting to feel apprehensive, but Houghton had briefed him thoroughly on what was required in one of their recent routine calls. He made his way through the reception, and there was a line of taxis immediately outside the hotel. The porter hailed one and opened the door for the guest.

"Le Chateau Music Bar, er... Parapet," said Fellows, remembering Aliyev's instructions. He slid along the back seat. There was a nod of acknowledgement from the driver.

Fountains Square is a popular tourist destination with numerous bars and, as the taxi reached the area, Fellows could see hundreds of people milling about; it was busy for a Monday night.

A few minutes later, the car pulled up outside an impressive building, probably dating back to the early nineteen hundreds. The driver got out and opened the door for Fellows, who gave him ten Euros to cover the fare and tip. The taxi drove away, and Fellows checked his surroundings. He looked up at the architecture; Greek colonnades in ochre stone and red-brick infill. It reminded Fellows of some of the old bank buildings back home; most of which were now also bars, ironically.

He walked through the entrance and he could hear the sound of music coming from inside. It was busy and there was a bottle-neck to get through the entrance to the entertainment.

He pushed his way through the melee and checked his bearings. A live band was playing on a stage to the left to a crowd of about two hundred or so raucous fans. Flashing strobe-lights added to the ambience; the noise was deafening.

He looked to his right where a bar stretched half the length of the wall. It was fronted by at least twenty high stools, most of which appeared taken. With the majority of people heading for the stage area, the bar was less busy. Behind the serving counter, were several staff members; some serving, some chatting; one was washing glasses. Fellows walked up to the counter between two people who appeared to be staring into their respective drinks and attracted the attention of the nearest bartender. He ordered the beer as instructed.

"Sorry, we have only Belgian lager," the barman replied

in English, albeit with a strong local accent.

Fellows was confused, but then became aware of someone standing immediately behind him.

The man spoke to the barman. Fellows turned around.

"Do not worry, my friend, the Belgian beer is just as good," said the man.

The barman returned a couple of minutes later with two large schooners of beer and handed them to the man who paid in Euros.

He handed Fellows one of the glasses. "Tural Aliyev?" enquired Fellows.

"Just Aliyev is fine. Come, we talk," said the man.

Fellows took a sip of his lager and followed Aliyev out of the bar and up a wide flight of stairs, trying not to spill his drink. The staircase was the epitome of grandeur with ornate bannisters and expensive-looking carpet.

At the top, there was a Mezzanine, and in the middle, another entrance door guarded by two bouncers.

Aliyev walked up to one of them and spoke in Azerbaijani.

"Come," he said again, and Fellows followed him past the security and into a gaming room.

It was much darker and quieter than the downstairs area; the main illumination coming from the five tables providing the entertainment. The hush of concentration was only broken by the occasional voice of the croupiers and the rattling of plastic chips. There were two roulette wheels and three card-games in play with a huddle of people around each. There was a purveyance of cigar-smoke in the air.

Fellows chuckled to himself at the thought of James Bond, a cliché but apposite. Many of the men were dressed in dinner jackets and bow-ties. Very attractive girls in revealing dresses prowled the tables looking for custom. Fellows took it all in.

"Over here," said Aliyev.

Fellows followed him to an area of the room away from the gamers. There was a leather settee and two smaller matching armchairs around a glass-topped coffee table. A wall-light was set in a small alcove behind them, creating shadows. It was quiet in this corner, well away from the general hubbub.

"Do not worry, it is very safe," said the man, noticing Fellows unease.

Fellows waited for Aliyev to be seated and chose the adjacent armchair. He looked at his contact. He was smartly dressed, as required, in a white shirt, sports jacket and trousers. His face suggested an outside occupation, lined and weather-beaten, with a dark neatly-trimmed beard. His hair was greasy, thinning and grey at the sides.

He took a mouthful of beer and placed the glass on a beer mat on the table; Fellows did the same.

"So, tell me, Mr Pettigrew, you say to me you need a boat."

"Yes, you got the message ok?"

"Yes, of course. What sort of boat do you want?"

"A fishing boat would be ideal."

"I can do that. You have money?"

"Yes, how much?"

"That depends. Where do you need to go?"

"Bandar-e Anzali."

"Anzali? In Iran, yes?"

"Yes."

The man picked up his glass and took another slug of

beer; his face adopting a grave expression.

"Hmm, Iran, very difficult, very dangerous, and you will have cargo to return, yes?"

"Yes."

"Drugs?"

"No, no, not drugs," said Fellows, looking offended at the suggestion.

"People, yes?"

"Yes."

"How many passengers?"

"Five."

"Do you know what the Iranians do to people smugglers?"

"No."

"They sink the boats with the people on board; many, they drown. Very dangerous."

"Hmm," said Fellows, processing the reality check.

"Fifty thousand," said the man.

"Euros?" clarified Fellows.

"Yes."

"I can't do that much. Forty?"

"Forty-five or I go now and leave you to play the tables."

"Yes, yes, ok, forty-five," said Fellows, recognising his bargaining position was not strong.

"When do you want to leave?"

"We need to return Thursday night. How long will it take?"

"That depends on how many times we get stopped. Eighteen, maybe twenty hours. Bring some Euros to pay the patrol."

Fellows took a drink; he was thinking of the possible timeline. As long as he was in Anzali for Thursday night, the journey time didn't matter."

"So how do we play this?"

"Tomorrow you will come to my boat in the harbour; I will write the address, you can take a taxi, twenty-minutes, maybe, and you bring money."

"Yes, ok, what time?"

The man was writing on a piece of scrap paper from his pocket. He gave it to Fellows who read it out aloud.

"Namiq Quliyev, Derya Fish House, South Bay."

"Yes, we meet there, one o'clock; have some food, and then I will take you to my boat. Do not worry the taxi will know it. It is very famous in Baku."

"Yes, ok, tomorrow, one o'clock," replied Fellows,

"Good, good and now we enjoy ourselves, yes?"

"I need to get back and get some sleep," said Fellows.

"You are here in Baku; you should enjoy yourself. The girls, they are very beautiful, from Russia. Give you a good time."

"Another time maybe," said Fellows. He finished his beer and got up; his business was concluded. "Can I get a taxi here?"

"Yes, yes, of course, outside, thirty meters, you will see." He demonstrated with his hands.

Fellows shook hands with his host. "See you tomorrow."

"Yes, nice doing business with you, Mr Pettigrew."

Fellows turned and walked towards the gaming room exit and watched as Aliyev headed for the tables; he was immediately approached by two girls.

On his return to his hotel room, Fellows took out his laptop and sent an email to Houghton.

'Tiger Lily on track, leave Wednesday for B.A. Meet as arranged.'

Hyatt Regency Hotel, Baku, Azerbaijan - Tuesday April 25th – 12:15 p.m.

Andy Fellows left his hotel and took the first available taxi, armed with the scrap of paper containing the destination. He gave the information to the driver. "Yes, it is no problem, I know it; everybody knows it," he said, and drove off.

Fellows took an interest in the passing city as the car moved down to the port, past the ferry terminal and the funicular, towards the docks. Here the scenery changed. Rusting hulks of tankers and other boats were squeezed together at their final moorings awaiting rescue or cutting for scrap. Discarded cranes and the detritus of other dockyard facilities suggested the area had seen better times. Eventually, they reached the restaurant.

It was a long wooden building; at the back, there was an additional alfresco seating area. It was clearly a popular place with the capacity for probably over a hundred and fifty covers. Through the window, he could see there was a children's playground, and, beyond that, a wide pedestrian promenade skirting the sea wall. Giant boulders had been placed at the water's edge to keep the tides at bay and prevent erosion. Men were fishing from them.

The restaurant was reasonably busy with probably half the seats taken, many with families. He looked around and saw Aliyev at one of the tables with an ocean view. The man waved, and Fellows walked over to join him. Several waiting staff were moving between the tables and the kitchen; Fellows had to dodge a couple to reach his host.

"Hello," said the man, and he got up to shake hands.

"Hi, I hope I haven't kept you waiting," said Fellows.

"No, I am here early. It is very busy here sometimes, and I wanted to have a table. Please, sit, the food here is very good. We eat, then I take you to the boat."

It was over an hour before they finished their food, and it certainly lived up to the billing. During the meal, Fellows gave Aliyev more detail about the mission. As he described what was required, Aliyev responded with a sharp intake of breath. There was no doubting the challenge ahead of them.

They left the restaurant and Fellows followed Aliyev to a large Toyota pick-up truck.

"Get in, I will show you the boat."

It was only about five minutes or so down to the old docks; everywhere there were more signs of industrial decay. They reached a pontoon. Aliyev stopped at the entrance and got out; Fellows joined him, and they walked along the landing stage past two other moored vessels.

Fellows looked at the boat as it bobbed up and down in the choppy waters. There was a name on the bow painted in Cyrillic script which Fellows couldn't translate. It was definitely a working vessel and in serious need of a lick of paint. It reminded Fellows of Quint's boat in the film Jaws; it was about the same size. He hoped it didn't suffer a similar fate. He didn't think there were any Great White Sharks in the Caspian Sea, but he couldn't be completely sure.

Aliyev went on board.

"Come," he said and beckoned Fellows.

Fellows walked along the short gang-blank and followed Aliyev into the wheelhouse. It was littered with maps and old papers. There was a large ship's wheel in the middle overlooking the front deck with various dials and switches either side; to the right, a radio.

"It is ok, yes?" said Aliyev.

"Yes, yes, it looks fine," said Fellows running his fingers down the flaking décor.

"Come, I show you more," said the captain, pulling open a door at the back of the wheelhouse which led down a short flight of stairs. It opened out into living quarters; a room with seating around the perimeter which converted into beds. Aliyev demonstrated for Fellows. "It is good, yes," he repeated at every opportunity, seeking reassurance from his customer that it would suit requirements. In the corner, there was a small galley.

"Plenty room for five people, yes?" said Aliyev.

"Yes, it looks fine," said Fellows.

"There is a bathroom through there," said Aliyev pointing to a door on the other side of the room. Fellows decided not to look too closely.

"Come," said Aliyev. "You have something for me I think," he added as they returned to the wheelhouse.

"Yes," said Fellows, and he put his hand in the inside of his jacket, took out an envelope and handed it to him.

Aliyev opened it and looked at the notes. He took them out and counted them. His expression changed.

"What is this?" he exclaimed. "It is not enough."

"It's twenty-five, you will get the other twenty when we dock in Iran."

The man's face turned from anger to a grimace. "You British, you trust no-one."

"It helps keep us alive," said Fellows. "Do not worry,

you will get the rest as agreed. I am just protecting my investment."

The grimace turned into a smile. "Yes, it is how you say? Cool," and Aliyev offered his hand.

"Come, I will take you to taxi. Tomorrow, you be here early, six o'clock; you bring plenty Euros to pay the patrol boats."

"Yes, ok, I'll be here," said Fellows and the pair left the boat and headed back to the Toyota.

Old Docks, Baku, Azerbaijan – Wednesday April 26th – 5:55 a.m.

It was a ten-minute walk from the main road, where the taxi left Fellows, to the pontoon where the boat was anchored. He was carrying a large duffle-bag with his toiletries and clothes and a sling bag around his shoulder containing his wallet and papers. He had dressed for the journey in an old tee-shirt, jeans, and deck shoes; his interpretation of what an Azerbaijani sailor might wear. It was a million miles from the power-dressing culture of Vauxhall Cross.

He retraced his steps from the previous day and reached the vessel. He could see Aliyev on the front deck looking in his direction.

He reached the boat, threw his bag to Aliyev and crossed the plank.

"Good morning," he said and shook hands with Aliyev.

"Come, we will leave now. Do you know what to do?"

"What do you mean?" said Fellows, thinking for a moment that he was expected to take the wheel.

"You can release the ropes, yes?"

"Yes, I can do that," said Fellows.

Aliyev stowed Fellows' bag in the wheelhouse as his passenger released the two ropes from the capstans that were securing the boat to the dock. Fellows jumped back on board and pulled in the gang-plank. He had reached the limits of his seamanship.

Aliyev put the engine into reverse and slowly opened the throttle. The boat slowly backed away from the pontoon. After about fifty yards, Aliyev made the turn and headed out into open waters.

For the first hour, Fellows sat next to Aliyev on what looked like an old bar-stool, as the captain steered a southerly course. The weather was fine and the sea calm. There was a gentle chug from the engine and Fellows was feeling good; the port of Baku was slowly disappearing in the distance behind them.

Fellows went to the galley and made some coffee; Aliyev had taken care of the food supplies with the money Fellows had given him the previous day. He returned to the wheelhouse carrying two metal mugs and handed one to Aliyev.

"I noticed the name of the boat, I don't read Cyrillic script, what does it mean?" asked Fellows, trying to make conversation.

"Azadlıq Ruhu? In English, it means 'free-spirit'. A good name, yes?"

"Yes," replied Fellows.

Five hours into the journey, the initial excitement and novelty had worn off. There was nothing of interest outside; the distant coastline to their right changed little;

the occasional mountain range, a coastal town went by as they continued south. Fellows kept polite conversation with his host to pass the time. The highlight of the journey was a school of dolphins that joined them for twenty minutes, keeping pace with the boat before they too appeared bored and moved off in a different direction. Aliyev said it was a good omen; Fellows hoped he was right.

Another five hours passed; it was four o' clock.

"Here, it is your turn," said Aliyev.

"What do you mean?" asked Fellows.

"It is your turn to steer. I need to sleep for some short time."

"But I don't know what to do."

"You do nothing. You keep the boat in that direction. Thirty minutes I will return; you do not have to steer very much; just keep straight."

Aliyev demonstrated for Fellows. "There; it is no problem. It is easy," said Aliyev and left Fellows clutching the wheel nervously."

After ten minutes, Fellows was getting used to the feel of the boat and found the experience exhilarating. He started singing quietly to himself, Rod Stewart. "I am sailing, I am sailing, home again, 'cross the sea, I am sailing, stormy waters, to be near you, to be free." He couldn't remember the second verse, so kept repeating the first; it was helping his concentration.

Thirty minutes went by, and there was no sign of Aliyev. He caught a glimpse of a small vessel on the horizon. They had seen several ships; the Caspian Sea was a busy waterway, but this was different; it appeared to be heading their way.

He called out. "Aliyev! Aliyev, there's a boat coming.

Can you come up?"

He called again and then heard movement behind him. The door opened and Aliyev came into the wheelhouse doing up his trousers.

"Why are you shouting? What is the problem?"

"Look, there," said Fellows pointing to the vessel which was now much nearer and closing in on the fishing boat.

Aliyev checked his charts. "Yes, we are now in Iranian waters; it will be a patrol boat. You have Euros?"

"Yes," said Fellows. "How much?"

"Five hundred is usual," said the captain.

"Right, ok," said Fellows and went below.

Ten minutes later, the patrol boat was less than fifty yards away. There was a shout from a loudhailer in English.

"Fishing boat. Stop your engines, we are coming alongside."

Aliyev looked at Fellows. "Do not worry, it is usual. I know many of them. Go below, I will deal with it. Give me the money."

The ship pulled alongside, and an armed officer leapt onto the deck, securing a rope. Another armed officer followed. One approached the wheelhouse while the other stood on guard with his AK-47 engaged.

"What is your purpose here, Captain?" said the first officer on reaching the cockpit.

"I am collecting supplies from Anzali," replied Aliyev.

"Papers?"

Aliyev gave the officer a manifest of items from a chandlery in Anzali, which he had prepared for this eventuality. He was familiar with the process.

The officer scrutinised the documents. "They seem to be in order," he said and passed them back. "You have the customs payment?"

"Yes," said Aliyev and he handed the man the five-hundred Euro note provided by Fellows. "That is the usual fee, yes?" added Aliyev.

"Yes, I think that will cover everything."

The officer had a cursory glance around the wheelhouse and left.

Minutes later, they had returned to the patrol boat and it moved away. Feeling the engines start up again, Fellows returned to the wheelhouse.

"Was everything ok?"

"Yes, no problem, we should be fine now," replied Aliyev.

It was nearly three am as the Free-Spirit chugged into the Iranian port of Bandar-e Anzali. Streetlights twinkled along the seafront, which in daytime would be busy with walkers and fishermen. It is a large city of over a hundred and forty thousand inhabitants, and its main claim to fame is that it is one of the largest producers of Caviar in the world. Fishing and associated industries are its primary source of wealth.

Although not a regular visitor, Aliyev had been here before and knew his way around. He had secured a berth for two nights at one of the commercial docking areas.

The weather was chilly now, and both Fellows and Aliyev were wearing jackets. Fellows watched as the captain steered the boat through the outer harbour and into the mouth of the Sefid River. They passed the ATC Oil Refinery on the left which seemed a hive of activity despite the hour, with its numerous arc-lights creating an impressive industrial landscape. Then the huge grain terminal appeared before the river narrowed.

Fellows spotted a military area in front of them where several patrol boats and two larger warships were at anchor. Given the present state of alert, illumination was confined to onboard lighting, which gave them a ghostly appearance in the dark.

Aliyev steered right into a smaller tributary, and ten minutes later, he was expertly guiding the boat into a berth between two other large fishing boats.

"Pettigrew, the ropes," ordered the captain, and Fellows dutifully went onto the forward deck and retrieved the mooring rope. As soon as the boat slid against the dock, Fellows jumped onto the concrete jetty and looped the rope over the capstan. Having secured the bow, Aliyev was waiting at the stern and threw the line to Fellows. Free-Spirit was safely secured.

Fellows climbed back on board.

"Now, we sleep. There are no bars open here," said Aliyev and started to laugh.

Bandar-e Anzali docks, Northern Iran – Thursday April 27th – 7:30 a.m.

The accommodation was basic, to say the least, but after concentrating for almost twenty hours, Fellows managed to grab about four hours sleep, despite the snoring of his companion.

The day was going to be long and boring; there was little to do until Houghton arrived with the passengers. The Anzali dock area was extensive, and Fellows needed to provide

Houghton with the exact location. He opened up his phone and sent a text. '*37.472024; 49.448963*'.

Moments later, he received acknowledgement; Houghton would know what to do.

Aliyev would never consider himself to be a chef, but he managed to prepare a fry-up for breakfast in the meagre galley. The living quarters soon smelled like a truck-stop, but Fellows and his unlikely travelling companion enjoyed the 'full-English'.

"We need to get fuel today," said the captain, after they had finished and cleaned up.

"How will we do that?" asked Fellows.

"There is a place, one, two kilometres away, we get gas, yes?"

"Yes," replied Fellows. "Whatever you say."

"You have the Euros you owe me?"

"You need it for the fuel?"

"Yes, we pay Euros."

"Yes, ok."

As far as Fellows was concerned, he'd struck up a good understanding with the Armenian on the inward voyage and was happy to pay the rest of the money earlier than he had intended. He unzipped his duffle-bag and retrieved an envelope, opened it and counted out the remaining balance, then handed it to Aliyev.

"I guess we're going to need some Euros for the return journey in case of patrol boats," replied Fellows.

"Yes, that is true," said Aliyev and started to laugh. "S'ok, Mr Pettigrew, I will see to it. No problem."

"Ok, thanks," said Fellows.

Aliyev folded the notes and put the money in his trouser

pocket.

"We go, five minutes, get gas, then return, ok? Today, we must be very careful. The Iranians, they patrol here all the time. They arrest many people and they are never seen again."

Fellows was beginning to appreciate this was a totally different environment to Azerbaijan and was on high alert.

The captain went up to the wheelhouse and Fellows followed. It was a bright, warm day, and with the benefit of daylight, Fellows was able to check his surroundings. They were moored on a long concrete quay on the river which was about a hundred meters wide at this point. There were boats of various descriptions immediately in front and astern. Fellows wondered how on earth Aliyev had managed to locate the place in the dark, a credit to his seamanship.

The adjacent area was built up, with warehouses and dockside cranes; it was a working river. A narrow service road separated the riverside from the buildings. The opposite bank seemed to be open land; the sea was about half a mile away, but out of view.

Fellows jumped onto the jetty and released the stern line and then the bow; he stood on the deck while Aliyev gently eased the boat out of the berth and into the river. The tide was flowing upstream aiding the propulsion; it was only a short journey to the filling station. The industrial buildings continued, some run-down others working. Forklift trucks moved between the factories loading and unloading.

After about ten minutes, there was a bend in the river and the service area came into view. Aliyev drew up alongside a row of three diesel pumps; the same as you would see on a garage forecourt, but with longer hoses.

Again, Fellows secured the ropes and Aliyev left the boat and went to the office behind the pumps. Fellows returned to the wheelhouse. He could see the captain chatting to someone inside and then handing over cash. There seemed to be a discussion over the price; it didn't appear to be friendly.

Aliyev emerged, looking angry. He went to one of the pumps and connected it to the boat's fuel intake. While it was pumping the fuel, he jumped back onboard.

He looked at Fellows. "How you say? Fucking robbers," he said and took two large cans which were secured to the side of the wheelhouse. After the pump had finished dispensing the diesel, Aliyev filled the containers.

Fellows watched the activity with curiosity. Then, he spotted two uniformed officers coming around the corner of the office. Fellows dropped down out of sight. He could feel his heart rate increase; he didn't know what to do. If he was discovered he would almost certainly be taken in for questioning. He had no entry documents; his passport was British and in a false name. He peered over the top of the wheel and watched as the men approached Aliyev. There appeared to be some sort of a discussion. He could see one of the officers point to the boat. Fellows dropped down.

He went down the steps into the living quarters; the smell of the fry-up still lingered.

He went to one of the benches and raised the top; inside there was some bedding. There was just enough room. Fellows jumped inside and pulled down the top. He lay there with barely an inch clearance. His breathing was fast; he could hear footsteps; someone was on board.

He heard the wheelhouse door open, then more footsteps as someone descended the stairs into the living quarters.

He could hear Aliyev; the discussion continued. Fellows couldn't understand what was being said. He held his breath.

Then the footsteps returned, ascending the stairs; more muffled discussion, then quiet.

Fellows exhaled, then heard someone descending the stairs.

"Pettigrew?"

Fellows pushed open the top of the bench and sat up; it was like Dracula emerging from his coffin.

Aliyev started laughing. "Very good, Mr Pettigrew, very good. Do not worry all is, how you say? Cool."

Fellows extracted himself from what he thought at one stage would be his tomb.

"What happened?"

"They wanted to check for illegal immigrants. It is ok; I paid them some customs money; now they leave us alone."

"Five-hundred?" said Fellows.

"Yes, it is how things are done."

Fellows took out a five-hundred Euro note from his trouser pocket and handed it to Aliyev. "Here, you better have this," he said, and the captain took it.

"Wait, I will check they have left."

Aliyev returned to the wheelhouse and called Fellows.

"They have gone, can you release the ropes and we will go back."

Fifteen minutes later, Aliyev was guiding the boat back to the original mooring where they would stay until the passengers arrived.

Chapter Eighteen

British Embassy, Tehran – Thursday April 27ᵗʰ – 9:00 a.m.

Today was going to define Houghton's career as an MI6 operative and maybe even his life. Days of detailed planning were about to be tested.

Houghton had been at his desk since seven o'clock, checking and rechecking, visualising every eventuality and planning contingencies. David Dexter had also been up early, and they had travelled to the embassy together in the Jaguar. The MOIS surveillance team had lost interest in the compound; nothing had happened for days and morale was deteriorating. They had taken little notice of the exit apart from logging the activity; the early departure had not registered any undue attention.

Houghton had spent what he hoped would be his last night in Tehran with Dee; it turned out to be a very emotional evening. In the morning, he had cleared his apartment, and his suitcase and carry-on were in the corner of his office. He needed to travel light today and would just use the holdall which Dee had acquired for him. The rest of his clothes would be sent to London by the embassy.

Dee was in the comms room checking MOIS traffic in case there had been any change that could affect their plans; so far, so good.

The good news was that Hassan Mahabadi was safe with his family. The bad news was that he was being watched closely. Fortunately, this was something that Houghton had factored in and was the reason behind the chosen method of exfil.

The previous two days had been taken up with briefings. Tuesday, he had met Mayflower in one of the new malls and spent over an hour going over the plan; her part in the operation would be critical. It was a nerve-wracking moment given his previous experience, but this time, there were no dramas.

The same day, Dee had visited Leila and managed to inspect the vehicles. The ambulance was looking in good shape and, externally at least, would fool the surveillance teams. There was no medical equipment inside apart from a stretcher which Leila's father had provided. "There's even a blue light," said Dee when describing the van to Houghton on her return.

Wednesday morning Houghton and Dexter had spent time with Afareen. She had also been introduced to Dee so she would be familiar with those involved in the mission. Houghton did have concerns; she was extremely nervous following her encounter with MOIS, and at one stage, she broke down in tears saying she could not go through with it. Gradually, however, Houghton managed to boost her confidence and, with her husband there to give her support, he felt she would be able to deliver her part.

Houghton had been buoyed by the texts from Fellows. He was relieved that this part of the operation appeared to have gone without a hitch. Houghton had written down the coordinates and closely studied a map of the area to find the exact location. He had committed the route to memory; he

could not afford to be found with maps of the important sea-
port in his possession. Fortunately, it was less than a mile
from Route 49, which was the one he would be taking from
Tehran.

Houghton was not good with inactivity; he just wanted to
get the mission underway. His nerves were obvious; tapping
his desk with his pen, walking around the room, picking
up pieces of paper then placing them back again without
reading them.

Dexter knocked and entered; Houghton was glad of the
company.

"Take a pew," said Houghton.

Dexter pulled up a chair. "Nick, can you go over the plan
again with me; I want to make sure I understand exactly
what you need me to do."

Houghton went over the plan again.

"Yes, got that, but I think you might have a problem."

Houghton felt an adrenaline rush.

"Problem? What problem?"

"You want me to be with you to help as a stretcher-
bearer, yes?" said Dexter. "And you're going to drive the
ambulance."

"Yes. Why?" said Houghton with a concerned look.

"Doctors don't drive ambulances. If the Mahabadis' place
is being monitored, as I am sure it will be, then it's possible
they could spot it. It wouldn't look right."

Houghton thought about it for a moment.

"Hmm, I take your point, but it will be pretty dark by
then, so I'm hoping they won't take much notice."

"I think an ambulance turning up at the Mahabadis'

apartment will definitely create some attention," countered Dexter.

"Can you think of an alternative plan?"

"It's simple enough. We swap roles, I'll do the driving, and you can be the passenger."

Houghton looked at him, immaculate suit, clean-shaven, short hair, the very essence of the diplomatic corps.

They were interrupted by a knock on the door; it was Dee with her morning delivery of croissants and coffee.

"Hi Dee," said David, as she came in and handed out the goodies.

"Thanks," the men acknowledged.

"Let's see what Dee has to say," said Houghton removing the lid of his coffee cup.

"About what?" said Dee.

"David wants to drive the ambulance tonight," said Houghton.

Dexter explained his concern at the present plan.

"Actually, I think David's right," said Dee. "Doctor's don't drive ambulances."

"Yes, I can understand the logic, but I'm worried about David's appearance. If David's driving then he's going to need a uniform of some sort. Where are we going to get a medic's uniform from?"

"Well, we can improvise," said Dee. "Anyway the ambulances I've seen, the drivers don't wear a uniform, it's more a white shirt with a badge of some sort on the sleeves."

"Wait a minute," said Houghton. He went to his cupboard and took out the white coat from the hanger which Mayflower had provided for him. "You mean like this?"

At the top of the sleeve, there was a badge with a shield

and logo.

"Yes, that's it. I've seen them in town," said Dee.

"How are we going to get one of those?" posed Dexter.

"Well, I could draw one with a marker pen. No-one will notice from a distance," said Dee.

"No. Hang on, wait, we're over-thinking this. We don't need a badge, just the white shirt. As you say, no-one will notice. You have one of those, David, you're wearing one," said Houghton.

"Yes, and I have some dark trousers."

"Ok, yeah. That's settled then, and thanks," said Houghton.

"No problem," said Dexter. "Just glad I can help."

The day dragged.

Houghton kept consulting his timeline; they would need to leave at five o'clock to pick up the vehicles. Dee made several visits to bring Houghton intel updates; there had been no messages that would concern them or the integrity of the mission. Then at three-thirty came a bombshell for Houghton. It was Dee who brought the news.

"Hi, I thought you would like to know; that Egyptian guy, you know, the one from Esfahan?"

"What about him?"

"They executed him two hours ago."

"Jeez, no," said Houghton and put his head in his hands.

"Yes, would you believe they videoed it? It's been a while since we had a public execution here; they were obviously sending a message. Quite gruesome. They've been playing it on Iranian TV. I couldn't watch it. It was a crane hanging; the human rights lobbyists will be up in arms again; not that

that will make any difference."

Houghton could feel the anguish, but it was something he would have to live with.

"Are you ok?" asked Dee and went around the desk and hugged him, then they kissed. "I'm going to miss you, Nick Houghton, I really am. I love you; you know. There, I wasn't going to say it."

Houghton looked at her. "When this is all over, apply for some leave and let's meet up in London."

"Yes, ok, I'll do that," said Dee and kissed him again.

There was a knock on the door, and Dee quickly went back to the other side of the desk. David Dexter walked in. "Oh, sorry, I hope I wasn't interrupting anything," he said, seeing Dee in a flushed state.

"No, no, of course not," said Houghton. "Just some last-minute tweaks. You heard about the Egyptian?"

"Yes," said Dexter. "There's going to be an almighty political fall-out over this, that's for sure. I've just heard they've recalled their Ambassador – the Egyptians."

"What about his family, do we know?" asked Houghton.

"No, there's been no news that I've heard," said Dexter.

"No, there was nothing on the broadcast," said Dee.

"Anyway, what do you think?" said Dexter as he stood up to show off his uniform for his new role as an ambulance driver.

"Well, it looks like a diplomat with a bad taste in shirts," said Houghton and the three laughed.

"No, I'm joking, it's fine," said Houghton. "What do you think, Dee?"

"It's good," she replied. "But you might want to make it more lived in. They don't sell Ermine Street tailoring in

Tehran."

"Good point. Let me work on it," said Dexter.

Houghton checked his watch.

"Ok, that gives us about an hour. We'll meet in the lobby. I've ordered one of the minibuses for five o'clock."

"Yes, ok, see you there at five, and I'll do some work on the shirt."

"See you later," said Dee, and they both left the office.

Houghton put his head in his hands; the death of the innocent Egyptian was playing on his mind.

British Embassy, Tehran – 5:00 p.m.

And so it began.

Houghton walked up the stairs from his office for the last time. His clothes and laptop had been safely packaged ready for return to Vauxhall Cross. He was wearing a white shirt, dark trousers and was carrying his holdall with a change of clothes and the kit he would need, including his doctor's disguise, hospital pass and the Mahabadis' passports.

He reached the reception area and could see Dee waiting, dressed in her 'going-out' clothes, which included a grey silk scarf across her head and wrapped around her shoulders. She had applied make-up.

"You look good," said Houghton as he approached her.

"Thanks," said Dee.

Dexter came down the stairs from the first floor in his dark trousers and, now lived-in, white shirt.

"What do you think?" said Dexter as he walked over to the pair.

"Yeah, you look fine," said Houghton.

There were more nervous glances.

"Right, come on, let's get this thing done," he added.

They left the embassy building; the minibus was idling outside with Kazem at the wheel. They got in; Houghton had his holdall on his knees; Dee, a shoulder bag. Dexter was travelling very light; just some emergency cash in his trouser pocket.

"Sa'adi?" asked the driver.

"No, Imam Hussain Hospital on Mandani Street." Houghton noticed the driver's expression in the rear-view mirror; he wasn't expecting the new destination.

Dee looked at Houghton with a quizzical look. Houghton just nodded.

The rush-hour traffic was relentless, and it took over twenty minutes to reach Mandani Street.

As they passed the Safa Grand Mosque on the left, Houghton leaned to the driver.

"Just here will be fine," he said, as they approached a layby in front of a fast-food shop.

They were directly outside the front entrance of the hospital on the opposite side of the road. Dee smiled at Houghton; she recognised where she was. Dexter just looked confused.

The driver got out and slid open the door to let the passengers out. They waited on the kerb-side for the minibus to disappear in the traffic. Braving the vehicles, Houghton led the way across the road.

"You are very clever," said Dee.

"I wasn't taking any chances," said Houghton.

"Can someone let me into the secret?" said Dexter.

"You will see," said Houghton.

It was a large hospital and the buildings stretched a quarter of a mile before they reached a side turning, Farvardin Street. They turned right, following the hospital perimeter for about a hundred yards then crossed the road into another side-street. It was a mix of houses and small commercial units. Then on the right-hand side, there was a garage repair shop.

"We're here," said Dee.

"Your directions were great," said Houghton.

The shutters were down and to the right, there was a door. Dee walked up to it and rang the bell.

It was Leila that answered it dressed casually in jeans and top. There was no headscarf.

"Hello, come in."

The three walked inside, and Leila and Dee embraced. "Thank you for helping us," said Dee.

"It is my father you must thank."

Just then, a man in his fifties joined them from a back room. Dee made the introductions.

"Nick, this is Ervin, Leila's father."

Houghton shook his hand. "I can't thank you enough for your help."

"Sorry, my father doesn't speak much English," said Leila and translated what Nick had said.

The man responded.

"My father says it has been an honour to help."

"Come," said Ervin in English.

The three walked through a workshop; parked outside, were the two vehicles. Houghton looked at the ambulance. He walked around it and stroked his hand down the bonnet as if it were a favourite dog. He looked at Ervin.

"This is amazing, thank you so much," said Houghton

Ervin nodded in acknowledgement and gave Houghton the keys, then spoke.

"My father says to open it and check everything is how you wanted," translated Leila.

Houghton unlocked the door and opened it, then handed the keys to Dexter. "What do you think, David? Can you drive it?"

"I don't see why not, everything's the wrong way 'round but otherwise it's similar to ones I've driven back home. I used to deliver parcels part-time when I was a student."

Dexter was clearly nervous, despite his bravado.

Houghton checked the back. It was basic, but there was a space for the stretcher which was rolled up along the side. Ervin spoke.

"My father asks if it is ok," translated Leila.

"Yes, it's excellent, thank you," said Houghton and shook hands with Ervin. No translation was necessary, and the man embraced Houghton.

"Come," said the man and they walked behind the ambulance, leaving Dexter to master the controls.

A new-looking Khodro Peykan was parked. "It is good, yes?" said Ervin in his faltering English.

Houghton stood back and examined it more closely. Dee was standing next to him. "What do you think?" asked Dee.

"It looks fine, as long as it doesn't break down," said Houghton.

Ervin handed the keys to Houghton who passed them to Dee.

"Are you ok with this?" asked Houghton. "I do have a contingency?"

"I wouldn't miss it for the world," said Dee and squeezed Houghton's hand.

Houghton checked his watch; six-thirty. They had some time to kill.

He turned to Leila. "Is it ok if we stay here for a while, I'm expecting a phone call around seven."

"Yes, of course, would you like some coffee?"

Dexter re-joined them after familiarising himself with the controls of the ambulance.

"Yes please," said Houghton and Leila led them into a small room at the side of the workshop.

"Can I use the toilet?" asked Dexter.

Leila indicated the way. "Of course."

The Mahabadi Residence – 6:30 p.m.

Afareen Mahabadi was feeling the pressure.

Her husband was in his favourite armchair reading. Although not outwardly showing it, he was overjoyed at being back with his family for the first time in months. The children were playing in their room, Afareen's mother was in front of the TV.

Afareen looked at the clock. Time seemed to be standing still, but she knew, like the tide, it could not be held back.

She turned to her husband. "Are you sure we are doing the right thing?" she asked, not for the first time today.

Her husband looked up from his book.

"Yes, I am sure, my dear. We will be much safer in England. We must think of the children and their education. I want them to be free."

"Yes, I know you are right, but it just seems so hard."

"We must do what they have asked; they are risking their

lives to help us."

Afareen went into the kitchen and took out the syringe containing the drug which Houghton had given her the previous day. It had been hidden in the refrigerator at the back behind some milk. She remembered the demonstration she was given by Houghton. Pull the plunger back, squeeze a little to expel the air and inject into the arm.

She walked back into the living room. The children were following her, confused about what was happening.

At ten and six-years-old, Afshin and Kiana were bright. Hassan had taught them English and they were excelling at school. Afareen had explained to them that they were going on a long journey, which had created excitement, and now, they were impatient to leave. Afshin tugged his mother's arm. "When are we going; I'm bored."

"It won't be long, darling. Take your sister into the bedroom and make sure she is ready. I will need you to look after her."

"Oh, alright," said the boy, not really appeased, and he returned to the bedroom holding his sister's hand.

Afareen looked at her mother. There was no way she could make the journey but leaving her was going to be the biggest heartbreak. Afareen had not told her all the details, just that she was going on a long holiday with her family. Her mother acted dumb, but deep down, she knew what was happening; it had been something that had been discussed many times before.

Afareen checked the clock again; it was time.

"Hassan, it is time," said Afareen. He looked at her and stood up; then they embraced.

"It is ok, dear, we must do this," said Hassan.

He rolled up his shirt-sleeve. Afareen's hands were shaking as she positioned the syringe.

"It is ok, my dear. I love you."

"I love you too, Hassan," she said and pushed the hypodermic into her husband's arm. He winced as he felt the needle break his skin; he watched the phial empty. With all the contents discharged, Hassan wiped away the small trace of blood with his handkerchief and rolled his shirt sleeve back down.

"Now we wait," he said and sat back down on his chair.

While they waited for the drug to take effect, Afareen returned to the bedroom and hid the hypodermic in one of the pillows. She looked around the room one last time. Her clothes, collected over many years, hung in the wardrobe; her shoes, much loved and well-worn, were on the floor where they would remain until her mother decided their fate. She checked her jewellery box. She had taken out all her most valuable items and hidden them in the clothing she was wearing in case they needed money. There were just a few trinkets of little value remaining.

The children's things had proven more of a problem, especially toys, and explaining that they had to be left behind had caused a great deal of upset. Afareen had allowed them one item each which she thought would not raise any alarm bells with the ever-watchful secret police. They were both dressed warmly for their journey with several layers of clothes.

The effects of Flunitrazepam is usually visible within fifteen minutes of administration, and by twenty-past seven, Hassan had drifted to sleep; he appeared to be mumbling incoherently.

Afareen took out her phone and dialled the number.

Rostami Auto Repairs, Farvardin Street, Tehran – 7:23 p.m.

Back at the garage, Houghton, Dee and Dexter were being entertained by Leila and her father when the call came through. There were just three words.

"It is time."

Houghton had changed into his doctor's coat; his stethoscope was in his pocket and his hospital pass was hanging around his neck by the lanyard. He rang off and stood up.

"Ok, guys, this is it. Good luck," said Houghton.

They said their farewells to Leila and her father and there were hugs all around.

Dexter got into the driver's seat of the ambulance and started the engine. The driver's window was open. "I'll see you later," he said to Leila, who was standing closest.

The plan was to return the ambulance to the garage after the mission; Ervin would dispose of it.

"We will wait for you," replied Leila.

Dee walked up to Houghton and kissed his cheek.

"Are you ok? You know where to go?" said Houghton with genuine concern.

"Yes, I'll be there," she replied. Ervin was holding the door of the Khodro for her to get in.

"Can you look after this for me? I won't need it in the ambulance," said Houghton, giving Dee his holdall.

"Yes, no problem," she responded, as she settled in the driving seat and examined the controls of the unfamiliar vehicle.

He opened the boot and stowed it while Dee was manoeuvring the gear stick, practising the change sequence. Then, she depressed the clutch and started the engine. Ervin closed the door.

Houghton climbed aboard the ambulance.

The vehicles were heading in different directions.

Houghton knew that the next hour or so was likely to be the most dangerous of the whole exfil plan. Some of the events were going to be outside his control.

He was in the passenger seat, giving directions to Dexter as they headed to the Mahabadis' residence. They decided not to use the flashing blue light, mainly because Dexter hadn't worked out which was the appropriate switch.

"You seem to be getting the hang of this, David," said Houghton, as he swung the ambulance expertly from the side road onto the main highway that would take them to the Bahar district.

"Yes, they say it never leaves you," he replied and smiled. There was still much nervous energy.

The Mahabadis' apartment was due east of the garage and Houghton had estimated the journey would take about twenty minutes. Several vehicles pulled to one side, seeing an ambulance behind them and Dexter accelerated past.

It took slightly less than Houghton's prediction and, as they pulled up outside the residence, he noticed a van with blacked-out windows parked on the opposite side of the street; there was activity inside.

Dexter turned off the engine, and Houghton went to the

back and retrieved the stretcher.

He looked at the apartment block trying to work out which was the Mahabadis' and then he spotted Afareen waving from the second-floor window.

He pointed so Dexter could see, and then they ran into the building.

It was two flights of stairs and they were both breathing heavily when they reached the door. Dexter was carrying the stretcher.

Afareen was waiting for them, and they went inside.

Hassan Mahabadi was now unconscious in his chair. Afreen's mother had no idea what was going on and was ululating creating an awful noise. Afareen admonished her. "Be quiet mother, Hassan will be alright now, he is in safe hands."

Dexter and Houghton managed to lift Hassan onto the stretcher.

"Ok, let's go, make sure you have everything you need we won't be coming back," whispered Houghton to Afareen.

The two children were also confused. Kiana, the six-year-old was crying. Again, Afareen offered reassurance.

"Come children, we must go with Papa to the hospital." Afareen's mother started wailing again. Afareen went to her. "Don't worry, mother, we will be fine. I love you."

"I love you too," said her mother in between deep sobs.

Dexter and Houghton carried Hassan out of the apartment. He was heavy, and they quickly realised that getting him down the stairs was not going to be easy,

Afareen led the stretcher party slowly to the top of the stone steps and then froze. Two armed, uniformed officers were coming up towards them. Afareen thought quickly and spoke in Farsi.

"Quick, quick, please help us. My husband, he has had a heart attack."

The soldiers reached the stretcher party and took over. Houghton nodded to them and walked in front, guiding them down the stairs like a concerned doctor. Dexter was bringing up the rear with Afareen and the children.

They reached the ground floor and left the block. Houghton opened the rear door of the ambulance, and the men guided the stretcher into the secure position. He took out his stethoscope and checked Mahabadi's chest, then looked at Afareen with a grave face and started CPR.

The two soldiers watched the charade. Afareen shouted at them in Farsi.

"The Mardom Hospital, quickly."

Two motorcycles were parked next to the surveillance van and the men mounted and kickstarted. One of them shouted at Dexter.

"He wants you to follow them," said Afareen, who was now sat in the back with Houghton and the two children. They were both now crying. "Papa, papa," said Afshin, looking at his father with an expression of anguish.

Dexter started up the ambulance. The motorcyclists accelerated away using their horns to alert other motorists. On a road where you were lucky to make twenty miles an hour, Dexter suddenly found himself weaving through cars at fifty, taking all his powers of concentration. The passengers in the back were being thrown from side to side and Houghton was holding on to Hassan to make sure he stayed on the stretcher.

It was around five kilometres to the hospital, and in less

than ten minutes, Dexter was pulling up outside the main entrance.

There was a flurry of activity. One of the men had opened the back door, and Houghton could see a friendly face waiting with a trolley. He smiled, but more in relief.

Eliz shouted at the men, and they gently extracted the stretcher and lifted Hassan onto the trolley.

"Thank you, we will take it from here," said the nurse.

One of the men slammed the ambulance door shut and banged twice on the back with the palm of his hand. Dexter drove off, away from the hospital and back to the garage.

Twenty minutes later, David arrived back where they started, and Leila came out to meet him.

"Hi," said Dexter, as he got out of the ambulance.

"Was everything ok?" she said.

"I hope so. We've done all we can."

"Do you want my father to take you somewhere?"

"No. Thank you, that's very kind. I'll be fine. I'll head back to the main road and get a taxi."

He handed Leila the keys.

"Thank you for everything," said Dexter.

Dexter retraced his earlier steps and soon reached Mandani Street, next to the Imam Hussain hospital. Five minutes later, he was in a taxi heading back to the British Compound, experiencing the most incredible adrenaline rush.

Back at the hospital, the mission was reaching its most crucial stage. Mayflower had taken charge. She called over two porters, and they immediately started trolley-pushing duties. The two officers had remounted their bikes and driven away.

The nurse led the way through reception to a large lift to the right of the admin desk. Houghton was playing his part as the concerned medic and holding Hassan's wrist as if checking his pulse; his stethoscope was around his neck. He was careful not to make eye-contact with anyone.

They got in the lift, rode one floor and walked down a long corridor. The nurse stopped at the door on the left-hand side and opened it, a vacant treatment room. Afareen and the children followed them inside.

Mayflower dismissed the porters. She went to the door and looked down the corridor. There was no-one around.

"Ok, we need to treat him now," she said to Houghton. "Have you got it?"

Houghton had the antidote; he thought it was safer for him to keep it. He fumbled in his pocket for a moment, then pulled out the small phial. The nurse took out a syringe from her apron pocket and filled it with the Flumazenil, then injected it into Hassan's upper arm.

"Ok, it should start taking effect in about ten minutes, but he will not feel well for maybe a day, maybe two. You must watch him carefully," she said to Afareen.

"Thanks for everything. We couldn't have done it without you," said Houghton.

Afareen went up to the nurse and hugged her.

"Ok, as soon as he starts coming round, we need to get him to the car," said Houghton.

The tension was unbearable as they waited for Hassan to come out of his induced unconsciousness. Mayflower kept checking on the patient as Houghton watched the corridor from the door, making sure no-one entered. The children were dazed and confused and Afareen was doing her best to look after them.

Gradually, Hassan started to make moaning noises.

"Wait, I will get a wheelchair," said Mayflower and she left the treatment room.

Houghton could feel the tension; every moment they stayed in the hospital was a moment of danger. He was pacing up and down the room, then peering out of the small circular window in the door watching for anyone who might pose a threat. He had no idea what he would do. Several staff walked by but, thankfully, no guards.

"Come on, come on," he said under his breath as he waited for the nurse to return.

Five minutes later, the nurse returned, pushing a wheelchair, and between them, they manhandled Hassan into it. He was decidedly disorientated.

"Right, we need to go. Can you take us to the exit we discussed?" said Houghton to Mayflower.

"Yes, follow me. I will take you a different way, not reception – too many people."

They left the treatment room with Houghton pushing the scientist; his wife and children were in close attendance. Mayflower was leading the way.

They passed several more treatment rooms. More doctors and nurses were about but took little notice of the family.

They arrived at a smaller lift and the nurse pressed the button. "This one is for maintenance and laundry, but it is ok, staff use it."

The lift arrived and the group got in. The children seemed much better on seeing that their father was starting to recover.

They reached the ground floor, and the nurse looked left and right.

"It is ok, quick," she said.

Houghton vaguely recognised the corridor and quickly located the fire door.

"Quick," said Houghton. "Through here."

The nurse pushed the bar, and a blast of fresh air hit them as they left the stuffiness of the hospital.

Houghton looked left and right, nothing; no sign of Dee and the car.

Where was she? Had she been stopped? Had the car broken down? Questions were running through his mind. He felt sick. Afareen looked at him. "What is happening?" she asked.

"I don't know," replied Houghton. "The car should be waiting."

Eliz, too, was looking anxious.

Houghton glanced at his watch, then behind him at the emergency exit expecting it to open any minute by armed guards. "Come on, come on," he whispered under his breath.

Then suddenly around the corner came the unmistakable shape of the Khodro. Houghton exhaled loudly. Dee waved and pulled up alongside the waiting party.

"I'm so sorry, there was an accident. The traffic was backed up for miles," said Dee.

"Thank goodness you're here," said Houghton, which didn't come close to the relief he was feeling.

"Quick, give me a hand."

They managed to get Hassan off the wheelchair and onto the back seat. He was conscious but had still not fully recovered his motor skills. The children sat either side and

Afareen got into the passenger seat.

Mayflower had turned and was walking towards the open emergency exit pushing the empty chair. Houghton quickly caught up with her.

"Eliz, wait a sec. Thanks for everything you have done. Keep safe, yeah."

"Yes Nick, I will. I am glad I could help."

"Here, you better have this; I won't be needing it," said Houghton and handed her the stethoscope.

She smiled and took it, then turned and walked through the door. Houghton watched it slam shut. There was so much more he wanted to say.

He went to Dee, who was holding open the driver's door.

"Will you be ok?" he said.

"Yes, I'll be fine. I'm just going to get a taxi from the front; there'll be plenty. You take care, won't you? I love you, Nick Houghton."

They kissed. "I love you too," said Houghton.

He waited for Dee to turn the corner before returning to the car. He opened the boot, took off his doctor's outfit and pass, stuffed them into his holdall, then closed up and got into the driver's seat.

"Everybody ok?" he asked and started it up without waiting for a reply.

He breathed a little easier as he drove along the service road towards the main road. He was trying to familiarise himself with the Khodro's controls as he drove; it felt sluggish and the steering was heavy.

Unfortunately, they weren't yet out of the woods by any means.

Chapter Nineteen

The Mardom Hospital was on the east side of Tehran which meant Houghton needed to cross the city to get to Route 2, and the road north-west to the port. He was on high alert. There were rumours of random police checks; he just hoped that tonight he would not run into one.

Fortunately, the directional signage was in English as well as Farsi, and he was able to follow the signs for Karaj, the first major town on his route. It would be around two-hundred and thirty miles to Bandar-e Anzali, and he estimated that it was going to take at least six hours.

He had been on the road for about twenty minutes and was close to the start of the freeway when in front of them he could see a line of cars.

He checked the back; Hassan and both children were asleep. Afareen saw the queue. "Oh no, it's the police," she said. "What shall we do?"

"Stay very calm, let's see what they want."

Houghton had no idea whether Hassan's medical emergency had triggered any concerns within the Ministry; they would have certainly been informed of events.

The cars moved forward, some were being checked, others were being ushered by. The temporary control-post consisted of a police car positioned sideways across the road, blocking one carriageway; it was guarded by three armed officers. As vehicles were checked, the cars were directed around the stationary car.

There were two cars in front. Houghton could feel the beads of sweat running down his forehead. He wiped them away with the back of his sleeve.

One of the officers approached and said something. Afareen turned to Houghton. "Papers," she whispered.

Just at that moment, Hassan reached across his son and pulled on the rear door handle. It swung open, and he leaned out and vomited over the pavement. He moaned and gasped.

"Please officer, my husband he is not well, we need to get him home."

The man looked through Afareen's window and shone a torch. Hassan was sitting back up, but there were stains of vomit down his shirt, both children were crying. He pushed closed the back door, then shouted to Afareen.

"Ok, you go,"

Houghton pulled out around the car in front and past the patrol car. He was back on the open road and breathed a huge sigh of relief.

"How are you dear?" said Afareen looking at her husband on the back seat.

"I will be ok," he said.

They had left the city environs and were now on the freeway; traffic was light, and Houghton was able to keep a reasonable pace. He checked the time and then pulled into a layby.

"One minute," he said to Afareen. He took out a bottle of water from the receptacle in the driver's door panel and handed it to Afareen.

"Make sure Hassan drinks plenty; I have to send a message."

Before he had travelled too far from the city, he needed

to update Fellows. Mobile phone coverage was extremely limited, and reception almost exclusively confined to large cities. He checked his phone; he barely had a signal but sent the message. *'Package secured. ETA 2:30'.*

Moments later, he received an acknowledgement.

MOIS Headquarters – 10:00 p.m.

Commander Fallahian, head of the Eagle 2 field agents, was in his office trying to make sense of some news that Hassan Mahabadi, one of Iran's top nuclear scientists, was in hospital having suffered a heart attack. He read the reports from the two motorcyclists who had escorted the ambulance an hour earlier. They contained details of the emergency transfer. One of the officers had expressed concern that he might even be dead. The death of a prominent technician certainly came under his remit. He called the Mardom and was surprised to learn that no one had been registered in that name.

He quizzed the receptionist who admitted that it was possible that he could have been taken for treatment without being registered if the condition was life-threatening. She would speak to someone and check.

An hour later, he called again. Still nothing; there was no trace of him. He checked his watch and made a decision. It was late and he'd been on duty for fourteen hours. He would follow it up in the morning.

Route 49, Northern Iran – 11:00 p.m.

Houghton was tired. He had been on the road for the best part of three hours and the Khodro was a nightmare to drive. His passengers were quiet. Hassan and the two children were asleep and Afareen was staring at the road ahead; dark and featureless, just the stars and the occasional approaching headlights.

Houghton needed to stop but was wary of possible police patrols. Having made it this far, he did not want to jeopardise the mission now.

Qazvin is a large city with almost half a million inhabitants; he could see the glow of streetlights in the distance as he approached. On the left, he noticed a truck-stop and made a decision. It was still open and there were several lorries outside.

He pulled onto the gravel and turned off the engine. The children woke; Hassan was still not fully focussed but looked around.

"We have stopped; why have we stopped?" he said.

"It's ok," said Houghton. "Just need to use the bathroom, and I'll get some food. I don't know about you, but I'm starving."

"I will come too," said Afareen. "I need the bathroom, and I can translate."

She checked on the children, who were awake but very dopey.

"I want to pee-pee," said Afshin.

"And me," said his sister.

Having been cooped up for the best part of three hours, Houghton relented. They left Hassan on the back seat and the four walked towards the café. Houghton was breathing deeply, taking in the night air. It had a reviving affect. As they entered the building, they were immediately hit by the smell of cigarette smoke. Houghton blinked to get his eyes accustomed to the illumination.

It was a large café with bench-style seating with about thirty people taking refreshment. There were no females.

Houghton spotted the signs for the toilets and the group walked through the café. Houghton went inside the men's room and splashed water on his face to freshen up, used the toilet, then waited for Afareen and the children. He could hear complaints coming from inside the ladies as Afareen attended to them.

Houghton kept checking his watch; he was pacing. "Come on, come on," he was saying under his breath.

Then Afareen appeared, holding her daughter's hand with Afshin following behind.

"Be quick, we need to go," whispered Houghton, and they walked to the counter. There were sandwiches of various descriptions; Houghton picked up a selection. The children started arguing about their choices, and Afareen scolded them. They settled on some crisps and chocolate bars. There were takeaway drinks, and Houghton ordered two coffees, raising two fingers and pointing. Afreen picked up three large bottles of water.

Behind the counter, a woman in a burka was preparing food, another, in more contemporary dress with a headscarf, was serving; a man in a white shirt and dark trousers was behind them and didn't appear to be doing much. Houghton paid and they carried their purchases out of the café. One or two customers watched as they left but merely out of curiosity. It was late for a family to be travelling.

As they opened the door, Houghton noticed two motorcyclists in black leathers and crash-helmets slowly pulling into the parking area. They stopped near the front entrance.

He quickened his pace; Afareen also spotted the danger and grabbed her daughter's arm. Afshin trotted behind.

They reached the car. Afareen opened the back door for the children as Houghton got in and tried starting the engine. The car made a strange grinding noise. Houghton turned the key again; just a discordant sound. He felt his anxiety levels rise.

He reached down to see if he could find the bonnet opening mechanism. The interior light cast shadows and it was difficult to see under the dashboard, but he found a lever which he pulled. There was a clunk as the hood raised a couple of inches. He got out and lifted the bonnet completely, securing it with the metal holding-rod and staring at the car's innards. It was dark and he couldn't see very much. In the ambient light, he started fiddling with the wires in case one had come loose; he was not a mechanic and didn't really have a clue what to do.

He became aware of a presence at his shoulder.

Afareen had seen him and got out of the car ready to translate, knowing Houghton's lack of Farsi.

Houghton looked down; he could see a side-arm and leather riding boots. This was no casual rider.

The man spoke in Farsi.

"What is the trouble?"

"The car, it won't start," said Afareen. Houghton looked up at the man and shrugged his shoulders.

The man took out a torch from his pocket and shone it at the engine. He found the starter motor and gave it a sharp rap with the side of his torch.

"Try," said the biker.

Houghton understood and got back inside and turned

the ignition key. There was a triumphant roar as the engine sparked to life. The man dropped down the bonnet and secured it. Afareen was showering appreciation. Houghton walked up to him, shook his hand and nodded with a broad smile.

The man spoke. "No problem, safe journey."

Afareen translated for Houghton back in the car.

Houghton was shaking as he eased the Khodro out of the truck-stop and back on the main road. He was cursing the Iranian car industry under his breath. The children were unconcerned and content with their chocolate and crisps. Hassan had gone back to sleep. Afareen passed Houghton one of the paper coffee cups and he took a long gulp.

It took nearly half an hour to get through Qazvin. Houghton was following the road signs, which took all his powers of concentration. He was not planning on stopping again and just hoped that the car would last the trip.

As they reached the open road again, he checked with Afareen; the children were asleep, but Hassan was awake and feeling more comfortable.

Fortunately, there were no other emergencies; they stopped twice more for comfort breaks, but Houghton kept the engine running, relieving himself beside the car.

It was ten-to-three as they reached the city of Bandar-e Anzali. Route 49, which they had used since Qazvin, skirted the centre and Houghton recalled the way to the docks from the co-ordinates that Fellows had given him. After about ten minutes, there was a sign indicating a right turn ahead; 'Docks'.

Houghton made the turn and was trying to remember the directions. He needed to be sure before going any further; getting lost in the myriad of backstreets around the docks was not an option. He stopped under a streetlight and, checking no-one was about, went to the boot of the car. Inside one of the pockets, there was an innocuous scrap of paper. To anyone reading it, it just looked like a shopping list, but Houghton could interpret the code.

He checked his bearings and looked ahead; he was on the right road.

Fellows had been on deck since two-thirty, anxiously awaiting the arrival of Houghton and the passengers.

It was dark along the quayside with only the occasional streetlight providing any sort of illumination. He checked his watch yet again; three-ten. Then, he spotted headlights in the quayside road about a hundred metres away.

Fellows was holding a large torch and shone it towards the car. He just hoped it was Houghton.

The car turned towards him and then the headlights flashed in acknowledgement. Fellows felt a deep feeling of relief; he wanted to jump for joy.

The Khodro drew up alongside the boat and Houghton got out. Fellows walked down the gangplank and shook hands warmly with Houghton. Afareen opened the back door and was trying to wake the children who were now in a deep slumber. Hassan was awake and attending to his son. Gradually, the passengers exited the car. Afareen was carrying her daughter on her shoulder. Hassan was holding his son as he rubbed his bleary eyes.

They collected the rest of their belongings and walked

towards the boat. Houghton retrieved his holdall from the boot, locked the car and followed them. Captain Aliyev was also now on deck, and Houghton introduced the family.

"Ok, you come," said Aliyev, and led them through the wheelhouse and down the stairs into the living quarters. While they were waiting, Fellows had converted the furniture into make-shift beds. Afareen checked the room and started allocating the sleeping arrangements. It would not be particularly comfortable, but it would do.

"What about the car?" said Fellows looking at the Khodro parked on the opposite side of the road.

"Whoever wants it is welcome to it, the heap of junk," said Houghton and threw the keys in the car's direction.

Fellows pulled up the gangplank and released the mooring lines from the capstans as Aliyev started the engines, then joined Houghton in the wheelhouse. The boat bobbed and swayed for a moment before it achieved forward momentum; with the load onboard, it was low in the water. Having completed the fuel stop upstream, the boat was facing down river and, with the tide now flowing seaward, they were soon in deep water and heading for the harbour.

A fishing boat leaving at this time of night was not a usual occurrence. Aliyev was careful not to open the throttle too wide and allowed the current to take the boat along to avoid any undue noise. Eventually, the boat was clear of the river.

"We are near entrance to harbour," said Aliyev pointing ahead.

Two long concrete walls protected the mouth of the harbour like a pair of arms, with a gap of about a hundred metres in between, allowing boats to enter. On the end of each arm were two towers about thirty feet tall with warning lights flashing on the top.

"Tonight, maybe not good," said Aliyev, indicating a waving motion with his hands. Houghton and Fellows watched anxiously as the boat passed between the two beacons and headed for open water.

Immediately, Aliyev released the throttle, and the familiar rhythmic chugging returned.

There was a sharp breeze, and the sea was not as calm as it had been on the inward journey. The tops of the waves were white in the darkness and spray lashed the wheelhouse. Downstairs it was uncomfortable; the roll of the boat was now causing the children to feel nauseous. Hassan continued to experience the effects of the drugs and had vomited again, but at least he'd managed to reach the toilet.

Afareen went to the wheelhouse and explained the situation.

"Here, take the wheel," said Aliyev to Fellows and he led Afareen back inside.

"I didn't know you were a sailor Andy," said Houghton, admiring his confidence at the steering.

"Oh, you know, did a bit of rowing in my youth. Thought it would come in handy one day," he said and started laughing.

Downstairs, Aliyev found the medical chest in the galley and handed Afareen a packet of pills.

"One half of one pill only. They will sleep for four, maybe six hours. They will be fine."

Afareen helped the children take the pills with some water, and within a few minutes, they were sleeping soundly.

Hassan was feeling restless and couldn't settle. He was suffering from stomach cramps and extreme fatigue; Afareen was trying to look after him as best she could.

They had been at sea for over two hours. Houghton was sat on one of the stools in the wheelhouse; Fellows had the other. Aliyev was steering a northerly course. On the starboard side, the easterly glow on the horizon heralded the approaching dawn. It was cold, but the wind had dropped, and the rolling was now a gentle sway. Aliyev was keeping the coastline to port, about twelve miles away.

Suddenly, in the gloom to the west, he noticed movement. It was distant but appeared to be closing.

"Pettigrew, Pettigrew, you awake?"

Fellows had drifted into a seated-sleep and the alarm jolted him. Houghton heard the call and was watchful.

"What's the problem?"

"Patrol, I think, coming this way. We must hide them. Quick, take the wheel."

With Fellows back on steering duties, Aliyev went downstairs.

"Wake up," he said to Afareen. "Quick, you hide."

He lifted the lids of the seats to reveal the storage compartment.

"Quick, children inside, now."

They were both sound asleep. Afareen lifted the children one-by-one into the compartment and closed the top. Neither had woken.

"You, and you," pointing to Hassan. "Toilet. Stay until I say."

Hassan struggled to get up and Afareen helped him to the back of the boat and into the small toilet. Aliyev closed the door.

The patrol boat was closing in. It was about fifty yards

away when the searchlight started scanning the fishing vessel.

"Fishing boat, stop your engines. Prepare to be boarded," came a voice over loud-speaker. It was in English.

Aliyev cut the motor, and there was a bump as the two boats collided side-on.

An armed officer jumped onto the front deck and wrapped a rope around the capstan to tether the boats together. A second officer jumped aboard.

The first man was wearing a uniform and holding an assault weapon close to his chest; he approached the wheelhouse.

Houghton looked at Fellows. "Stay calm," he whispered.

"What is your business?" said the officer.

Aliyev was playing the same game as the inbound journey.

"Collecting supplies," he said and handed the man the chandler's docket.

"I have customs money," said Aliyev, and showed the man a five-hundred Euro note.

The officer grabbed the money and put it in his pocket. He looked at Houghton and Fellows suspiciously.

"You and you, papers."

Neither Houghton nor Fellows were in a position to argue. Unfortunately, neither were in a position to hand over their passports either; there would be significant questions about two British nationals in Iranian waters. They would be arrested at the very least.

Houghton looked at the man and shrugged his shoulders and pointed to the cabin. The officer waved his weapon indicating for Houghton to go below.

"You go," he shouted at Fellows.

Fellows followed Houghton; The officer was behind them with his rifle poised. Houghton went to the left and picked up his holdall and made the appearance of a search. Fellows went right and was rummaging through his baggage. The move divided the officer's attention, but then a child's voice sounded followed by a shriek. The noise and movement in the cabin had woken Kiana.

The officer was momentarily distracted.

In one move, Houghton picked up the nearest heavy object, a flashlight, which was on the table, and slammed it into the officer's face. He fell to the floor, dazed, and dropped the weapon. Fellows picked it up.

Houghton went behind the man, grabbed him around the neck and twisted his head sideways. There was a clicking noise and he went limp. Houghton let him drop to the floor.

The wailing noise from the cabinet continued and Houghton opened the top. Kiana was sobbing bitterly with her arms outstretched, calling for her mother. Afareen heard the commotion and left the hiding place to comfort her daughter.

"What do you want to do?" said Fellows.

"We've got no option; we're going to have to take them out."

They crept slowly up the short staircase and opened the door to the wheelhouse. Aliyev was stood next to the wheel.

Houghton put his index finger to his lips to indicate silence. He was on his hands and knees and peered around the wheelhouse entrance until he could see the other officer. From his crouching position, Houghton took aim and fired. The force of the hit sent the man backwards and into the sea.

Houghton immediately aimed right and let off another burst at the patrol boat, shattering the windows of the wheelhouse. He leapt aboard; Fellows followed. Houghton rushed the wheelhouse; there was a body on the floor with a bullet wound to the head and one to the shoulder.

Houghton paced the top deck. The wheelhouse was full of sophisticated gadgetry; he had no idea whether their presence had been called in or not. He opened the metal door to the below-deck area and slowly descended the steps. The layout was not dissimilar to the fishing boat, but the furnishings were more modern and robust.

He heard a noise, then another officer appeared with a rifle. Before he could move, Houghton let off another burst of gunfire in his direction and he went down.

Fellows joined Houghton. "Is that all of them?"

"We need to check," said Houghton and together they searched the rest of the vessel.

Satisfied that there were no more on board, they dragged the two officers onto the deck and threw them over the side.

"What about the boat?" said Fellows.

"I have an idea," said Houghton. "Do you know how the automatic pilot works?"

"No, but I'm sure Aliyev will."

"Can you get him?"

Fellows leapt onto the fishing boat and collected the skipper. He joined Houghton in the patrol boat control room.

"Do you know how to use the auto-pilot?" asked Houghton.

"Yes," said Aliyev, surveying the impressive array of dials. "What do you want to do?"

"I want to set a course north-east, away from land. It will

continue until it is out of fuel, by which time we should be well away."

"Yes, I know this," he said and started keying in co-ordinates.

"Ok, Andy, you need to release the rope, and I'll set the throttle."

"You'll need to be quick, once it's disconnected, it's going to take off."

Aliyev jumped back on board the fishing boat, followed by Fellows. He went to the capstan, removed the line and threw it back over the patrol boat. Houghton released the throttle and immediately the patrol boat lurched forward.

It was already five feet away from the fishing boat. Houghton threw the rifle onto the boat and then jumped. He was well short and ended up in the water between the two vessels. It was freezing cold, and the shock took his breath away. He thrashed around for a moment, then started swimming to the fishing boat which was now maybe twenty feet away

Fellows threw him a lifebelt. Houghton grabbed the ring and Fellows hauled him to the side of the boat.

Aliyev gave Fellows a hand, and between them, they managed to drag Houghton unceremoniously on board. The patrol boat was running merrily on its way north-eastwards.

"Thanks," said Houghton as he recovered from his dunking, "Let's get out of here. There could be more about."

They entered the wheelhouse and Aliyev started the engines.

"Andy, can you give me a hand, we need to dispose of the other body?"

They went below where Afareen and Hassan were

comforting the children. They dragged the dead officer up the stairs and into the wheelhouse. They were about to push him over the side when Aliyev shouted.

"Wait!"

He went to the man and rummaged through his pockets and found the Euro note. He took it out and smiled at Houghton and Fellows. "Now, is good."

They rolled the body over and into the sea, then collected his weapon and added it to the other one at the back of the wheelhouse. Houghton hoped they wouldn't need them.

"How long before we are outside Iranian waters?"

Aliyev checked his watch. "About five, six hours," he replied; that was little comfort. "But Iranians they don't take notice. We need to watch carefully."

Aliyev reset the course for Baku. Houghton went below to change into some dry clothes.

MOIS Headquarters – Friday April 28th – 7:00 a.m.

Commander Fallahian was briefing the General on the disappearance of Hassan Mahabadi.

"I checked the hospital again this morning, there is no record of Mahabadi receiving any treatment there."

"I have read the agents' reports; it seems his family were with him," said the General.

"Yes," said the Commander.

"Does that not seem strange to you?"

"What do you mean?"

"If Mahabadi had had a heart attack, would they not have left the children at home?"

"Hmm, I see what you are saying."

"You need to visit the house; see what is happening."

The Mahabadi Residence – 8:30 a.m.

Commander Fallahian arrived at the apartment with two officers and hammered on the door.

Afareen's mother was in the bathroom, and it took two further urgent knocks for her to reach the door.

"You remember me?" said the Commander.

"No, who are you? Why are you banging on my door at this time of day?"

The three officers barged in.

"I am Commander Fallahian, Ministry of Intelligence, where is Mr Mahabadi?"

"They went to the hospital last night; he has not returned. I think he must be dead."

She raised her arms and started wailing.

The Commander looked at his officers. "Search the apartment."

"You, woman, be quiet."

She complied straight away and sat down in her chair; her eyes red from crying.

The Commander looked around the living room, searching for clues, anything that might give light to their whereabouts.

A few minutes later, the men had completed their search.

"Well?" said the Commander.

"Nothing, they are gone, but their clothes are still here."

What about personal stuff, jewellery, children's toys?"

"Yes, they are here."

"Hmm," said the Commander.

"Where have they gone?" he shouted at the woman.

"They are at the hospital. Hassan is dead," she said and

started wailing again.

"Ok, let's leave her," said the Commander. "We need to go to the hospital."

The Mardom Hospital – 10:30 a.m.

The Commander and his two officers arrived at the hospital and went into reception.

"Who is in charge?" he said to the receptionist, flashing his identity card.

"One moment," said the girl and picked up the internal phone and spoke to someone.

"Doctor Modarresi will be with you in a moment."

It was five minutes before the white-coated doctor appeared.

"How can I help you?" he said, approaching the officers.

They walked away from the desk and were talking in the middle of the waiting area. There were curious looks from seated patients.

"I want to know about Hassan Mahabadi."

"Yes, yes, you have been asking about him; I was informed."

"He was brought here last night."

"So I understand, but there is no record of him being here at all."

"You have CCTV?" said the Commander pointing at the cameras.

"We have cameras, but no film. No money," he said and shrugged his shoulders.

"Damn! Who was on duty last night? Do you have a list?"

"Yes, I can find that out," said the doctor. He turned and

walked towards the admin area, behind the reception desk.

British Embassy, Tehran – 10:00 a.m.

Dee was with David Dexter in his office reflecting on the mission; the atmosphere was flat. She'd been in the office since seven-thirty checking for any messages that might indicate the success or otherwise of the mission. There was nothing; they considered this to be good news.

"I've been thinking Dee; we need to get you away and back to London; we've no idea what the fallout from this might be once they realise what's happened. You may have been caught on a camera somewhere. They're no fools; I'm sure they'll work out Mahabadi's escaped sooner or later."

There was a knock on the door and one of the admin assistants entered with an envelope.

"There is a woman in reception, said I must give you this urgently. She is downstairs."

Dexter opened the letter. *This is to introduce you to Eliz Bashi, codename Mayflower. She has been instrumental in the extraction of the Mahabadi family and should be offered every assistance.'*

It was signed by Nick Houghton on British Embassy notepaper.

Dexter showed the letter to Dee.

"Nick said he had a contact here who was helping. He wouldn't give me too much information but said she worked at the hospital. Wait… She must be the one who was pushing the wheelchair last night. We were in such a hurry I didn't take much notice at the time"

"Can you bring her up?" said Dexter to the assistant.

A few minutes later, there was a knock on the door and

the assistant was back with Eliz.

Dexter stood up. "Come in," he said and introduced her to Dee. "How can we help you?"

British Embassy, Tehran – 5:00 p.m.

There was still no news from Houghton. It had been twenty-four hours since they set off on their mission, and for both Dexter and Dee, the waiting was agony. They realised they would have no contact while they were at sea, but, at this stage, they had no idea whether they had even made the boat. The good news was, there had been no 'chatter' from the Iranians which would have heralded the capture of a British agent.

Dexter had done some calculations and, providing everything went according to plan, he believed it would be between ten o'clock and midnight when the party would reach Baku.

Dexter was in the comms room, waiting for information. He was with Ryan Hudson.

Dee came into the room and joined them.

"I'm staying, David, there's nothing for me back at the compound; I won't be able to settle," she said and went to look at the teleprinter which was rattling away with messages.

"I'm staying too," said Hudson. "I want to see it to its conclusion."

As the person responsible for communicating between the embassy and Vauxhall Cross, Hudson had an outline knowledge of the mission.

"We better get some food," said Dexter, "It's going to be a long night."

Granting Mayflower political asylum had been straightforward. After her arrival, Dexter had contacted Vauxhall Cross and, explained the approach. The response came from Commander Jenkins herself. Given Eliz's role in the escape and the potential penalties if she were caught, her application was approved. She would remain inside the embassy in the emergency accommodation quarters until transport arrangements could be made to fly her out of the country.

Chapter Twenty

Fishing boat, 'Free-spirit', the Caspian Sea – 10:00 p.m.
Tural Aliyev was almost dead on his feet having been steering the boat for most of the seventeen hours. Fellows had taken the wheel a couple of times to enable Aliyev to get some rest. Luckily, the weather had stayed calm; it was cloudy but bright.

Now, it was pitch black, just the dim light of the wheelhouse for illumination. Aliyev called over to Fellows who was dozing in his seat and pointed to the horizon in front of them. There were pin-pricks of twinkling lights.

"Baku," said Aliyev, triumphantly.

Houghton was on the floor with his head against the wheelhouse door. He stood up and peered through the window into the distance.

"Now, that looks good," he said and smiled at Fellows.

He went below. Hassan and Afareen were both resting; the children were asleep.

"Hassan, Afareen. Baku, do you want to look?"

Hassan was still recovering from the effects of the Rohypnol but was feeling much better and the nauseous feeling had gone. They both followed Houghton up the stairs to the wheelhouse.

Aliyev pointed at the horizon to the lights. "Baku," he said, "One hour, maybe less; the tide, it is good."

Just before eleven p.m., they chugged into the harbour

and made their way to the same mooring pontoon from where Aliyev and Fellows had departed a couple of days earlier. It pulled up to the jetty and Fellows jumped off to secure the ropes.

Afareen woke the children and collected their things. Hassan waited in the wheelhouse, and then the family walked down the gangplank into Azerbaijan.

Houghton gave Afareen the new passports. "Don't forget your new names."

Aliyev secured the boat and joined them on the quayside.

"What are your plans?" he said to Houghton.

"I'm going to get them to the Hyatt for tonight, then tomorrow, the embassy."

"I will take you; it is late – not so many taxis, I think."

The party followed Aliyev to his Toyota. The children were bemused by everything.

It was a tight squeeze, with Houghton and Fellows squashed into the passenger seat, the family on the seats behind, and the baggage on the back of the truck. Aliyev drove them to the hotel.

There were emotional farewells and expressions of gratitude as Aliyev left them.

The hotel was quiet. Fellows walked up to the receptionist; there was mutual recognition from his earlier visit.

"Hello, Mr Fellows; nice to see you back," said the desk clerk.

Fellows explained his requirements and introduced Houghton and the Mahabadi family; they were using their new passports. Houghton paid for the three rooms, and with the documentation complete, they followed a porter to the lifts.

Once in his room, Houghton sent a text. '*Package delivered safely*'.

A few seconds later, he got a reply. *'Great job'*.

British Embassy, Tehran – Saturday April 29th – 9:00 a.m.

Dexter received the text alert around midnight and immediately showed it to Dee and Hudson who were still in the comms room. There was a whoop of joy and a huge sigh of relief. They could now sleep more easily.

The following morning, Dee was in the comms room, checking the intel traffic when Dexter walked in.

"Any news?"

"Not much. It seems they've found some empty patrol boat adrift in the Caspian Sea about seventy miles off the coast. Something of a mystery according to the messages. There'll be nothing on TV about it, that's for sure."

"Hmm," said Dexter. "I wonder what that was all about."

He moved closer, out of earshot from the other operatives in the room. "I also wanted to let you know, I've booked you on a flight out this afternoon; I thought you could travel with Eliz, you can keep each other company."

"Oh, ok, that soon? I'll need to collect my stuff from my apartment."

"I guess so. That's a pity, I would prefer you didn't have to go out again."

"I'll be careful," said Dee.

"No, it's ok. I'll come with you, we can take the Jag, it will be less suspicious."

"Yes, ok, great. Give me half an hour."

"Oh, before I go, I've also sent a message to the First Secretary suggesting you're relocated to a new assignment; it is too dangerous for you to stay here, and I've also recommended a commendation for the work you have done."

"Thanks David. I don't know what to say."

"It's me that should thank you."

Hyatt Regency Hotel, Baku, Azerbaijan – 9:15 a.m.

Houghton was desperate to contact Dee. He had always been self-sufficient but had found himself missing her, particularly on the long drive and even longer sea voyage. He also shared Dexter's concern about her safety. He took a chance and sent a text, hoping she would be in the embassy and away from any monitoring. *'Missing you, keep safe.'*

Moments later came a reply. *'Me too, going home today, contact me when you get back x.'*

He felt elated at the reply and left his room to collect Fellows from next door. The Mahabadis were walking along the corridor towards them.

"Hi, hope everyone is ok," said Houghton.

"Yes," said Hassan.

"And how are you feeling this morning?" said Houghton to Hassan.

"I'm much better, thank you."

"We're going on an aeroplane," said Afshin, excitedly.

"Yes," said Houghton. "I know; we're coming with you."

The boy smiled.

After taking a quick breakfast, they left the hotel, took the first two taxis in the queue, and headed for the British Embassy on Khagani Street. From the outside, it was a fairly non-descript building, certainly compared with Tehran. It just looked like an office block but with two Union Jacks posted outside the entrance.

The process of granting the Mahabadis' asylum had already been started by the Foreign Office in London, following details from Vauxhall Cross. The defection would be a huge coup for the British secret service. Mahabadi, it was hoped, would be a highly valuable asset in its nuclear power programme.

The ambassador himself came to greet the party when they arrived, and they were entertained in his office. The good news was that the family and the two agents were booked on a flight to London via Frankfurt that afternoon.

MOIS Headquarters – 9:00 a.m.

Commander Fallahian was briefing the General on the latest information on the Mahabadis' disappearance.

"We have received a list of all the staff who were on duty on Thursday night and we have been interviewing them; no one remembers seeing anything."

"Hmm, I am not surprised. They are all in it together, I bet. I have a good mind to arrest them all. Someone must know something. Interview them again; put some pressure on them. He can't have just disappeared. What about the mother?"

"She is no use, she is crazy."

"Hmm, and you have interviewed everyone at the hospital who was there that night."

"No, two were not on duty yesterday."

"Then go there and interview them; we must find out what has happened."

"Yes sir," said Fallahian and left the smoke-filled room.

Mardom Hospital – 10:30 a.m.

Fallahian was back at the hospital with Doctor Modarresi who was protesting vehemently at the continuous intrusion.

"Look, we have told you everything we know. You have interrupted my staff in treating patients, threatening them. This is not acceptable."

"The intrusion is necessary; we are dealing with a matter of national security and I am sure you do not want to appear unhelpful."

"No, no, of course not, but we have patients to look after."

"Then the sooner we get this matter resolved, the sooner you can see to your patients."

"Yes, yes," said the doctor.

"I have the list you gave me and there are two names here who we did not speak to yesterday. Are they here now?"

The doctor looked at the names.

"He is, but she is not. She has not arrived for work today."

"Is that usual?"

"No, not at all, Eliz is one of our most dedicated and best-qualified nurses. She was due on shift at ten o'clock."

"Can you give me her address?"

The doctor hesitated for a moment. The Commander looked at him sternly.

"Ok, one minute."

The doctor left the room and returned with a slip of paper and handed it to the commander. "I have asked for the other person to be available for you."

"Thank you, can you send him in please?"

The doctor left the room, and a few minutes later, the remaining name on the list was being interviewed.

After twenty minutes, it was clear that he knew nothing, and he was allowed back to his duties.

Half an hour later, Commander Fallahian and three guards were outside an apartment block. He checked the name again, Eliz Bashi, then the address; they were at the right place.

They walked the three floors to the apartment and banged the door; no reply. He banged again, nothing. Then a neighbour came out of their flat, disturbed by the noise.

"Eliz is not there. She has gone."

"Where?"

"I do not know. She said she was going away for a while and asked me to look after her things."

"When was this?" asked the Commander.

"Yesterday."

"When, yesterday?"

"Morning, I have her things."

"Let me see," said the Commander and the neighbour went back inside followed by the officers.

There were three cardboard boxes in the bedroom. The Commander opened the first one; it was just clothes and some pictures.

"Damn," he said under his breath.

"When did she say she would return?" asked the Commander.

"She didn't say."

"Did she say where she was going?"

"No, just said she was visiting friends."

"Ok, I want you to call me if she gets in touch; this is my number." The Commander presented the woman with his business card.

"Yes, of course."

MOIS Headquarters – 1:30 p.m.

Commander Fallahian was back at headquarters and in another meeting with his boss, considering the latest information.

"Have you got a photograph?" asked the General.

"Yes, they gave me one at the hospital, but it is not very good."

"I think we should send it to the airport; they can add it to their watch list. I assume they have details of the Mahabadis?"

"Yes General, I sent one yesterday. You think the nurse might try to leave the country?"

"I do not know, but it is possible."

Imam Khomeini International Airport, Tehran – 2:30 p.m.

Dee and Eliz were taken to the airport in one of the embassy's Jaguars. As members of the diplomatic corps, they were entitled to special privileges and were in the first-class lounge waiting for the flight to Heathrow to be called. Security and passport control had been routine formalities.

Dee had managed to collect her belongings from the compound and said her farewells to her colleagues, including the Ambassador who was still not fully aware of the role she had played in the Mahabadi defection.

The time seemed to pass slowly.

Dee looked anxiously around the lounge; she was becoming more and more nervous. The airport was crawling with MOIS agents and police; she felt vulnerable.

She had struck up a good friendship with Eliz and recognised that she too was feeling uneasy.

"Won't be long now," she whispered.

Eliz was sitting next to her, drinking tea. She nodded.

At three o'clock, came the announcement that the flight was ready for boarding. Dee breathed a sigh of relief. The pair picked up their baggage and left the lounge for the short walk to the departure gate.

Dee looked around; two armed police officers were standing next to the exit door to the aircraft. She fiddled with her boarding pass and passport.

As first-class passengers, they stood at the front of the queue and Dee watched as the door was opened and they were called forward. There was an assistant in an airline uniform checking the documents to the list of passengers. She also had a computer screen with the watch-list names. Dee was checked and ushered through.

The assistant took Eliz's passport, looked at her and the picture.

"Wait, one moment," said the assistant. Eliz held her breath as the girl checked the records.

"Ok, have a good flight," said the assistant. She ticked her manifest and handed the documents back. Eliz joined Dee and they made their way onto the plane. Forty-five minutes later, they were in the air.

Shortly after the plane took off, there was some commotion at the check-in desk. The watch-list had been updated and one of the clerks recognised the name. She referred it to her supervisor, who immediately contacted MOIS headquarters.

Commander Fallahian had some bad news for the General.

MI6 Headquarters, London – Sunday April 30th 2006 – 11:00 a.m.

Commander Jenkins was in her office with agents Fellows and Houghton. They were all drinking coffee from bone-china cups.

"Well, I admit I had my doubts. I didn't think you would pull it off," she said. "It's been a credit to the service; I've even had a message of congratulations from the Foreign Secretary."

"Thank you, Ma'am," said Fellows.

"So what's happening next?" asked Houghton.

"Well, the Mahabadis are in a temporary safe house until we find them a suitable place. Then we need to find the children a school and get Hassan Mahabadi in touch with the Atomic Energy Institute; they are very keen to meet him."

"What about Mayflower?"

"Yes, the same; she's ok. She's in an apartment. With her qualifications, the NHS will be crying out for her. Once she's settled, we'll find the nearest Hospital Trust and get her interviewed. She's been granted asylum and given a work permit."

"Thanks, Ma'am," said Houghton.

"Anyway, you two deserve some leave. I'll see you back here a week tomorrow."

Houghton looked at Fellows and grinned. "I think I need a beer."

They were soon outside and after a short walk, were in a

café-bar.

"What are you having, Nick?" said Fellows as they approached the counter.

"A beer please, just need to make a quick call."

He dialled a number. "Hello," came the reply.

"Missed me?" he said.

"You'll never know," said the voice.

"What are you doing tonight?"

"Anything you want," said Dee.

Epilogue

Three Years After Exfil

The nuclear crisis in Iran rumbled on but with less intensity. Ironically, the joint uranium enrichment deal with Russia agreed on April 20th, 2006, collapsed nine days later when Iran confirmed that it would not move all activity to Russia, thus leading to a de facto termination of the deal.

Back in the UK, both Houghton and Fellows were based out of Vauxhall Cross working on intelligence gathering and risk assessment; they had been relieved of field-work duties for the moment.

Houghton had been in the comms room in Vauxhall Cross when a message came through that immediately grabbed his attention.

'Antonio Alvarez, a Mexican national, accused of spying for the USA, has been released as part of a deal with the Mexican Government.'

Within a few weeks of returning from Iran, Houghton and Dee had set up home together and were eagerly awaiting the arrival of their first child.

Dee remained a close friend of Eliz Bashi, helping her adjust to her new life in London. Eliz was now a senior theatre nurse at Islington General Hospital.

Settling into the UK had been more difficult for the

Mahabadis.

Afareen was missing her mother and felt guilty at leaving her behind. Despite sending many letters, she had not had any contact with her.

Hasan's health had suffered, and he spent some time in hospital after his arrival from Iran. Afareen blamed it on the stress of the exfil. He was, however, reunited with his brother in Cambridge and had met up with him several times.

After six months, Hassan started working in London as an adviser to the Atomic Energy Commission and was appointed to several influential committees.

The children were more resilient and fared slightly better. They were now in good schools and achieving high grades.

Once Hassan's health improved, Afareen started doing voluntary work supporting other immigrant groups.

Hassan's appearance in London, however, had not gone unnoticed in Tehran.

London – June 2009

There's a familiarity about a well-travelled journey; the daily commute, the school-run, the dog-walk. It allows us to day-dream; a cognitive paralysis that takes us out of ourselves.

Hassan Mahabadi was making such a journey; he had a meeting in town.

He walked down the footpath and opened the front gate of his comfortable detached house in a desirable London suburb. His forty-five-minute journey always started with a short walk to the Tube station. Faces recognised and acknowledged with a simple nod, the feigned politeness as everyone tries to position themselves for the comfort of a seat.

It was not raining, but the air was damp, amplifying the smells in the carriage; stale clothing, unwashed hair, body smells and the diesel-oil that permeated the train.

He could count the stops in his sleep, seven, then a short walk to the next platform for the final leg.

He watched the electronic destination board; 'next train 2 minutes'; 'next train 7 minutes'.

The yellow line at the edge of the platform resembled the start-line of a hundred-metre race. Everyone remained behind the marker, ensuring an equal chance of getting a seat, provided you were at the front and the carriage door opened directly ahead of you. Mahabadi was at the front and knew exactly where the doors would open. The destination board indicated one minute. The air-pressure changed, a blast of cold air picking up discarded newspapers as the approaching train rattled into view.

Then, an almighty force came from behind him; he was unprepared, and there was nothing he could do to prevent the momentum as he was pushed. He was hurled into the abyss; the pit of litter, metal, and white electrical conductors.

Then oblivion.

The End

Lightning Source UK Ltd.
Milton Keynes UK
UKHW011043131019
351525UK00004B/116/P

9 781913 170134